WIREMU DU ROSE

The Hana Du Rose Mysteries

(Generation Z)

K T BOWES

DEDICATION

For Haydn. My boy.

WOULD YOU LIKE TO BE PART OF IT?

I'm a believer in 'try before you buy.'
There's nothing worse than forking out your hard-earned cash
on a doozy and regretting it.
I don't want stinky reviews.
I want you to love my work and feel like you got value for money.

If you'd like 4 free eBooks, then join me.
I will take care of your email address and won't be sharing it or
spamming you.
Ain't nobody got time for that.
You can unsubscribe at any time.
I promise not to send Rohan Andreyev after you…maybe.
Join at my website, ktbowes.com

1

HAMMER PIN

The knot in Wiremu's chest grew to the size of a boulder as the police car positioned itself behind him on the narrow road. Flashing blue and red lights strobed against the pine trees lining the hill to his left, creating a haze of alarm. Other motorists streamed past, crossing the centre line to avoid clattering with the officer emerging from his vehicle as he settled a fluorescent yellow jacket over his shoulders. They slowed to give them enough time to peer at the unfortunate teenager in the borrowed truck, but the darkness and glittering headlights masked the embarrassed flush lighting Wiremu's cheeks.

With shaking fingers, Wiremu hauled on the handbrake and knocked the truck out of gear. It took two stabs of the button near the door handle to force the side window to lower. He scrabbled in the jacket laid on the passenger seat, extracting his wallet and flipping it open. The cocky face which peered at him from the laminated driving licence looked like a different person. A lot had changed in three years.

"Good evening, sir." The police officer bent to get eye contact with him and Wiremu held his breath. "Can I see your driving licence, please?"

Wiremu held it out between them and the officer took it. He shone a torch onto the photograph before glancing back at the driver with a furrow appearing between his brows. "Du Rose," he murmured. "Why do I know that name?"

Wiremu cleared his throat to alleviate the pressure from the boulder, which had forced the air into his gullet and made it difficult to breathe. "I don't know, officer," he replied, keeping his tone deferential. He didn't want trouble, knowing it would cause him to fall at the first hurdle. "Did I do something wrong?" he risked asking, his chest rising and falling faster than usual.

"Is this your vehicle?" The cop bent again at the waist, the fabric of his jacket rustling in the sharp breeze blowing up from the south.

Wiremu pursed his lips. If he told the truth, the officer might call his uncle, but if he lied, then what? His mind stalled on the notion of lying and what kind of lie might smooth the way rather than making it worse.

Nothing. His brain produced nothing helpful.

He cleared his throat again. "It's my uncle's. He lent me a fleet vehicle for my new job."

"Here?" The man raised a dirty blond eyebrow and glanced ahead of him along the darkened road. No streetlights softened the eerie lane, with the pine trees rustling in the breeze.

"Yes sir." Wiremu swallowed. "I'm working at Horse's Farm on the Pirongia Road starting tomorrow."

"Right." The officer took a step back and licked his lips. "For Vaughan?"

"Yeah." Wiremu nodded with more enthusiasm. "General farm work."

"Wait here." The sleeves of his jacket crinkled as the officer tapped the driving licence against his opposite palm. "What's your uncle's name?"

"Logan Du Rose." The boulder slipped into his stomach as he said the name, failure burning like a hot coal in his gut.

The officer's boots crunched against loose grit as he walked back to his patrol car and sank into the driver's seat. He closed the door against the wind and turned on the interior light. Wiremu watched in the rear-view mirror as the man's lips moved in conversation with the control operator. He braced himself for the inevitable crushing of his dreams as the chance encounter threatened to unravel his carefully made plans.

"Idiot!" he rebuked himself. "Should have refused the truck." He shook his head, knowing he couldn't have done that without suspicion. The boulder of worry grew until it pressed against his spine and threatened his circulation. The cop opened his door and stepped out of the vehicle. His easy gait carried him back to Wiremu's side.

"That all checks out," he concluded. Long fingers with wide knuckles handed back the driving licence. Wiremu almost dropped it as he accepted the smooth plastic card, his fingers shaking.

"Why did you stop me?" His tone carried an edge of suspicion. The police force had worked hard to expunge the poisonous thread of racism from their ranks, but living with darker skin often attracted an insipid unconscious bias.

The cop nodded towards the back of the truck. "Dodgy taillight. Might be a loose connection." He lifted his chin and pointed to the lever next to Wiremu's right knee. He displayed his knowledge of the vehicle type by knowing of the lever's existence, though the darkness hid it from view. "Pop the trunk and I'll take a look."

Wiremu's fingers scrabbled until he found the lever, though he had to dip his head to ensure he pulled the right one. A clunk indicated the unlocking of the rear tailgate, and the cop scrunched around to the back of the truck. Unsure whether to get out of the vehicle, Wiremu followed at a safe distance. He released the catch for his seat belt and slid down from the driver's seat, careful not to appear threatening. Already over six feet tall and with muscles created from manual labour, he could intimidate smaller men without trying. He edged around the back of the truck and watched the cop's deft fingers as he peered into the flat bed of the truck.

"Can you hold that for me?" The cop glanced back at Wiremu and held out his torch.

"Okay." Wiremu took a step towards him, grasping the heavy light and leaning over to shine it into the cavity. He used his other hand to raise the canopy and afford them more room.

A click sounded and red light beamed from the unit in the police officer's hand. "Got it," he said with a satisfied sigh. "These Toyota utes suffer from faulty connections sometimes. The plastic gets brittle in the heat. You'll need it replaced at your next service."

"Thanks." Wiremu waited until the cop lifted the tailgate and set the canopy back into place. He tapped the metal chassis with an index finger before accepting back his torch.

"Nice truck," he commented. "Few people would trust someone your age with one of these."

Wiremu nodded in acknowledgement of a truth. "He's a good bloke." A sharp intake of cold air cut across his confession before he could make it. Logan's faith in him wouldn't last, not when he found out what he'd done. What he wanted to do.

"Is that all, sir?" he asked. The moment contained an awkwardness back lit by the patrol car's lights, still strobing into the darkness. Another motorist edged around them, crossing onto the other side of the road and slowing. Wiremu jerked aside as the cop raised his hand, turning it into a wave at the last minute. The passing ute driver pipped the horn in acknowledgement.

Embarrassed by his obvious suspicion, Wiremu floundered. "Thanks for your help," he gushed, his words tumbling over themselves in his haste to escape. "Please, may I go now?"

"Yeah, sure." The cop nodded and held out his hand. "Welcome to town. It's not much, but we like it."

Wiremu stared down at the pale fingers as the red and blue lights kissed the man's skin and gave it a purple hue. He took his hand and gave it a moderate shake, careful not to crush the fine bones.

"Wiri Du Rose," he replied, his voice wavering. He'd told his employer a different surname, adopting his mother's maiden name to avoid awkward questions. But the cop had seen his driving licence, and it created the first of many cracks in Wiri's story. He forced a smile onto his lips and prayed he didn't cross paths with the cop again.

They parted company, the cop deactivating the strobing lights and pulling onto the road with the roar of a diesel engine. Wiri gave the man a feckless wave, his complexion pale and sickly through the side window. As the taillights of the patrol car disappeared along the lane, he pushed his shaking palms beneath his thighs and rested his forehead against the steering wheel. The exhaled breath took his recriminations with it. "Should have said no to the truck," he murmured.

2

DRAWBAR

His phone's satellite navigation picked a fight with him five painful minutes later. The irritating female voice told him he'd reached his destination, her tone becoming more hysterical with each reminder.

"I haven't!" he complained. His mind flicked back to the email from his new boss in which he'd given rough directions. "He said fifteen minutes out of town and on the left." He slowed the truck to a crawl and peered through the darkness. His headlights lit up the road ahead, crossing to a point in the distance. Switching them onto full beam provided little relief, showing another stretch of empty road identical to the last few kilometres. Headlights shone on the horizon, tiny pinpricks from an approaching vehicle.

"You have reached your destination," the soft voice intoned.

"I haven't!" Wiri ground his teeth until his jaw ached. The screen zoomed out to show a dense green area, a lake and the narrow, snaking road south. Wiri closed his eyes and imagined the algorithms rationalising the information. When he looked up, he found the view hurtling towards the bright red pin stuck into the road on the screen as though attempting to prove the narrator spoke the truth. He wondered if a secret club of artificial intelligence navigation narrators ever got together in an alternate reality and laughed at the stupidity of their drivers. He pulled the truck onto the narrow verge and retrieved the mobile phone from its cradle, cursing as his wallet fell from the passenger seat to the floor and bounced against the carpet.

"You have reached your destination." The female voice added more emphasis, as though pleading with him. Her heavy twang hurt his teeth and jarred with the softer vowel sounds of home.

"Let's check the email," he muttered, pressing the icon on his screen. He groaned at the complete lack of a signal as the app refused to load. The map worked on a stored memory of the route which he'd set the day before in secret.

Headlights flared like a sunburst in his peripheral vision and a diesel engine slowed. Wiri glanced up to find the police car stopped next to him. "Are you lost?" the cop asked.

Wiri's reluctant nod oozed failure and defeat. "Yeah." He sighed.

"You have reached your destination." The sentence contained hope as though appealing to the police officer for affirmation.

He smiled, displaying perfect white teeth. "I don't know why that always happens here." A light laugh slipped from his chest. "But Vaughan's place is about two kilometres further on and to the left. It's not signposted but look for the lights on the hill and turn into the gateway. You'll go over a cattle grid and onto a dirt road. Drive up to the house and he'll hear you if he's around."

"Thanks." Wiri dropped his useless phone onto his jacket. He exhaled and viewed the road ahead. "Again."

"No worries. Catch you later." The cop waved a hand through his side window at the same moment his dashboard radio crackled. He pressed on the gas and eased the patrol car along the road towards the town.

"Not if I see you first," Wiri whispered under his breath. He pulled onto the road and increased the truck's speed, raking the view ahead for signs of a gateway. The forestry block ended with such abruptness, it took Wiri's breath away as the Milky Way burst to life overhead. The contour of the road flattened and the breakneck bends gave way to a gentler camber.

Lights twinkled as though suspended in the air as Wiri pushed the truck along a straight piece of road. Unlike the glaring whiteness of the stars, these held the yellow hue of man-made bulbs. He slowed in time for his headlights to catch the glint of a metal pole to the left and a wide gateway yawned over a cattle grid.

Nerves vied with relief as he made the turn and clanked over the heavy steel poles. The truck juddered and shook and his phone joined his wallet in the foot well. His headlights bounced over post and rail fencing. A cool breeze filtered through the open window and stroked dry the sweat on his brow.

The house grew in size as Wiri followed the steep driveway through the foothills of the mountain. It lifted its chin with pride at the valley below, though as he drew closer, Wiri spotted the tell-tale signs of neglect. The chimney sagged, not lining up with the front door next to it. An outside light cast the lines of the house into sharp relief, exposing all its faults with the combination of glow and shadow. Wiri ground his teeth, choosing not to care as he parked behind an ancient truck with an old-fashioned number plate. He'd made his choice and he would walk in it, no matter what looming disaster befell him.

Like a reprimand, the GPS blocker he'd plugged into the cigarette lighter flashed once, the telling red light stopping his uncle from tracking the fleet vehicle. He'd been unable to refuse Logan's generosity without making a scene and so he'd relied on the internet purchase to provide a temporary solution.

Killing the engine and taking a deep, fortifying breath, Wiri climbed from the driver's seat. He left his fallen phone and wallet and activated the central locking, tucking the key fob into the front pocket of his jeans. A sleek Mercedes saloon blocked the path he should have taken. Squaring his shoulders, he navigated it and walked the short distance towards the front of the house. A ranch slider lead onto a new deck, the pine still fresh and untreated. Wiri frowned at the stark contrast with the dilapidated building. Ghostly net curtains fluttered through an opening in the ranch slider and he paused and debated whether to knock on the window or continue towards the front door. "Door," he whispered to himself, channelling the English woman who'd raised him. "It's politer." He angled his boots towards the peeling blue paint, the flickering porch light creating crawling shadows over the neglected surface. The scent of fresh wood filled his nostrils as he sprang up the two new steps and onto the deck.

He jumped aside as the ranch slider drew back with a hiss to create a yawning mouth. The net curtains made a bid for escape. A dark shape appeared, moving at speed sideways as it tangled with the flimsy material.

"Get out!" a male voice yelled. "And don't come back or I'll break your bloody legs! Then I'll shoot you in the face!"

The shape became a person, shunting against Wiri in its attempt to remain upright. He released a grunt of pain and shoved with both hands, tipping the man's balance and sending him off the edge of the deck. The man landed with a wail and sprawled in the dirt, the yellow glow of the porch light picking out the highlights of an expensive suit fabric. The net curtains lifted in the breeze and a briefcase flew beneath them before the boot which had drop-kicked it settled back to earth. "Take your crap and go," the same voice growled. The case sent up a puff of dirt and the man grabbed it before turning onto hands and knees and using it to push himself upright.

"That's assault! I'm calling the cops." He dusted filth from his knees and closed his fingers around the handle of the case. Rising, he jabbed a finger at Wiri. "He's my witness. You saw him assault me."

The barrel of a shotgun poked through the gap in the ranch slider and the man gasped. A giant fought his way past the net curtains, his feet encased in boots heavy enough to have glued Wiri to the floor. The butt of the gun rested between the man's shoulder and collarbone as he stepped over the metal frame of the ranch slider. Relaxed fingers supported the barrel and Wiri noticed what the panicked man didn't. An index finger caressed the trigger guard without slipping inside it. He planned to scare but not to injure, despite his verbal threat. "You saw nothing, did you boy?" The gunman addressed Wiri without looking at him, his steps pausing for a reply.

Deciding he'd already told enough lies to send him straight to hell and into his ma's bad books, Wiri added another, bigger one. "No sir," he replied. "I saw nothing."

"Liar!" the other man wailed. "Just you wait!"

"Go away Hendricks!" The giant ducked his head to sight his prey, and the man yelped and skittered backwards.

"You've done it now!" he called over his shoulder, though he didn't elaborate on what the gunman had done besides kick his briefcase and threaten him with a gun. Wiri winced and his mind flicked back to the police officer just a few kilometres away. The giant snorted and swore. He lowered the shotgun, and the jointing clicked as he used the break-action to disable it. The other man fumbled with his car key before unlocking the Mercedes. Lights flashed both outside and inside the vehicle, illuminating it like a Christmas tree as he hurled himself into the driver's seat and slammed the door. The engine fired, but he stalled it twice in his haste. Wiri held his breath as the man reversed at speed, narrowly missing swiping his truck as he performed a messy nine-point turn. Dust and grit peppered the deck as he stamped on the gas and careened along the bumpy driveway towards the road.

With a snort of disdain, the giant set the shotgun over his shoulder before wiping his hand on his jeans. Then he held it out to Wiri. "Wiremu Kingii?" he asked.

Wiri nodded and accepted the huge fingers in his hand. The man's bulk made him feel like a child again, his hopes and fears overwhelming as they whirled around his head. An inner voice begged him to go home, confess, ask for mercy, and take his punishment. The voice sounded female, and he hardened his heart against her pleading. "Yes sir," he replied. "I'm looking for Vaughan Hōiho."

The giant smiled to reveal even teeth marred by a chip in the front left incisor. Glittering hazel irises held humour, crow's feet creasing to join the curve of his cheekbones. "Well, kid, you found him," he stated, dropping his hand to his side. "Welcome to Horse's Farm in the ass end of nowhere. I hope you brought some wet weather gear with you, because the forecast says we're in for a doozy of an autumn."

He didn't give the teenager a chance to reply. He yanked the net curtains to the side and pushed the gun through first, holding the fabric open for Wiri to follow.

3

Stock

W iri blinked against the light from a bare overhead bulb. A dilapidated sofa sagged along the back wall of a lounge and tattered rugs formed stepping stones across stripped boards to the kitchen. He jerked his thumb behind him. "I'll fetch my gear," he said, his voice sounding loud in the silent room.

Vaughan shook his head and propped the shotgun against the TV stand. "Na. I've put you in the house next door. Corey lived over the shed, but my wife wants to renovate the space."

"Right." Wiri focused his gaze on a line of wallpaper hanging halfway down the wall. It curled over as though in defeat, its mates on either side already gone to leave tufts of lining paper sticking to the plasterboard. Vaughan spun to follow his gaze.

"Leilah's been stripping the wallpaper." He ran a hand through his dark fringe and winced. The toe of his boot caressed a steamer parked haphazardly to his right. Water sloshed inside the drum. He exhaled, as though his wife's renovations cost him more than financially. Then he looked up at Wiri and smiled, his face morphing into something akin to pure elation. "Women, hey?" he commented, and his eyes softened.

Wiri nodded, his mind flicking back to home and Logan and Hana. He'd seen the same goofy expression on his uncle's face. Irritation bowled over by love. He cut off the image before it could remind him of Phoenix and everything he felt for her. "Who was that guy?" he demanded, his eyes narrowing to slits. "What did he want?"

Vaughan rubbed his right eye with the back of his hand. He let his fingers drop to his chin, the skin scratching across the stubble as he considered his answer. Then he sighed and shook his head. "He sells finance for farmers," he said, his tone stilted. Dipping his body, he seized the shotgun and jerked his head towards a narrow hallway leading from the kitchen. "Let me lock this away, then we'll head over to your place. Leilah went over to tidy up, so we'll take your truck and I'll come back with her." He nodded at Wiri before his heavy tread took him out of sight.

Wiri spun on the spot, staring around him at the room. He'd taken the job after a series of emails, never considering that Vaughan might not be able to pay him. The financier's visit after dark suggested he'd tried to catch the home owner at other times and failed. Wiri tapped nervous fingers against his thighs and stilled as his smart watch indicated a missed call on the phone still in the truck. He lifted his wrist and spun the dial at the same moment that his phone received a text and mirrored it through the Bluetooth on his watch. He relaxed upon seeing his cousin's name.

'*All good here,*' Mac said. A smiley face reinforced his confidence in the ruse. Wiri blew out a breath and sank onto the sofa, wincing at the way the cushion dented to leave him sitting on the wooden board underneath it. Macky wouldn't give him away unless his life depended on it. Limited hearing had isolated him from birth, but keen observation skills made him a silent witness to most of Wiri's mischief. He knew about Phoenix and approved.

Wiri sighed as the air left his lungs. No one could withstand the might of Logan Du Rose. Not even Mac. If his uncle got wind of what he'd said and done, they'd all be in more trouble than any of them could imagine. The problem was that none of them really understood why.

"Ready?" Vaughan appeared in the doorway and strode across the kitchen. He snatched up a set of keys from the counter next to the kettle and jangled them against his palm.

"Yes, sir." Wiri rose and dug his key fob from his jeans.

Vaughan blinked in surprise, long black lashes brushing against his unkempt fringe. "Na mate!" he exclaimed. "Just call me Vaughan."

"Okay." Wiri stepped towards the ranch slider and he slipped through the gap. The cool breeze nipped at his exposed arms and wound around his neck like icy fingers tightening a noose. He waited as Vaughan locked the door and turned towards the porch with a sigh.

"You'll find the weather colder down here," he commented, his tone soft. "Crazy when we're still in the Waikato."

Wiri nodded and stepped off the porch. He hadn't lied about the work he'd done on the mountain farm, creating an impressive CV from his experience. Toby got him to write his own reference, signing it on the bonnet of a farm ute and leaving a messy signature scrawled through a line of dust. Asking Logan posed too much of a risk and would lead to questions. Guilt nibbled at the back of Wiri's neck at how he'd taken advantage of Toby's illiteracy to force through his plan.

Vaughan settled into the passenger seat of Wiri's truck, dipping forward to collect the fallen wallet from the foot well. He placed it into the cup holder with the phone he'd retrieved from the seat. "It's ringing," he said, jerking his head towards the buzz as he fastened his belt.

"It's fine." Wiri started the engine, alarmed to see Logan's name flash on the screen. "I'll get it later."

Vaughan stared around the truck with a frown, inhaling the newness before peering at the silent dashboard display. "Didn't you connect it?" he asked, his fingers twitching as though he wanted to fix an unknown problem.

Wiri shook his head and cranked the gear lever into reverse. "Na. No point. I'm just borrowing it."

Vaughan's gaze dropped to the device plugged into the cigarette lighter and he frowned but didn't ask. Instead, his attention turned to giving directions as Wiri bumped the truck along the driveway towards the road. Wiri exhaled with relief, driving with care, hoping to impress his new employer. He'd plugged in the jammer after reading the instructions which came with it in the box. The disjointed translation of the Chinese content suggested the device could inadvertently mess with the efficacy of his phone's signal. The crazy, roundabout journey which the Google navigation subjected him to had proved the point. He'd only found the general location of Vaughan's farm by stopping at a local garage and asking the attendant.

Reaching the main road and traversing the bone jarring cattle grid, Wiri checked the road twice before taking Vaughan's direction to turn left. He sent a silent prayer to heaven that he wouldn't encounter the police officer again in a hurry. Experience told him the cop's curiosity would unravel his story within minutes.

He couldn't risk that.

4

FORESTOCK

The house next door made no sense. Wiri dumped his bag in the double bedroom and stared around him with a frown. He jumped as a woman stepped through the open doorway. Mahogany curls bounced in a ponytail at the back of her head, and her blue eyes sparkled in her slender face. She pointed at the pile of bedding folded into a tower on the mattress. "I'll leave you clean sheets each week and there are towels in the airing cupboard in the hall." She cocked her head and stared at him. "Is everything okay?"

Wiri nodded. Vaughan had made him remove his trainers on the porch and place them on a rack. After his disregard for the house next door, it had seemed a stark contrast in behaviour. But as Wiri looked around his new bedroom, it made perfect sense. The threads of a plush grey rug pressed through his socks to caress his toes. "It's nicer than I expected," he admitted. "I figured you'd shove me in a loft somewhere."

The woman released a soft laugh. "That's what my husband intended, but I have plans for the big shed. The lodger said he didn't mind sharing. It makes his rent cheaper, and you'll find it handy for work." She took a step forward and Wiri noticed a woodenness in her stance. She used her right palm to cradle her left elbow as though it hurt. "I put some basics in the fridge to carry you through until you can visit the supermarket. Jet's doing a run of night shifts, so you won't see much of him until his rotation changes."

"Right." Wiri swallowed and his brow creased with a frown. He struggled to formulate the sentence in his head, hating to reject the woman's hospitality at their first meeting. "I'm trying to raise money," he said, the words tumbling over his reluctant tongue. "I can't afford this." He licked his lips and stared at an elegant painting on the wall behind her head.

The woman's lips flattened into a line of sympathy. Her ponytail bounced as she shook her head. "Nothing's changed from the earlier terms," she said, her tone soothing. "Vaughan will pay you what he agreed." Her blue irises glittered like diamonds in the white light from the bedside lamp. "We have money. We don't need to cheat you."

Wiri swallowed. Her statement rankled against everything he'd already observed of Vaughan. He'd arrived to find his new employer drop kicking a financier onto the driveway of his dilapidated house, yet his wife oozed ready cash and privilege. He gave himself a mental shake and sank onto the mattress, choosing to focus on his own problems instead of the stranger's.

"Thanks," he said, realising she'd waited for his answer. "I forgot to ask Vaughan what time he wanted me to start work in the morning." He blinked against the scratchiness of his eyes as stress and exhaustion nipped at his psyche.

The woman turned to leave and stopped in the doorway. "Walk across the paddock at seven o'clock. You can have breakfast with us." Her tentative smile lit up the room. "I'm Leilah, by the way. I hope you'll be happy here."

She left before giving Wiri a chance to reply and he sat on the bed and listened to her steps pad along the hallway towards the front of the house. He jumped as Vaughan's head appeared around the door. "You find everything you need?" he growled.

"Yeah, thanks." Wiri rose and dug his thumbs into his back pockets. The stance felt awkward, and he straightened his shoulders and tried to appear less afraid of the situation he'd walked into with such care and planning, but now regretted. "I'll see you tomorrow at seven o'clock."

Vaughan nodded and withdrew his head, closing the door behind him with a click. Wiri sank onto the mattress and pressed his fingers against his eyes. He'd grabbed his phone from the truck and stuffed it into his jeans pocket and it buzzed against his thigh. Wiri groaned.

Tugging the device free, he saw his aunt's smiling icon flashing on the screen, her phone number strobing below it. Taking a deep breath, Wiri answered her call, keen not to raise suspicion. "Hey, Ma," he said, forcing joviality into his voice. "How are you going?"

"Good sweetheart." She sounded bright. Wiri swallowed the confession rising into his throat, realising too late how dangerous the interaction might prove. He'd never been able to lie to Hana. She possessed an uncanny foresight and saw through his deviousness in record time. "Did you have a safe journey?" The question held a veiled rebuke. He'd promised to text her.

Wiri cleared his throat. "I got a bit lost. The farm is quite hard to find." He glanced around him at the plush bedroom. "The house I'm staying in is amazing," he gushed. "They just finished renovating." He'd said too much and knew it the moment her silence reached him.

"Oh," she managed. "Aren't you staying with the family?"

Wiri squeezed his eyes closed tight enough to create spots of lights which flashed behind his eyelids. "Yes." He steered a more careful path through the truth, acknowledging the safety of staying as close to it as he dared. "They have two houses next door to each other." He omitted the presence of a wide paddock between them.

"Logan didn't mention that." Hana exhaled with a sigh. "But I don't think he's visited for many years. How much warmer is it in the north?"

Wiri imagined her next sentence containing a threat to visit him and held his breath. His words emerged with a jolting edge to the consonants. "It's not much different," he said, crossing the fingers of his left hand behind his back. "I think there's rain forecast for the next few days."

"Boo," Hana replied, and he sensed her lips turning down in sympathy. "The house is quiet without you. Mac is walking around like a left shoe looking for the right one."

"Oh." Wiri clenched his knees together to stop them from knocking. "How are Edin and Phoe?"

Hana snorted a laugh. "You only left this morning, sweetheart. Edin's meant to be getting ready for youth group but started prettying herself an hour ago and hasn't reappeared. Phoe went riding with Logan. I think it helps to clear her head after all the upset of the last few weeks."

"Yeah." Wiri dropped his head back to stare at the immaculate ceiling. The glow of the lamp cast shadows around the ceiling rose, stretching it into an oval and distorting the embossed plaster. He hated thinking about it, dwelling on thoughts of Phoenix kissing another boy. He swallowed, remembering how she'd almost died, the boulder rising through his stomach to press against his heart.

And then she'd kissed him, given him hope and presented him with her gift.

His fingers strayed to the top pocket of his duffel bag and he tugged the bracelet free. The beads shifted around the elastic, clinking against his fingers. He clasped it to his chest and released a sigh. A silence made him pull the phone away from his ear and glance at the screen. Then Hana's voice crackled again. "Signal," she said.

"Pardon?" Wiri brought the bracelet to his lips, the irony not wasted on him. The token of Phoenix's forbidden love taunted her mother, nestling against the phone as she asked more questions.

"I said, the signal is terrible. Tell me something about your new job before we get cut off."

"I'm not sure yet what he wants me to do," he managed. "I start tomorrow. Just general labouring, I guess. The other guy left. But they seem like real nice people."

"That's great." The connection crackled again. "I'm surprised it's such a poor reception," Hana repeated. "The signal keeps coming and going. Are you far from Kerikeri?"

Wiri held back the snort which threatened to escape. He wanted to confess he was miles away from the northern town, further in fact than her. Logan had made enquiries with the family member who ran a beef farm before leaving the rest to Wiri. He'd never said where he was headed, but nor had he stopped their naive assumption. "Yes," he replied, steering close to the truth. "Miles away from Kerikeri. The signal is dodgy, but I'll call when I can."

"Okay sweetheart." Hana sounded sad. "Keep us posted about how you're doing." She lowered her voice as Edin complained in the background. She said something about her fake eyelashes sticking to the mirror instead of her face. "I miss you," Hana whispered.

"Thanks Ma." His voice wavered. "I miss you too." The statement formed the closest one to the truth of their entire conversation. The call ended, and he stared at the screen, knowing he missed her and wishing he could just throw himself on her mercy and beg for her help.

He shook his head and pressed the bracelet to his lips again before hiding it beneath his pillow. Hana might have understood his agony, but she'd prove no match for her husband.

No one would ever be good enough for his Phoenix, least of all the bastard son of the man who cut him open with a machete. And laughed as his intestines spilled out onto the dusty earth.

5

TRIGGER GUARD

Wiri woke before dawn the next morning, his watch alarm buzzing until he turned the dial. He lay on his back and imagined himself at home in his own bed, listening to Phoenix stretch and yawn in the room next door. He closed his eyes and imagined the way her hazel curls brushed her shoulders. She'd stumble to the bathroom, her ponytail askew from sleep and her nightdress twisted around her torso until the buttons lay over her left hip. He couldn't remember a time when he didn't love her.

Hana had raised him alongside her own children, scooping him up when his father absconded and the men in white coats came for his mother. He'd never doubted her love for him, and the notion of betraying her set off the familiar gnawing sensation in his guts.

Remembering Leilah's promised breakfast, he forced himself to rise and hoped he could eat as the creature in his stomach clawed and bit.

Padding to the bathroom, Wiri sensed the presence of someone else in the house. He listened and a soft snore reached his hearing. The door at the end of the long hallway had stood open when he explored the night before, but someone had closed it while he slept.

Wiri rose onto his toes to deaden the sound of his steps as he continued his journey to the bathroom. He used the toilet and winced as the loud flush spat foaming water into the septic tank. Washing his hands and cleaning his teeth, he peered at his reflection in the mirror. The tiled wet room boasted a complicated control panel for the shower and he delayed investigating it until evening. Waking his flatmate after a night shift seemed a bad way to meet. He padded back to his room and dug in his duffel bag for a work shirt and jeans. His fingers coasted over the tattered fabric of his favourite shirt, its green and red checks faded from wear. Shaking his head, he tugged free a newer tee shirt and unrolled it on the bed. He added jeans and clean boxer shorts, but after pulling back the curtains; he added a heavier work shirt over it. He fixed a belt around his waist, winding the leather through the loops on his jeans. The brass horse head covered the junction of his zipper. His father's belt buckle. He gave it a nervous tap and dropped his shirt down over it.

It worried him he knew nothing about the lodger. He straightened the bedding and tucked his truck key inside the pillowcase. Wrinkling his nose, he took his phone off charge and jammed it into his jeans pocket.

He left the house without making too much noise. After locking the front door with the key Vaughan left for him, he fixed the attached carabiner on his belt loop. and pushed the key into his pocket.

A bush cockroach skittered from his left boot as he lifted it from the rack on the porch. Wiri wrinkled his nose and shook out both before fitting them onto his feet. He eyed his trainers with caution, hoping he remembered to check them before he wore them at the weekend.

His phone offered a decent stream of torchlight as he looked for a gate into the adjoining paddock. Not finding one, he used the top rail to spring over the fence and set off through the long grass towards the yellow lights in the distance. After a few minutes, he found a flat area where the grass grew closer to the earth. It improved his speed of progress and he followed it across the paddock.

The brim of his hat lifted in the wind which attacked the openness of the slope, and he tugged the strap beneath his chin. It smelled of Poppa Alfie's tobacco and Nonie Leslie's perfume and served as another reminder of his deception. They'd been so proud of him striking out on his own. Alfie had presented him with the battered hat as a token of home. Nonie pressed twenty dollars into his palm and told him to buy himself lunch at the service station north of Auckland. Wiri's eyelashes fluttered as he pushed away the memory. He'd almost broken then and told them the truth, wanting to believe in their loyalty.

"Yeah," he murmured to himself as he disturbed a mob of grazing cows. They lurched away from him, barrel like bodies on sturdy legs. "But Nonie tells Ma everything. It wasn't worth the risk."

The lower slopes of the mountain curved upwards to his right as he trudged along the well-worn path. A terrace had formed from the constant traffic and Wiri's phone torch picked out the cloven hoof prints in the dust. He wondered about the link between the two properties which seemed so separate and yet linked. It threw up thoughts of home and the two halves of the mountain which Logan had united after his father's death.

Divided in lust and united in blood.

Wiri picked up speed as the scent of bacon reached his nostrils. He rubbed a hand across his growling stomach and turned off the phone's torch as daylight sneaked like a thief through a crack on the horizon.

6

Receiver

The ranch slider slid open as Wiri bent to unlace his boots on the porch.

"Leave those. The floor is disgusting." Leilah beckoned him inside. Wiri took a step over the threshold before shaking his head and withdrawing his foot.

"It feels wrong," he murmured. "It only takes a second."

Leilah held the net curtain back with her hand as Wiri dipped to unlace his boots and kick them off onto the pine slats of the porch. He paused to stuff the neck of one into the other to prevent unwanted home makers and sat his hat over the top.

Moths fluttered above his head, drawn by the lure of light and warmth. Leilah batted them away with her hand as Wiri stepped into the lounge. She closed the door and dropped the fabric with a flourish, leaving the creatures to beat their wings against the windowpane. "Eggs?" she asked, glancing back at him as she sprang ahead.

"Yes, please." Wiri gave an enthusiastic nod, ignoring the sickness which threatened his appetite. Everything reminded him of Phoenix, especially eggs, which she hated with a vehemence unless her mother turned the yolk to a rubbery yellow.

"Grab a seat." Leilah jerked her head towards the table where three place settings sat ready. Wiri glanced down at hands which had touched the fence, his boots and numerous other things. He wanted to wash them, but Leilah occupied the cramped space behind the kitchen counter. He faltered, staring at his fingers and feeling ridiculous. The stockmen ate in the bush all the time, swallowing sweat, dirt, and bugs without a second thought. He'd spent most of his life doing the same. But the rules had always been different inside the house, and he yearned for the safe normality of Hana Du Rose.

Wiri wiped his hands on his jeans and took the seat on the opposite side of the table to the kitchen. He realised his mistake as he stared at the neat place settings, which would force Leilah and Vaughan to watch him eat.

As though summoned by Wiri's thoughts, Vaughan arrived in the kitchen. As tall as Logan Du Rose, he almost hit his head on the frame as he powered beneath it and closed the door behind him. He slid into the kitchen without disturbing Leilah and grabbed three mugs from a shelf. Keeping them in one hand, he wrapped the other around her waist and she stilled as he kissed the top of her head. Wiri watched from beneath his lashes, pretending to study the image on the place mat as Leilah tilted her head back to bump his shoulder. The air crackled with their intimacy and the boulder slumped heavily over Wiri's heart.

He closed his eyes and replaced the couple with him and Phoenix. Would she stand in a dilapidated kitchen one day and make him rubberised eggs for breakfast?

His brain ran the question on a loop and his quest took on a futile flavour. He'd broken away from the Du Roses on purpose, severing the threads to make it on his own without their money or influence. Like Dick Whittington and Robert Smythe, he'd forge his own path in a different town, hoping to make his fortune and return to breathe truth into his promise. Vaughan had advertised a fair wage and low rent for manual work Wiri could perform in his sleep. Phoenix would celebrate her sixteenth birthday in ten months and he figured if he worked hard, he could save enough to support them both until they could marry.

"You still asleep?" Wiri snapped his eyes open to find Vaughan staring at him. The bigger man wrinkled his nose. "Sorry, were you praying?"

Wiri exhaled and forced his muscles to relax. He released his clenched fingers beneath the table. "Something like that," he replied.

Daylight sneaked through the ranch slider and cast orange flecks across the worn rug. It betrayed the loose threads and fading pattern with a dignified glee. Leilah arrived at the table bearing two plates filled with bacon, eggs, fried bread, onions, and tinned tomatoes. She leaned across to place Wiri's on the mat, the plate tilting enough to cause the juice from the tomatoes to bleed into the egg. "Sorry," she breathed. She handed the other plate to Vaughan before rubbing at her shoulder and turning back to the kitchen.

Returning, she carried a plate containing two rounds of toast spread with jam. She settled at the table next to Vaughan. "This isn't usual," she said, groaning before bouncing up again and fetching a tea pot. She dumped it in the middle of the table and went to the fridge for a carton of milk. By the time she returned, Vaughan had poured the amber tea into two of the mugs. He jerked his head to Wiri and with nothing else on offer, he nodded.

"Yes please."

Leilah sat again in her seat and dumped milk into her tea. "We don't do this every morning," she began, closing her eyes as she sipped the hot drink.

"What?!" Vaughan's brow furrowed and his jaw dropped as though in shock. Then he laughed, the crow's feet appearing in the corners of his eyes and his irises sparkling like hot coals. "Just kidding." He winked at Wiri. "Leilah refuses to play the role of the farmer's wife." He shot her a sideways glance filled with humour. "She's much too high society for that game."

"Too right." Leilah bit into her toast with a crunch. Her face lit up with an amiable smile. "We wanted the opportunity to get to know you is all."

"Great." Wiri sliced up the bacon and took time over his first mouthful. The first lie invited a second and a third. He chewed, saying, "This is nice. Thank you," before adding another piece of bacon.

"How big is your farm in Northland?" Leilah took another sip of her tea.

"My uncle's? Two hundred hectares." Wiri paused with his fork in the air. He'd planned it all out, so the information he provided couldn't lead back to Logan. He knew how small and insular the New Zealand farming community could feel. His tenuous plan wouldn't tolerate mistakes. "Mainly beef but also horses."

"Horses?" Leilah cocked her head. Long curls from her ponytail covered her left shoulder and reminded him of Phoenix. She frowned and pierced him with perceptive blue eyes. "I saw that on your CV. Do you have your own?"

Sadness pricked the back of Wiri's eyeballs, and he shook his head. "Not anymore." Something about Leilah's easy maternalism tugged at the loose threads within Wiri's heart. She was younger than Hana, not yet forty, but she carried the same infectious empathy. He took a deep breath and let the words spill free. "I had a gelding for the last ten years. He developed a tumour on his lung a few months ago." The next piece of bacon tasted like ash in his mouth. He'd insisted on staying with the horse while the vet administered the drug to end his suffering. It wasn't the farm's usual method of disposal, but he'd wanted something more dignified for his friend. The vet's visit cost him from his own pocket, but he hadn't cared. Phoenix's tears had stained his shirt and, in his grief and confusion, he'd lost himself and used her as the lifeline to rescue him. He'd kissed her, fulfilling the desire he'd held forever and making promises he couldn't yet keep.

Realising he'd grown silent and morose, Wiri spun the conversation with the skill learned from his uncle. "What about you?" he demanded. "How did you both meet?"

Vaughan smiled and dropped his gaze to his plate. Leilah exhaled and picked up her second piece of toast. "School," she said. Her lashes swept down and then up again to Wiri's face. "But circumstance forced us apart, and we only met again at the start of last spring."

"Circumstance?" He repeated the word, his body dipping forward as her words captured his interest. An intensity entered his demeanour and Leilah jerked back at the force of it. She glanced sideways at Vaughan, and he shrugged.

"Someone will tell him," he murmured.

Leilah exhaled and dropped her toast onto the plate. She sat back in her seat. "Vaughan grew up here with his Uncle Horse and my father raised me on the farm next door." Her lips curved upwards into an attractive smile.

Vaughan breathed out through his nose. He reached for his mug and gripped it as though wanting to crush it into a thousand pieces. "No one in this town was good enough for Hector's daughter." His tone held a rueful quality. "Especially not me."

Leilah shrugged. "But we loved each other."

Wiri shook his head. His chest filled with desperation as a mirror image of his own situation played out before him. "But you didn't stay together?" His voice croaked at the end of the sentence and he glared at the egg yolk hardening into a stain on his plate. The impossibility of The Plan made him want to run, to forget Phoenix, and learn to love someone else. He glanced up to find Leilah staring at him with a perception which made him uncomfortable.

"No." Her soft voice reached him, cutting through the pain of the boulder ricocheting around his stomach like the ball from a pinball machine. She reached across the table and closed her fingers around the shaking wrist, which gripped the fork in his left hand. "But I wish we had. I wish we'd fought for what we knew, because then we wouldn't have wasted the last twenty years."

Wiri's gaze found hers across the table and he grounded himself in the sensation of her gentle fingers wrapped around his bony wrist. Vaughan studied their interaction with a frown, his analytical nature locking him outside the emotional moment. Leilah smiled at him and withdrew her hand. She moved on as though she hadn't just tuned into the cry of Wiri's soul and flayed it bare. "I'm sorry about your horse," she said, her tone soft. "It's always very upsetting."

Vaughan glanced sideways at his wife before resuming his breakfast. Leilah lowered her voice and whispered, "Just eat what you can manage." He nodded and Wiri saw the flash of a smile he afforded his wife.

Wiri consumed his breakfast with more energy than of late. He'd received Leilah's message loud and clear. Like a call to arms, she'd told him to fight.

Fight with everything he possessed.

For Phoenix Du Rose.

To stop them laying waste to two decades of their lives.

The boulder settled in his gut as he drew The Plan back to the forefront of his mind. He used his bread to clean his plate before rising with a smile at the same time as Vaughan. "Thanks for everything," he said to Leilah.

And he meant it.

7

MAGAZINE

"First job is repairing the fence by the road." Vaughan strode off the deck and clamped a baseball cap over his hair. He glanced back at Wiri. "I'll get the gear to tighten the wires. Then we'll drive to town to get some posts."

"Okay." Wiri stood still and listened to the gentle clank of crockery as Leilah cleaned up the kitchen. She'd waved off their offers of help with an easy flap of her hand. If he closed his eyes, he could imagine Phoenix loading the dishwasher and the steady hum of voices as the Du Roses readied themselves for the day. He missed them all with a tangible ache.

Vaughan opened the roll door to the huge shed after navigating the front bumper of the old-fashioned truck. He disappeared inside, but emerged seconds later with a pair of pliers in his hand. Jerking his head towards the main road in the distance, he turned along the rutted driveway and bid Wiri to follow.

They walked side by side without speaking, the soles of Wiri's boots loud in the morning's silence. Afraid of revealing more of himself than he could bear, Wiri trudged next to

Vaughan without attempting to start a shallow conversation about nothing. Vaughan's shoulders lost their tension, and it occurred to the teenager that his employer didn't appreciate idle chatter, either.

They operated together with an effortless grace, as though the alliance held no newness. Vehicles sped by on the fast road and two of the drivers honked their horns and waved. A knot of curious calves watched their activity, ears forward and feet splayed as the men fixed a bad sag in the fence.

Wiri hauled the wire taut, wearing a borrowed pair of work gloves which protected his fingers. He stretched it past the post and created a loop, twisting the wire to create a join. Vaughan used the pliers to press the twist and prevent the wire from recoiling. Between them, they pulled the loop around the post. Vaughan shoved a bolt through the end, which he drew from his back pocket with an impressive sleight of hand. He used it as a lever to twist the loop around the strand of wire until it tightened to create a decent barrier. "Good job," he said, rising with a grunt and admiring their work. "Only four more to go."

They repeated the exercise on each of the runs until the whole fence had regained its integrity. The cool breeze remained, but the sun had risen high enough to negate its bite.

Vaughan wiped his forehead with the back of his hand, catching the brim of his hat and knocking it to the floor. He dipped to retrieve it, but rubbed his stomach with a wince as he rose. "We'll grab Leilah's truck," he said, turning to walk across the paddock towards the driveway. "Then we'll nip into town for the posts."

Wiri removed the gloves and shoved the knitted wrists into his back pocket. They flapped against his buttock as he walked like a series of inappropriate butt slaps. Vaughan reached the driveway first, his long legs traversing the paddock gate rather than opening it. Wiri pressed his fingers on the top rail and prepared to follow when Vaughan released an indecent exclamation.

"What's up?" Wiri paused with his right boot on the bottom rung.

Vaughan grunted and pressed himself against the gate, obscuring his view. Curiosity made him slide sideways to observe the expensive utility vehicle turning into the driveway. The indicator light flashed orange and as the black vehicle made the turn and straightened, Wiri spotted the immaculate horse trailer bouncing along behind it.

The ute stopped next to Vaughan and the tinted driver's window lowered to reveal a stunning redhead with perfectly aligned features. She looked from Vaughan to Wiri and then back again, the light catching her irises to make the colour indiscernible. "Hi," she said, lifting her chin as she considered Vaughan. Wiri set her age around twenty, the porcelain tones of her skin still revealing the perfection of youth.

"Hi." Vaughan lifted his right arm and placed it across his stomach, the flat of his hand resting over his ribs as though for protection. Clearing his throat, he said, "Leilah is still up at the house."

"Thanks." She didn't smile when she continued, "I'll check in with Deleilah and then find somewhere to put Ruffian. I picked him up this morning on my way through Hamilton." It seemed to Wiri that she emphasised Leilah's full name with a determined arrogance.

Vaughan nodded for a whole ten seconds before any words emerged. He waved his hand towards the paddock behind him. "Your horse can go in here, if you like?"

The woman snorted. "No thanks, not with cows! I'll find somewhere closer to the house. I'm guessing you'll shove me next door in Grandpa Hector's house again."

"No." Vaughan shook his head and pushed himself away from the gate. "We weren't expecting you." He jerked his thumb over his shoulder in Wiri's direction. "My new lad moved in yesterday. The lodger is still in the master bedroom. You can stay with us."

As Wiri absorbed the information that this was Leilah's daughter, he watched her top lip curl back into an ugly sneer which destroyed her proportioned face. It wreaked a horrid kind of havoc, drawing her brows together into an angry line and creasing the bridge of her nose. "Great!" she snarled, her tone sounding anything but thrilled with the solution. She stamped on the gas and the ute lurched away, dragging the horse trailer behind it. A clatter and a snort revealed the occupant being taken by surprise at the sudden forward momentum.

"Wow." Wiri struggled to stop the word from escaping his lips. He realised his error as Vaughan's face darkened and his eyes took on a gimlet hard appearance.

"Don't even think about it," he said, misunderstanding Wiri's disgust for admiration. "She'll eat you for breakfast."

Wiri's mouth opened to correct him, wanting Vaughan to understand that Leilah's arrogant daughter was far enough away from Phoenix's gentleness to revolt him. But the right words wouldn't form on his tongue and so he followed in silence, trudging back up the winding driveway in the wake of the woman's dust.

8

FRONT SIGHT

Vaughan kept silent on the drive to town. He frowned as he cranked the gears and pushed the old truck through the foothills of the mountain. Wiri leaned back against the worn leather seat and let his mind turn to Phoenix. He wondered if she'd made it to school on time or if she thought of him. He tugged his phone from his jeans pocket and activated the screen, his heart lurching at the sight of the text icon.

'*Good luck today. You'll do great.*' Logan's good wishes in text form were both unusual and a gift. Two months ago, Wiri would have basked in his uncle's approval, but his relationship with Phoenix threw all that yearning into sharp relief. When Logan discovered their duplicity, he'd use his many resources to hunt them down and drag his daughter home. They couldn't marry without consent until she reached eighteen, which meant Wiri needed to earn enough cash to remain hidden until it was too late.

He jumped as the truck hit the curb, his phone tumbling onto the floor of the cab.

"Sorry," Vaughan grunted. He looked over his shoulder to reverse the vehicle back into the traffic and start the process again. "I always forget to back this thing into parking spaces," he said with a smirk. "Leilah nails it in one. Maybe we won't tell her I bailed again."

Wiri nodded and unlatched his seatbelt. He snatched his phone from the floor and jammed it back into his pocket. His shirt parted to reveal the brass horse head and Vaughan's brow knitted. "Nice buckle," he said.

"Thanks." Wiri dropped the hem of his shirt and turned away. Stepping from the truck, he found himself on the main street of the town. It looked like any other small New Zealand township, with shops lining either side of the road. Metal rods attached to the front of the buildings held awnings over the pavement to protect pedestrians from the weather, casting the huge flagstones into shadow. Wiri spotted dress shops, a hairdresser and a cafe in the first twenty metres. He spun on the spot, allowing himself to imagine bringing Phoenix there to live in obscurity. No one would know them and they could disappear. His heart filled with an uncharacteristic lightness, and his fingers brushed the fabric of his pocket above his phone. He compiled the text in his mind before dropping his hand.

He'd made promises to her.

She had only kissed him.

Perhaps it didn't mean what he thought it did.

"It's a decent town." Vaughan joined him on the pavement, tucking his shirt into his jeans.

"You grew up here?" Wiri pushed Alfie's hat higher on his head to shade his eyes from Vaughan's gaze. The rawness of his dreams needed time to fade.

"Yeah." Adding nothing more, he jerked his head towards the cafe a few metres away and pushed open the door. The scent of warm bread filled the air as Wiri followed him inside and looked up at the bell, which jangled a warning at their presence.

An old man hogged a counter facing the window, and he touched the brim of his hat as Vaughan nodded to him. Gnarled fingers held a pie and steam curled from it towards the ceiling. The man dipped forward and blew on his pastry, sending out more spray than breath. Wiri looked away in haste, focussing his attention on Vaughan.

"About bloody time." A woman hurried from a kitchen behind the counter before stopping at the sight of the men. "Oh," she said, disappointment lacing her tone. "Where's Leilah?"

"Delayed." After issuing the single word, he turned to leave. Wiri altered the trajectory of his feet, ready to follow him back into the street.

"Wait!" Elfin and wizened, the woman bustled around the counter, straightening the apron wrapped around her thin body. She raised a crooked index finger and dug it into Vaughan's powerful biceps. "She promised she'd drive me to the cash and carry in Hamilton. I'm running out of flour."

"Sorry." Vaughan frowned at Wiri and jerked his head towards the door in a silent command to bolt. "Seline turned up at the farm with a new horse. We didn't expect her."

"Oh." The woman's head jerked back on her neck. Her left hand wound behind her and she loosened the tie on her apron. "I want to see her." Her brown irises glittered with a sudden moistening and Vaughan clattered Wiri in his need for escape.

"No," he growled. "I'm not your chauffeur and I've got stuff to do."

"Ten minutes," she begged, her tone wheedling. "My old car doesn't like the hill up to your place." Wiri noticed pink gums occupying the space where teeth should be and her lips slapped when she spoke. He gulped as she noticed him and jabbed her finger in his direction. "He can manage."

Vaughan snorted. "No, he can't. He works for me, Mari. We're doing important bloke stuff." The cloudy darkness in his face shifted as he winked at Wiri beneath the cover of his fringe. But the old woman persisted.

"I want to see Hector's grandbaby! He doesn't have to cook nothing. Just stand behind the counter and look pretty." Her eyes narrowed at Vaughan and her lips tightened. "You owe me after what you did."

The old man in the corner snorted, coughing as he inhaled flaky pastry through his hairy nostrils. "Get real, Mari!" he barked. "That young dude couldn't look pretty if you covered him with icing sugar and called him a muffin."

Wiri watched in horror as a tear rolled from the woman's face and dampened her bronzed cheek in its tracks. "You just got married without me. I'm her only family and you didn't even invite me. I'll never forgive you for this, Vaughan Hōiho. Never. You don't deserve your Uncle Horse's name."

"I'll do it." Wiri raised his hand and swallowed, amazed at the instant transformation. Her eyes brightened, and she scrabbled at the trailing cords from her apron before he'd finished his sentence. "I'll stand there for ten minutes." He glanced up at Vaughan before pointing towards the cash register. "If that's okay with you?"

The man in the corner hooted, crumbs from his pie tumbling to the tiled floor. "Sucker!" he cackled. "She saw you coming." He cocked his head and stared into space. "Not that she sees much anymore. Blind as a bat."

Vaughan inhaled and released the breath with a shake of his head. He winked at the old man. "For once, I agree with you, Ted," he said. "She did see him coming."

"Here!" Mari shoved the balled apron against Wiri's chest, not waiting for him to catch hold of it. She primped her hair with her fingers, a fringe of white curls graduating to grey and then brunette at the back of her head. Blinking up at Vaughan, she said, "Come on, boy! I don't got all day!"

Vaughan twisted his lips before withdrawing the truck keys from his pocket. He shook his head at Wiri. "Thanks for that, mate," he said, before walking back through the front door and onto the street.

9

BARREL

"Get me a beer." The old man in the corner waved his pie at Wiri. "And I want a good head on it an all."

"Right." Wiri strode behind the counter and examined the various shelves. He kept his hat on and didn't slip the apron strings over his head or around his waist. The hands on the wall clock showed a little after nine thirty, and he figured he'd missed the breakfast crowd. He hoped Mari reappeared before the start of an anticipated morning tea rush.

After examining the shelves and the glass fridge behind the counter, Wiri stepped through an archway into a cluttered kitchen. It dawned on him as he inspected the contents of a small walk-in chiller that the old man might have punked him. Fixing a demure smile over his irritation, he walked to the back of the shop and stood next to him, avoiding the widening circle of crumbs littering the tiles. The old man was still blowing on his pie. "I don't think the aunty sells beer," he announced, keeping his tone light.

The old man cackled hard enough to burst a blood vessel and a dollop of dripping cheese left the pie and added itself to the crumbs on the floor. Opening his mouth wide revealed not a single tooth in his head. "Old Ted here got ya good!" he roared. "What a dickhead."

"You or me?" Wiri kept his tone polite. "The dickhead."

The old man's laughter faded like water down a drain. "Well, we're sharper than we look, aren't we tama?" He used the Māori word for boy or son and the taste of home robbed Wiri of a ready reply. Instead, he nodded.

"Can you make a decent coffee for old Ted?" He squinted up at him as a lump of steak splatted onto his stained shirt front.

Wiri nodded. "Yes, koro," he replied. The familiar term of address bathed the old man in a warmth which transformed his features.

"Āe," he replied, his amber irises sparkling. "Ka pai." Good.

Wiri returned to the counter and navigated his way around the coffee machine. Evenings and weekends spent working as a barista at his uncle's hotel paid dividends as he produced a half decent flat white. He took it across and placed the mug next to Ted's plate. The old man switched from blowing his disappearing pie to breathing spit over the froth on top of the coffee.

Wiri waited for Ted to taste the drink, his own sense of achievement demanding praise. The old man sipped before clattering the mug against his plate. A line of milk froth covered his dark moustache and the underside of his hooked nose. "Very good," he admitted. "Mari's coffee tastes like bathwater. Deleilah Dereham makes a great cappuccino." A bushy eyebrow rose as Ted peered from beneath his eyelashes. A slyness entered his body language and Wiri stiffened. "Sit with me." Ted's crabbed fingers patted the wooden counter which ran parallel to the window. He hooked a stool with his right foot. Wiri glanced at the cafe door and prepared to make an excuse. Ted waved it off before he could formulate it. "Nobody comes in until ten," he said. "Just me."

"Okay." Wiri perched on the offered stool, but he didn't relax.

Ted inhaled and stared through the window into the street, his view obscured by the word 'cafe,' backwards in an arched font. "I've sat here for sixty years," he announced. "Right back from when Mari's mother worked in the kitchen. The woman from the post office owned it and she didn't like brown workers on show. Upset her good when Mari's mother bought the place from her." He jerked his head towards a bench beneath the window. "I had to sit outside in those days on account of the concrete on my boots." His lips rose in a smirk. "But I know everything about this town. My mother gave birth to me here, and I ran my business here." He grunted. "Sold it to a man who ruined it in under five years." His gaze slid sideways to Wiri, and he sighed. "I seen Horse and Hector Dereham knocking ten bells outa one another in that street. And their kids screwing each other on the riverbank thinking nobody knew." His lips flattened into a line. "Te Mutunga Iho, they called this town. You know why?"

Wiri shook his head. Feeling awkward still wearing his Jackaroo, he removed it and set it down on the wooden surface. Made from swamp kauri, the long counter bore the scuffs and dents of age. He ran his fingers over its face and winced at the stickiness caused by the cleaning products Mari used to clean the tables.

Ted continued, his pie cooling alongside his coffee. "You speak Te Reo, though?"

"Yeah," Wiri replied. "It means end of the day."

"Āe." Ted shifted on his stool, his curved back releasing a series of painful sounding pops. "My tīpuna hid in the caves here during the Waikato Wars. My ancestors birthed the next generation in the darkness. Not just the darkness of the caves, but of the times for Māori." He removed his battered cap to run a hand through sparse greying hair. "The English drove them from the banks of the Waikato River and they fled until they couldn't walk any further. The soldiers rode boats up the river, shooting cannons at the tribes along the way. They didn't care about killing innocent women and babies." He leaned sideways and bumped Wiri's shoulder with his. "But one captain didn't agree with the war. He sailed real slow to give them a chance to run. They called that boat The Swan with the Broken Wing."

Exhaling, he lifted his drink with a shaking hand. Brown streaks snaked over the rim and down the sides to leave a ring on the kauri surface once he replaced it. "At the End of the Day is the name of this town in Te Reo. Because the tribe couldn't run anymore and camped here. It's a stronghold, see." He patted the kauri surface next to his plate. "Government wants to change it to something more palatable." A slow blink punctuated his next sentence. "Ain't gonna happen."

Wiri nodded. "Thanks, koro," he said, acknowledging the old man's time and history. He winced as an elderly woman fought a tiny old-mobile into the parking space Vaughan left in front of the cafe. She used the entire distance which the truck had occupied to go back and forward and still abandoned the vehicle at a strange angle. Its rear bumper poked into the traffic and her white-haired companion struggled to exit the passenger door and clamber up the high curb.

Ted jerked his head towards them with a cackle. "Except them," he said, as though to himself.

"Sorry?" Wiri leaned closer with a frown.

Ted grinned, displaying his pink gums. "I should have mentioned how they come in every day before ten to play dominoes with me. They'll want a cooked breakfast, so you might need to get your apron on over them muscles."

"Seriously?" Wiri gaped at him and Ted's body shook with the force of his enjoyment.

"Āe," he replied. "Mari's done you right dirty."

"Yep." Wiri rose from his stool with a sigh. "Hasn't she just."

10

Cylinder Flutes

The bell over the front door jangled and Wiri glanced up from the coffee machine. He'd managed to work out the rudimentary functions, finding it similar to the one at his family's hotel. He wiped the wand, which funnelled steam into the milk, using a clean cloth he found folded on the counter. "Be with you in a second," he said, failing to register the identity of the new customer.

"I hope you're better at making coffee than you are at lying," a voice said. A nasty chuckle accompanied it, and Wiri's shoulders stiffened. The nasal tone grated on his nerves and he narrowed his eyes to glare at the man Vaughan had ejected from his house. He didn't dignify the slight with an answer, but its content bothered him. Wiri flattened his lips and channelled Logan Du Rose's innate severity as he faced the man.

"What can I get you?" he asked. "It's cash only."

Hendricks shrugged. He dug into his back pocket and pulled out a black leather wallet. The zipper scraped across the metal surface as he peered inside. "You're in luck," he growled, drawing out a five-dollar note from a wad stuffed between the card holder and the coin purse. He flapped it between them, protruding knuckles stretching the pale skin over his fingers. "Large flat white to go. Keep the change."

Wiri reached out and took the note, every nerve ending recoiling against the man who'd touched it. He jammed it into his jeans pocket and spun to wash his hands before firing up the machine.

Hendricks turned to survey the empty cafe, his gaze settling on Ted. The elderly sisters had gone home when denied their cooked breakfast and Ted remained in a sulk. "All right, old timer?" Hendricks called.

Wiri punched coffee into the portafilter and frowned as Ted shifted in his seat, presenting his back to Hendricks. A vile swearword issued from his lips, and he dragged his mug from the wooden bench and faced the window. Hendricks laughed. "Suit yourself," he cackled. "You still owe me, old man. You have one more day before I tell your lady-love the whole sorry tale. I have standards, remember?"

"Hey." Wiri's hand froze, the portafilter poised beneath the brewing grouphead. "Leave him alone. Do your business elsewhere."

Hendricks snorted and dipped his body to lean his elbows on the counter. The aggressive stance left him observing Wiri from beneath bushy grey eyebrows. He lowered his voice to a hiss. "Don't give me orders, kid." Wiri jerked as the man rose at speed and whirled around to face Ted's stiffened back. "Hey Ted, what do you think of Mr Kingii here?" He glanced back at Wiri and his glittering eyes held a warning within their coal black depths. When Ted continued to ignore him, he moved his body around in a slow arc, using his middle finger and thumb to flick a stray sugar sachet across the counter. It hit Wiri in the stomach before plummeting to the tiled floor with a plop. Hendricks jerked his head towards it. "You might wanna pick that up, son," he said, his eyebrow quirking upward again. "Wouldn't want to report Mari's nice cafe to my mate at the council for health and safety violations." His gaze slid back towards Ted's rigid spine. He patted the counter with his hand. "Mind you, what's the point, eh Ted?"

Wiri set the portafilter on the counter and considered his next move with care. A well-timed punch could lay the man out flat on his back on the floor. His uncle taught all his children how to do the most damage with the least effort. Economy of scale, he called it. Wiri calculated the width of the counter and the length of his arm, knowing if Hendricks anticipated the move and stepped back, it would leave him sprawling. He imagined knocking the smirk off the shaved chin, choosing between the man's mouth and throat to inflict the most pain. He remembered his first encounter with Vaughan and the big man's steady hand on the gun, and sympathised.

A sweet scent drifted across the counter, irritating Wiri's senses with the mix of pine needles and expensive cologne. Hendricks' lips peeled back in an even wider grin, baiting him to fulfil the desire he read in his eyes. "Come on then, Kingii," he whispered and Wiri sensed in that moment that somehow, Hendricks knew the truth about him. The man nodded. "That's right, kid. I know a Du Rose when I see one." His tongue appeared between his teeth and he wrinkled his nose. Wiri flinched as the man's hand rose and jabbed towards his own temple. Hendricks leaned forward. "See this scar? Reuben Du Rose gave me that in a bare knuckle fight over a woman."

"I don't know him." Wiri issued the retort through clenched teeth. His soul ached with the effort of denying his whakapapa. The power drained from his body as his father's lies tainted him as they often did, drenching him with the stink of deceit and hatred. His fingers shook within the balled fists at his side, his wrists trembling and his whole body aching to strike.

Hendricks snorted. He jabbed an index finger towards Wiri's face, his courage growing from the other side of the counter. "Whatever, kid. Your genetics and grey eyes say different." He shook his head, his brown irises dancing with delight. "Which one are you then? Reuben only bred losers." He cocked his head to the side and his finger stilled in the air. "Apart from the last one." His eyes narrowed to slits, and the smile drooped. "Maybe I'll leave you alone if you're out of that one. I'd have met my match there." He whirled around again to address Ted, though the old man continued to ignore him. "Service is lax today, isn't it Teddy boy? Not quite the usual speed."

"Get out." Wiri found his voice. He saw in his peripheral vision how Ted's head turned and his ears twitched backwards like a nosy gelding's. Wiri unclenched his fists and capitalised on Hendricks' fear of Logan Du Rose. He raised his hand and pointed towards the door. "Go," he told the man. "Before I make you."

Disbelief rampaged across Hendricks' features, screwing them into a mass of ugly creases and ridges. Scorn replaced it at speed and he took a step towards the counter. Before Wiri could react, he swiped his hand to the right and knocked over the metal cup containing spare sugar sachets and stirrers. They cascaded across the counter like a waterfall, a jumble of paper and plastic sticks slapping against the tiles as they spread far and wide. Hendricks squared his shoulders and jerked his chin downwards as though drawing an invisible battle line. "So, we have it," he said, his voice low. He lifted his hand and pointed at Wiri's chest. "I see who you are," he growled.

He whirled around on expensive, shiny shoes and hauled on the door handle. Pausing, he delivered another glare at the back of Ted's head and glowered at Wiri. "Say hi to your flat mate for me, won't you?" His lips peeled back from his teeth in a snarl. "Tell him roulette is for grown-ups." The door clanged shut behind him as quick steps took him outside onto the path. The pine scent remained behind him as a reminder of his presence long after the bell over the door ceased its irritating jangle.

Wiri swallowed, his muscles refusing to work at his bidding. A deep ache consumed the pit of his stomach and the boulder rolled into the void it created. He hated that Hendricks saw right through him to his black, defective core. The filth of Kane's genetics made him want to run and hide, to keep running until he somehow left himself behind as though shucking a second skin. He envied Mac and Phoenix, carrying Logan's whakapapa their entire lives without giving it a passing thought.

A wooden leg scraped against the floor and he glanced up to see Ted shifting his stool back to face the view of the street beyond the window. His claw-like fingers clenched around the handle of his mug as he set it back on the counter. He didn't look at Wiri or attempt to discuss what he'd heard. Wiri licked his lips and retrieved the portafilter from the counter where he'd left it. He cleared up the sachets and the sticks, throwing the latter into the sink in the kitchen for washing. His hands shook as he wiped coffee powder off the counter and smiled at the new customer stepping through the front door. The man waved to Ted in the corner and this time, he waved back at him.

11

COMB

Wiri glanced up half an hour later to see Vaughan's truck blocking the main street. Mari clambered from the passenger seat at a pitifully slow pace. The bell jangled as she pushed open the door and looked at the crowd gathered around the counter.

"He makes a nice coffee," a man commented, lifting his take away mug in a salute. "But he won't do my cooked breakfast."

Mari ignored them all, powering through the bodies and around the counter. She disappeared into the kitchen without speaking to anyone.

"Is my chai latte ready?" A teenage girl wearing a school blazer leaned low enough over the counter to give Wiri a view of her lacy bra. A series of loud honks issued from the street and Wiri stuck his head through the archway.

"I need to leave, Whaea," he said, urgency in his voice. "It's my first day and I can't afford to mess up."

"Tēnā koe." Mari faced the tiny window in front of the sink. She lifted the hem of her blouse and dried her damp eyes. "Coming now."

Wiri paused as the horn of Vaughan's truck sounded over all the others. "Are you okay, Aunty?"

Mari nodded and her face crinkled into a series of lines as she fixed a fake smile in place. She waved her hand in his direction. "Thank you, boy. I wish I could say it was worth your trouble."

"Right." Wiri searched in his mind for platitudes, but they strayed away as invisible threads. Vaughan honked again. He dug into his jeans pockets and produced a flurry of coins and notes. "I didn't know the code for the register so I took cash." He closed his eyes to list the number of coffees he'd made in the fifty minutes since she left. A shrug accompanied his shy smile. "I sent them to the cashpoint, and they didn't like it. And another guy paid, picked a fight and left without his drink." He turned to leave and grabbed his hat from the corner of the counter, halting and spinning on his heel.

"What guy?"

Wiri's jaw tightened. "Hendricks?"

She swallowed and avoided his gaze. "Right."

"Oh, and that old man in the corner refused to pay for his drink. He said he pays in kind." Wiri pursed his lips as Mari's eyes narrowed to slits.

"In his dreams," she growled. "Stupid old fossil."

"Okay. Bye." Wiri pushed his way through the crowd and a general hum of unease arose as Mari stepped behind the coffee machine. He jumped onto the truck's runner and opened the door. "Sorry," he puffed as he hurled himself into the passenger seat. He grappled with the seatbelt and Vaughan waited for him. Glancing in the side mirror, Wiri saw a tail back which stretched the length of the main street.

"All good." Vaughan seemed unconcerned. He depressed the clutch and cranked the gear lever into first, letting the truck drop forward before it built up speed. A wave of his arm through his open side window ended in a two-fingered salute to the driver behind him. Wiri pressed himself back against the seat and clamped his teeth over his lower lip.

Vaughan turned left onto a side road and headed out into open country. He glanced sideways at Wiri. "How did you cope?" he asked. "You got quite a crowd in there. Someone sent out a text saying there was decent coffee for a change. Think the town and his wife turned up to see if it was true."

Wiri snorted. "Yeah, I reckon they did. I don't mind making coffee, but everything I cook tastes like burnt sausage."

"Even burnt sausage? Impressive." Vaughan grinned and released a sigh the further they travelled from the town, as though the increased distance allowed him to breathe.

After ten minutes of silence punctuated by the tyres rumbling against the asphalt, Vaughan cleared his throat. Wiri jumped. He'd closed his eyes and rested his head against the seat, and the jarring sound startled him. "Sorry." Vaughan kept his gaze on the road ahead, but his jaw worked against his cheek, creating a harsh line through his dark stubble. "It's complicated, but Mari wanted to see Seline." He exhaled and shook his head. "I'm sure you'll work it out for yourself, but she hates me."

"Mari?" Wiri sat up straighter and replayed the scene in the cafe. His eyes narrowed in confusion as he'd watched her touch Vaughan's arm and tease him with a twinkle in her eye.

"No. Seline." His Adam's apple bobbed as he swallowed and gnawed on the inside of his cheek. "She won't accept me. I don't think this is a friendly visit."

"But you're married." Wiri faced the windscreen and worried at his lower lip. "Don't people leave you alone once you're married?" The Plan depended on the deep-seated belief. He didn't know if he could cope if Vaughan disproved the existence of his trump card.

Unaware he destroyed Wiri's world in four simple words, Vaughan snorted. "Who told you that?" The truck slowed with a guttural roar as he indicated left and turned into the lumber yard. The scent of drying pine filled the truck's cab as Wiri pushed his hands beneath his thighs to stop them shaking.

Vaughan chose timber to replace the rotting fence posts on another side of the property. Wiri helped to load the wood, his mind elsewhere as his hands worked on autopilot. He toyed with the idea of going home and picking his life back up, labouring for Logan and living in the room next door to Phoenix. Tears of defeat prickled behind his eyelids as he challenged the shaky premise on which he'd built his plan.

Poppa Alfie legitimised his relationship with Nonie Leslie through marriage.

Kane, his birth father, had done the same by marrying Caroline.

Wiri slammed the tail gate and leaned against it as the lumber worker straightened his fluorescent vest and shambled back to his fork lift. The truck shuddered as a post settled against another and stilled. Wiri squeezed the bridge of his nose between a finger and thumb. The borrowed gloves rendered the action ineffectual, and he tugged them off and jammed the cuffs into his back pocket. Repeating the pressure against his nose brought no extra relief. The Du Roses didn't get the opportunity to object to Hana before Logan jammed a gold band on her slender finger. Theirs was the love story of their generation. Wasn't it?

Wiri sank down until his backside rested on the rear bumper. The boulder seemed to occupy his chest, cutting off his circulation and stopping him from extending his lungs. He scrabbled in his pocket for his phone and pulled it free.

She answered on the third ring, her voice clear and gentle. "Wiri," she said, and he heard her smile. "Are you okay?"

"No," he breathed. "I've made a terrible mistake."

"What's happened?" Her tone changed to one of alarm. "Are you hurt?"

"No." His reply held a strangled quality as though pressure tamped down his voice. He exhaled as Vaughan strode across the yard towards him. The shadow cast by the brim of his cap did nothing to diminish the thunder in his face.

"Did you mean everything you said?" Her tone contained a plaintive edge.

Wiri lowered his voice to a whisper. "I want to marry you, Phoenix." His ears strained against the extraneous sound, wanting to hear the beat of her heart.

"I miss you, Wiri," she replied without a pause. "Come back for me." A bell pealed in the background and she gasped. "Gotta go," she gushed. "You promise you're not hurt?"

"No," Wiri managed. "I'm okay."

The call ended, and he stared at the screen as her number faded from view. She'd always known what to say to him and how to soothe his angst. They'd lost each other in the weeks since her disastrous summer camp, but he believed in the inevitability of their union. He cleared his throat and shoved his phone back into his pocket, telling himself it would all turn out okay.

Vaughan didn't speak as he reached Wiri. A man in a battered weatherproof jacket followed, halting the fork lift driver as he clambered back into his seat. "Unload it," he called to him. "He can't take that until he settles his account for the last lot."

Vaughan's shoulders slumped as an aura of defeat shrouded him. Wiri sensed the waves of sheer humiliation as the fork lift driver complained about double handling the wood. Speaking to Phoenix had flushed a lightness of spirit through Wiri's soul and he dug in his back pocket for his phone. "Wait," he said, lifting off the cover and slipping free the emergency credit card he hadn't yet used. "Take this."

"Right." The man in the dirty jacket snatched it in fingers worn by manual labour. Black lines ingrained in his skin displayed a lack of fear of hard work. "You'll need to pay for last month's as well." He jerked his chin towards the load in the truck. "And this."

"Okay." Wiri didn't look at Vaughan as he followed the man to the office. The five-hundred-dollar bill went onto his credit card and as he pressed his code into the keypad, he tried not to panic. Though it depleted his savings to nothing before Vaughan paid him, the boulder lightened its weight in his chest and he sensed Phoenix would approve. He strode back to the truck and clambered into the passenger seat, allowing Vaughan time to deal with his shame.

They were almost back at the farm before Vaughan leaned in Wiri's direction and murmured a muted, "Thanks for that." He didn't say he'd pay him back and a tick of worry set itself whirring in Wiri's gut. Vaughan cleared his throat. "Please don't tell Leilah." He exhaled and his irises glittered with wounded pride. "I'm not ready for that yet."

"Right." Wiri cast his mind back to all the times Hana had expressed the same sentiment. It led to her never feeling quite good enough for Logan and damaged their marriage in those turbulent early days. He breathed out through his nose. "You should tell her. Make a plan together and decide what you'll accept. It'll save you a load of trouble in the future."

Vaughan stared at him too long and the truck crossed the centre line. His frown created lines in the forehead visible below the baseball cap. "How did you get so wise?" he asked. He shook his head. "Okay. I'll talk to her." His Adam's apple bobbed in his throat. "Thanks for what you did back there."

Wiri licked his lips and nodded. "I don't need to pay it for a couple of weeks. She'll be right."

"Well, thanks." Vaughan drove back to town in silence, passing back along the main street and out the other side towards the farm. The truck shook against the rails from the cattle grid and bounced to the top of the hill. Vaughan exhaled and swore at the sight of a bay mare trotting around the paddock nearest the house. She shook her head and lifted her black tail towards the gelding grazing near the fence.

"What's wrong?" Wiri jumped from the truck and followed Vaughan's gaze.

"Seline put her gelding in with Hinga," he said, his voice a low growl. "I keep her separate for a reason. She's had a rough time and I'm trying to recondition her." He shook his head and slammed his door. "Leilah knows that."

His disappointment in his wife's inability to challenge her daughter rankled Vaughan for the rest of the day. They dragged the heavy poles up the mountain using ropes attached to an ageing quad bike and dug the holes by hand. Wiri neared exhaustion by the time they finished for the day.

He trudged back across the paddock towards the house with every muscle aching in his body. "I want a bath," he said to himself, using the track to set his course and concentrating on putting one foot in front of the other. Approaching from the side, he didn't see the patrol car sitting just below the deck or the two police officers talking to each other at the front door.

He didn't see them until he was almost on top of them. Then his heart froze in his chest and the boulder in his stomach slipped against the bottom of his left lung to impede his breathing.

12

Muzzle

Wiri froze at the end of the deck, the steps up to the front door seeming insurmountable. A blond man in a police officer's uniform leaned against the balustrade, his stance casual and without alertness. He jerked his chiselled jaw upwards in acknowledgement of Wiri's presence. As tall as Vaughan and just as wide, he'd let his expanse of muscle degenerate to leave a flabbier appearance. The way he'd tightened his belt to cause his stomach to bulge a little over his waistband indicated a man who didn't yet want to address what the mirror told him. The other officer sat on a bench beneath the lounge window, his legs stretched out in front of him. Wiri swallowed his panic, letting it collect in his throat as a lump before traversing the first step.

"Hey," he said, looking from one to the other. "Is there a problem?"

"Hi again." The officer on the bench rose and nodded to Wiri. The patrol man from the previous night stared at him through amused blue eyes. "I left my key at work. Figured I'd wait for you to let me in." He jerked his head towards the other man. "This is my brother, Tane. He runs the local watch house."

Wiri forced his head into an awkward nod at the other man. He hauled the carabiner off its loop and held out the key. "You're Jet," he said, his tone sombre.

"Thanks." The officer took the key and grinned at his brother. "He's fast, bro'. No flies on him."

"Don't be a dick." Older by at least half a decade, the officer leaning on the rail shot Wiri an apologetic look, his brows furrowing into a line. He forced his lips into an amiable smile. "He could have lived with me and my wife," he said as an explanation. His shrug betrayed his disappointment. "Ah well." He pushed himself off the rail. "You both have a good night."

Jet waved at the same time as he pushed open the door. "Thanks for the ride," he called after Tane.

His brother stopped on the bottom step. "See you for dinner tomorrow night. Don't be late. You're back on day shifts now, right?"

"Yep." Jet emerged from the doorway and handed back Wiri's key. He saluted Tane with two fingers. "Thanks for requisitioning my day off."

"Yeah, sorry." Tane didn't look sorry as he strode from the deck to the patrol car and slid behind the driver's seat. Wiri forced an inane grin onto his lips and managed a feckless wave as the patrol car moved through a precise three-point turn and cruised along the driveway towards the main road.

Jet eyed Wiri through eyes which sparkled with amusement. He folded his arms across his muscular chest and raised a blond eyebrow. "So, Wiremu Du Rose," he said, twisting his lips into a smile. "It seems we're house mates for the next few months."

Wiri nodded, his brain failing him with anything sensible to say. Jet exhaled and turned towards the house, his shiny boots carrying him across the threshold and into the hall. Wiri took a moment to let his panic subside. He took time to remove his hat and his boots before placing them on the rack on the porch. The size nine trainers nestling in the cubby above his shifted into context as Jet's. Wiri jumped as the man appeared next to him.

"Don't tell Leilah I forgot," he grunted, thudding onto the bench to remove his boots. He glanced up at Wiri from beneath his lashes. "You don't seem like a snitch."

"I'm not." Aware of the defensiveness in his tone, Wiri dropped his shoulders and moved towards the front door. He ignored whatever Jet said next, striding to his bedroom and shutting the door. Leaning against it, he closed his eyes and let the vibration of his panic wash over him. His situation couldn't be worse. He'd lied about his name to Vaughan and Leilah, only to discover he lived with the cop who knew the truth about him.

Wiri gnawed on his lower lip and contemplated phoning Phoenix again. He sensed she'd know what to do. His fingers moved over the black phone screen and he imagined listening to her soothing voice as she worked through the problem. But when he activated the screen, it gave the time as after five o'clock. She'd be at home in the kitchen, surrounded by her family. Answering the phone to him would force a fracture. She'd need to leave the room and avoid Edin's nosiness to speak to him.

He threw the phone onto the bed and took a step away from the door, jumping as a fist hammered against the wood. "Hey," Jet shouted. "Do you wanna clean up and go to town for dinner?"

"Not really," Wiri whispered to himself. But he licked his lips and pushed confidence into his voice. "Okay. Give me twenty minutes for a shower and some clean clothes."

The hallway swallowed Jet's reply and Wiri felt the floorboards vibrate with his movement as he slammed his own bedroom door at the other end of the corridor. His sense of fatalism threw the calamity into a chance for opportunity. Getting the police officer on his side could prove advantageous. He just needed a few moments to work out a plan.

"OOh, is this all that's left?" Jet blinked in surprise. He jabbed his index finger towards the sparse array of leftover pies. They'd used Wiri's truck to drive back into town and he nodded to Mari as they stepped into the cafe. Jet's damp fringe flopped over his eyes and Wiri sighed as he watched him peer into the cabinet. The police officer took longer than Phoenix to ready himself for the outing. Such a cloud of aftershave had wafted through the house, Wiri had retreated to the front deck to wait for him.

"Well, look what blew in with the last storm," Mari said, walking from behind the counter. Her crabbed hands reached out to squeeze Jet's wrist, but she slipped her free arm around Wiri. He stilled in shock at the way she singled him out for attention, her affection unwarranted. Then she qualified her reasoning. "Apparently this boy makes the best coffee in the town." She tightened her grip until her shoulder bumped the defined biceps bulging from beneath the sleeve of his clean tee shirt. "His skills are only outclassed by his kumu, according to the girls from the high school." She cackled and dropped her hand to pat Wiri's backside. He jerked away in shock, his eyes widening in horror.

Mari went back behind the counter, shaking her head at him. "Most entertaining too," she murmured, only loud enough for Wiri to hear. She clapped her hands, the short nails stained with the distinctive purple of late beetroot. "What are we having today, then?" She jerked her head towards the lighted cabinet. "You can have anything from there on the house."

"Awesome! I'll take a steak and cheese then, please." Jet hauled on the door of the drinks chiller and pulled out a bottle of soda. "You want one?" he asked Wiri.

"Please." Wiri watched him grab an identical bottle and set it on the counter. Mari got busy with tongs, her movements deft as she lifted out a pie and stuffed it towards a paper bag. She squinted, concentration shuttering her expression as she missed at the first attempt.

"She said what do you want?" Jet nudged him from his momentary lapse and Wiri found both him and Mari staring at him.

"Same, please." He gave himself a visible shake and stepped closer to the counter, taking one of the drinks to keep his fingers from worrying at his clothing.

"You can eat in here," Mari said, wiping her hands on her apron after she placed Wiri's pie next to Jet's. "But don't make a mess. I'm closing up in five minutes."

The men sat at a table in the corner as Mari switched the sign on the door to indicate she'd closed. She clicked the snib on the lock and returned to her kitchen. Jet sank his teeth into the pie with a sigh.

Wiri took tiny bites, his lack of trust affecting his appetite. When he lifted his drink, the soda gushed into his throat too fast and made him cough.

Jet finished his pie and leaned back in the wooden seat. A chalk board above the counter listed the special dishes and Wiri focused on it to avoid conversation. Mari clattered around in the kitchen. She spoke to someone, and an external door opened and closed. Wiri caught sight of her hefting crates of fresh vegetables into the chiller, her biceps straining with the ease of someone who repeated the task every day. He read the chalk board from one side to the other until he'd memorised every price and then started over, testing his brain for errors. He stilled as Jet spoke.

"We need to talk," he said, leaning his elbows on the table. He'd changed into a clean tee shirt and jeans and firm plates of muscle showed through the fabric.

"About what?" Wiri swallowed, the pie crust edging its way down his throat by slow degrees.

"I don't live with Tane for a reason," Jet said. He rocked back on his chair as though the discussion cost him, listing as it teetered on the back two legs. Fearful of Mari's rebuke, he glanced towards the kitchen and then righted it. "I dream," he said with a sigh. His blue irises flashed, and he studied Wiri's reaction, the darkening of his expression expecting something painful.

Wiri shrugged. "So?"

Jet exhaled. "So, I sometimes wake up in other parts of the house."

"Oh." Wiri nodded, relief flooding his bloodstream. "Night terrors, you mean?"

Jet swallowed. "Kinda." His fingers knotted and twisted on the table. "I served ten years in the army. I saw some stuff. Nobody knows." His jaw protruded through his cheek in the same way Vaughan's had earlier, a similar level of internal pain inducing the grinding action of his teeth.

Wiri shook his head. "It's okay. My ma has them real bad. She screams and runs around because of the bad stuff that's happened to her. My uncle deals with it. It doesn't bother me any more."

"Right." Jet nodded and leaned back in his seat. A pink bloom rose into his cheeks, flushing through the tanned skin of his neck and forming spots of colour above his jaw. He exhaled. "It's only fair I tell you something else," he said, lowering his voice and shooting a precautionary glance at the kitchen. Mari hummed a lazy tune inside, clattering crockery and containers as she prepared to leave.

Wiri's fingers stalled with his pie half way between his mouth and the table. "What?" he whispered, though he already knew.

"Vaughan thinks your name is Kingii." Jet leaned forward, his fringe flipping to cover the bridge of his nose. "I stopped your vehicle, so it gave me a reason to check you out on our system. You're Wiremu Du Rose like your driving licence said." His lips twisted as though the next revelation caused him discomfort. "You come from money, man. So why are you earning minimum wage on a nothing-as farm at the back end of nowhere?"

13

CHAMBER

Telling the truth proved cathartic, and Wiri stuck close enough to it he didn't need to remember complicated lies. He detailed his turbulent upbringing until the moment Hana absorbed him into her tight-knit family, and listed the events which had sullied the Du Rose name during his lifetime.

Jet gave an affirming nod as they balled up the paper bags from their pies and carried their drink bottles from Mari's store. She clicked the bolt on the door behind them and dropped the blind. "I thought I knew the name," he concluded. He nudged Wiri's shoulder with his as they stopped on the curb facing the main street. "Can you give me advanced warning if you feel like murdering someone?"

"I'll think about it." Wiri grinned and shook his head. "I don't look for trouble, dude. It just finds me."

Jet snorted. He tilted his head back to swallow the last of his soda before shoving the empty bottle into the street bin. "If I had a dollar for every criminal who says that, I wouldn't need to work."

Wiri tossed the remains of his uneaten pie into the bin, and he kept the drink bottle in his hand. Jet's low key reaction reinforced his faith in him, but he didn't regret keeping his relationship with Phoenix to himself. He couldn't bear to listen to another's speculation on whether they would make it. They had to make it. He had no Plan B.

Once in the truck, Jet guided him to a supermarket on the outskirts of the town. He made excuses for his lack of car ownership, not that Wiri cared. They separated at the front doors and Wiri bought basic supplies and enough packet meals to last him for the rest of the week. He wandered the aisles, marvelling at the cost of basic foods in a tiny town held captive by the store's proximity. He regretted not stopping in Hamilton and stocking up on supplies in one of the more competitive chains.

Phoenix's favourite cereal soothed his angst as he picked up the yellow box and turned it over in his hands. A cartoon character paraded across the front, a spoon lifted to his teddy bear mouth. His lips parted at the astronomical price and he set it back on the shelf with the others. The boulder pressed against his lungs, causing him to take shallow breaths. If they headed off the beaten track to hide from the Du Roses, he'd need even more money for The Plan than he'd anticipated.

Wiri shoved a packet of cheap oats into the trolley and kept pushing. He'd slather on cocoa powder and chopped banana in Hana's kitchen, but he flicked through his mental shopping list and discarded both expensive items. Powdered milk with an unknown brand dropped into the trolley as he continued searching for food, which wouldn't break the bank. He rounded the end of the aisle without looking up and a metallic clash cut across the classical music piping through the overhead speakers. "Sorry!" he gushed. "My fault."

The man sneered at him from behind the other trolley. Wine bottles and packet meals slid towards the front end to reveal junk food and a lonely lettuce. He lifted an eyebrow and tilted his head as though looking into Wiri's soul. Then he leaned his forearms over the trolley handle and surveyed the teenager with disdain. "What are you sorry for?" he asked. His tone held a hidden depth, something black and sticky beneath the smooth surface. He raised a quizzical eyebrow as he peered into Wiri's trolley. "So, kid," he said, "why are you in our town? They've cast you out of the whānau, or you're on the run. Which is it?"

Wiri swallowed. His skin prickled with the exposure, like a spider beneath the microscope of a boy known for pulling off their legs. "Excuse me," he managed, keeping his voice light. He drew the trolley back and tried to angle it around the man and his feast for one.

Hendricks shifted his trolley forward with enough speed to block Wiri's route. "Which is it?" he growled. "I love a good mystery."

Wiri ground his teeth. "No mystery." He forced a laugh into his voice. "I'm nobody. Just here to work."

Hendricks pressed his lips together, and they disappeared, leaving white, bloodless lines in their place. "On the run then," he said. His eyes danced with the unexpected intrigue delivered from a routine supermarket visit. Wiri moved his feet and Hendricks shoved his trolley again, anticipating the power bunching in the teenager's muscles as he prepared to push through the non-existent gap by force. "What are you running from, young Mr Nobody?" he whispered. He cocked his head and studied Wiri's face. "A crime? A debt? An angry father with a shotgun?"

His laughter rang out through the supermarket. It echoed off the metal shelving. An older woman pushed her trolley around the corner, took one look at Hendricks and reversed. She gave Wiri a tight-lipped look of sympathy, but didn't offer assistance.

A thwack made Wiri jump. He turned to find the yellow box of cereal face down on the smooth linoleum floor. He turned on wooden limbs and stalked back to right it, abandoning his trolley. It took all his resolve not to keep walking, to arrive outside in the car park with nothing to show for his foray into the adult world. The yellow box teetered at the edge of the shelf, the cartoon bear appealing to him for rescue. Wiri walked back to his trolley, sensing Hendricks boring holes in him as he returned. The man's gaze burned and Wiri sensed hatred gaining a foothold in his heart.

He let it, drawing on the reserves of power it afforded.

Reaching for his trolley, he seized the handle and gave it a mammoth shove. Metal ground against metal as Hendricks released his trolley, and it flew by him. His eyes widened as it cannoned past the end of the aisle and kept going, pinging off a chilled shelf containing shrink-wrapped meat. Wiri's trolley chased Hendricks', crashing into it again until they parted ways and disappeared in opposite directions.

"Better now, Mr Kingii?" Hendricks squared up to him, although Wiri acknowledged it wouldn't be a fair fight. But as he looked down at him, he saw the man's eyes held an unhinged quality which he'd seen in his mother. She'd had nothing to lose, either. Except him, and that hadn't seemed enough to stop her.

His fists balled by his sides and his jaw worked with a mixture of anger and fear. Hendricks lifted a sharp finger and jabbed Wiri's chest muscle. "I had intended to leave you alone, kid," he hissed. "Even though your truck is registered at CircleLine Holdings Ltd. I pitied you down here all alone." He leaned closer, his breath warming Wiri's chin and snaking up into his nostrils. "Especially now I know you're from the stupid side of the family."

The teenager forced himself to stop his lungs from inhaling the other man's acid. Hendricks flicked his finger like an old dad joke, catching Wiri's nose with his fingernail. Then he laughed. "You'll keep," he said with a chuckle. "Another time." He winked at him, mirth dancing in his eyes. "Next time, you won't see me coming."

He took a calculated step backwards, not taking his gaze off Wiri. Rage boiled in the teenager's chest like lava contacting water. The moment consolidated all his pent-up angst, the disappointment he anticipated from the Du Roses, and the permanent terror of loss combining into a volcanic misery. As Hendricks stepped out of range, Wiri played through a mental forecast of how he'd kill the man. He'd run at him, catching his flaccid stomach with his head. Once he'd got him onto the ground, he'd beat him to death with the neat rows of plastic milk bottles until Hendricks drowned beneath the white powder.

Wiri drew in a gigantic breath which filled his lungs and puffed his chest until it strained at his shirt. An inner voice, which sounded a lot like his mother's, urged him on. It dismissed the consequences as incidental as long as it banished the pain for an hour. A minute. A millisecond.

Anger made his stride longer and fury infused his fingers with power. Hendricks baulked at whatever he saw in Wiri's eyes, perhaps recognising the signs he'd pushed him too far. His eyes bulged like boiled eggs in his pink face, as Wiri lifted him by the throat and jammed him against the shelf. The structure shook beneath the force. Hendricks tore at Wiri's hand with his nails, drawing blood as he sought to release himself.

"No, boy." The gentle timbre penetrated the red mist which coloured Wiri's vision. A firm hand landed on his shoulder and squeezed. "Let him go, son. He's not worth it."

Locked in a war with his own soul, Wiri didn't command his fingers to release the man and the soles of Hendricks' expensive shoes scrabbled for purchase on the lowest shelf. He kicked over cartons of long-life milk, scattering them like fallen bricks across the aisle as he struggled to take the pressure off his throat.

The hand of the newcomer moved along Wiri's shoulder and tapped the bulging biceps doing all the work. "Stop!" he snapped. "Put the man back on his feet."

The pincer of Wiri's fingers and thumb snapped open and Hendricks sank to the floor. He slid until his head sagged against the edge of the second shelf, his spine collapsed and contorted on the linoleum like a discarded toy. Wiri's fingers remained open and in mid-air, twitching as though still drawing energy and pleasure from the action.

Hendricks flipped onto his hands and knees, scrambling to his feet with an air of panic. His jacket parted at the back to expose his fitted shirt tucked into his trousers. Striped boxer shorts poked above the waistband. It reminded Wiri of a child at school who'd tucked every item of clothing into the next layer. Trousers into socks. Shirt into underwear. Jumper into trousers. He glared at the man who'd intervened. "Whatever, Ted!" he snarled, like a teenager brawling with a classmate. "You still owe me."

Wiri's body trembled as the adrenaline withdrew from his system. He tested the urge to kill Hendricks and found it dissipating like fog. The rational side of his brain hard wired him back into the discomfort of the boulder and reasserted The Plan. A prison sentence would mark the end of its feasibility forever. He gulped, the sound loud despite the overhead crescendo of a maniac on a piano. Regret laced his vision as Hendricks reached the end of the aisle and passed out of sight.

Ted slapped Wiri on the back. "Don't be a dickhead all your life," he growled. "That man will always win, no matter what you do to shake him. He'll be hurling curses with his last breath." With that insightful piece of information, Ted spun on the rubber heels of his gumboots and stamped away. His cap clung to his wispy hair and his boots made a hollow, echoing appeal as he moved out of sight. At the end nearest the cashier, he used an experienced sleight of hand to pocket a fistful of chocolate bars and an energy drink.

Wiri ran a hand across his mouth, the fingers jerky and shaking. He forced a stabilising breath into his lungs and commanded his feet to go in search of his trolley. Hatred took hold in his heart, not just for Hendricks, but for himself. He'd spent years taming the beast in his soul, forged by his parents' inappropriate union. Kane had terrified him. Anahera had mystified him. He'd wanted love and received only violence and confusion.

He reached the end of the aisle, finding his trolley slewed across the main thoroughfare. The bottle of fizzy drink he'd allowed himself lay on the bottom, bubbles rising in a threat to burst as soon as he touched the lid. He took time to stand it up again, leaning it against the metal struts and putting a block of cheese and a loaf of bread in front of it to hold it still. He wheeled back to the site of his failure, his loss of control evident in the scattered cartons of milk. Picking each one up and placing it on the shelf, he vowed not to let Hendricks get the better of him again.

He rose after placing the last box back onto the shelf and turning it so its label faced the aisle. His heart lurched at the sight of Vaughan striding towards him. Small town gossip travelled fast, but if someone had summoned his employer already, it had excelled. "Hey." Vaughan jerked his chin upwards in greeting. He carried a cauliflower under one arm and three zucchinis bunched in his right hand. "Leilah's making soup. You want some?"

Wiri choked on his reply, licking his lips before answering. "We went to the cafe," he stammered. "I had a pie."

"All good." Vaughan continued past him, oblivious to Wiri's inner turmoil. "See you tomorrow then."

Wiri bent double and placed his palms on his knees. His breath caught in his chest. The swearword which leached from his lips just made him dirtier.

Jet waited for him outside, a single plastic bag sitting next to him on the asphalt. He shrugged as he eyed his supplies against Wiri's. "I eat at my brother's a lot," he confessed. "You should come over with me one night."

Wiri gave an upward jerk of his head but didn't commit to anything. He had no desire to spend an evening shooting the breeze with two cops. It would only be a hop, skip, and a jump to a link with Hana's son. One wrong word and Detective Inspector Bodie Singh Johal would be on his doorstep to investigate the lie.

Darkness nipped at the mountain as they travelled back to the farm. A yellow glow lit up Vaughan's house as it perched on the lower slopes. Wiri drove with care, keen not to invite criticism from his passenger. Their house blended into the mountain and Wiri regretted not leaving at least a bedroom lamp shining. The shadowy structure created a stark contrast to Hana's house with its teenage voices, light and endless supply of hot water and food.

In the seconds before Wiri indicated and turned onto the driveway, he discerned the smallest flicker of light at the front of the property. He must have made a sound because Jet turned to face him. "What's wrong?"

Wiri wrinkled his nose. "Just tired maybe. Thought I saw something on the deck at the front of the house."

Jet leaned forward to peer through the windscreen. The headlights picked out the fence line and the reflection of cow irises as they raised their black and white heads to stare at the truck's progress. "On the deck?" Jet's body stiffened and Wiri frowned.

"It's probably nothing, mate." He waved away the cop's concern and released the yawn playing at the corners of his mouth.

But it wasn't nothing.

As Wiri locked up the truck and the men walked towards the house, they smelled tobacco smoke. The man from the supermarket leaned with his elbows on the balustrade. He kept his gaze directed towards the glow of the town in the distance. Lifting his right hand, he took a hard drag on the cigarette lodged between his index and middle finger. Wiri realised he'd seen the resulting orange flare from the road. He glanced at Jet, looking for direction.

"Hendricks." Jet spat the word as though he'd swallowed something unpleasant.

"Officer." The man turned and Wiri's heart sank when he jerked his head towards him. "I'm here to make an assault complaint." He dragged the baseball cap from his head to reveal a mop of tangled greying curls which didn't fit the neat suit into which he'd poured his body. "It's in the public interest. Can't have folk going around attacking the good people of this town. Can we?" He grinned at Wiri like a horror film clown.

Wiri swallowed, The Plan screaming at him for his stupidity.

Jet shrugged and shifted behind him towards the front door. He removed a bunch of keys from his pocket and jangled them. "Come to the station tomorrow. The desk sergeant can take a statement."

"I wanna do it now." Hendricks spoke to Jet but kept his gaze fixed on Wiri. His gimlet eyes sparkled in the death throes of the sunset. The blackness of night and of something else clung around his shoulders like a cloak. "I might have another incident to report, too. Or perhaps my new friend here can help me."

"I'm off duty." Jet maintained an even tone, not allowing the man to push him into doing his bidding. But Wiri observed the rigidity of his shoulders and sensed something deeper at play between the men. "Go to the station tomorrow." Jet didn't turn around, but the man hadn't finished. He tapped the brim of his cap against his thigh.

"So, you don't mind being my witness, do you, Wiremu Kingii?" His irises glittered in reflected light as the moon slid from behind a cloud.

"What?" Wiri cocked his head and his brows formed a line of confusion beneath his fringe. "I don't know what you're talking about, sir." He kept on the right side of politeness but infused enough dismissal into his tone to make Hendricks wince as though he'd hit him.

"Is that right?" Hendricks took a step towards him and the air crackled. "Nice of you to clear Vaughan's debt at the lumber yard, son." Wiri got the sense that he'd stepped into a crucial conversation without realising and had missed the first important markers. He held his breath as the man took another drag of his cigarette and exhaled into Wiri's face. "Wish you hadn't done that." He stared up into Wiri's eyes, his expression angular and his irises flickering. "You can make it up to me, can't you? You witnessed Vaughan point a gun at me." He jerked his head towards Jet. "Tell the nice police officer what you saw."

This.

Logan had trained him for this.

Wiri played catch-up in his brain, understanding the veiled threat and preparing himself for whatever came next. He'd made a mistake at the supermarket, allowing Hendricks to catch him by surprise. This time, he'd finish the confrontation as a winner. Logan expected nothing less, especially from him. It would always be different for him because of his genetics.

He was a Du Rose.

Du Roses didn't lose.

Wiri allowed himself a slow blink which took in Jet still by the front door. His right hand rested on the key in the lock, but he'd turned his body to face them. His eyes glinted in the light from the hallway, which he'd flicked on with his left hand. They radiated confusion and a laser sharp awareness of danger. Wiri hardened his jaw. "Get off our property," he said to Hendricks. The raspy depth of his voice registered the warning in Hendricks' brain as he paused in the process of flicking ash onto the deck. His body straightened as though in shock.

"But it's not your property, is it Wiremu Kingii?"

His persistent use of Anahera's maiden name seemed to light a fuse deep in Wiri's gut. His mother's depression had coloured the earlier years of his life, but he chose to believe she'd loved him. Still loved him perhaps. The fuse burned to the point of pain and he yearned to knock her precious name out of

Hendricks' mouth, to pound his smug face until he chewed on his own teeth. Wiri's quick brain ran through a lightning speed version of how he'd put the man on the ground.

Step back, balance, fists up, right hook to the nose, throat, guts and then groin. He gave himself three seconds to drop the man on the deck and another to push him between the posts holding up the balustrade. Then he glanced at Jet and saw him give the slightest shake of his head. It was enough to stall the angry clamour in his mind.

Wiri grimaced as though he'd vomited in his own mouth. He took a long step towards Hendricks, landing close enough to put them toe to toe. The stench of cigarette smoke curled around his head as he stood over the man, taller by at least the length of his old school ruler. He left him no personal space as he spoke into his face, their breaths mingling. "Piss off!" he growled.

The smug smile remained on Hendricks' lips, but to his credit, he tried not to display his fear. Wiri smelled it rising from him like a haze and a latent thread of satisfaction coursed through his body. The sense of victory shocked him, reminding him of his father's blood still occupying his veins. It would always be there, the dark thread of inherited sickness which encouraged vengeance, violence and mania. Kane Du Rose tore down his house with his own hands, over and over again, until his body failed him. Wiri plugged into his familial lack of boundaries as he glared at Hendricks and saw the moment the man glimpsed the craziness he projected.

Hendricks took a step back and Wiri had never felt stronger or more defiled than in that moment. The man edged around him, but not before flicking his cigarette over the deck and into the scrubby grass to the side of it. "Your funeral," he hissed. He traversed the porch steps in one jump and dug his hands into the pockets of his expensive jacket.

His heels crunched in the grit as he set off walking along the driveway. Wiri didn't watch him leave, too busy battling the monster unleashed from his soul. He closed his eyes and controlled his breathing, pushing his father's spirit back into Pandora's Box and slamming the lid. He hadn't heard Jet speaking and jerked away as the other man touched him.

"Wiri." Jet pinched his left biceps hard enough to cause pain. Wiri shoved at his hand and swore at him. He licked his lips as adrenaline surged through his body. He'd all but buried Hendricks in his imagination, and the chill it left behind seemed both familiar and frightening. It rocked his soul and challenged what he knew of himself.

A voice in his head told him he didn't deserve Phoenix. He shook the condemnation away and grappled with his right hand until he found the balustrade and gripped its angular edges. Its solidity grounded him and he blew out a ragged breath.

Jet swore again and ducked beneath the balustrade to the right. He disappeared and Wiri closed his eyes against the sound of him stamping out the cigarette as its heat took hold of the tinder dry grass in front of the porch.

Wiri had gathered himself together by the time Jet returned, but his knees shook with the nauseous fragility rampaging through his gut.

"Must have left his car on the main road," Jet said. He waited as Wiri removed his boots, his behaviour both attentive and concerned. "Mate?" He paused until Wiri looked up at him. Then he delivered his warning. "Don't get on the wrong side of that guy. Tane's tried and failed to get him to court. He's got some nasty connections."

Wiri snorted, the sound hollow and without mirth. "So have I," he replied, his tone hard. He realised his error as the police officer blinked back at him.

Not willing to talk any more, he waved his hand at Jet and jerked his head towards the corridor leading to his bedroom. "Night," he said, his steps laboured and his shoulders sagging. He closed his door and leaned against it. His mind's eye showed him a vision of his father, his handsome features screwed into a sneer. "No," Wiri sighed, lacking the energy to fight the image and knowing he'd appear to torture him in his dreams.

Conceived in spite and raised in deceit.

Wiri shook his head against his fate. He yearned for Hana's simple honesty to wash him clean. Fumbling in his pocket, he tugged his phone free and dialled, longing to hear her voice. He let his spine slide down the door as she answered, stretching out his legs and crossing them at the ankles. Her sunshine soothed his bones and chased the vileness from his blood. He was her son at that moment, and she was his ma. Nothing else mattered.

Later, as Wiri stripped and crawled into bed, he pushed his fingers beneath his pillow and felt for Phoenix's bracelet. He'd left it near the edge, knowing he'd seek it when his chest seemed most hollow, and not wanting to search his bag for it in the night.

"What?" he said out loud, flicking on the lamp and sitting up to tug the bedding free. The beads weren't where he left them. Sickness rose into Wiri's throat as he hunted, eventually finding them sitting on the skirting board beneath the head of the bed. He lifted them and pressed the plastic jewels against his lips, his heart still thudding with the anticipated sting of loss.

Another sense added itself without invitation. Fear.

Someone had searched his room and caused the bracelet to slip behind the bed. Gratitude filled Wiri's heart that they hadn't removed his treasure, but anxiety marred its deliciousness.

Who had trespassed into his private place?

Not Jet. They left together. Maybe Hendricks had a key to Leilah's house.

His eyes narrowed to slits of anger and his teeth clenched as his accusatory thoughts strayed towards the man on the deck. Wiri rolled the beads against his palm, lodging his second grievance against Hendricks. "I'll kill him," he whispered, pressing a kiss over the biggest bead clinging to the narrow elastic thread. It sparkled in the lamp light, a fake diamond patina glinting through the moulded plastic.

"That's my boy," his father's ghost chuckled. "That's my boy."

14

LOADING PORT

W iri grunted at Jet the next morning as they passed in the kitchen. The police officer's uniform put him on his guard and he shook his head at the misnomer which turned a friend into a foe by dint of his clothing.

"You sleep okay?" Jet fixed his epaulettes over the shoulder bars of his shirt. He gazed through the front window and fastened the top button. "Gonna be a hot one today. Heavy rain later though, or so the weather forecast said."

Wiri nodded and stuffed his sandwiches into a reusable bag. He shoved the package into a fabric cooler with corners tattered from age. He missed the lunches Hana made and the ease of feeling hungry and finding food in the fridge. "Yeah," he replied, though he hadn't given the weather a thought before that moment.

"I finish at six today." Jet straightened his waistband and smiled at Wiri. "Wanna go to the bar in town?" He frowned and shuttered his eyelids in a mental calculation. "Yeah, you're old enough, aren't you?"

"Yep." Wiri pushed his drink bottle into the cooler and closed the zip with a whizzing rasp around its worn corners. "Depends if all you want is a sober driver."

Jet snorted and shook his head. "Na, mate. Just some company."

"What about your brother?" Wiri's fingers stopped on the handle of the front door as Jet followed him into the hall. Through the glass on either side of the door, dawn broke behind the mountain range to cast an eerie tangerine haze across the land and pick out the chrome detailing on his truck.

Jet shrugged. "They're busy tonight. His kid has a thing at school."

"Right." Wiri pulled the door open. A yawn gripped his face as the frosty morning air stroked his skin. He finished fighting the spasm which overtook him, then glanced back at Jet. His jaw ached with the force threatened by the next one. "Can I decide later? I won't be good company if I'm knackered."

"Fair enough." Jet spoke from the cavity of the fridge, his voice muffled.

Wiri rubbed his eyes before pulling the door wide enough to slip through the gap. He closed it behind him and sighed at his boots sitting beneath his hat on the shelf. The night's fitful sleep hadn't refreshed him. Waking at every creak and groan of the house left him feeling ragged and unprepared for the day. He sat on the bench to lace his boots and clamped the hat over his hair. Alfie's scent surrounded him and provided a modicum of comfort.

A glance at his watch told him to hurry as the digital hands moved past the hour. He sped up, the cooler strap digging into his shoulder and the bag bumping against his hip. It didn't just contain his sandwiches. His wallet nestled next to the bracelet inside a zip-lock bag. Unable to trust the sanctity of his bedroom, he'd carried with him everything that mattered. A closer inspection of his duffel bag in the light of the overhead bulb had shown his clothing in disarray. Even the book he'd brought had lost the bookmark from the last page he'd read. Someone had done a thorough search of his belongings and it worried him. The intruder possessed a key because they'd done no damage on entry. Wiri had prowled the house after midnight when he couldn't sleep, searching for signs of a break in and found none. Jet mentioned nothing about his gear being disturbed, which meant the visitor had targeted only Wiri.

He trudged across the paddock towards the lights of Vaughan's house, the mystery playing out in various scenarios in his mind. The cows tumbled away from his footsteps just as they had the day before, their limited brains forgetting they'd seen him make the same journey yesterday.

Wiri hopped the perimeter fence with limbs as heavy as lead. He didn't make it as far as the porch before a voice hailed him from the shed on the other side of the house. At least, he thought it hailed him.

"Hey, boy, come here!" The female tones held a petulant quality. Wiri looked around him, half expecting a child to appear. "Hey, whatever-your-name-is, come and help me."

A security light flickered on and Wiri spotted the woman who'd greeted Vaughan the day before with such disdain on the driveway. His steps ground to a halt and he stared at her.

Auburn hair tumbled over shoulders covered by a tee shirt made for a child. Neat breasts pushed through the fabric, and even in the dim light, Wiri noticed the outline of protruding nipples. Her bare stomach displayed a glittering jewel in her navel. His lips parted in surprise at her revealing attire. Her eyes glittered in victory as she walked towards him, marking every step with an exaggerated sway of her hips. "I need your help," she said, her tone becoming silky now she had his attention.

Wiri swallowed and glanced towards the house. "Vaughan's expecting me." He forced himself to concentrate all his focus on her glittering eyes, not letting them drop below her cheek bones. The sunrise gained traction behind her and its rays set her hair on fire.

Like a warning beacon.

She shrugged in dismissal and her top lip snagged upward to create an ugly sneer. "I'm sure he'll cope for a few minutes."

Wiri inhaled and released the breath as a sigh. He'd been here many times before and extracted himself, keeping the best of him for Phoenix even before she knew he loved her. He jerked his head towards the house. "Even so, I'll check with the guy who pays my wages."

She snorted. "Have you seen any of that yet?"

There it was again. Her inference sneaked past Wiri's defences and doubt crept into his thoughts. The plan only worked if he earned enough money to sustain two people in hiding for a prolonged period. The cooler bag bumped against his hip as a reminder of yesterday's naivety. He'd removed the credit card from behind his phone, placing it in his wallet and pushing it below the bottom panel of the cooler. He wouldn't take it out again, his emergency fund well and truly gone once the bill arrived.

Removing his gaze from the woman proved unwise. During his momentary lapse, she stepped close enough to invade his personal space. She leaned forward and her breasts brushed his left arm as she breathed his air. "I need your help with my horse." Her hand rose, and she cupped his cheek in her palm. Her pupils dilated as last night's stubble scraped against her skin. She dragged her hand lower until her fingers gripped his chin. "I heard you're good with horses," she whispered.

The boulder in his chest toppled to press against his heart hard enough to cause him pain. Wiri skittered back out of range, his cheek and chin burning as though she'd poured lighted gasoline over his face. "I have a girlfriend," he growled, the words dragged from a secret, covetous place in his chest. He'd always imagined saying the sentence, playing it over and over in his mind like a fantasy across the years. Grey swirls streaked across the sunrise as a warning of rain, reminding him of the storms which drifted across Phoenix's irises when he made her angry.

Confidence infused him as he rejected Leilah's daughter. He recognised the moment of impact as her chin lifted and her jaw tightened with hatred. The flash of spite in her face revealed a woman not familiar with the word 'no' or its connotations.

"Seline?" Leilah's gentle call issued from the house at the same time as the ranch slider hissed on its tracks. The woman tossed her hair and dropped her chin to glare at Wiri from beneath her brows.

Wiri answered when she didn't. "Hey, miss. It's just me." He turned away from the bile spewing like a black cloud from her psyche, his boots scraping against the baked earth. "Is Vaughan ready?"

"Hi Wiremu." Leilah's brightness tinkled in the dawn. The yellow glow from the cheap bulbs behind her threw her into silhouette, emphasising her gentle lines and angles. Slight and elfin, she contained a beauty which she projected from the heart. Wiri forced himself not to glance back at her daughter, marvelling at how certain qualities seemed able to miss a generation. He stepped up onto the porch and readied his smile to greet her. When he looked back, Seline had gone. Leilah wrinkled her nose and blinked out into the darkness. "I don't suppose you saw a young woman?" she said, a furrow appearing in her porcelain brow. "She went out ages ago to check on her gelding."

Wiri lifted his chin in an easy action, hiding his discomfort of her daughter's ambush. "Security lights are on," he replied. "Someone's moving around in the shed."

"Thanks." Leilah hauled the ranch slider open one handed to allow him entry. Her eyelashes fluttered, and Wiri's heart ached for the vulnerability he recognised in her eyes. It called to him like a familiar nemesis, threatening to burst through the cage of her heart and meet his in mid-air. He doubted regular cleaning products could ever expunge the mess it made. Leilah blinked, and the perception in her smile rendered Wiri speechless. "Take a seat." She pressed her fingers against his spine and guided him in the general direction of the dining table. "Vaughan's just coming."

Wiri sank into the same chair as yesterday, conscious of his work boots inside her home. He placed his cooler on the table and watched the strap slither over the side like liquid. Battered and innocuous, it contained his worldly possessions. The wallet betrayed his identity as a Du Rose and the bracelet formed the totem for his existence. Absorbed in his musing, he jumped to find Leilah dumping a mug of strong coffee onto the table in front of him. "You came prepared," she said, jerking her head at his bag. "You can leave it here, if you like?"

Wiri thanked her for the fortifying caffeine, but avoided her offer to safeguard his bag. He had no intention of letting it out of his sight.

And not because he was a fan of rubbery cheese and inferior pickle sandwiches.

Not unless Hana made them.

15

SAFETY

"You want me to go down there?" Wiri peered through the small manhole cover into the cavernous depths of the water tank. His voice echoed through the narrow tunnel and returned to him from the concrete void. He stepped back and studied the tank, uncomfortable with the three metres of earth which surrounded it from neck to base. Only fifty centimetres protruded above ground, clover and late daisies kissing the mottled grey sides. He stamped on the pitched concrete roof, testing its solidity.

"Don't do that!" Vaughan objected. "You'll be fine down there. It's one of the safer ones. Made by a local guy."

Wiri groaned. "Why does it have the tube thing on top? I don't mind going into the tank, but why do I need to squeeze through the hatch thing?"

Vaughan shrugged. "It stops nosey people falling in, I guess. You've got to want to go in there. On purpose. It's a safety feature. Cost my uncle a fortune when they first came on the market."

"I don't care. I don't want to be in there. On purpose or otherwise." Sweat streaked Wiri's brow, and he hopped down from the tank's pitched roof and leaned against the side of the truck. The super-heated chassis burned through his tee shirt at the shoulder. Exhaustion nipped at his ankles. He'd already dug twelve holes in the baked earth and helped to bury new fence posts. His right hand ached where stretching the wire had stressed the tendons. Dirt caused a scratch on the back of his right hand to smart. He figured Hendricks left it there in the supermarket when he'd scrabbled for release from the choke hold.

Vaughan shrugged. "It's an hour's job. Less if you hurry up and get on with it. We'll stop for lunch afterwards." He held out a rope attached to a fabric harness. "Come on, chop chop." He pushed the bundle into Wiri's hands.

The teenager's brows tugged into an anxious line. "You go down there if it's such a quick job. I'll make sure you're okay." Carabiners clanked together in his arms.

"I already went down there." Vaughan jerked his head towards the hole. "Who do you think cleaned the bugger in the first place?"

Wiri swallowed, hiding his shaking hands beneath the mess of rope and harness as Vaughan strained to lower the ladder into the vault. It clattered against the sides of the tunnel, the sound reverberating off the walls until it intensified in his mind like a continuous vibration.

"There you go." Vaughan stepped back and nodded towards the hole. "I can't plaster to save my life. You said on your CV that you'd done maintenance jobs." He raised a black eyebrow as though in challenge. "Prove it."

Wiri blew out a ragged breath and licked his lips. "Fine!" he growled. "How will you pass the stuff down to me once I get in there?"

Metal clattered as Vaughan lifted a bucket from the back of the truck. A piece of rope attached to the handle contained a tub of ready-mixed cement and a trowel. A heavy torch balanced on the top of the motley implements. "I'll lower and raise things in this." His black eyebrows waggled beneath the brim of his cap. "I might even send down your lunch if you don't shift yourself."

With no alternative, Wiri stepped into the harness and Vaughan tied the safety rope onto the anchor beneath the truck. "That's going nowhere," he said, rising with a sigh. Not trusting his safety to another, Wiri checked the knot and used Vaughan's distraction to hide his phone beneath the loose base inside his cooler bag. He delayed, tugging on the rope and frowning until Vaughan's tone became snippy. "Just get in, dude!" he exclaimed. "There's a ladder and a rope. You need an escort as well?"

Wiri stepped up to the tank and clambered onto the angled roof. The rope trailed along the ground behind him, slithering in his wake. Long enough to allow him to descend and walk around the tank's interior unimpeded, it represented a lifeline to freedom.

The presence of the narrow circular chimney created a slender viewing window for assessing the contents of the water tank. The ladder narrowed the aperture even more. Wiri rested his palms on the lip of the tunnel and peered down into the void. "You sure it's totally empty?" He held his breath and dragged his courage to the fore, knowing he'd need it once he descended into the dark space. "Have you disconnected the feeder pipes?" He squinted at a white tube which left the concrete, made a ninety-degree turn and disappeared beneath the earth.

Vaughan shook his head. "No need. This takes the water from the hay barn over there." He lifted his muscular arm and pointed at a building less than fifty metres away. Its open side revealed a season's worth of hay stacked to ceiling height. The narrow pitch of the roof finished in a length of guttering to collect the rainwater from its wide expanse. It fed into a down-pipe fixed to the front right wall. Vaughan snorted. "If you piss in there, you'll have to drink it because it supplies your house."

Wiri sighed as he inspected the blue sky with a shrug. A single cumulus cloud hugged the highest of the mountain's three summits. Like a cherry on a cake. He peered into the void below the inspection hatch and resisted the urge to yell into it like a child and revel in the echo of his voice.

The edge of the ladder protruded from the opening, reducing the width his body would need to fit through and descend. Wiri wrinkled his nose, wondering how Vaughan had pushed his muscular torso down through the gap in order to stand at the bottom and hose the walls.

The vibration of hooves echoed around the tank, knocking against the concrete and rising to his ears like a drum beat. Wiri rose with a violent exhale, almost losing his footing on the pitch of the roof.

"Hey guys." Leilah drew up next to the truck, free riding a bay mare whose rolling eyes displayed an inherent nervousness. Leilah's slender legs hugged the mare's burgeoning winter coat, her boots hanging without the stability of saddle or stirrups. A loose rope halter replaced a bridle, and she rode like a Du Rose. Healed scars covered the mare's body and the wrinkled corners of her tender lips bore colouration changes. Someone with hard hands had hauled on a snaffle until she'd bled. Wiri studied the mare and felt the familiar up-tick of his heartbeat at the sight of cruelty. He frowned and Leilah smiled at him. The sun rose in her face and Wiri found himself smiling back, appreciating the inner beauty which radiated from her. She fitted the mare, her body at one with the half ton of horseflesh which obeyed her will. "We didn't do this," she said, her tone soft. Holding the rope from the halter in her left hand, she used the other to pat the mare's sweating neck. Soft ears flicked back and forth in response.

"Who did?" Wiri demanded. Standing on the protruding roof of the tank put him at eye level with the mare. She tossed her black mane and stretched her muzzle towards the scrubby grass. Leilah lengthened the rope and let her nip the weak blades, her hand resting against her thigh.

"Long story," she replied, her gaze flicking to Vaughan. He blinked, his eyelashes grazing his cheeks as he cocked his head. His expression softened until he resembled an adoring puppy. Wiri swallowed as the intensity of their connection locked him out of their intimacy. Leilah's lips curved into a sad smile, dropping as she sensed Wiri staring at her. "Let's just say my husband rescued me at the same time as he liberated Hinga," she said, clearing her throat at the end of the sentence.

A second set of hooves pummelled the earth and Seline cantered her gelding over the rounded crest above them. Her horse wore an English saddle and bridle and she stood in the stirrups as they moved onto the downhill camber. A riding hat covered in black velvet ended in a neat chin strap and she'd swapped the indecent tee shirt for a blouse. The grey dappled Appaloosa suited her. "I thought you might fall off," she said to Leilah, her condescending words fitting around ragged breaths.

Leilah grinned. She appeared glued to the ribs on either side of the mare's spine, her posture relaxed. It looked impossible to separate her from the horse, but she didn't dispel her daughter's concerns.

"Wiri is just gonna mend the cracks in the tank." Vaughan waved his hand towards the concrete. "We can't afford for the winter rains to burst right through it."

Leilah nodded. She smiled at Wiri with gratitude. "Thank you." She said it as though her husband hadn't contracted to pay him for every filthy task. Her nose wrinkled. "It's a horrible job."

"He'll be fine." Vaughan brushed off her sympathy with a brusqueness, which made her frown.

"Well, don't let me catch you down there." Her tone held a warning. She jerked her head towards Vaughan's midriff. "If your stitches open up again, I'm calling an ambulance and making sure it drives slowly through town with the sirens on full blast."

Vaughan winced and Wiri read the discomfort in the down turn of his lips. He didn't strike him as a man who liked to advertise his weaknesses. As Leilah winked at Wiri, he sensed her playing to her advantage. His loyalty to Vaughan forced a response. He gave her a dismissive wave and, throwing his shoulders back, faked courage he didn't feel. Ignoring Seline's raised eyebrow, he turned back to the tank.

"I'm all good," he said, wishing the sentiment into reality. He jerked his head at Vaughan and dragged the rope behind him to create a decent length of slack. "Are we doing this, or what?"

16

Action Bar

An hour in the darkness proved more than enough for Wiri. He used the torch to isolate the hairline cracks which threatened the integrity of the concrete tank before filling them with the quick drying cement. The sun cast a fortifying circle of yellow on the floor beneath the manhole, the rungs of the ladder stretching long shadows through it as though they battled for dominance. The hooves vibrated through the earth and bounced off the concrete walls with a dull thud as Leilah and Seline left for home.

"You okay?" Vaughan's voice boomed through the structure, though he hadn't shouted.

"Yeah." The lie made Wiri clench his teeth behind the mask and force himself to focus on the task. "Can you pull the safety rope tighter? I keep tripping over it."

Vaughan grunted, and the coil slithered away until it hung from Wiri's waist and formed an arc towards the ceiling like a sagging washing line. Wiri sighed as he felt the tug. He wished he could go with it. But the sooner he filled each of the cracks Vaughan had marked, the sooner he could climb the ladder and escape to bask in the sun's warmth. Grit ground beneath his boot soles as he walked around the wide space. Each step threw up the scent of mustiness and the choking concrete dust. The mask covered his nose and mouth to prevent it polluting his lungs, but it didn't stop his nostrils becoming clogged with the smell of the awful darkness.

"You still okay?" Vaughan's voice boomed again and Wiri sighed. He appreciated his employer's care for his well-being, but wished he'd stop keep calling to him. The sound reverberated again around the concrete walls until fading into the packed earth beyond them.

"Yeah," he replied, struggling to keep the annoyance from his voice.

He'd started at the furthest point from the manhole, knowing the longer the task took him, the harder he'd find it to remain inside the tank. He worked in a clockwise direction, and each step closer to the circle of daylight infused him with a mixture of hope and desperation.

"Need a break yet?" Vaughan asked. "You can come up for a breather if you want. Leilah texted. She has lunch for us back at the house."

Wiri shook his head. He lifted the mask away from his mouth and damp air rushed between his lips like an invasion of fungus and bacteria, which made him choke. "No, thanks," he called back, hearing the stress in his voice. "I brought my own. And if I come out, I ain't getting back in again."

"Okay." Vaughan didn't challenge him, and Wiri sensed he understood the dilemma.

He squeezed cement from the tube, balancing the grey mixture on the point of the trowel before pushing it inside another crack marked by Vaughan's slanted hand. He'd denoted the start and end of the crevice with arrows in white spray paint. The cement dried within minutes, forcing Wiri to work fast. He pushed another blob inside the gap, leaning the elbow of his other arm against the wall to take the weight of the torch. A curse escaped his lips as the narrow beam picked out a bead of cement tumbling to the floor. Wiri edged the tube closer with the toe of his boot and dipped to squeeze another lump onto the trowel. The next lot went into the crevasse, sealing it against the water, which would rush in during the coming rainy season.

A flash flood or heavy rain had caused the cracks to widen over subsequent seasons, and Wiri flashed the torch over his line of repairs and hoped they held.

"Did you see the ones up near the ceiling?" Vaughan's voice boomed again into the hole.

Wiri shone the torch over his head and groaned aloud as he noticed the white arrows dotted above his eyeline. "No!" he called back, his tone testy.

"You'll need to use the ladder." Scraping sounded against the narrow entrance as Vaughan hefted the rungs until the metal feet rose above Wiri's head. His breath caught in his chest at the notion of being stuck in the hole without the ladder. Then Vaughan's voice returned. "I'll reduce the length so it can fit in the tank with you," he called. "But you'll need to catch it when I put it back in, or it'll fall and crack the wall."

"Okay." Wiri took a deep breath and walked towards the circle of light on the floor. A cockroach skittered away in front of him and he sidestepped it. As soon as the rains came it would drown anyway, trapped in the concrete prison. It would move higher and higher up the walls, traversing Wiri's repairs until it reached the ceiling. He swallowed and imagined the horror of such a death.

Laying the torch and trowel at his feet, he pushed the awful thought from his mind. Squinting into the darkness, he realised he'd left the tube of sealant on the floor and sighed. "I'll get it in a minute," he promised himself, closing his eyes and basking in the sun pouring through the hole.

Metal clanked as Vaughan fiddled with the connectors of the ladder, reducing the height so Wiri could lean it against the interior walls to reach the higher cracks. His head and shoulders removed the glow and cast Wiri back into darkness as he leaned over the tunnel. "You ready?" he demanded.

"Yeah." Wiri's shoulders slumped.

Vaughan disappeared and the sun which momentarily caressed Wiri's cheeks seemed to farewell him. The ladder fitted back through the narrow gap and Wiri shielded his eyes to look up into the light. Vaughan grunted as he supported its weight and lowered it into the void. He leaned through the gap, his stomach balanced on the concrete lip as his muscles strained to keep hold of the ladder. Then he swore. "I'm gonna drop it!" he shouted. "Move!"

His cry caused Wiri to step back. The ladder shot through the hole and plummeted down, pivoting on its two feet like a ballerina before tipping. The torch and trowel shot in different directions. Wiri estimated its trajectory and dove out of the way before the top rung crashed into the wall above where his head had been seconds earlier. The force of the impact caused it to slide until the bottom feet jammed in the join between the floor and the wall, the top rung scraping down until it stopped just under two metres from the bottom.

Wiri's throat ached with the pulsing of his heart and he pressed his palms against the wall on the other side of the tank from the ladder. He turned his body until his back slid down the rough concrete and his backside touched the heels of his boots. Controlling his next few breaths, he dragged off the mask and blew them out through pursed lips. Airborne dust pushed into his mouth and lungs until he coughed.

"I need to come out," he called up to Vaughan, straining his ears for a reply.

Nothing.

"Vaughan. I need to get out now." Wiri rose, his knees trembling enough to make him press his left hand against the wall. "Get me out!" he repeated.

A shape moved across the hole and cast a human shadow over the circle of light.

"Vaughan!" Wiri dropped to his hands and knees and crawled underneath the fallen ladder. He bumped his head on a rung and shifted towards the wider end of the triangle it created. He made it to the space beneath the hole and called up to the person looking down at him. Sunlight back-lit them, causing a blinding halo to surround their blurry shape. "Vaughan!" Hysteria entered Wiri's tone. "This isn't funny!"

A scraping sound reached Wiri's ears as concrete moved across concrete. The figure disappeared, and the sunlight returned. But only for a moment.

A grunt echoed around the chamber as the person at the surface dragged the heavy lid over the aperture. Wiri held his breath and his strangled cry reverberated around his head, tinged with panic and disbelief. "No!" His voice rose to a scream. "NO! Don't!"

The spot of light he knelt in winked out as though controlled by a switch. But not before the safety rope snaked down around him, the end slapping him in the groin. The inspection lid clanked as it completed the seal far above Wiri's head.

The disbelief grew as a knot in his chest as Wiri bent double and clutched his stomach. His breaths puffed into the mask, soaking his lips and cheeks and fogging his brain. The darkness reached out for him with tentative fingers, enveloping him and burying him with the unlucky cockroach.

17

Rib

The pitch-black darkness paralysed Wiri for longer than he could estimate. His brain worried too much about the why of his situation before he could distract it with the pressing matter of his survival.

"What would Logan do?" he asked himself, his whisper returning to him as though someone else asked the question. He imagined his uncle doing the mathematical calculations required to give him freedom to work. It pushed the notion of his inevitable death into the future and allowed him to breathe with more ease.

Wiri sat back on his bottom and grasped his knees to his chest. "Think, think!" he urged himself. The dead silence helped to settle him as he cast through half-forgotten biology lessons from school. "The average person breathes eleven thousand litres of air a day," he recited. "This is a twenty-five thousand litre tank. I have time." He relaxed his fingers and his legs stretched out in front of him. "I have time," he repeated. "Someone will miss me before then."

He reached his fingers above him, knowing the ladder was up there somewhere and not wanting to bang his head. When he didn't find it, he rose to his feet and squatted, still grabbing the air above him. His fingers contacted the rough metal, and he gave a sigh of relief. A cough ratcheted from his chest and he fumbled to replace the mask, setting it back over his nose and mouth. "Two things," he whispered to himself, raising his own spirits by charting his successes as he completed them. "Found the ladder. Still got my mask."

Keeping hold of the ladder, he eased himself to a standing position, following the angle to its highest point. He nudged it with his shoulder and tried to push it away from the wall. It resisted. The metal prongs ground against the concrete. The force of the fall had driven it into the side of the tank and wedged it across the space from one side to the other. When his feet tripped over the safety rope, he loosened the harness and slipped himself out of it to give him more flexibility. It fell to the floor with a clank of the carabiner clips.

Wiri kept one hand on the ladder and reached the other to his back pocket. The empty flap of fabric condemned him for leaving his phone on the surface with his lunch. He released a sigh and pressed his forehead against the metal ladder, feeling the cold leach through his skin. "Think," he urged himself. "Panic doesn't help." His uncle's familiar words returned to coach him, Logan's hatred of fuss discouraging his children from becoming hysterical in his presence. "Torch," he breathed. "Find the torch."

Replaying the scene as the ladder fell meant revisiting why Vaughan would want to seal him into the tank. Wiri tried to do the first without dwelling on the latter. He imagined himself emerging into the daylight to the sound of Vaughan's rumble of laughter. Shaking his head, he realised it didn't fit with what he'd already learned of the serious man. It wasn't his style. And anyway, shortening the ladder meant it wasn't long enough to reach the top of the tunnel.

Wiri flapped his hand in the darkness and planned how he would find the torch. Replaying the scene told him it had skittered to the right of the manhole. His escape route had taken him to the left, but following the ladder to its junction with the wall put him as far away from the shaft as he could get. Wiri raised his right hand and mapped out the landmarks. "The inspection lid is near the eastern edge," he said. The echo-voice repeated it back to him. "That means the torch went south. I'm standing in the west." He let go of the ladder and dropped to his hands and knees. "I'm going this way."

Wiri's wristwatch still showed the time but wouldn't connect with his phone from inside the heavy concrete structure. His wrist grew weak from flicking his hand to activate the screen and utilise the faint glow made by the display. Twenty minutes passed as he performed a fingertip search of the half of the tank bisected by the ladder. He found the trowel first, jamming the handle in his back pocket to save him from banging his knees against the sharp metal edge of the blade. His breath caught in his chest as his fingers brushed the plastic case of the torch and he paused before trying the switch.

Pushing himself back onto his heels, he prepared himself for the genuine possibility that it no longer worked. His thumb traversed the case until it rested over the button. "Now," he said to himself, willing it to burst to life and illuminate his situation. The bulb flared a faint yellow light indicative of failing batteries. Wiri had watched Vaughan replace them before they started and tutted as he inspected the broken glass in the torch's face. The various mirrors had shattered with the impact and the floor glittered as he shone the weak light on the space where he'd found it.

Wiri turned onto his knees and crawled one-handed, moving away from the broken shards and keeping the torch clutched in the fingers of his right hand. His reasoning diverged into two trains of thought. The first wanted to conserve the torch light, while the other warned it might not start again if he extinguished it. He trusted the latter and kept it shining.

The addition of light helped him to free the upper part of the ladder from the wall. It required a decent upward shove to release it, though it removed a layer of concrete in the process. Wiri shook his head at the two long grooves, deciding he no longer cared.

Desperate to rest but unable to risk wasting the torchlight, Wiri pushed the ladder as upright as he could manage. He walked it by keeping it leaned against his body. Using his feet to push each of the metal legs in turn like a father dancing with a child, he made slow progress. The ladder's ragged joins skinned his fingers as he gripped the torch and rungs. He paused at intervals to shine the light towards the ceiling and estimate his distance. At last, he stared up at the underside of the concrete lid above his head. The thought drifted across his mind that he might not be able to push it off the opening, but he dismissed it and tamped down the resulting fear. "I have to get there first," he told himself.

The impossibility of escape made itself known when the ladder failed to reach the ceiling. Vaughan had shortened it to pass through the hole and enable Wiri to lean it up against the interior walls. The design of the ladder meant he'd had to withdraw it from the tank and lay it down on the ground to alter the safety catches. Wiri didn't have enough room on the floor of the tank to repeat the exercise.

He used the fading torchlight to estimate the distance between the edge of the tank and the start of the inspection tunnel. Nearer on the eastern side, it presented him with the possibility of reaching from the ladder to the lip of the tunnel leading to the surface. Wiri shook his head. He'd have nothing to hold on to and no way of clambering as far as the lid, even if he could move it by himself.

Several attempts later, he'd extended the ladder by two rungs while standing at the lowest point possible while reaching above his head and pushing. But he needed to go further and the ladder already touched the point of the wall's junction with the roof. The apex of the ceiling meant he still needed more height to reach the manhole, but he'd been unable to fix the catches again properly and it weakened the ladder's integrity. Disaster struck as he stood on the fifth rung with the top of the ladder protruding into the inspection tunnel. He tilted it too far backwards, his hands busy shoving the top half of the ladder towards the ceiling and praying the catches caught to give him an extra thirty centimetres of height.

The whole thing tipped backwards, missing the bottom lip of the tunnel and pitching Wiri onto his back on the floor. The ladder wedged itself again between the sides of the tank, the top edge too high for him to push free a second time. Pain blossomed from the base of his spine and travelled through his neck to his skull as a thudding ache. He lay for a moment in the dust, not wanting to move in case he'd done something serious. His stomach roiled with nausea, but when he didn't vomit, he sensed it felt different from the time he broke both his arms falling from a horse. Phoenix had fed him scrambled egg from a teaspoon, laughing as the yellow yolk tumbled onto his shirt. "More serious or less?" he asked himself, unable to provide an answer.

The nausea passed, and he hoped it was shock and not a broken bone. "I'm good," he whispered, his words echoing in the empty cavern. "I've never known anyone break their ass."

Wiri pushed himself to a sitting position next to the feet of the ladder. Pain flared and he eased himself onto his side. He used the torch to inspect two of his fingers. He'd trapped them in the mechanism as he tried to manoeuvre the body of the ladder past the catches, the action causing the overbalance. The index finger of his left hand still moved under pressure, but a flap of skin protruded from the middle one.

"Don't give up," he told himself, "Not yet." The addition of the second sentence suggested there may come a time when he needed to contemplate it. "Not yet," he repeated. He angled his wrist until the screen activated, showing he'd used up another half an hour. The length of time surprised him. His battle with the ladder seemed to have taken hours, exhausting him until he had little energy left in reserve. The watch vibrated and Wiri closed his eyes, imagining it had notified himself of another hour passed. When it did it again, hope burgeoned in his heart.

He spun the dial to the left, willing it to connect to his phone above ground in the back of the truck. A message flashed on the screen.

'Are you two coming for lunch soon?'

Leilah! Leilah knew what they were doing. If they didn't return, she would question it.

"She already is," Wiri breathed. "She's texted Vaughan, and he hasn't replied."

He used the watch settings to type *'help'* into a message. He didn't risk elaborating, in case the tenuous connection with his phone ended as abruptly as it began.

It took two attempts to press the tiny icon, which allowed the message to send. Blood streaked the screen and caused Wiri's fingers to miss the mark. He held his breath as a miniature egg timer in the centre of the face spun and spun as the watch tried to connect with his phone.

It spun for long enough for the back light on the face to wink out and take Wiri's hope with it. When his phone vibrated again, he stared at the message on the screen.

'Unable to send. Check signal!'

"That's that then." He leaned against the wall beside the ladder and closed his eyes, letting his head drop back against the rough surface. The foetid air infiltrated his mask by degrees, sneaking into his nose and mouth and giving him a taste of how death might feel.

18

BEAD FRONT SIGHT

Scraping echoed around the chamber, disturbing Wiri from his nightmare. Phoenix stood over him, her features grey with grief. "I kissed him," she whispered. "It meant nothing."

He jerked away from her and clattered his head against the wall of the tank. A dart of pain shot through his neck and into his skull. It blossomed outward to encompass his ears before swan diving into his spine. He groaned and shifted position, blinking into the darkness as numbness turned to tingling in his buttocks and thighs.

"Wiremu?" A woman's voice echoed into the tank, her tone light and high. "Wiremu, are you there?" Her city accent shortened the vowel sounds, and he recognised Seline's voice. She grunted again and dragged the concrete cover sideways a little more. The surfaces grated together, a deafening, teeth grinding sound. "I can't lift the whole thing off. It's too heavy." She swore and a loud clang rung Wiri's head like a gong. "Sorry. It fell off the chimney-thing," she admitted. "It's dented the roof."

"I'm stuck," he croaked, coughing as his throat locked the words into his chest.

"Are you okay?" Her petulant tone demanded an answer. "Vaughan's hurt."

"Help!" he managed. "Get help." His tongue stuck to the roof of his mouth and he yearned to stick his face under a tap. "Water," he called, managing only the single plea.

As though heaven responded, drips pelted his nose and forehead where he lay. Seline withdrew her head and shoulders from the opening and Wiri groaned against the sense of aloneness which rushed to occupy the gap. But the absence of her shape seemed to make the drips heavier and faster, cascading into his eyes and his mouth with abandon. "Just a drink," he murmured. "Not a bath."

Water pattered over his forehead and ran down his neck into his tee shirt. It seemed just a few minutes before cold gripped his body in violent shivers and he wished it would stop. It seeped into the healing scratch on the back of his right hand and attacked the sore finger on the other. "No more," he rasped. "Too much."

But Seline didn't return to the opening and as Wiri's eyes adjusted to the light, he realised it wasn't still sunny above ground. As he lay staring up at freedom, he finally registered the angry clouds overhead and the occasional blinding flash of lightning forking through the sky. His pupils widened, and he saw it wasn't bright at all, but a murky, threatening grey. "Oh, God, help me," he pleaded. "Seline! Seline! Where are you?"

She didn't reply again. Wiri lay on his side at the bottom of the tank. It hurt too much to sit upright, his spine alternating between darting twinges and a breath-taking ache. The fresh air brought him comfort. She'd abandoned him, but at least Seline left the hatch open. Wiri bent his left arm and laid his cheek against it, stemming the panic by pretending he lay in his own bed in the room next to Phoenix. He closed his eyes and imagined the day he left, picking over their conversation before he set off on his journey south. It seemed a lifetime ago. She'd kissed him of her own volition, stepping from the graveyard and pressing her lips against his. Her passion ignited a spark in his chest and he'd clung to its warmth with a bone deep craving. It governed every decision he'd made since that moment. He coughed into the mask, his body rocking and pain locking up his lungs. Logic challenged him, reminding him he'd conceived The Plan on his last birthday. When they'd euthanised his horse. And he'd kissed her the first time. They'd both known in that moment it could be no other way. Wiri and Phoenix against the world.

Water soaked through his jeans and lapped around his head, breaking him free of the daydream. The graveyard disappeared from his inner vision like dissipating fog. Ice cold water and a stained grey darkness replaced it. Wiri pushed himself up onto his left elbow, seeking the hatch opening through the gloom. Rain spattered onto the concrete beneath it, adding its weight to the growing flood. He blinked in the darkness, sating his fear with the promise he'd imagined it. The rain entering from above didn't have the volume to create such a deepening pond. "It's in your head," he hissed to himself. "It's not real."

"He's down here!" The female voice grew louder as it reverberated off the sides of the tank. Other sounds joined it, a cacophony of noise and the vibration of movement overhead.

"Wiremu?" He heard the strain in Leilah's voice and scrabbled his feet against the floor. Grit skittered away to bounce against the broken shards of the torch. He eased himself onto his bottom with a groan and edged closer to the wall. Locking his spine against it, he used his legs to push himself to an upright position. It seemed to take forever until he could stagger back towards the circle of light near the edge of the tank. He bowed his head and covered his face, wiping rainwater from his eyelids. Noise sounded overhead, one indiscernible from another.

A siren.

Voices.

The clatter of something metal.

"Wiremu?" Leilah called again, her tone soft. "Are you okay?"

He squatted in the circle, reluctant to lose the light's embrace, but he couldn't lift his head to face the rain. "No," he admitted, his voice hoarse.

His eyeballs ached when he rubbed them, airborne dust leaving a coating over his skin. He kept his left hand close to his body. He'd sacrifice more if he needed to, but his finger already burned from the gash.

"An ambulance is coming to take Vaughan to hospital." Seline's voice returned and concern gave it a gentler lilt. "Mum will go with him, but I'll wait here with you." She paused for a heartbeat and continued when Wiri didn't reply. "Wiremu? Can you talk to me? I can hear the claxon for the volunteer firefighters. They're scrambling them now. Listen."

Wiri managed a reluctant grunt. The only thing stopping him from vomiting was the realisation he'd need to return to the darkness again to clear up his mess. It had stopped him urinating too, but not for Vaughan's sake. He didn't want to drink his diluted pee through the taps.

"Tell me something," Seline urged. "What's your girlfriend's name?"

Wiri's legs gave out, and he tipped backwards onto his bottom. His spine curved and the back of his head hit the floor. Gazing up at the light, he saw the silhouette of a woman, her pale arms waving in the entrance. Despite the seriousness of the moment, he laughed, the sound strangled and choking. He figured it beat the other alternative, sobbing.

"It's not funny." Exasperation entered her voice. "Are you hurt?"

Wiri blew out a breath and dragged the mask from his face. Warm air licked his skin like the first drips from a shower. "I've busted up some fingers." He cleared his throat, realising he sounded drunk. "What's wrong with Vaughan?"

Seline sniffed. "Not sure. Looks like he fell against the lip of the opening. The stitches in his stomach burst, and he knocked himself unconscious. Mum thinks he needs surgery." Her tone quieted and Wiri saw her in profile as she looked at something in the distance.

He shook his head, grit grinding through his hair. Logic prevailed. Vaughan didn't leave him there and close the lid. Wiri shut his eyes and remembered the cry Vaughan released as he dropped the ladder. Then the awful silence. "Just an accident," he said to himself, slurring his words.

19

BOLT

Seline disappeared again. When she didn't return, Wiri lay in the growing puddle and let the rain pound his face and neck. It seeped through his tee shirt and into his jeans as far as his boxer shorts. Exhaustion shrouded him in its persuasive cloak and encouraged his eyelids to close against the deluge from above him. It ran in rivulets between his lips, convincing him it tasted of soda so that he swallowed in shallow gulps.

His fingers throbbed and his head ached. The cold water soothed the bump on his crown, so he pushed his fingers beneath the growing pond, which lapped around the feet of the ladder. They smarted and then lost all sensation. Something bumped his elbow, and he squinted through one eye to see the tube of quick dry cement bobbing next to him. Water trickled into his ears and dulled all sound to a low boom. He tuned into it, liking the way it reminded him of the bath at home. His mask followed it, a white cone-island chasing the tube around his body like a surfer seeking the swells.

"You need to get up now." Her voice sounded so real, its tinkling timbre making his bones ache for her. "Get up, Wiri."

He opened his eyes and saw Phoenix standing over him. She'd dressed for her first prom, the one he escorted her to when she couldn't find a partner. He feared for the burgundy dress, which fitted her like a glove. The hem dragged in the water, a dark shadow rising through the fabric as it became saturated.

"I can't do this," he murmured. "It's all too hard." He exhaled, his torso convulsed by a violent shiver which intensified as it moved through his ice cold extremities. He knew he didn't just mean his current situation, but all of it.

The deceit.

The Plan.

The impossibility that Logan Du Rose would let him live for kissing his precious daughter.

Water filled Wiri's ears and paralysed him with the echoed bumps and clangs of life. He jerked as his left arm shook. His eyes hurt when he opened them. He raised his right arm to protect them against the brightness. A face stared down at him. A pale coloured safety hat glinted from behind a head torch. The man's lips moved, but the water distorted his voice. He tilted his face towards the opening above and shouted. Wiri's left arm shook again with the man's movement. "He's conscious!"

Rain weighed down Wiri's lashes, making it difficult to keep his eyes open. The water covered his ears and reached his chin, the newcomer's movements causing a tide which lapped as far as his lips. He spluttered, and a brawny arm slipped behind his head and lifted it above the water line.

"Hey buddy." A kind voice filtered through the sudden cacophony as the water drained from Wiri's eardrums. Every sound seemed louder than he could cope with, and he squeezed his eyes closed. "My name is Larry," the man continued. His gloved hand supported Wiri's head, keeping his face above the water. He knelt next to him and the tube of cement tapped against the side of his boot. "Pastor Larry until twenty minutes ago when my pager went off in the middle of a funeral." Creases showed in the corners of his eyes.

Wiri blew out a ragged breath. He'd prayed for help and God sent a vicar called Larry to rescue him. He sighed and his voice croaked in his throat. "I'll take it," he rasped.

"Do I need a back-board or a collar for you?" Larry asked. "This rain isn't stopping and I'm worried about a neck injury."

Wiri shook his head, and the rain attacked both cheeks, pouring through the opening to fill the tank. "I just got tired," he admitted. "There's too much water."

Larry chuckled. "Funny place to take a nap, dude. Did you fall or bang your head at all?"

Wiri let his mind perform a replay of the events, producing a jumble of movements.

Crawling, fighting the ladder, banging his head, falling on his backside, splitting his fingers.

The darkness seeping into his bones.

The cockroach already safe near the ceiling.

A vision of the broken torch vied with the memory of Phoenix in her ball gown and Hana crying at how beautiful her daughter looked in her finery.

Something brushed Wiri's leg, slithering across his knee before swishing away and he smiled. "She's getting her dress wet," he stammered. Though the sentence ended, his teeth continued to chatter as if having something of their own to say.

Larry removed his gloves and stuffed them into a top pocket of his suit. Deft fingers moved at the back of Wiri's neck, smoothing over his soaked body and dipping beneath the water level to continue their inspection of his spine and his limbs. Heavy drops cascaded through the open hatch and bounced off the fireman's helmet, soaking Wiri to the bone. "Why didn't you wear a safety harness connected to something at the top, dude?"

"I did." Wiri remembered the slithering rope and wondered where it had floated to in the deluge. The level rose, covering his limbs. "Too much water," he said again. "Pipe."

"Do you need the board?" A thickly accented baritone carried across the trickling and gushing of the flow. The new speaker's vowel sounds held the familiar colloquialism of the old Māori language, the dialect favoured by the Waikato tribes. It reminded him of Poppa Reuben in his rare moments of sobriety, when he sang songs, played his guitar and laughed. A tear leaked from Wiri's left eye, mingling with the rainwater and concrete dust until it became so diluted it negated his misery.

"You're all right, buddy."

Wiri blinked up at him, responding to the almost inaudible whisper which strived to hide his distress from the men at ground level. Larry smiled and Wiri blew out an agonised breath. "I don't want to die," he said, a swallow bisecting his sentence.

"Me neither." Larry tipped his head upwards towards the hatch and water pelted the brim of his helmet.

The man shouted again, his voice filling the tank and competing with the water. "Larry. The board is too wide for the manhole. I can send down a collar."

"No time!" he replied, his voice booming. "I can't find any bone breaks but it's filling fast down here."

Still supporting Wiri's neck, Larry pushed himself onto one knee. "Can you stand?" he asked him.

"Yeah." Wiri replied without knowing if he could. His hands scrabbled against the submerged floor of the tank, slipping and sliding without gaining purchase. His numb fingers flailed without effect.

"Easy does it." Larry pushed against Wiri's shoulders until he could sit. His spine behaved more like a rubber band than a series of bones. "Can you support yourself?"

Wiri nodded and a dart of pain robbed him of words. It shot from his tail bone to the back of his head and he tried to breathe through it until it lost its grip. He balanced on one arm as Larry rose and released a rope from around his waist. As Wiri squinted up at him, he saw it trailing overhead until it disappeared through the opening above them. Every time the man at the top peered through the hole, he caused the rain to change direction, cascading off his helmet like a waterfall. As Wiri stared up, he noticed the strobing of a red light mingling with the lightning. He covered his eyes as light flooded the tunnel and the tank, bouncing and reflecting off the water surrounding him. "Lightning," he murmured to no one in particular.

"Floodlight." Larry grunted as he fixed a series of knots into the rope, forming a circle which dangled from the trailing lifeline. He looped it over his elbow and dipped at the waist to hoist Wiri to a precarious standing position. "They finally got it working." He raised a bushy eyebrow, which disappeared beneath the yellow helmet like a retreating slug. "Rookies." His teeth glinted in the refracted light from his head torch as he grinned. "How many men does it take to change a light bulb?"

Wiri recognised the joke but he couldn't remember the answer. It was one of Alfie's, and he smiled on cue. The correct response refused to fall into place in his brain. He inhaled and fixed his wavering focus on the fireman. "I need to tell you something," he said, his words juddering against the chattering of his teeth.

"What's that then?" Larry slipped the circle of rope over his head and tightened it beneath his armpits. Wiri groaned as it pressed against his spine and sent a blast of pain into his head. His knees buckled, and he stumbled sideways. Larry swore and tipped his body to support him. "Where's the blood coming from, buddy?" he asked, his tone urgent. Diluted pink liquid trailed across his palm. He swore again as Wiri's head lolled. Tilting his face towards the opening, he called to the man peering through the gap. "We've got blood. I think it's a head injury."

"You want the collar?" he called back. "We shouldn't risk it."

"No time." He supported Wiri with a gargantuan strength. "The rain's already covered the floor. I daren't lay him back down on it. I thought you knocked off the inlet valve. It's still coming from somewhere."

Wiri swayed as water lapped at his shins. Every time Larry moved, the water hit the sides of the tank and returned with more force. "Need to tell you something," he said again, his mind whirling the thought away with the water. The cement tube bumped against the side of his leg and he instructed his fingers to retrieve it. They refused the command, fluttering against his soaked jeans in a feckless, twinkling movement as though he performed the actions for a nursery rhyme. Logan detested waste and Wiri listed as he reached again for the tube, estimating it still contained a quarter of its contents. The man above moved, and the floodlight picked out the white tube in its beam. Wiri noticed the missing lid and groaned.

"Not long now." Larry misunderstood his angst and tugged twice on the dangling rope. He guided Wiri's body as the tension increased against his ribs and spine until the pain became almost unbearable.

The moment came when Larry's grip dropped from Wiri's dangling feet and he was alone, suspended from the ceiling like a mullet hoisted from the sea on a fishing line. His arms dangled by his sides, the pressure of the rope beneath his armpits making it impossible to raise his hands to clear the water from his eyes. His spine throbbed, the pain originating from a hot spot near his tail bone.

He didn't want to die.

In the space of the six metres between the bottom of the tank and the surface, Wiri renewed his zest for life and his determination to win Phoenix. He made peace with himself and with his decisions.

The Plan.

Rivers deluged through the lace holes of his boots as gravity commanded the tributaries back to the growing lake beneath him. A pipe to his right gushed like a waterfall and then ceased as though a hidden hand turned off the tap.

A voice from above echoed around his head, bouncing off every bone in his skull. "All good, Larry. Bert disconnected the down pipe on the barn. We'll get the kid up and then send the gear back for you."

"Yep." Larry's voice called back, concern edging his tone. "He needs a neck, head and back x-ray. Said he didn't fall, but he's confused." The floodlight blinded Wiri as Larry continued. "There's blood on the wall here." He sighed. "Should have used the collar."

"We're fine!" the man at the top assured him. "You've done well."

Warm air stroked Wiri's cheek and the delicious scent of grass filled his nostrils. Life never tasted so fresh as careful hands hauled him through the narrow tunnel and into the eerie grey daylight. Someone ordered him to stay still as they lifted his head and slid a collar around his neck. He hated the restriction of the board they strapped him onto, but tolerated it. A sharp scratch on his right hand injected a powerful painkiller into his system. He heard Seline's voice speaking through a growing fog, a hint of hysteria fraying around the edges. "I'll ride with him," she said.

A floral scent enveloped him, and he turned his eyeballs to squint at her as she leaned across. The vehicle's movement shifted her body from side to side as the ambulance bumped over the rough ground. Her lips tightened until the haughtiness faded, and she looked truly afraid.

20

Grip

Wiri seethed against the indignity of being dangled over a
hole by a group of volunteer firemen.

Shame reddened his cheeks and raised his heart rate enough
to alarm the paramedics, who monitored his vitals on the way
across the bumpy paddock. Humiliation flooded his veins,
reminding him of the time Logan rescued him from a mob of
stampeding cattle during a muster. He'd yanked him up by the
waistband of his jeans and slapped him over the horn of his
saddle like a sack of grain. The stock men laughed about it for
months. Seline made the current situation worse.

"Oh, my goodness!" she wailed. She leaned across the
ambulance to speak to him and he squirmed against her
heightened sense of drama. "I ran down to the road to direct the
fire engine." She wiped her eyes with the back of her hand. Water
had plastered her red fringe to her forehead. "Then the lightning
started and the torrential rain. I didn't even think about the tank
filling." Her breath stuck in her chest and a paramedic slipped a
foil blanket around her soaked shoulders. "Mum sent me over to
see if you wanted us to bring lunch." Her eyes widened. "She's

gone with Vaughan. He's hurt real bad." Her voice wavered, but an intensity entered her eyes as though she hid deeper emotions.

Wiri's watch vibrated on his left wrist. He screwed his head sideways to see the screen flash to life. *'Message sent,'* it told him. Then the light winked out, and the watch died. Shower proof but not drown-proof.

Wiri groaned and stopped fighting the restriction of the collar. The paramedic lifted a syringe filled with clear fluid. "Don't move around, Wiremu," he said, his tone kind. "We'll get you up to the hospital and they'll see what damage you've done to yourself." His words suggested Wiri had intentionally sealed himself inside a water tank below ground and thrown himself around just for kicks. His pulse rate rose again and the steady clip-clop of the monitor measuring it flashed as though surprised.

The clear liquid warmed the site where the cannula entered the vein in the back of his right hand. Wiri felt it snake up his arm and his view of the ambulance blurred. "Phone," he heard himself murmur. "Phoe."

"What's he saying?" Something soft swished across his cheek and the scent of floral conditioner filled his nostrils.

"Sit back, miss." The paramedic rebuked her in an authoritative tone. "He won't make much sense for a while. I need to keep him still until we get to the Waikato hospital."

"He's asking for someone called Fiona." Seline's words contained an element of pique. "That must be his girlfriend."

"That's not you, then?" A cold spray hit Wiri's damaged fingers, and he tried to recoil them, finding himself unable to work the joints. The drug made his muscles and tendons release their hold on his joints. He floated free like a bag of empty skin in his mind. The image repulsed him and he commanded his body to curl into a ball. It disobeyed, and his mind panicked.

A cool hand laid across his forehead and his imaginary image of Phoenix leaned over him, her stone-coloured irises dancing in her beautiful face. "You'll be okay now," she promised. He relaxed as she leaned over and kissed his cheek. He forced himself to focus on the delightful curve of her lips and the way her black curls sneaked past her shoulder. They lapped against his chest with the movement of the vehicle over the rough ground. His fingers ached as the paramedic splinted the bones and wrapped a bandage around the ragged skin.

"I love you," he whispered, his heart filling with an elation he'd never experienced.

Her expression morphed into one of surprise and Wiri gaped as Phoenix became Seline. Her eyes narrowed and her lips pursed in confusion. But her blue irises danced with danger and Wiri shuttered his gaze with hastily closed eyelids. The swearwords which loosed inside his head would have shocked Hana to her core. When laughter reverberated around the interior of the ambulance, he realised he'd said them aloud.

* * *

Wiri dropped into consciousness with the force of a slap. One second he floated with Phoenix in the warm waves of the Tasman and the next, he stared at a white tiled ceiling covered in fly crap. A single overhead strip-light flickered like a strobe. He tilted his head to the side, relieved to find the restrictive collar gone. He commanded his left hand to rise and this time, it obeyed. A ridiculous white bandage covered the middle finger like something from a cartoon. Logan's stock men would have laughed up a lung at the sight of the foul gesture it created, separating the fingers on either side of it into a fan.

Disgusted, Wiri used his other hand to tug at it. But the medic who wrapped enough gauze around the wound to pack an artery had stuck tape to his knuckle with something akin to super glue. The activity of his right hand dislodged the cannula someone had pushed into his vein and the pipe connected to it dropped below the correct level. The clear fluid changed colour as the pipe filled with his blood.

A breeze ruffled the patterned curtain surrounding Wiri's cubicle and voices issued from beyond its fabric wall. He tilted his head to find himself wearing a hospital gown. Closing his eyes against the horror of strange hands undressing him, he prayed it wasn't Seline who'd removed his boxer shorts. He imagined trying to explain that to Phoenix and a blurred memory surfaced of him telling Seline he loved her.

Swearing, he pushed himself onto his right elbow, breathing through a dart of pain which shot from his tail bone into his spine. He pushed off the waffle patterned blanket and sheet covering his lower half, grimacing at the grit and dirt collected between the downy hair covering his shins. The tube running from a drip by the bed hung lower and filled with more blood. Wiri scrabbled at it with his left hand, the cartoon finger rendering the action impossible.

By the time the curtain swished back and a nurse entered, Wiri had stripped off the white bandage and disconnected the drip. "Stop!" she said, her tone filled with horror as his index finger and thumb closed around the nub of the cannula. Quick steps took her to the side of his bed.

The fabric of her blue scrubs brushed against his elbow as she bent to retrieve the pipe leaking pink fluid onto the tiled floor. "Just wait, Mr Kingii," she said, her rubber shoes squeaking against the tiles. "Please don't undo all my good work."

"Sorry." Wiri's throat croaked as he spoke. He brushed his lips with the back of his left hand, finding them cracked and painful. Blowing out a ragged breath, he dipped forward to look at the floor, discovering the action took the pressure off his spine.

A ruffled piece of pink fabric held the nurse's blonde hair back from her face in a neat bun. She smiled at Wiri and her lips flattened into a line. "I get it," she soothed. Deft fingers lifted his right wrist and placed his hand over his thigh. "You can leave after you've seen the doctor."

Wiri shook his head and winced at the ache at the back of his skull. "I need to get out of here," he croaked. He tried to lift his right hand to worry at the site of the pain and the nurse tapped it before setting it back on his thigh.

"Let me take this out first," she said. She epitomised the definition of competence as she removed the cannula from the back of his hand and pressed a sticking plaster over the tiny hole. Her fingers moved through a series of processes with the ease of experience.

"What's wrong with my head?" As soon as she released his hand, Wiri pressed his fingers over a piece of fabric covering the sore spot. His eyes widened at the stubble on either side of it. "You shaved my hair!"

His shocked expression drew a laugh from the nurse. She tapped his shoulder, her lips fighting not to make his mortification worse. "It'll grow back," she soothed. "Keep it dry and clean for a few days. The doctor put in four stitches and some medical glue."

Wiri groaned and contemplated removing the gauze. His fingers picked at the tape, but the nurse's narrowing eyes forced him to drop his hand. Around Hana's age, she infused him with a sense of safety created by her maternalism. She jerked her head towards his fingers. White strips covered the black stitches knotted across a cut which ran from knuckle to knuckle. A red line snaked around his finger to end at a black point on his nail. "Don't pick those off," she warned, raising her right eyebrow. Wiri saw how grey flecked the blonde as she dipped to inspect the wound.

He allowed her to raise his hand, forcing himself to relax against her grip. Her breath coasted across the skin and she nodded once before releasing it. His hand felt heavy without her support, and it crashed down against the mattress. She froze and stared at him, her lips straightening into a line. "I might get the doctor to look at you again," she stated, her tone serious. "They x-rayed your spine and there's nothing broken, but you might have nerve damage."

Wiri shook his head, and the gown rode up above his knees as he slipped from the bed to the tiles. His toes delayed their obedience, refusing to bend on cue, and he crashed onto his heels without control. He groaned as his tail bone hit the metal bed frame and his toes slipped forward until they contacted the nurse's rubber shoes. Wiri's humiliation deepened as she grabbed him beneath the armpits and hoisted him back to a sitting position. "Wait there!" she commanded. "I'm fetching the doctor." The curtain swished open, and another nurse stuck her face through the gap.

"Can you give me a hand?"

Wiri's nurse nodded before turning her attention back to him. "There's a cop waiting to see you." She forced him to accept her help, to set his legs back on the mattress. He looked away as she raised the sides of the bed and squeaked away on her sensible soles to assist her colleague.

"Are you decent?" Jet's face appeared around the edge of the curtain. He glanced at the thunder in Wiri's eyes and winced. "Oh. Sorry."

Wiri exhaled. He shoved his elbow at the bed rail. "They're treating me like a child," he grumbled. He frowned at the casual tee shirt and jacket covering Jet's upper body. Shifting sideways, he spotted jeans and trainers. A frown set deep lines into his forehead as he lifted his left wrist and cursed at his dead watch. "What's the time?" he demanded. "Why aren't you at work?"

Jet glanced at his wrist and wrinkled his nose. "It's just after eleven."

Wiri blinked. His sense of time wrapped the hours around themselves and met him on their circuitous way back through his mind. He shrugged, the action hurting his spine. "In the morning?" His memory flicked back to his cooler bag and the sandwiches he'd took such trouble over making.

"At night." Jet pursed his lips. "Leilah is still here with Vaughan. She asked me to bring you some stuff." He hoisted a cloth shopping bag. Bulges pressed through the fabric. "I went through your bag. Hope that's okay? Just grabbed the basics."

"Yeah." Wiri exhaled. "You're not the first."

"What?" Jet frowned and cocked his head.

"Nothing." Wiri opened and closed the fingers of his right hand. "Quick, help me with this bed rail. I need to get out of here before the nurse comes back."

Jet winced and backed away as though he thought Wiri contagious. "Na, man. Don't do that."

Wiri ground his teeth and his grey eyes flashed in warning. "Unless you want a ringside view of my ass when I crawl over this kiddy rail, then help me!" he growled. "I'm not joking!"

The busyness of the hospital played to Wiri's advantage as laboured movements got him out of the gown and into his clothes. The nurse didn't return as beeping alarms and the demands of a wailing woman in the next cubicle occupied her attention. Jet slumped into a plastic visitor's chair and read emails on his phone. He refused to assist other than to put down the safety rail on the bed.

"Help me fasten my jeans," Wiri pleaded after the fifth attempt to push the buttons through the holes.

Jet swore at him and waved off his request. "I don't think so." His casual tone grated on Wiri's nerves. "Imagine the headlines, dude. Local cop caught feeling patient's nads on hospital ward."

"Fine." Wiri slipped a clean tee shirt from the bag and wrestled his sore head through the neck. "Pity you didn't think I'd need underwear because I'm gonna flash at everyone walking towards us." He spun in a circle, hoping to find the clothes he'd arrived in. "Can you see my boots anywhere?"

Jet rose with a sigh and opened the cabinet next to the bed. He hauled out a transparent plastic bag containing a jumble of soaked items. Pointing at Wiri's boots on the bottom, he grimaced. "I didn't think to bring shoes, either. Can you wear these?" He parted the lip of the plastic and recoiled at the smell from its interior. "Yuk! You might need to bin this stuff."

Wiri straightened the bedding and sent a silent apology to the nurse for his lack of appreciation for her craft. "I'll go barefoot," he declared. He glared at Jet. "And commando, so thanks for that. Where's your car?"

Jet blinked back at him. "I don't have one."

Wiri closed his eyes against an image of himself sitting on a night bus, barefoot, with his fly undone. Temper flared in his chest, momentarily dispelling the various pain signals which occupied his brain. "How did you get here?" he asked with a sigh.

"I used your truck." He winked at him and hoisted the bag. "Delightful ride Mr Du Rose."

"Shut up!" Wiri released a ragged breath. "That's the other reason we need to get out of here. Someone told them I was Wiremu Kingii. They won't find me on any of their medical systems." He exhaled and rubbed his good hand over his ribcage. "She said something about a cop waiting to see me. Is that you?"

Jet grinned back at him as he peeked through a gap in the curtains. Grey water dripped from a corner of the bag, leaving a trail behind him as he sneaked between the fluttering edges of fabric. "No," he replied. "I said I was your flat mate." He waggled his eyebrows. "And that, my friend, is why nothing good comes from lying." He jerked his head at Wiri to follow, his shoulders shaking with a low, irritating chuckle.

21

EJECTORS

Jet's police experience made him an efficient but careful driver. Wiri sensed it wouldn't have mattered if he'd driven like a maniac, as his body protested every bump and bend. He relaxed as much as he could to prevent his muscles tensing at each jolt, the driveway to the house giving him more pain than the route south from Hamilton.

Jet stopped the truck next to the deck and Wiri released a sigh. He glanced left towards the single porch light shining from Vaughan's house and worried. Rain dribbled down the window to distort the light. "Did you hear how Vaughan's doing?" he asked, chewing the inside of his cheek.

"Staying in hospital for tonight." Jet cracked open the driver's door and looked back at him. "Leilah said he bust open the wound across his stomach again. He had surgery recently for Crohn's disease."

Wiri nodded. "He struggled to lift the ladder back through the gap. I heard him grunt in pain just before he dropped it on me."

Jet frowned and paused with one hand on the door and the other still on the steering wheel. "Why did he take the ladder out in the first place?"

Wiri ran a hand over his face and leaned his crown against the seat, wincing as a dart of pain shot from the cut and clamped his entire head in a vice. "Ow!" he groaned. "I needed to use the ladder to reach the higher cracks near the ceiling of the tank. He'd extended it to its full length so I could climb from above ground to the floor so it poked out of the hole. I needed it shorter to manoeuvre around inside the tank. Vaughan hauled it out, shortened it and I waited for him to lower it back down for me." He closed his eyes and frowned. "That's when it all went wrong. I guess he caught his stomach on the lip of the inspection tunnel."

Jet shrugged. "How do you think he split open the back of his head?"

Wiri screwed up his eyes and drew his brows into a line of confusion. "The back of his head?" He blinked at Jet. "I don't know. I figured he hit his forehead on the tank and passed out."

Jet gave himself a shake as though to dispel his uncertainty. He exited the vehicle, and it seemed an age as Wiri watched him walk onto the porch and unlock the front door. "Tell him," he whispered into the dark vehicle. "Just tell him." The knowledge burned behind the bridge of his nose. Someone had disconnected the rope from the truck's tow bar and replaced the hatch. It seemed possible they'd also wiped out Vaughan before doing it.

Wiri swallowed as the hall light bloomed and Jet appear back on the porch. His footsteps thudded across the wooden boards and Wiri tensed. A memory returned to him as he waited for Jet to reach the passenger door to help him out of the vehicle. He'd waited for him another time, too.

On his first night at the house, Jet had taken longer to get ready and Wiri had hung around, jangling his truck keys with impatience.

So, as Jet offered his arm to help him stand and locked up the truck behind them with care, Wiri said nothing.

If Jet searched his bedroom that first night with Wiri just metres away, it showed he didn't mind taking a risk. It also placed him in the frame for causing the tank disaster, and putting both Wiri and Vaughan in hospital.

Refusing further help, Wiri limped through to his bedroom. With no internal locks on the doors, he jammed an armchair beneath the handle and sank onto the mattress fully clothed. He didn't expect to sleep, but the intravenous painkillers continued their work and his eyes closed almost immediately.

Wiri woke before dawn, having dribbled on his pillow. Sleeping on his side had alleviated the pain in his spine but added a neck ache to his list of ailments. He rolled onto his back and groaned, wishing he hadn't but lacking the energy to correct his position. The ache in his head had dulled from a roar to the occasional stab. He lay still and observed the light change from its pre-dawn grey to a murky purple.

Rolling onto his side gave him enough momentum to sit up, but the trailing charger cable reminded him of his absent phone. The dead watch on his wrist sent a flicker of misery through his tired brain. Logan and Hana gave him the device for his last birthday, and he'd loved both its usefulness and the thought behind the gift. He tugged the buckle free and set the watch on the bedside cabinet, wondering if the kitchen cupboards contained any rice. "Should have done it last night," he murmured with a sigh, adding another regret to his growing list. Then he remembered the bag of soaked clothing and his work boots still sitting on the porch where Jet dropped them. He sat the watch on its charger and crossed his fingers, growling as it irked his stitches.

Wiri used the bathroom and inspected his various bruises and cuts in the mirror over the sink. Blood had seeped through the stitches on his finger to stain the strips of medical tape. He washed his hands with difficulty, trying not to wet that one finger but failing, anyway. Dark circles of tiredness ringed the eyes of the man who stared back at him. A weeping cut over his left cheek matched the one on his jawline. His whole body hurt and Wiri rested the heels of his hands on the side of the sink. He bent at the waist until the cold porcelain cooled his forehead. It stretched the kinks from his spine and he took slow, fortifying breaths through the pain.

Channelling the indestructible spirit of his uncle, Wiri forced himself to get ready for work. Logan Du Rose showed up bright and early every day despite the haemophilia which bruised and scarred his body in a relentless tide of injury. Wiri gritted his teeth and sorted out his sodden clothing, loading it into the washing machine and setting it on a cycle. His boots stank. He rinsed them under the tap in the laundry, adding washing powder and soaking them for a minute while he caught his breath. He rinsed them again before opening the front door and sitting them upside down on the porch to dry beneath the eaves.

Rain still threatened as black clouds rolled across the lightening sky. Wiri stared at the paddock between the porch and Vaughan's house and decided not to ruin his remaining footwear in the wet grass. Unable to bend to tie his laces, he shoved them beneath the tongue of his trainers. He returned to his room for his truck keys, hearing a digital alarm sounding behind Jet's door. The front door clicked shut behind him and he eased himself into the driver's seat of his truck with gritted teeth. He missed the comfort of Alfie's hat. His fringe bounced against his eyelashes as he hoped someone had rescued it from the bed of Vaughan's truck.

Not just his hat.

His phone, credit card, and the bracelet.

22

Notch

Leilah stared at him through a gap in the net curtain before hauling open the ranch slider. Her mouth hung open, and she shook her head, her eyes narrowing as she blinked out at him. "I didn't expect to see you today," she said, her tone hushed. A shaking hand lifted to tug at the loose ponytail from which most of her hair had already escaped.

Wiri shrugged. "How's Vaughan?"

She exhaled and her shoulders slumped. Her head tilted back, and she stared at something on the ceiling while she picked through sentences for something suitable. Wiri watched her eyelashes flicker and noticed again that effortless beauty she possessed. He wondered if she knew it.

Leilah shook her head. "Come in, Wiremu." She pushed the door wider and waited for him to step through the gap. She flapped her hand towards the table. "Sit down for a minute. Would you like a drink or something to eat?"

Taller than Leilah by a head and shoulders, he stopped just shy of the table. He licked his lips before speaking. "He's not dead, is he?" His voice faltered.

Leilah's eyes widened, and she rested her right palm over her heart. "No! Gosh, no!" She collected her emotions into a more manageable pile in her chest and released a sigh. "Sorry. I didn't mean to make you think that. He's just ropeable, is all."

"You haven't slept?" Wiri pointed to bloodstains on the cuff of her blouse, noticing she still wore the clothes from the day before when he'd seen her riding.

Leilah shook her head and tugged the hair bobble free. Mahogany curls tumbled around her shoulders like a hood before she scooped them back into her fingers and retied them. Stray tendrils disobeyed, floating around her face like a halo. "I stayed at the hospital with Vaughan until the staff moved him onto a ward." She waved her left arm towards the sagging sofa. "I slept there. He needed surgery in the night to sluice out his scar and put in more stitches. I just phoned, and he's sleeping." She blew out a breath through pursed lips. Then her body jerked, and she held up an index finger. "Oh, wait. Pastor Larry drove the truck back to the house for me. He rescued your cooler from the back and left it here for you." Staccato steps carried her into the hallway, rapping out a beat as she hurried through the house.

Wiri remained by the table, eyeing the chair as though it represented an insurmountable obstacle. By the time Leilah returned, he'd already decided not to sit down on it. She handed him the bag, and he ripped open the zipper and inspected its contents. Withdrawing the bag of sandwiches, he held them aloft. "These still look fine," he said, forcing a smile onto his lips. He chewed the inside of his cheek as he pulled the bag containing his phone from beneath the bottom layer. Phoenix's bracelet clanked against it as he lifted it up to the light. "It's dry," he said, his chest relaxing as he spotted his credit card. "Thank goodness."

"I dried the bag out in the airing cupboard overnight. Have a seat." Leilah indicated the chair again and Wiri shook his head.

"I'm good, miss," he replied. "I'll head up to the top paddock and feed out the cattle. It might take me longer today." As he turned, Leilah inhaled at the sight of the gauze still stuck to the back of his head.

"You're bleeding," she whispered.

Wiri shrugged off her horror, and the haunted look which appeared behind her eyes. "I've had worse," he said, adding a fake laugh to cover his embarrassment. "I'll do my best for you today, miss. Might have to catch up tomorrow." His trainers squeaked as the soles turned on the threadbare carpet and he limped towards the ranch slider. The laces weren't tight enough and they slopped around his feet. It seemed to take too much effort to haul the ranch slider open, and he focused on putting one foot in front of the other.

He didn't push his thoughts towards the many jobs awaiting him, taking his time to walk towards his truck and lower himself in the driver's seat. The cooler bag slumped against his thighs as he dug out his phone and pulled it from the zip-lock bag. He plugged it into the car charger and sighed with relief as the screen lit up to cast an eerie glow over the truck's interior. His fingers coasted over the bracelet before pushing it back into the safety of the bag.

"Wait!" Leilah's knock on the window made him jump, and he squinted up at her. He started the engine before using the button to lower the window. Leilah pressed her fingers over the sill. "Seline said she'd work on the farm today. Do you want to wait for her?" She jerked her head towards the old truck sitting in front of the shed. "You don't need to use your own vehicle. Borrow ours."

Wiri breathed out a sigh and shook his head. "I'm good, miss," he replied. A laugh escaped with more sarcasm than he'd intended. "I already got sat down here and I don't think I can face getting out again for a minute." He wrinkled his nose at his lack of tact and pursed his lips.

Leilah nodded. She removed her hands and backed away from the truck, wrapping her arms around her torso. "Okay, thanks," she said. Swallowing, she struggled to release her next sentence. "I had a call yesterday while I was at the hospital." She gulped and a tick of panic started in Wiri's chest. His mind somersaulted through various possibilities, which ended with Logan discovering his treachery. He held his breath until his chest ached.

"What?" he whispered, his eyes wide. "Who called you?"

"WorkSafe." She said the word too loud and the nervous bay mare whinnied from the gate. The orange of the sunset picked out the halo of hair around Leilah's face and turned it to flickering flames of doom. "Perhaps the fire department alerted them to the accident. Maybe it's procedure." She waved it off as fact, though her expression held a veiled accusation.

"I didn't call them." Wiri saw the heightened colour bloom on her cheeks as daylight turned her expression into a readable page. Whatever she saw in the hardening of his face made her take another step backwards. Wiri sighed and ran a hand over his chin. The stubble scraped against his palm. "I wore a harness, and we attached it to the truck. The ladder was sound." He wanted to tell her it all, to confess he saw the figure who looked down at him before they sealed his fate. But the words stuttered in his chest because although instinct told him Leilah wasn't the one, he couldn't be certain. Instead, he gave a definitive nod of his head. "Don't worry," he offered. "It was just a stupid accident."

Leilah swallowed and tears sprung into her eyes. She licked her lips and nodded, turning away from the truck to hide her emotion. "Thanks," she called over her shoulder as she stepped up onto the deck.

"WorkSafe," Wiri muttered with a sigh as he raised his window and turned on his headlights. A weight rested on his shoulders. He couldn't lie to a government safety inspector and his plan would crumble at the first interview. It would be bad for him, but worse for Vaughan. The farm was obviously already in difficulty, but WorkSafe had the power to shut it down altogether.

Wiri turned the three-point turn into a mess of stopping and starting. His tail bone complained about the pressure of the seat and he struggled to curl the fingers of his left hand around the steering wheel. But he made it to the gate on the other side of the house and steeled himself to get out and open it, knowing another six waited for him along the uphill climb beyond it.

23

RECOIL SHIELD

Wiri laboured through the first few hours after sunrise, finding he fared better if he kept his muscles moving.

He loaded hay bales from the barn into the bed of his truck and drove through the many gates to the cattle on the upper ridges of Vaughan's land. Lifting the bales one handed to avoid opening the cut on his fingers took longer than usual. His muscles strained and his back seemed to creak at a point level with the waistband of his jeans. But he kept going, remembering the route from the day before and feeding two mobs of Vaughan's cattle before taking a break.

Seline's help never materialised and as the sun grew high enough to chase away the scudding clouds, he remembered he'd forgotten to bring a drink. He missed Poppa Alfie's hat as sweat dripped from his fringe into his eyes.

As the steers tugged at the hay, he stood for a moment and watched the bales collapse into defined slices. He'd pulled off the orange twine and should have spread out the hay to stop them from jostling, but he'd run out of energy long ago. A shard of guilt lodged in his chest as he watched them nudge and bicker to get to the food.

"Fine!" he growled, shooing them aside for long enough to kick the slices around in a wide arc. "Sorry about the foot in your breakfast, but it's the best I can do." Hay wedged in the holes for his laces and stuck to his socks.

He returned to the truck and rested his elbows on the bonnet, leaning down to stretch out his spine and release the niggling ache of compression. A male voice made him jump, and he groaned at the various stabbing pains which set off in a series through his body.

"Sorry, mate."

Wiri exhaled and rose, screwing his head around to face the newcomer. He squinted, recognising the man's face but not able to place him. "Hey," he replied, noticing the rasping of his breath.

"Larry." The man held out his hand and waited for Wiri to accept it. His mind took him straight back to the tank and the rushing water, which threatened to bury him beneath its swirling grey blanket.

"I remember." Wiri nodded. "Thanks for getting me out of there." He tutted as one steer kicked out at another and sent the mob scattering. They ranged too close to his truck, and he cursed, remembering too late that Larry also served as the local pastor. "Sorry," he added. His fingers closed over the door handle and he gave an ineffectual tug. It resisted, and he tried again. "I should carry on," he said. His gaze raked the paddock as far as the gate, and he cocked his head at Larry. "Did you walk up here? I can give you a ride to the bottom if you like?" The door opened on the third attempt.

Larry spread his arms to encompass the mountain and the stunning views of the valley. "I'm here to help, my friend. Leilah called. She's worried about you."

Wiri let the door close and braced his right arm against the truck's chassis. He drew in a deep breath and eyed the pastor's clothing. He'd dressed for work, paint splatter staining a pair of tattered jeans and holes in the checked shirt, which looked too big for him. Though a baseball cap covered his grey hair, he carried a battered Jackaroo in the fingers of his right hand. Wiri sighed. "You didn't call WorkSafe on Vaughan, did you, man?" He heard the tiredness in his voice and wondered if he'd care. He needed help, and only his pride would reject it on behalf of a misplaced loyalty. But he hoped anyway.

Larry's face creased, and he shook his head. "Someone called WorkSafe?" he replied.

"Yeah." Wiri blinked into the sun's watery glare and held out his hand for his hat. "If you drove Vaughan's truck, you must be okay to drive a gear shift. Please, can you drive mine because the clutch on this is killing my back?"

W iri settled into the passenger seat with a sigh of relief. "I'll do the gates," he offered, keeping his eyes closed.

"Na, don't worry." Larry revved the engine. "Those automatic gear boxes don't have the same torque for off-roading, do they?"

"No." Wiri squirmed against the pains in his spine. "I forgot to bring water. And my painkillers."

Larry grunted as he turned the truck downhill. "Leilah didn't think you'd show up at all this morning. She said you looked terrible."

"Thanks." Wiri snorted. "No worse than her. She said Vaughan was ropeable."

"Yeah." Larry drew out the word. "That man doesn't enjoy being cooped up. He's a law unto himself."

"How long have you been in the town?" Wiri shifted position and turned his head to watch Larry's expression.

"Two months tomorrow." He grinned. "The other guy retired. It's a pleasant town. Lots of stuff going on below the surface."

Wiri raised his eyebrows and thought of home. The township beyond his family's hotel seemed no different. Whispers and gossip drove the economy with as much clout as hard cash. "What about the fire service?" He shuddered at the memory of the rushing water filling his boots. His toes scrunched up inside his trainers.

"I've been doing that since my twenties. It's all hands to the pump in a small town with no retained fire service. I trained as a volunteer thirty years ago." He winked sideways at him and crinkles appeared next to his eyes.

Wiri nodded. "Some of my uncle's stock hands were volunteers. It's difficult to respond when they're in the middle of nowhere, stuck up a mountain on horseback." He sighed. "I thought about joining, but I knew I'd move on elsewhere as soon as I left school so there seemed little point."

"You also need a sympathetic employer who doesn't mind you disappearing half way through a job. Wait there a second. I'll get this gate."

Larry drove and Wiri guided him through the route Vaughan took on the previous two days. They fed the various mobs of cattle dotting the mountain's lower slopes and took a break next to a paddock containing horses. Wiri strained to heft the bale over the post and rail fence which surrounded them. They ran to it and he waved them away before bending with difficulty to cut the twine and push it into his pocket. Larry hung back on the other side of the fence. He tilted his head to watch Wiri as he worked without concern at the half tonne horses which milled around him.

Wiri clambered onto the fence and sat on the top rail. He released a groan of relief as his aching back stretched and the thin fence took his weight across the top of his thighs instead of his tail bone. "Feels good," he said, closing his eyes and tipping his head back to accept the kiss of the sun. "It definitely hurts more than two broken arms." His lips curved into a smile as he remembered Phoenix's careful attention as she fed him his dinner on a spoon. He'd loved how her mouth moved, as though chewing the food for him as she mirrored his movements. The few weeks of inconvenience and frustration had been the best of his entire life.

Larry gave a low whistle and leaned his elbows on the rail. The fence line trembled with his movement and Wiri winced. Oblivious, Larry stared at the horses as they stamped away late flies and nuzzled through the hay. "I don't like horses," he confessed. "They always struck me as being a half tonne of unpredictability."

Wiri snuffed and nodded. "Yeah. They are sometimes. My uncle had this white mare for years. Part station bred and part Appaloosa. I've seen Sacha chase people she didn't like, but she adored my aunt and uncle and turned to mush when they were around her." He squeezed the bridge of his nose between the finger and thumb of his right hand. Hay dust shrouded him and made him want to sneeze. He blamed it for the watering of his eyes and his need to wipe them on the back of his hand. History weighed on his shoulders and the essence of home called to him, the whispered voices of his ancestors issuing a karanga because he'd strayed too far in his pursuit of The Plan.

Shrugging his sore shoulders to hide the shiver which rode his spine, Wiri hopped down from the fence and bent his knees to take the shock of the hard ground on his feet. "We'll give them the last bale as well," he said, his voice not much more than a sigh. "I brought one too many."

"Can I throw it over to you?" Larry's lips peeled back into a grimace, which displayed neat white teeth. "You can spread it out for them."

Wiri shook his head. Reluctant steps took him to the bed of his truck. "Na. You'll spook them." He jerked his head at a dappled Appaloosa mare who'd pushed her way into the throng.

Her stomach hung below her like a barrel. Her roan colours sparkled in the sunlight as though God had sprinkled her with gold. "She's pregnant. Vaughan intends to move her into the paddock near the house." He hefted the last bale and buried the grunt of pain by breathing out by slow degrees. "Pass it over to me but don't drop it." He retraced his steps over the fence and took the bale, which Larry balanced on the top rung. His thick biceps protruded through his shirt as he took the weight and lifted it down onto the grass.

The twine popped beneath the sharp blade of his pen knife and he spent time splitting it into slices. "Here you go," he told the mare. She followed him away from the others, nosing at his jeans and his trainers before settling her muzzle into the hay. Wiri took the opportunity to check her over, running his hands over her powerful body and lifting each of her dinner plate hooves in turn. Bending to check the frogs tucked against her hoof wall made his back twinge, and he rested a hand on her ridged spine as he rose for the last time. She inhaled and blew out a gentle, peace filled breath. Wiri ran his right palm over her rounded belly and bit his lower lip as a tiny hoof moved against his touch. "I wish I could afford your foal," he whispered, resting his forehead against her ribs. "I think it's going to be stunning."

He closed his eyes and imagined himself training a rose-coloured yearling in the round pen at home. His former companion's absence left a void in his emotions, which riding and mustering once occupied. Numbness remained. He ran his fingers over the ridge of hardness and something flickered to life in his chest.

With his back to Larry, Wiri pressed a kiss to the mare's ribs and wished that life didn't need to be so hard. Once he'd claimed Phoenix, the round pen and the mountain would no longer welcome him home. He'd become an outcast, a pariah.

Just like his Poppa Reuben.

24

Top Strap

Larry forced him to take a break after he'd checked the other horses. He waited with a frown as Wiri clambered back over the fence. "You look wrecked, dude," he said, his tone soft. "Leilah doesn't expect you to bleed for the job."

Wiri snorted and squirmed in the passenger seat of the truck. "That's ironic coming from a guy whose boss did exactly that."

Larry laughed, the raucous sound filling the vehicle and carrying across the mountain. The nearby horses started, and he covered his mouth with his hand, immediately contrite. "Sorry. But you're smart." He squinted at Wiri sideways, one hand resting on the steering wheel and the other on the gear stick. "And you're churched too. Always a bonus."

Wiri nodded. He removed Alfie's hat and ran his right hand through his fringe, pushing it away from his eyes. Sweat kept it stuck to the top of his head, but he lacked the energy to care. "Yeah. My ma took us all to church. Phoenix just came back from a Christian summer camp." He pursed his lips and frowned. The hardships she'd endured there weren't his to tell.

He felt guilty because he couldn't regret they'd happened when they'd changed her enough to accept his affection.

"Pleasant experience or bad?" Larry cocked his head and Wiri wrinkled his nose.

"Mostly good. The pastor is a neat guy. My cousin always wanted to follow in his footsteps, but things changed over the summer." He licked his lips and clamped his jaw closed to stop him from revealing too much to the attentive man watching him with such avid interest.

Larry inhaled and Wiri tensed, expecting a different sentence. "You said yesterday that you wanted to tell me something." Larry smiled, and a dimple appeared in his rugged cheek. He removed his cap and grey curls tumbled free, unruly enough to make him appear less like the rigid clergyman which perhaps the small town had wanted. "That's why I'm here." He turned in the driver's seat and gave Wiri his full attention. "What did you want to tell me?"

Wiri tensed and fixed his gaze on the roan mare. A bay gelding approached her depleted pile of hay and she turned her backside towards him in warning of a swift kick. Even the scudding clouds seemed to still as though waiting for Wiri to dig himself out of a different kind of hole. The rain-soaked grass had dampened his trainers and his toes squirmed in protest. Larry said nothing, waiting with enough patience to suggest he encountered many walls of resistance in his line of work. His mana filled the truck's interior, projecting outward as trust, confidence, and honour. Wiri exhaled and forced himself to face Larry, the boulder he carried in his chest seeming to lighten at the prospect of sharing its weight. He swallowed and licked his lips. "It's a bit of a long story," he said, his tone flat and devoid of emotion.

Larry shrugged. "Then let's go somewhere and get comfortable," he said.

Pastor Larry lived in a villa next door to the Anglican church. He left his beaten up Toyota on Leilah's driveway and tucked Wiri's truck between two hedges, which cried out for a trim at the vicarage in town. Wiri sat in the passenger seat and gazed up at the filigree details in desperate need of a lick of paint. He imagined bringing Phoenix home to their own place, and a warm sensation trickled through his limbs. The Plan required enough money for them to survive and he worried about where that might take them. His heart sank at the unwelcome reminder of the credit card bill which would land in his emails in the next few weeks. Vaughan had thanked him for saving him the embarrassment of unloading the lumber, but he hadn't actually mentioned repaying him.

"I think one of Mari's pies is in order," Larry said, his voice filling the truck's interior as though he readied himself to preach a sermon. Wiri jumped and his concerns settled back on his shoulders as a dead weight. "Take my key." Larry's work-worn fingers held out a bunch and Wiri took them with a sigh. "You might find the lounge sofa comfy enough to lie on while I fetch us some kai." He dipped his head and frowned from beneath bushy grey brows. "You look beat my friend."

Wiri stared down at his fingers, stretching them out to study the warm earthy undertones of his skin. The cut on his middle finger smarted, and he sighed. "Thanks." He accepted the key, testing the weight in his palm as Larry released it. Remembering his manners, he pushed the cooler bag with the toe of his damp trainer. "I have some cash in my wallet."

"Don't worry." Larry waved a hand in dismissal. He picked up the truck key and dropped it on top of the one for his front door. "You sort yourself out and I'll fetch us some food." He exited the vehicle, and the truck rocked as he slammed the heavy driver's door. Wiri took his time clambering out of his seat and reaching back into the cooler for his phone and wallet. He pushed them into his jeans pockets before retrieving the bracelet, which he secured in a bag pocket.

His legs ached as he climbed the steps of a wraparound porch. The truck locked automatically as the key moved out of range of its internal sensor.

Larry's house had a sparseness, which took Wiri by surprise. He let himself in through the front door and groaned as he bent to release his laces. Leaving his trainers in the wide hallway, he padded through the rooms one at a time in search of the promised sofa. Christian artifacts hung in prominent spots on the walls. Larry had introduced little of his own personality into the space and generic, abandoned furniture occupied the downstairs rooms.

Wiri found the lounge at the back of the house. He eased himself with care onto a corduroy sofa the colour of diarrhoea. He got himself comfortable and then stilled, listening for the sound of Larry to clatter up the porch steps in his work boots. Unable to relax in someone else's house, he leaned against the cushions and stared at the textured ceiling. Original features called out from the ornate fleur-de-lis pattern overhead to the intricate details surrounding the single light bulb, which dangled beneath a ceiling rose. "Phoenix would love this," he sighed to himself.

Larry arrived back in a cloud of bluster, bringing pies and take out cups of Mari's dubious coffee. Wiri heard him slam the front door before kicking off his shoes and padding towards the back of the house. "Here you go," he said, holding out a white paper bag with grease seeping through the cheap wrapping in a grey arc. "Steak and cheese." He placed a cardboard holder on a low coffee table and wrinkled his nose. "The coffee isn't great, but it's drinkable."

"Thanks." Wiri's stomach sent a coherent message to his brain, telling him it wasn't hungry and warning him what might happen if he pushed his luck. The painkillers caused acid to burn below his ribs and he reached out for the coffee Larry handed him, placing the pie in the space it vacated. "I'll just try this for now," he said, smiling up at the pastor.

Larry sank into the only other seat in the room, a sagging brown armchair with the kind of fraying which suggested a cat used it as a regular scratching pole. He sipped his coffee and bit into his pie with a sigh. His eyelids fluttered closed with pleasure. "This is good," he breathed. Crumbs scattered around his stomach and landed in his lap. Wiri sipped his coffee and forced away his concern about the mess. Untidiness and disarray triggered his uncle's fastidiousness and the Du Rose children had learned to clean up after themselves if they wanted dinner on time.

Except Edin.

Perceptive and devious, she'd realised early that if she left a mess, someone else would take care of it without her needing to lift a finger. Wiri's mind conjured an image of his half-sister and he wondered if she missed him. An involuntary shrug of his shoulders told him she wouldn't.

"So, what did you want to tell me?" Larry wiped his mouth with the back of his hand, leaving a line of pastry dappling his right cheek.

Wiri sipped the strong coffee, sensing the moment the caffeine hit his lagging brain. He blew out a ragged breath and stared across at Larry. "Can I trust you?" he asked, his tone low. The moot question seemed laughable. He had no one else to tell.

"Vicar's honour." Larry held up the fingers of his left hand and performed an enviable Vulcan salutation. Wiri snorted.

He set the coffee cup on the table and released his muscles against the back of the sofa, each one sending out messages of discomfort until his body stilled. "Okay," Wiri said. "Well, this starts a while ago and ends up with someone trying to kill me yesterday."

25

FRAME

Larry listened to the sorry tale which began with Wiri's feelings for Phoenix, and his formation of The Plan. He interrupted a few times, but not often enough to disturb Wiri's flow.

"So, you're Wiremu Du Rose?" He raised a bushy eyebrow. "Why do I know that name?"

Wiri released a sigh which he blew through puffed cheeks. "My uncle owns a hotel just below Auckland. It gets dragged into the news every time something happens to anyone with the Du Rose name."

"Right." Larry leaned forward. He balled up his pie wrapper and bounced it onto the table where it pinged off Wiri's cup. "You're sure someone untied your safety rope and dropped the hatch over the tank?"

Wiri nodded. Excitement and wariness caused his spine to twinge in complaint as he mirrored Larry's stance. "Yes! And Vaughan has an injury to the back of his head. But he fell forward as he took the weight of the ladder." Wiri flapped his hands. "He needed to support it until I reached it and shared the weight. Then I could lower it to the floor and lean it up against the interior wall. I heard him cry out and then the ladder hurtled through the hole and I dived out of the way." He exhaled. "It smashed the torch and almost landed on me. When it tipped, the feet lost traction and shot far enough to hit the join where the wall meets the floor. It fell and wedged itself across the tank at an angle. I retrieved it once, but I needed to lay it down to extend the rungs enough to reach the inspection hatch." He held up his wounded finger. "I did this trying to do it the hard way."

Larry frowned. "But you saw the person looking into the tank?"

"Yes!" Wiri leaned forward as he projected his certainty. He ignored the low burn consuming the base of his spine. "I thought at first it was Vaughan."

Larry shook his head. "Na. The paramedics said he was out cold with an egg on the back of his skull. What you see is what you get with Vaughan Hōiho. I've never known him fake anything and it would take acting skill for a bear like him to go floppy enough to fool a couple of experienced paramedics." He shrugged. "Leilah was distraught. She told me that herself. He couldn't fake through that. The guy adores her. I should know, I married them last month."

Wiri blew out a ragged breath and forced himself back into the moment. His toes twitched against the sensation of the water lapping over them, and he closed his eyes against the darkness. "Seline." He frowned and remembered the effort it took for her to lift the concrete hatch. "Seline arrived first, and I heard Leilah." He exhaled. "Maybe I should ask what made her check in the tank after she found Vaughan."

Larry shrugged. "Ask her. She knew you were up there with him."

Wiri nodded. "Yeah, but the rope wasn't visible because the same person who sealed the hatch threw it down on top of me."

He sighed. "I'll ask her. But the trouble is, I don't know who to trust."

"Because someone searched your room?" Larry gave a slow nod. "Yeah, I hear ya. Otherwise you could tell that cop who lives with you. He seems like a decent bloke."

"He is," Wiri agreed. "But not if he tried to kill me."

Larry clapped his hands together and tilted his wrist to check his watch. "I should get cleaned up ready for the Women's Institute meeting." He blinked and grinned at the same time. "I realise how bad that sounds, but they meet in the vestry." He pressed his fingers against the arms of his chair. "You can rest here for as long as you like. Just pop the key next door when you want to leave."

"I'm good." Wiri's socks scrabbled against the bare boards and it took him two attempts to push himself upright with enough stability to stand. "I'll head up to the farm and see what's happening."

"Ooh!" Larry dug an older version flip phone from his jeans pocket and poked at the screen. "Let's swap numbers."

"Okay." Wiri unlocked his phone and entered a new contact. His finger hovered over the name, wondering whether to give the pastor his full title. He opted not to and instead, just added him as Larry. They exchanged numbers and Wiri lifted his truck key from the coffee table. He collected his uneaten pie and the remains of the coffee. "I'll let you know if I find out anything else now that I have your number."

Larry grinned. "And I'll take care of your soul by hassling you half an hour before every service." He waved his phone in the air.

"What?" An edge of hostility entered Wiri's tone. "You wouldn't!"

"No. I wouldn't." Larry's body rocked in a series of guffaws.

Wiri limped towards the door leading to the hall, his fingers reaching for the door frame to stabilise him. "Has anyone ever told you how you laugh like Father Christmas?" he grumbled.

Glancing back, he saw Larry standing with his head cocked. The pastor's eyes narrowed to slits, and he gave an exaggerated wince. "I hate to break it to you, but you know he's not real, don't you?"

Wiri cursed and blasphemed in a single sentence as he edged nearer the front door. Larry's heavy steps followed him. "Wait up!" he said. Wiri jumped as a hand rested on his shoulder. "I need to pray for you real quick," Larry said.

Wiri sighed and stopped his forward motion with regret. He'd never met a cleric yet who knew the correct definition of 'real quick.' Closing his eyes and bowing his head, he waited for Larry to drone them both past the hour. He jerked in surprise when the pastor squeezed his shoulder and dropped his hand. "Are we done?" he asked, awe in his voice.

"Yup." Larry reached forward and his fingers closed around the front door handle. He tugged it open and its hinges creaked. "God invented shorthand. And besides, women are waiting for me."

A snort accompanied Wiri's exhale. He pushed his feet into his trainers but couldn't face bending to tie them. The shuffle along the deck and down the steps seemed even more fraught with difficulty because of the trailing laces. Wiri glanced up as a vehicle slowed on the street beyond the scrubby garden. Long and sleek, it crawled past so the driver could stare at him with a smirk on his tight lips.

Larry arrived next to him and lifted his hand in a wave. He spoke sideways through a fake smile. "Watch that guy," he said as his wrist bobbed from left to right. "He's dangerous."

Larry stepped across the rubble between the house and the church, navigating what might once have been a low wall. Wiri paused with his hand on the door of his truck, preparing to walk around to the driver's door. Having seen whatever it was he wanted, Hendricks pressed his foot to the gas pedal and his car cruised towards the main street.

26

BASE PIN

Wiri plugged his phone back into the truck charger and started the engine. He tilted his wrist out of habit and regretted the absence of his watch. The clock on the dashboard showed almost eleven, and he pursed his lips and sent a text.

He smiled as his phone rang in his hand and he sighed with relief as he connected the call and let the truck speakers project Phoenix's voice around him. Its warmth chased away the horror of the dark tank and the tang of impending death. "Hey, Wiri." Laughter sounded around her and he imagined sitting beside her on the low wall surrounding the school soccer field.

"Hey," he replied. "I wanted to catch you before the end of interval."

"Aw, that's nice." She exhaled, and he closed his eyes and allowed his muscles to relax against the seat. It hurt, but not as much as earlier. "How's the new job?"

Wiri paused. He hadn't just lied to Logan and Hana. Phoenix didn't know he hadn't gone north to the family either. He toyed with the idea of telling her, but stopped himself at the last minute. Phoenix couldn't lie to save herself. But Mac could.

"It's okay," he said. "I'm earning money, so that's positive." He held his breath. That had been his intention, but he'd wound up in more debt than he'd started. And injured.

He heard her gulp and the smacking of her lips as she toyed with a question. "Will you still come back for me, Wiri?" A plaintiveness entered her tone. "I miss you. I shouldn't have stopped you speaking to Papa before I went to summer camp. If I'd let you then, things might have been different. I'm sorry about that, but not for kissing you." A bell sounded behind her to signal the return to class and she breathed into her phone. "I need to go. You won't forget about me, will you?"

"Never." Emotion infused his tone with a gruffness which locked up in his throat.

She whispered something he didn't catch and disconnected the call. He pictured her running to class, her rucksack loaded down with text books and her mind already soaking up information like a sponge.

Doubt slapped him around the head and not for the first time. Phoenix was intelligent and loved learning. How could he justify stealing her away from a promising career and forcing her into hiding? The weight of the boulder pressed down on his head and he groaned beneath the impossibility of a combined future. He couldn't push it free and it dogged him as he drove back to Vaughan's farm.

Seline pulled the ranch slider open in response to his gentle tap. She smiled at him, her eyes sparkling with something he couldn't discern. "You knock like a cop," she said, her lips turning down into a pout.

"Right." No ready response presented itself, and he stood on the porch and stared at her. He wondered how she knew what differentiated a police officer's knock from a farm labourer's. He squinted as his mind failed at the mental gymnastics required to solve the riddle. Then he figured she referred to Jet. "Is Leilah around?"

"Dee." All traces of humour faded from her expression. Her lips tightened to create a thin, colourless line. "Or Deleilah."

Wiri frowned and lifted Alfie's hat from his head. It tugged the gauze and aggravated the stitches at the back of his scalp. Impatience grew in his chest and he lost the sentence he'd rehearsed to thank her for saving his life. "Whoever," he growled. "I don't really care. Please tell your mother I've fed the cattle on the slopes and the horses in the lower paddock. I can't do the fencing alone, but I'm happy to do other jobs if she wants to text them to me." He blew out a breath and turned to leave. His laces trailed around his feet. "How is Vaughan?"

Seline's face lost all trace of beauty. Wiri recoiled from the naked hatred in her down turned lips and the sullenness which tugged at the corners of her eyes. "Don't know. Don't care!" she snarled.

Heavy footsteps took Wiri from the steps to the gritty driveway as he tried not to trip. Seline watched as he climbed into the driver's seat of his truck, his expression a mask of pain. "Deleilah, Leilah, Dee. Why the hell should I care?" he muttered to himself, firing up the truck and feeling the vibrations from the diesel engine rumble through the seat and into his painful spine. He glared at her as he made the turn to face his truck in the direction of the road. The lack of a turning circle forced him to perform a three-point turn which extended past three and into the realms of ninety. "What a bitch," he said out loud, the sentiment only adding to his anger.

At the junction with the road, he turned left and then left again, labouring up the mountain to the shared house and the hopes of a lie down on a comfortable mattress. He promised himself he'd just shut his eyes for a minute as a reprieve from his pounding headache.

He woke from a deep sleep and struggled to orientate himself. His lids grated against his eyeballs as he forced them apart with reluctance. The greyness of the light filtered through the tinted window and threw the ceiling into a pattern of high points and shadows. He didn't recognise the shade shrouding a single energy bulb above him.

He'd drifted off after lying on his back on the mattress, not bothering to undress or pull the covers over himself. It hadn't seemed necessary when he expected a text from Leilah or Vaughan at any minute. His trainers dangled off the end of the bed.

Wiri checked his wrist again and groaned. He shifted his head to look at his watch, still on its charger. A green light at the bottom suggested it might not be as dead as he first believed. He sighed and tested his muscles one at a time. "The odds are definitely against me," he murmured to himself. "I bet that watch is still buggered."

Rolling onto his side, he pushed his legs over the mattress until the toes of his right trainer connected with the floor. Then he forced himself into a sitting position. He dipped forward to stretch the muscles of his spine and grappled on the bedside table for the packet of painkillers. His empty cooler box tumbled to the rug. "Maybe I shouldn't have taken them so soon," he said, yawning and resisting the urge to stretch up his arms.

The sound of a fist rapping against glass took his breath away, and he inhaled in shock. He turned his body towards the noise, starting at the sight of a man peering through his bedroom window. Blond hair sprouted from his head, beginning at a cow lick on his forehead. The genial expression he'd worn the last time Wiri saw him had disappeared in favour of a grimace. He hammered again on the glass, using the balled side of his fist. "Open the door!" he shouted. "Now!"

A watery sun dipped low in the sky behind his angry face and Wiri blinked in surprise. A prickle of guilt played at the edges of the fog that he'd slept through the entire afternoon.

Wiri eased himself to a standing position, anxious at being caught with his trainers still on his feet. He shuffled along the hallway, hoping he wouldn't find Leilah standing on the door mat with the angry man who strode around to the front of the house to meet him. She'd gone to great lengths with her renovation of the old property, and he imagined her dismay at his shod feet. The laces trailed behind him like a wake.

Wiri leaned against the wall next to the front door and used his right hand to turn the catch. The handle depressed from the other side and he jerked away from the door, which cannoned open into his face a second later. He only just dodged the force of it, listing sideways and scrabbling to hold on to the wall.

Jet's brother filled the gap, his neck bending as his head just cleared the lintel. He filled his police uniform with a wall of muscle and the faint burgeoning of a rounded stomach.

"What's wrong?" Wiri leaned against the wall to remain upright and dragged a hand across his scratchy eyes.

"I've been knocking for the last ten minutes," Tane growled.

"Sorry." Wiri blew out a ragged breath. "I took some painkillers and fell asleep." He gasped. "What's the time? Oh, no!" He patted his pockets and remembered putting his phone on charge after its night in the cooler. "Did Leilah send you? Has she tried to call me?" He exhaled and colour flooded his cheeks. "Damn! I'll lose my job. I left a message for her to text me with the tasks I needed to complete."

Tane shrugged. "Leilah didn't send me. That's not why I'm here."

Wiri gaped up at him, his tired brain limping through a series of plausible explanations. After a moment of wrangling, he sighed. "Sorry, mate. I got nothing." He released a hiss through his teeth. "Can I get my phone and see if Leilah sent me some jobs by text?" He ran his palm along the wall for a few metres until the clearing of Tane's voice caused him to turn back to face him. Every movement made his muscles shriek their protest into his brain. "What?" A tremor entered his voice.

Tane's expression mirrored one he'd seen before.

Logan wore it when he informed Wiri his dad was dead. So, he'd kept quiet then, not sure if his uncle knew the truth. And then his dad really died and his tent pegs had pinged free from the whenua, as though casting him adrift without an anchor.

Wiri leaned back against the expensive flock wallpaper which Leilah loved but wouldn't live with. He spread his fingers over the embossed pattern and held his breath. "What's happened?" he asked, his tone wavering. "Just tell me. And then please, can you lace up my trainers for me?"

27

LOCKING LUG

He didn't expect Tane to take him to the police station. Not quite under arrest, but definitely under duress.

The sky-blue building at the end of the main street looked more like a residential house. Only the ramp up to the front door suggested a nod to disability equality, although the roughness of the wooden slats would make any wheelchair journey hazardous. Wiri tripped twice on his way up the ramp, pausing to catch his breath as his fingers gripped the hand rail. His index finger smarted at the contact and he withdrew his hand and tucked it beneath his right arm. Tane waited for him, his manner brusque and frustration drawing deep frown lines across his forehead.

Jet stood in the centre of a reception area. He looked at something belonging to an elderly woman, nodding in a show of feigned sympathy while his attention wandered towards the front door. "Hey, bro'." He jerked his chin upward as Tane walked through, but he blinked at the sight of Wiri limping after him. "What's going on?" He tried to press the sheet of white paper back into the woman's hands, but she missed her cue and it fluttered to the ugly yellow linoleum beneath their feet. "Why is he here?"

"Good question." Wiri found his voice and locked his knees, halting his momentum just inside the front door. The old woman reminded him of Leslie, her breasts balanced on a shelf-like stomach, which made her dress shorter at the front. She turned to face him, her eyes massive behind spectacle lenses like magnifying glasses. She blinked, and he forced himself not to laugh, confusion, nerves and pain conspiring to create an uncharacteristic giddiness. The woman smiled at him and he realised she'd mistaken his inane grin as a greeting.

"Are you drunk?" Jet took a step towards him and Wiri shook his head. The room wavered as though supported on a thin thread, like the nest of a paper wasp.

"No." Wiri rubbed at his eyes. "I took those powerful painkillers from the hospital." A glance at Jet's widening eyes suggested he didn't mention that the police officer had snagged them from the nurse's station on the way out and they weren't actually prescribed. "My back is killing me." He lifted his right hand to touch the gauze on his crown and he sighed. "And my head. And my fingers." He tutted and eyed a row of orange plastic chairs lined up against the far wall. "Can I at least sit down?"

Tane exhaled and jerked his head towards a fire door next to the reception desk. "Through here," he grunted. Wiri blinked three times before deciding it was the door which leaned backwards at an angle and he should stop worrying about his eyesight. Tane pressed a code into the keypad and pushed it open, waiting for Wiri to shuffle through before him. Then he strode ahead and paused outside a bedroom converted into an interview room.

Another plastic chair awaited Wiri as he walked gingerly through the doorway. Its orange bucket seat appeared less appealing at close quarters. He eyed it as though the moulded frame contained barbed wire and razor blades, worrying about collapsing against it and finding himself unable to stand in a hurry. He ran a shaking palm over his face and realised he'd never needed Logan Du Rose's clear head more than in that moment.

"Take a seat." Tane indicated the orange chair with an outstretched arm before walking to the opposite side of the table and sinking into its twin.

"I don't think I can." Wiri shuffled towards the wall, resting a palm against its cool surface and then shifting his hip so he could rest his backside against it.

Tane leaned back in his chair until it tipped onto the rear legs. It seemed a strange, juvenile habit for a man in his late thirties, especially one who ran a police station. Wiri picked through Logan's repertoire of casual stances aimed at putting opponents at ease and recognised a similar tactic in Tane's behaviour. He exhaled and concentrated on remaining upright. "So, where did you go this morning?" the officer demanded. He lifted a tablet from the end of the table and raised it for Wiri to see. "I'll just flick this on and play it back for you when we're done." He fiddled with buttons and the screen flared to life. "Then you can make a written statement based on what we discuss."

"You're recording me?" Wiri swallowed. "Don't I need a lawyer?"

Tane shrugged. "Do you?" He jerked his head towards the flashing eye of a security camera fixed to the ceiling. It looked like the most expensive thing in the room, its presence jarring with its dilapidated surroundings.

"I don't know. What do you think I've done?" Wiri's voice rose, and he sensed the boulder tipping in his chest. It rolled against his empty stomach, which burned from the painkillers. Nausea rose and then descended like a tide. "You said someone died, but I don't know anyone here. I only arrived on Sunday."

Tane pushed the record button and extended the stand at the back of the tablet so it could perch upright on the table. As though it wasn't enough, he seized a pen from his top pocket and withdrew a notebook from his trousers. Wiri sighed. He'd heard enough stories from Logan and Tama to purse his lips and remain silent until Tane looked up at him in expectation. "What's your full name?" he asked.

Wiri stared up at the ceiling and considered his options. Then he exhaled, slowing down the breath, so it hurt less. "I can just say, 'no comment' all day if I need to, sir. But that won't help either of us much. Tell me why I'm here and we can start from there." He shrugged. "Otherwise, I'll just get a lawyer and you can do your worst. I've done nothing wrong and I know I can prove it. We'll waste each other's time and Leilah Hōiho's money."

Bluster. All bluff and bluster.

He didn't know any local lawyers and couldn't involve his Aunty Liza. She'd run straight to Logan. Vaughan and Leilah hadn't paid him anything. Yet. The looming threat of the credit card bill made Wiri swallow his fear of the future. It festered at the bottom of his pile of other, bigger worries. Like this one.

He listened to the words spill from his lips and observed the change in Tane's stance. His rigidity lessened, and the officer pursed his lips and leaned back in his chair with a sigh. Logan always advocated calm and reason before a smack in the mouth. Both worked, but the former involved less of a clean up afterwards. Wiri studied Tane's expression and sensed the mention of Leilah had induced the change. He wondered if they grew up together, Tane, Leilah and Vaughan. His quick brain filed the knowledge. Just in case.

Tane folded his arms. "It's an offence not to provide a police officer with your full name on request," he stated. His blue irises flickered beneath the glow of the strip light. His aftershave filled the room by degrees, as though triggered by the sweat of nervousness. Wiri breathed in the pine scent and tried not to focus on the fact he still wore last night's clothes. He leaned his shoulder blades against the wall and took the weight off his right hip.

"Wiremu Lincoln Du Rose," he said, failure nipping at his psyche. He hadn't even managed three days with his mother's borrowed name. Although Jet had rumbled the lie within minutes of arriving in town.

"Du Rose?" Tane stared up at the ceiling in thought. "Why do I know that name?"

Wiri sighed. "We're a big family, sir," he replied.

"Right." Tane licked his lips and focused on Wiri's face. He jerked his head towards the orange chair. "You might feel better if you sit. Do you need a doctor?"

Wiri wrinkled his nose. "If I sit down, I don't think I'd manage to get up again." He closed his eyes and let his awareness wander to all his different pain sites. Then he nodded. "I think I need a doctor," he concluded. "But can you tell me who Donovan is first, please?"

28

Bolt Face

"So, Donovan is Donovan Hendricks?" Wiri blew out a breath. "Right."

Tane's gaze burned a hole in Wiri's forehead as he sifted through the facts. "Leilah's daughter found him dead a few hours ago."

Wiri spread his hands in front of him. "Yes, but where? And that doesn't explain why I'm here."

"It's an investigation." Tane rocked back on his chair again. "I'm investigating."

Wiri's shoulders slumped. "So, there's a new brown guy in town. Let's fit him up for any new local crimes, huh? Nice." He shook his head. Disappointment coursed through his veins as his tired brain searched and found no other explanation. Defeat ricocheted around inside his skull, telling him he didn't deserve hope or a future because of his minority status and the melanin in his skin.

Tane tutted, drawing Wiri from his thoughts and shaking his head. "That's not who I am," he began, his fingers tapping an agitated beat on the table. "I resent that accusation!"

"Good. Because at least it's on the record." Wiri jerked his head towards the tablet and the red flashing light at the bottom of the black screen. "This is who you are to me." He held out his right arm to encompass Tane and his makeshift interview room at the back of someone's old home. "Yesterday I thought I would die in a flooding water tank and today I'm in a police station defending myself against a murder charge."

Tane lifted an index finger in protest. "I haven't charged you, Mr Du Rose. I haven't even mentioned charging you. Don't jump to conclusions." He peered beneath the table at Wiri's feet. "I might need to confiscate your shoes for evidence." His blond eyebrows rose in a wince of disbelief. "Although someone let the cows into the paddock and they've made a right mess of the ground around the water tank."

Wiri groaned and ran the fingers of his right hand through his fringe. He'd lifted his arms at the same time but let his left hand rest on the top of his head to spare the stitches. "I shouldn't have come here," he sighed, his chest filling with regret. "It's been a disaster from the minute I arrived. I came to earn some money and gain work experience. Now, I have a massive credit card bill and after yesterday, I can't even manage a full day's work to pay it." He bent his knees and his spine slid down the wall, the pressure building into a crescendo in his head. When his backside hit the floorboards, he vomited.

❧❧❧❧❧ ❦❦❦❦❦

The doctor arrived from the surgery across the street. He nipped over between patient appointments and examined Wiri's injuries in another room containing a flimsy medical stretcher and a blood pressure machine. Young and dynamic, he provided yet another mismatch in a town which oozed tradition and rigidity.

"You say the x-ray showed no broken bones?" He touched the skin above Wiri's waistband and tutted. "The bruise is huge. Are you sure I can't look at the site of impact?"

"No!" Wiri hauled his shirt down over his ears and caught both his finger and the gauze at the back of his head. Exasperation laced his tone. "I had enough people staring at and photographing my ass in the hospital, thank you."

The doctor smiled, his hazel irises dancing against the contrast of his umber skin. "That sounds against hospital policy." He dug in his black briefcase. "What painkillers did they prescribe?"

Wiri closed his eyes and focused his memory on the foil wrapper on his bedside table. "Something strong. I have two left."

The doctor raised his black eyebrows. His tweed jacket rustled as he moved. The leather patches at the elbows reminded Wiri of Poppa Alfie. He produced a cardboard wrapper from the depths of his case and held it up. "Lay off the potent stuff. Stick to plain old Paracetamol. You might have a concussion. I'll redress that head wound and put something over your finger to keep it dry and clean. Pop over to the surgery if you need anything else."

Wiri's finger moved less freely after the doctor finished wrapping a gauze bandage around its circumference. But he strapped it to his index finger, so it lost the cartoon appearance which the hospital favoured. He removed the fabric pack from the back of his head and murmured to himself.

"Pardon?" Wiri turned to face him and he tutted.

"You have stitches in the back of your head too. Didn't you realise?"

"No." Wiri pushed out his bottom lip and frowned.

"The emergency doctor will have written it on your discharge papers. Do you have them with you?" He lowered his voice and glanced towards the open doorway where Tane lurked. "It might help you if they mentioned concussion."

Wiri exhaled. The Plan already required so many lies, he didn't have the mental faculty for more. He licked his lips and turned on the thin bed, his feet dangling off the side. "I didn't exactly wait for them," he whispered. "I sort of did a runner."

The doctor blew out a breath and took a step backwards, a pair of angled scissors poised in his left hand. "Sort of did a runner," he repeated, his tone leaden. Then he nodded. "So, the painkillers weren't prescribed?"

Wiri winced, lifting his hand to ease a burgeoning bruise on his cheekbone. "No. They sort of kinda fell into my hand from someone else's."

The doctor shuttered his eyes closed and pursed his lips. Tane spoke to someone in the corridor, his voice rumbling through the walls. Then the doctor stepped closer, using Wiri's body to shield him from the view of the doorway. "Hendricks was a hideous individual, but I don't think for a minute you killed him. Not in this state." He jerked his head towards Wiri's feet and he followed his gaze with a frown. "Your trainers are on the wrong feet."

Wiri swore and released a heavy sigh. "That cop laced them for me and he didn't say a word," he hissed. "And I spent the morning with Pastor Larry and he never mentioned it. What's wrong with this town?" He squeezed the bridge of his nose between his finger and thumb. "I wish I'd never come here. It's been a living hell since the minute I drove over the boundary."

The doctor grinned. "Why do you think the elders called it The End of the Day?"

"I have a few ideas," Wiri grumbled. He exhaled. "Thanks for your help. I feel a little better now." He shifted his weight until he could slide off the high mattress and onto his feet. His mismatched trainers made him look like a four-year-old.

"Just stand there a second." The doctor pulled a pointed device from his pocket before touching various points on Wiri's spine. "I've done some chiropractic studies over the years. Perils of working as a small town practitioner. You learn to fill most roles. The older folk don't want to go to Hamilton in case they don't come back again. They think it's where they go to die. To be honest, it usually is." He clicked the device around Wiri's back and shoulders, causing pain to blossom outwards from wherever he touched. He poked and prodded, but the general aches eased. Satisfaction made his irises dance as he stepped back and admired his work. "That looks better. You have lots of swelling and water retention around the bruising. I'm sorry if that hurt." He cocked his head. "Are you sure you didn't break something when you fell? Everything is telling me you did."

"It feels a little easier to move." Wiri dodged his question. "I'm grateful."

"Awesome!" the doctor exclaimed with a sigh. He stuck out his right hand, the fingers almost touching the buttons of Wiri's shirt. "I'm Gareth, by the way. Nice to meet you."

Wiri accepted the handshake with a nod. "Thanks. Wiremu Du Rose." His eyelashes fluttered with guilt. "But I'm using my mother's maiden name. Kingii."

Gareth cocked his head. "Du Rose. Why does that name sound familiar?"

Wiri flattened his lips into a thin line. "That's the reason I'm not using it."

"Fair enough." The doctor patted his shoulder. He accompanied him to the doorway where Tane waited. Wiri stuffed the cardboard packet of pills into his back pocket where they nestled against Phoenix's bracelet.

"All good, Gareth?" Tane raised a blond eyebrow. "I just need to finish asking him some questions."

Gareth hefted his briefcase in front of him as though creating a shield. "He didn't do it, Tane," he said, his tone flat. "We both know that. The kid couldn't tie his own shoelaces. He's spent the morning tripping over them and look at his feet. There's no way he got into a fight with Hendricks, killed him and threw his body in there." He gave a snort of disgust. "You need to look elsewhere."

Gareth's sensible soles squeaked along the corridor and through the heavy door into the reception area. Wiri stood in the doorway and watched Tane's expression change from resignation to defeat. He exhaled and his chest deflated, straining the buttons across his chest. His voice held a lacklustre note. "Just make a statement, please," he said. He jerked his head back towards the interview room.

"Okay." Wiri nodded. "Can I swap it for a ride back up to the farm?"

They settled back in the office and Tane didn't object when Wiri remained standing and supported himself against the wall. He didn't turn on the tablet but reached for his pen and paper. His mood and his behaviour seemed different. "Let's run through your morning and see if you know anything that might help." He tapped the pen against the pad.

Wiri exhaled and stared at the ceiling. "I drove to Vaughan's and spoke to Leilah just after seven o'clock." He paused and sifted through his tasks, blinking in surprise when most of them descended into a blur. "I loaded my truck with hay and drove up to the cattle we fed yesterday." His spine twinged at the memory of the endless gates, opening, closing, sitting back in the driver's seat, getting in and out in a constant wall of aching bones and muscles. He sighed. "It took ten times longer than usual because I struggled to lift the bales. Larry walked up to meet me but I don't know what time he arrived. We fed another two mobs and the horses." He frowned. "I need to tell Vaughan his mare looked ready to drop soon. He wanted to move her next to the house." He blinked against the distraction and continued. "Larry drove my truck to town, and we went to Mari's cafe." He lifted his finger. "No, we didn't. He drove to his house, and he walked to the cafe and got pies and coffee. Ugh. I left my pie in the truck." His nose wrinkled as he imagined the grease sinking into his passenger seat cover.

"When did you last see Donovan Hendricks?" Tane stopped scribbling notes and looked up at him, his blue irises flashing against his tanned complexion.

Wiri stared at the flaking paint on the ceiling, ordering his thoughts into an orderly procession. "This morning. He saw me leaving Larry's place and slowed down to stare at me." He shook his head. "I don't know where he went. Larry walked into the church and I drove to Vaughan's place. Seline answered the door and roasted me for asking for Leilah." He blew out a breath and ran a hand over his chin. "I drove home, put my phone on charge and collapsed on my bed."

Tane nodded. "Give me timings for things. When did Hendricks drive past you?"

"Just before eleven o'clock. I phoned my cousin, girlfriend." He winced. "My cousin is also my girlfriend. I phoned her." Stating it out loud sent a flicker of pleasure zinging from the pit of his stomach to the roots of his hair. He wished he'd used it under different circumstances, but it felt good. The boulder in his chest squirmed, and he realised he hadn't asked her yet. But he would. Soon. When he had some money and felt as though he deserved her trust.

"Can you show me your phone, so I can verify that?" Tane raised a blond eyebrow but dropped it when a knock on the door heralded Jet. He walked in without waiting and shot Wiri a glance loaded with curiosity.

"I'm going back out on patrol," he said. "Need me to do anything before I go?"

"No, thanks." Tane dismissed him without looking up from his notes.

Jet withdrew and closed the door behind him. Wiri stared at the brush marks showing in the substandard paint job which didn't quite hide the turquoise layer beneath the white. Jet's glance had contained something else he couldn't discern. He exhaled, tiredness and pain wearing at the edges of his resilience.

"I left my phone at the house. You can check it when you take me home."

"Okay." Tane pushed his chair with the backs of his knees and rose. He seemed keen to get rid of Wiri now he'd failed to incriminate him. He stuffed his notebook and pen back into his top pockets, giving himself the illusion of odd shaped breasts. The pen protruded beneath his name badge and created a lop sidedness which didn't fit with the man's general neatness.

Wiri eased himself away from the wall. "How did Hendricks die?" He narrowed his eyes and cocked his head at Tane. "What did the doctor mean? Threw his body where?"

Tane pursed his lips and his chest muscles stiffened. He winced twice, and a scar appeared and then faded next to his left eye. "Leilah's daughter found his body in the water tank on Vaughan's farm this afternoon. She went out riding and saw the inspection hatch open." He held up an index finger as a knock sounded on the door. "Wait here."

His boots padded across the floorboards making little sound. For such a tall, bulky man he had uncharacteristic grace in his movements. Wiri remained as instructed, tightening each of his muscles in turn and trying to decide which hurt the most. Tane returned in less than a minute, a clear plastic bag in his right hand. He closed the door with his heel, blocking Wiri's view of the officer in the hallway. Tane's expression held more severity, the features flattened to create harsher shadows. He held the bag out to Wiri. "Do you recognise this?" he asked, his tone stern.

Wiri took the bag and peered at the label, not understanding the strange mix of numbers and letters. But when he looked through the plastic covering, he saw a shirt pressed flat against it. Someone had folded it with care as though displaying it in a shop for purchase. The frayed collar showed uppermost, the name tag evident.

'W. Du Rose,' it said.

29

SPRING

The plastic bag rustled as Wiri let it fall against his right thigh. The wet fabric stuck to the inside of the bag to create distorted pockets of moisture against the surface. His hand shook, causing the bag to shiver. His shoulders slumped, and he moved his chin from side to side, keeping the movement minimal to avoid extra pain. "It's mine." He frowned. "Ma sewed tags into all our clothes for school camps." He shrugged. "I use this shirt for rough jobs."

"Where did you see it last?" Tane shifted in his chair and leaned forward, his pen poised above the ruled lines printed on his pad.

Wiri closed his eyes and leaned his head back to give him thinking time. His eyelashes flickered as he contemplated the ride home he'd almost had and now lost. "Ma washed it for me. I packed it into my duffel bag before I left. Figured I might need it for some real dirty jobs. I would have worn it to go into the tank, but Vaughan didn't give me any warning."

Tane dipped his blond head and gazed at Wiri through his loose fringe. "So, you last saw it in your bedroom? Does anyone else have access to your possessions?"

Wiri snorted. "Probably. I went out with Jet after work on Monday night and someone searched through my gear."

"Who?" Tane frowned and his jaw tensed to create a hard line through his skin. "You live with my brother. Are you suggesting he took your shirt?"

"No." Wiri exhaled. "I know someone rifled through my bag, but the shirt was there when I checked later that night." He blinked, holding onto the next sentence for fear of Tane's dismissal. "It sounds stupid, but someone moved my pillow and perhaps lifted the mattress. I wondered if Hendricks had a key to our place."

Tane's head jerked forward and his eyes widened. "Explain."

Wiri limped towards the orange chair. He dumped the bag onto the table between them and the metal legs of the chair grated against the floor as he hauled it backwards by degrees. He inspected the bucket seat before easing himself into it. A flurry of tingles shot up his back and into his neck. "My girlfriend gave me a bracelet she made. I put it under my pillow before we left for town. When I got home, I found it on the floor under the bed."

"Could you have knocked it there?" Tane tilted his head and observed Wiri, his expression a millisecond away from morphing into the disbelief Wiri feared.

"No." He forced certainty into his tone and added a reluctant shake of his head. "I know where I put it. Someone shifted things around and poked through my bag. They tried to do it carefully, but I know how I pack. I roll things a certain way and they'd moved them."

"Right. Let me get this straight, you don't think it was Jet?" Tane pressed on with the unexpected line of questioning, causing Wiri to gape in confusion. He paused, not yet ready with a suitable answer. He wanted to mention finding

Hendricks on the property after they arrived home, but Tane seemed more interested in vindicating his brother.

Tane leaned sideways and placed his finger over the tablet's screen. He blinked at the lack of activity as though only just remembering he hadn't restarted it. He shot a nervous glance at Wiri and then back at the screen before licking his lips. Sweat beaded on his forehead and he wiped it with the back of his hand. The pen bounced in his fingers and he appeared momentarily lost. He cleared his throat. "You don't think my brother took your shirt?"

Wiri sighed. "I don't believe so. He could have gone through my gear that first time because I waited for him outside on the deck and he took longer to get ready." He shrugged. "But why would he bother? He's a cop. He can find out anything he wants to about me." The memory surfaced of Jet admitting to using the force's national computer to chase down details about his new flat mate. Wiri leaned forward and rested his elbows on the table. The evidence bag crackled at the contact with his elbow. "I don't understand what's happening here."

Tane released a tired breath through his nose. "Nor do I, son. Nor do I."

"Can you help me?" Wiri swallowed, the words sticking in his throat. "I think someone is trying to kill or frame me. I'm not sure which."

Tane inhaled, his chest rising and falling and his serious expression growing darker until it seemed to lose all its natural highlights. "Let's go back to the shirt," he said again, his tone flat and without intonation. "When did you last see it?"

"Yesterday." Wiri pictured the scene of his rude awakening that morning. "I'm wearing the clothes Jet brought to the hospital for me last night. I woke up late and needed to wash my boots before work." He tutted, the sound reminding him of how dry his mouth had become. "Actually, I guess Jet searched through my bag last night, anyway."

"To bring your clothes?" Tane made a note and his index finger flexed over the pen. "Right." He covered his disquiet with logic. "I'll ask him if he noticed the shirt then." His shoulders slumped as he leaned back against his chair. The plastic creaked beneath his muscular bulk. "Look, Wiremu, it's like this. Hendricks died in the tank. The same tank you got stuck in yesterday. The doctor gave an initial time of death and a cause of drowning, but the coroner is on his way from Hamilton. He'll verify the facts. My officers found your shirt in the tank with him."

Wiri nodded. That explained the saturation of the fabric and the darker colour of the checked pattern. He'd kept the shirt because Phoenix bought it for his sixteenth birthday. She loved to see him wearing it and he'd lacked the detachment to throw it away after it frayed at the cuffs and collar. He'd relegated it to farm work in order to justify keeping it. As he watched the liquid pool in the bottom corners of the bag, he wondered how the forensic examiners would stop it going mouldy. The issue prevented him from facing the fact it would never arrive back in his possession.

His heart ached with the familiar sense of loss and he jumped as Tane cleared his throat. "Sorry," he breathed. "My girlfriend gave me the shirt. I never wanted to get rid of it." His fingers crept across the table's scarred melamine surface to touch the bag. "Will I get it back?"

Tane's paw closed over the folded edge and he moved it out of range, where it sighed like a deflating lung and flattened itself at the other end of the table. "I don't know." His tone became brusque. "Let's go back over your movements this morning?"

Wiri groaned and pushed his backside towards the rear of the seat, taking the pressure off his tail bone as he dipped forward. "Okay," he conceded.

Tane picked up his pen again. "Don't tell me you drove straight home after leaving Larry. I stopped a speeding vehicle outside your gate at twenty past eleven. Your truck wasn't in the driveway and I didn't pass you on my way back to town." He raised a blond eyebrow. "So, where did you go?"

"Nowhere." Wiri shook his head. He wracked his brain for a memory of seeing a patrol car heading in the opposite direction. He would have noticed and checked his speed in a reflex action of guilt. "I drove to Vaughan's house and spoke to Seline." A plaintive strain entered his tone. "Ask her. Maybe you stopped the vehicle while I was up at the house. It's possible we missed each other. Did you notice my truck in Vaughan's driveway?"

Tane shook his head. "I wouldn't, would I? The driveway dips next to the house. If you parked by the porch steps, it's hidden from the main road. Vaughan's house protrudes further than Leilah's on the ridge. His Uncle Horse dug it out years ago to put in the equipment shed." He stared at Wiri from the other side of the table and he shrugged. "Unless Leilah's daughter vouches for you, you're toast."

30

ASSEMBLY

"How long does it take to get from the edge of town to Vaughan's place?" Wiri cast around for answers, his quick mind picking over his movements earlier that day. A fog descended over his memory and cast a haze of confusion.

"About five minutes less than it takes to get from town to yours." Tane raised a quizzical eyebrow. His phone beeped, and he frowned as he inspected the text.

"So, about twenty minutes to Vaughan's and another five to the rental place?" Wiri peered through the mind-fog. "Well, I drove from Larry's to Vaughan's house. That's twenty minutes. Seline answered the door and got weird when I asked for Leilah. I already told you that. I hung around for a few minutes and then drove home. Another five maybe."

Tane cocked his head, the intensity of his blue irises ramping up to indicate more than a passing interest. "Okay. Weird in what way? Because I have to tell you that my officer just texted me to say she's denying your visit happened."

Wiri flapped his hand. "She's lying!" he protested. "I asked for Leilah and she got snippy. She wanted me to call her Dee or

Deleilah, but not Leilah." He exhaled as the memories tumbled over one another. "I stayed for a minute or two, told her to get her mother to text me and drove home. I don't understand what she meant about her mother's name. Or why she would deny seeing me."

"Right." Tane jotted down a note. Wiri peered at it but had never succeeded with upside down writing. "How long do you suppose you stayed at the house? I want an exact time."

Wiri let his mind run over the visit, replaying Seline's change in attitude and the way she'd rebuffed his question about Vaughan. He pursed his lips and added up the minutes it might have taken for him to drive up and down the bumpy driveway and have the tense conversation with Leilah's daughter. "I drove real slow because the potholes hurt my back. She made me get out of the truck and walk right up to the door, although I suspect she maybe watched me do it." He shifted the fingers of his right hand against the table, grateful for the fresh gauze the doctor had added over the ugly stitches. "We spoke for only a couple of minutes. Two at the most. I got the feeling she wanted rid of me. It took a while for me to get the truck turned around to head back to the road." He sighed. "I'm uncertain how long it all took. I'd need to do it all again and time it." He scrubbed at his eyes with the back of his right hand. "But it's irrelevant. Hendricks drove past Larry's house, so he was still alive then."

Tane nodded. "I'm just gathering the information for now. I'll visit Leilah's daughter myself and ask what she remembers. We'll go from there."

"Okay." Wiri stifled a yawn behind his right palm. "She saved my life yesterday. There's no reason for her to lie."

Tane made a sound like a grunt and leaned forward with his elbows on the table. "A witness saw you in a physical disagreement with Hendricks a few nights ago in the supermarket. What would you like to tell me about that?" He jerked his head towards the healing scratch on the back of Wiri's right hand.

Wiri groaned. "Yeah, that's true," he admitted. He blew out a ragged breath. "Perhaps I need Aunty Liza about now."

"Who's Aunty Liza?" Tane's jaw dropped lower and wrinkles appeared around his shirt collar.

Wiri shrugged. "Judge Eliza Du Rose. Aunty Liza."

A bubble formed on Tane's lip and popped. He poked out his tongue and ran it in a circular movement as he bought himself time. "I've met her," he admitted. His cheekbone showed as a grim line. Then he swallowed. "It doesn't matter what I say now, does it?" His tone lost its victorious edge.

"She won't come herself."

"No. She'll send a lawyer who earns more in an hour than I clear in a month."

"Yeah." Wiri blinked up at him. "And you didn't record this part of the interview."

Tane pressed his lips into a flat line. "Talbot versus the Crown. 2019."

"Sorry." Wiri meant it. "Can you imagine the embarrassment of answering exam questions on your aunt's cases in Legal Studies at school?"

"No." Tane shook his head. "Do you want me to call her?"

Wiri swallowed. A sigh hissed from between his lips. "I didn't kill him, Tane. I should call her, but I know I'm innocent."

"Tell me about the fight." Tane reached across and activated the recorder setting on the device. He spoke into it, leaning forward with his tone formal and less defeatist. Wiri waited for him to finish.

"Hendricks approached me in the supermarket. He knew my grandfather, or so he said. I believe he was hunting, actually."

"Hunting?" Tane tapped the end of his pen on the pad. "With your grandfather?"

Wiri considered his words, ordering them into something which made sense. "No. I believe Hendricks gathered dirt on people from anywhere he could. Hunting. He dropped something contentious into a conversation and then mined whatever he got from the reaction. Then he blackmailed them as it suited him. He was trying to find out why I came to work for Vaughan. I got the sense he didn't want me here." Wiri dipped his head. "Yeah, I shoved him. The cameras in the supermarket will show you that." He frowned. "Ted stopped me. Hendricks left."

Tane cocked his head. "I have the footage. It looked like more than a push." He jerked his chin towards Wiri's right hand. "Did he do that?"

Wiri nodded. A frown closed his expression. "Will you test his fingernails for my DNA?"

Tane rolled his eyes. "He scratched you two days before he died. Besides, he'd been in the water tank for a few hours when the girl found him. When did you see Hendricks again?"

"He showed up at our place. Jet can tell you. But he was still walking and talking when he left. I saw him outside Pastor Larry's earlier today. He slowed down to watch me leaving." Wiri shrugged. "I didn't see him again. If he drove up to Vaughan's place and walked across the property to the tank, where's his vehicle? That flash Mercedes wouldn't handle the rough ground. Even on foot, it means he was still alive for at least an hour after I last spotted him."

"So, regardless of what Leilah's daughter says, you have no alibi. You claim to have slept through his death. If it took Hendricks an hour from seeing you to getting to the tank, that's still a total of five hours which you can't account for until you answered the door to me. I'll need to check out everything you've said." Tane leaned sideways to the recorder as though giving stage directions before pressing a button to deactivate it. He rose and stowed his pad and pen back in his pockets. "I'll start with Leilah's daughter," he said. Wiri noticed how he referred to Seline without saying her name, as though he nursed a kernel of dislike for her. He ached for the simplicity of home. For Phoenix's sunny presence and Mac's silent stoicism. He even missed his complicated half-sister, though he'd shown no affection for Edin despite their shared father. Her tinkling laughter and solid right hook would stand up against the spiteful streak which hid beneath the veneer of beauty behind Seline's delicate features. Edin would rout her in seconds.

"What's the matter?" Tane leaned forward and his fringe disobeyed the hand which seconds before had pushed it backwards away from his eyes. It dipped low enough to touch the bridge of his nose.

Wiri sighed. "Missing home," he replied, the truth hitting him in the solar plexus like a kick. His voice wavered as he stated another, more pressing truth. "I should never have come here."

31

FiRING PiN

Wiri remained silent as Tane drove him through town in the patrol car. Headlights twinkled against the storefronts to create a strobe which made his head ache. Even the darkness didn't stop his wave of shame as a dog walker stopped to watch the police car's progress as Tane turned left at the end of the main street. Wiri saw the man tug on his mutt's leash and give a shake of his head.

He released a sigh as buildings and traffic gave way to rolling paddocks and the craggy mountain slopes snaking towards the low cloud. Night had already eaten the ridges. Rain dotted the windscreen and sent up a scent like a wet dog. He pictured his shirt lying in his duffel bag and searched his memories for anything odd which might account for its appearance inside the tank with Hendricks' body. Tane hadn't charged or bailed him. He let him go and even drove him home. Wiri wondered if the threat of Aunty Liza had directed the odd course of action.

"How is it living with my brother?" Tane maintained a sedate pace, as though wanting to extend the agony for his passenger.

"Sorry?" Wiri shrugged and forced his face into a nonchalant expression. "I haven't seen much of him."

"Oh?" Tane frowned. "Right. I thought you both hung out last night at the bar in town." Then he clicked his fingers. "Sorry. That was the intention, but you ended up in the hospital."

Wiri nodded. "Yeah. Best laid plans and all that." He frowned and sat straighter in his seat. "You reminded me of something," he said, musing over his tussle with Hendricks on the deck. "Ask Jet if he remembers Hendricks saying, 'It's your funeral.' He said it to me before he left the other night. I already think he went through my gear. What if he also hit Vaughan and trapped me in the tank?"

Tane blew out a breath. "I'll ask him," he promised. "But with Hendricks dead, I don't fancy my chances proving he did anything to anyone." He shook his head. "It's not like I haven't tried." His lips flattened into a line and he returned to the subject of Jet. "It's good having him back in town, where I can keep an eye on him. You're welcome to come with him for dinner if you like? He eats with us most evenings, but flagged it last night to go out with you."

Wiri stilled in the passenger seat. Tane's account didn't fit with Jet's. He cleared his throat, curiosity overriding his need to stay out of other people's business. "Didn't you go out of town last night?"

Tane's instant reaction looked too natural to be fake. He jerked his head in surprise and screwed up his features. "No. My youngest expected Jet to help with making some cardboard thing for school. He cried off at the last minute. I got roped into making a replica of the Sky Tower from toilet roll holders."

"Right." Wiri swallowed down a lump in his throat, which made further conversation difficult. Loneliness wrapped its arms around him, hugging and compressing his chest until it robbed him of oxygen. He closed his eyes and yearned for the security and comfort which Phoenix gave him without even trying. Just her proximity seemed enough to fill the empty well in his soul. His fingers twitched involuntarily at the muscle memory of calling her and he craved the soothing sound of her voice. A glance at the clock on Tane's dashboard gave the time as after nine o'clock in the evening. His stomach growled, and he covered it with his right hand.

Tane's lips parted and Wiri cringed, anxious about the cul-de-sac of disaster he'd walked himself into with the cop. "Do you ever see your mother?" Tane asked, the question both unexpected and unwelcome. It told him he'd done some serious digging for information while he kept Wiri waiting in the tatty reception area for his ride home.

His aching spine gave a twinge of warning as he tensed every muscle in his body. He didn't want to talk about Anahera, especially not there and not while he still felt under suspicion. As he formulated a polite but dismissive reply, the radio on the dashboard crackled. A voice with a tinny quality filled the vehicle with its static.

"Go ahead." Tane replied to the call sign and dropped his conversation with ease. Wiri turned his face towards the passing trees and landmarks which blurred before his gaze. He used the valuable reprieve to blow out a relieved breath. Tane dealt with the mixture of code and English words in a strange conversation with the controller. Wiri zoned out and allowed his mind to check on the more painful parts of his body, touching each tender nerve ending with a tentative thought. His backache seemed worse, but the doctor had warned him that the next twenty-four hours would be painful.

"Hey." Tane nudged his forearm with a gentle hand.

Wiri snapped back into the moment with a start. "Sorry."

Tane shook off the apology. "No, I'm sorry. I just got a call and I need to leave real quick. Bring your phone into the station tomorrow and ask for me. I'll verify what you said about calling your girlfriend."

There it was again. Real quick. So much could change in a brief space of time.

Lose a mother.

Lose a father.

Break a bone.

Gain a soul mate.

Wake up fine in the morning and go to bed different.

"Right." Wiri blinked, trying to work out whether Tane meant to abandon him on the deserted country road. He looked up as they passed Vaughan's house perched on its outcrop. It clung to the mountain, its windows projecting a weak glow as a series of sparkles. It oozed a precarious vulnerability, as though if Wiri looked away, the house might slide into the valley.

"Can I drop you here?" Tane stabbed the bonnet of the vehicle into the driveway leading up to the rental house. Dust rose in a haze on either side as he jammed on the brakes.

"Yeah." Wiri fumbled with the door catch and inhaled dust as he half fell from the passenger seat and onto the narrow lane. Turning to close the door, he saw Tane's lights already strobing red and blue. By the time he'd stumbled out of the way, the police car had already backed out onto the main road and set off away from the town. The powerful engine whirred and hummed along the road. Wiri held his breath as Tane activated the siren, the shrill warning searing through his eardrums and into his aching skull.

He sighed and contemplated the long, uphill walk to the house. His toes ached inside his trainers, but at least he knew the reason. He wished he'd switched them over while Tane questioned him in the dim interview room, but he'd lacked the energy then and realised he still lacked it now. The cattle grid proved more problematic in the darkness than he'd anticipated. He lengthened his stride and balanced on the metal rungs. It took more presence of mind than he could muster to navigate them without losing his footing and falling sideways. His cousin had broken his collarbone, trying to run across one at home. Mac had overextended and tipped as the trench swallowed his right foot. The unforgiving rungs had cracked the bone on impact.

Wiri hunched his shoulders and dug his hands into his front pockets. His finger smarted, but his spine appreciated the support. He trudged up the long driveway, promising himself he'd retrieve his phone from its charger and call Phoenix. Then he'd speak to Mac. He missed them both in an ache which merged with all the others.

Phoenix's sunny expression encouraged him up the slope, crying encouragement as she had when he won the inter-school cross country in his last year as a student. She'd run alongside him for the last hundred metres, her dark curls bouncing against her shoulders and her face alight with pride.

It took longer than it should for Wiri to reach the ridge, which held Leilah's renovated home. He passed a wooden plaque he'd never noticed before and stopped to catch his breath. Moonlight stroked the grainy wood, giving Wiri a chance to read the words burned into its rugged surface. Someone had written 'Hector's Whare' in a cursive hand, the capital letters the same size as those in lower case. Clover and daisies covered the point where the plaque met the ground, interspersed with flowering puha and other edible weeds. They moved in the breeze as though squirming away from his gaze as a series of shadowy, bobbing heads. Wiri pressed his palms against his thighs and dipped his upper body, dismayed at how much the climb had depleted his energy. His chest heaved and sweat prickled against his spine and soaked into the fabric of his shirt.

"Nice to meet you, Hector," he murmured beneath his breath. His feet dragged as he reached the porch and closed his fingers around the sloping balustrade. The moon peeked through the clouds to kiss the wooden steps leading onto the deck. It guided his way before blinking out without warning.

Wiri tried not to tense as his backside settled onto the hard surface, finding it created less pain if he forced himself to relax. He bent double and hugged his knees, grateful for the stretching of the muscles and an easing of the ache. He contemplated his mismatched feet as he stared between his knees. Dropping his right hand, he loosened the laces and let them trail against the floor. Grass stains and dust coated the white leather surface, making the trainers appear older than their two weeks in his possession. He sighed and wished he'd spent the money on another pair of work boots.

The sound of fabric flapping disturbed his reverie. He screwed his neck around without sitting up, trying to see where it originated from. The hem of a lacy net curtain sneaked through a gap between the frame and the window. Safety stays prevented the window from being yanked open from outside and the curtain had caught around it. It struggled for escape like a shadowy mullet trying to free itself from a fisherman's cruel line. Wiri watched its futile movement for a moment, seeing his mother's agony in its pointless flapping.

He closed his eyes and rested his chin on his knees, tuning in to the low keening of an owl further up the mountain. Another sound added a backdrop to the melee, the natural hum conspiring to sound like a conversation. Wiri focussed on the resonance and pace, idly trying to isolate it from the gentle breaths of a nearby horse. He'd found himself spooked more than once by voices in the bush which, once analysed, became bird song, or a trickling water course.

Wiri concentrated, realising the scraping of shod hooves and snorted breaths sounded nearer than he expected. He pushed himself to a position which irked his tail bone and prepared himself for the painful rise to standing. Then he heard it. The whispered conversation returned to him, not misinterpreted bush noises, but a woman's voice. It came from beyond the open window and Wiri froze.

32

Ejector Spring

Fight or flight proved an ineffective reaction, as he was in no shape to perform either. He experienced a moment of utter powerlessness as he perched with his backside on the porch steps. A bung finger added to his woes.

Someone was inside the house.

A dull glow moved around beyond the window as though the owner of the light paced the lounge.

"It's Leilah," he reassured himself, his lips tripping over the words. Reason returned, and he forced himself to relax. Cocking his head, he strained to listen harder to the conversation, tuning out the other local sounds.

"Kingii," the woman's voice said. Wiri detected a note of strain in her low tones. "No, he's a nobody. Just a farm hand." He jerked backwards with a sneer, recognising Seline's voice.

"Who does she think she is?" he hissed. Anger dulled the pain as he closed his fingers around the banister and tried to haul himself to standing. His legs refused to extend and his spine sent a blossom of pain radiating its entire length. Wiri unfolded onto the porch steps like a rug being softly unrolled. He balanced the back of his neck on the point of the top step, waiting for the ache to subside. Seline's voice carried through the wooden slats of the deck as her voice rose in temper.

"Don't tell me what to do! I'm here, aren't I? I'm doing my best." She paused to listen to the person at the other end of the call. "No, this new guy lives in the room I had last time. Mum moved the furniture around and I can't get to it." Again, the dramatic silence as she waited. "I know you took care of the other thing," she said. "But you made everything so much worse."

A frantic edge entered her voice and Wiri recoiled at the blackness which issued from the spectre hovering over the house. It tried to settle on his head, sucking the air from his lungs and threatening every wonderful memory left in his tortured brain. He closed his eyes and lifted his arms as though warding it off, grateful for the prayers Hana covered him with every day since she'd taken responsibility for him. Pure nastiness drifted through the open window and tangled with the flapping net curtain. "You know what I'm talking about." A low wheedling underscored her conversation. "Fine, I guess we shouldn't talk about it over the phone." Then, "Yes, I'll do it," she snapped. "Don't worry. He won't see it coming." Her bark of laughter seemed so disconnected from Leilah's sunny countenance and soft giggle, it made him wonder at their blood connection. Footsteps sounded on the floorboards inside and reverberated through the house and deck.

Wiri tutted and curled his lips back from his teeth in a grimace. He wanted nothing to do with the woman who'd provided his rescue the previous day. Something unhinged communicated itself to him and he quailed at the voice, which screamed in his mind for him to hide from her.

He hauled himself to a standing position and edged around the side of the house, using the balustrade and the weather boards to support him. The back of his head hit the wall as he leaned against it and he froze, not wanting Seline to discover him listening to her conversation. Instinct made him continue his journey, conscious she may come outside to see what made the bumping sound. He covered the ground with slow steps, tripping over the bobbing heads of flowers as he chose the soil over the loose pebbles, which formed a meandering path. Darkness hindered his journey on the unfamiliar terrain. Wiri stuck close to the building and reached the far corner, ducking past Jet's bedroom window.

At the back of the house, he found Seline's transport. The gelding scraped at the ground with a lazy front hoof, slewing through the dust which rose around his ears. The glow from the laundry light picked out highlights and shadows across his shiny coat. He snorted out a long breath and nipped the heads of the nearest clump of daisies. Seline had tied his reins to the banister of the back steps. The horse lifted his head as he sensed Wiri, his eyes widening and his rear jerking around in a wide arc.

"Steady," Wiri whispered through the gloom. The moon slipped in and out of the overhead clouds as though teasing him. He hated not being able to approach the beast and introduce himself properly. He could have predicted the outcome, but it came sooner than he imagined. The gelding snorted at him and jerked backwards, his ears pricked and forward. Well-formed and muscular, he bore the brand of a thoroughbred on his left shoulder. "It's okay," Wiri whispered again, recognising the bunched tension in the horse's spine. "You're fine." His heart sank as the beast's eyes rolled in fear and the nose band strained as he tugged against the reins and dug his back hooves into the dirt.

Seline's voice rose to a shout inside the house, compounding the horse's nervousness. Conflict budded in Wiri's chest and snaked up the back of his neck into his aching head. He didn't want to reveal his presence to Seline, suspicious of her uninvited occupation of his home and now wondering about her appearance at the water tank. But he couldn't stand by and watch the gelding injure himself. He took a deep breath and prepared to approach the horse and attempt to soothe it, stilling his muscles and exuding confidence as he took a step towards it.

The screen door banged and the laundry light winked out in his peripheral vision. Wiri took a giant step backwards. His trainers tangled with the wooden edging of the flower border and he scrabbled to remain upright. He tensed and held his breath as he fell, the knotty stems of the cape daisies digging into his ribs and shoulders as he turned mid-air to deaden the impact on his spine. He landed with a dull thud and the breath released with a whoosh of pain.

The horse covered his noise with its own panic, drawing a creak from the hand rail as it hauled its body backwards towards freedom. Seline's footsteps pattered across the deck. "Steady, boy!" Her voice rose, but she remained calm. "Easy there." Her tone changed as she exercised control over her emotions with admirable skill. Wiri lay in the flowerbed and listened to an experienced horse woman bring her mount in hand, soothing the gelding's frayed nerves and talking to him in gentle, lilting tones. The buckles on the stirrups clanked as she hauled the leathers from where she'd hitched them. Wiri closed his eyes and imagined the scene beyond his vision. He heard the gelding blow out a breath as she tightened the girth. Something bumped against the rail and he recognised the grunt of her settling into the saddle. "Just wait." Her tone held humour and shod hooves scraped against the dirt and grit as the horse fidgeted.

The ground beneath Wiri vibrated as Seline pushed the horse into a walk and then a lazy trot. He used his right elbow to force himself to a sitting and then a kneeling position. Peering around the corner of the house, he made sure she'd gone. A head torch fastened to her helmet lit a narrow path ahead of her. Moonlight picked up the loop of the reins tapping against her thigh as she rose to a canter. Wiri sank onto his bottom and leaned his back against the wall. A cloud of pollen from the crushed daisies impregnated the air and made him want to cough.

Wiri shook his head and crawled the distance between the flower bed and the back steps. In her haste, Seline had left the rear door unlocked, and he wondered if she'd realise and return. His knees and palms carried him up the steps where he used the banister to haul himself to a stand. The horse's antics had caused the wood to separate from the post, and he worried about getting blamed for the damage.

One of his laces had come undone, and he used the other trainer to kick it free, leaving it where it lay on the back porch. Unable to face unlacing the other, he staggered through the house and planted himself face down on his bed. He didn't check his phone or wake to hear the three missed calls. His front door key dug into his hip and he slept away the night in a fog of misery.

33

EXTRACTOR

"She said what?" Wiri's fingers clung to the door frame as he kept himself upright. "She still says I didn't go to the house?" His voice wavered with the stress of Tane's revelation. He'd driven a patrol car up to the house at first light and Wiri's chest pounded with anxiety at Seline's untruth. He sensed Tane itching to take him back to the police station. "I told you she's lying. We had a conversation. She said I couldn't call her mother Leilah." His pitch rose, and he heard alarm bells pealing in the back of his brain. Logan's steady voice reminded him not to panic, but to plan.

Wiri settled the clamour in his mind and took deep breaths. He leaned against the wall and studied the delicate tassels at either end of the hall rug. Expensive and fragile, it mirrored his situation. Unsuitable for foot traffic, but there anyway. He exhaled and ran through the problem, reducing it to a series of tasks and calculations. Then he swallowed. "You can look at my phone," he said, his tone calm. "It'll show what time I called Phoe and how long the call took. I didn't start driving until eleven when the bell rang for her to go to class. The call log will show it." He turned and ran his hand along the wall as he walked, hearing Tane close the door behind him.

Wiri walked into his bedroom and wrinkled his nose at the heavy scent of sweat which hung near the bed. Hearing Tane's light tread in the hallway, he shuffled to the window and pushed it open. Cool air flooded through, stirring up the stillness and adding its own brand of meadow grass and daisy pollen. The net curtain flooded towards the narrow gap like water heading for a plug hole, reminding Wiri of his overheard conversation between Seline and the unknown caller.

Tane's shape blocked the doorway and obliterated the light from the hall. He stepped into Wiri's bedroom and stared around him. His keen eyes spotted the phone lying on the bedside cupboard, the charger cable trailing from the power socket near the skirting board. He frowned and crossed the room in three long strides, snatching it up before Wiri could object. "Unlock the screen," he commanded.

With a dramatic sigh of resignation, Wiri obeyed. His chest hurt as his fingers tapped in his code and he handed the device over to the police officer's scrutiny. "Do you need to read all my texts?" he grumbled as Tane scrolled through his private messages to Phoenix and to Mac.

"Yep." Tane's jaw tightened. "Who is this?" He spun the screen to face Wiri, and he sighed.

"My cousin, Mac Du Rose. Phoenix is his sister, and my girlfriend." There it was again. The staking of his claim. A prickle of pride warmed his chest.

"Right. You texted her, '*Hope you're having a great day. Thinking of you,*' at four minutes to eleven." He switched to the call log and read her name at the top of the list. "She called you a minute later, and you spoke for two minutes and five seconds. The call ended after eleven o'clock."

"Yep. Just like I said." Wiri sank onto the bed. He glanced down, noticing only one trainer on his foot. Yawning, he stared at his watch. "Dude! It's not even time to get up yet!"

"Jet's giving evidence in Hamilton. I'm driving him up there." Tane lifted the phone between them and waggled it. "Do you have GPS enabled on here?"

"Yeah." Wiri released the reply in a rush. He'd scrambled it on the truck because he didn't want Logan tracking him, but he'd never shared it with anyone on his phone. "Yeah, I do." He tried to rise and his legs failed him. A grunt escaped his throat as he bounced back onto the mattress.

"It's fine." Tane's fingers worked over the screen. He handed the device to Wiri, bending enough to observe his reaction as he spoke. "Unlock your Google account and pair my Bluetooth to yours. Then share your location map with me."

Wiri took back his phone and stifled a yawn behind his sleeve. He performed the functions like an automaton, his mind elsewhere. Tane's question made him jump. "What do you know about the deceased man?"

Wiri blinked. His mind processed the dilemma. Tane seemed so eager to blame him for Hendricks' death. He tutted as he saw the identity of Tane's phone and paired it with his own. "Nothing different from last night. I met him a total of four times and saw him through the car window just before he died," he said, keeping his tone light.

"Four times?" Tane's tone sharpened. "You accounted for two. In the supermarket and here."

Wiri sighed. "He came out of Vaughan's place the night I arrived." He didn't mention Hendricks exited face first with a gun pointed at him. "I met him in the cafe. Then in the supermarket when Jet showed me the town on the second night. We arrived home to find Hendricks on the porch." Wiri shrugged. "He left." Frowning, he cocked his head. "I didn't see a vehicle that time either. He walked back to the road along the driveway." The additional detail misdirected Tane from the reason for Hendricks' visit. He'd wanted Wiri to make a statement against Vaughan. Wiri's head bowed beneath the weight of complication. If Vaughan went to jail for assault with a deadly weapon, he couldn't settle Wiri's credit card bill. He looked up to find Tane staring at him. "Did you find his car?"

Tane nodded. "He parked it on the main road and walked up the hill across country. I just did it myself and it takes fifteen minutes." He looked down at the grass on the carpet and winced. "Sorry. That cuts down the estimate of an hour for him to get from town to the water tank." He cocked his head. "So, tell me about the meeting at the cafe." His blond eyebrow quirked upward to emphasise the importance of the question.

Wiri blinked and sifted through his memory of the cafe incident. He swallowed and picked his words as though stepping through rubble. "I worked in Mari's cafe for part of a shift while she nipped up to Vaughan's place to see Seline." A voice in his mind screamed at him to choose his next set of sentences with extreme care. "He came in for a coffee, said he knew my grandfather, and then upset Ted."

"Upset him how?" Tane's torso dipped as his interest grew. Wiri blinked at the speed with which the cop fast forwarded to Ted's involvement. He'd chucked that in as an afterthought, not wanting to incriminate himself further by admitting he'd thrown Hendricks out of the cafe without his coffee.

"Not sure." Wiri brushed off the question as Tane's phone chirped in his pocket. "It's asking you to pair your device with mine."

Tane's long fingers tugged his phone from his front trouser pocket. He unlocked the screen and jabbed his finger in line with a series of digital instructions. "Okay. Share your location app with me and take a screenshot of your call log and that text. Send those through as well." He waited with the device held in his large palm. "What exactly did Hendricks say to upset Ted?"

"I don't know!" Wiri's denial carried an edge of frustration. He didn't want to put Ted in the firing line. The old man's distress had radiated towards him from across the cafe, infusing him with the desire to protect him. "From what I saw of Hendricks, he took pops at everyone. He said something about

Ted's lady-love and the old boy turned his back on him and didn't engage." Wiri ground his teeth, feeling his blood pressure rising. "What does it matter? That dude is ninety years old! You think he drove up to Vaughan's place and chucked Hendricks down a man hole and into a water tank?"

Tane wrinkled his nose. "Ted doesn't own a vehicle." He exhaled. "His lady-love is Mari. He thinks nobody realises how much he cares for her, but the whole town has known forever. Unfortunately, she loved Leilah's father, but he wouldn't marry her and then the bugger died."

Wiri blinked and shook his head. His head felt like a bowling ball balancing on the thin stem of his neck. "Geez," he sighed. "It sounds like our town. They all have the same dad and he only had a bicycle."

Tane's laugh barked into the small room and Wiri jerked in surprise. "Yeah. Imagine trying to police all that swapping of bodily fluids."

"Ugh." Wiri gulped and forced his brain onto his own problems to avoid dwelling on the ramifications of Tane's statement. He took the requested screenshots and shared his location app, waiting for Tane's phone to ping once it received the digital items. He shook his head. "Ted just ignored Hendricks and went back to his coffee after he left. No biggie."

"Yeah." Tane exhaled and nodded in satisfaction as his phone vibrated. "Got all that now. I'll add it to the evidence log. You need to come in and make a formal statement regarding your movements and everything you saw relating to Hendricks."

"So, you know I didn't kill him?" Wiri cocked his head and lifted his right shoulder to take the weight of his head.

"I think I'd like it if you did," Tane replied, his voice soft. "That makes it nice and easy for me. Arrest the stranger, jail the stranger." He shrugged. "Small town policing sucks sometimes. I grew up with these people. It takes the fun out of it when you understand their rationale and sympathise with their motivations." Both eyebrows disappeared into his hair as he leaned closer and whispered, "Hell, I'm struggling to find anyone who didn't want Hendricks six feet under in a watery grave."

Wiri shivered, the motion starting at the back of his neck and rocking the mattress as it coursed through his muscles to the tips of his toes. He swallowed and looked up at Tane. "It's not a great exit strategy, I can assure you," he said. His mind filled with the remembered darkness and the sense of hopelessness as he tried and failed to extend the ladder. Desperation flooded his soul, as deep and bottomless as his memory of the pit. He winced and shook his head. "Bloody horrible way to die."

Tane frowned and bent his long frame in half to sit down on the mattress next to Wiri. "About that," he began.

34

BOLT BODY

"What about it?" Wiri tensed at Tane's proximity, afraid he might let something slip without meaning to. The details swirled around his head like cartoon sparrows, failing to make sense as they bobbed and dipped to peck his sore head.

Tane sighed, and the motion rocked the bed. "I spoke to Vaughan. He said he hurt his stomach as he fell forward trying to put the ladder back into the tank." Tane left a dramatic pause. "He's adamant he didn't pass out and remembers everything up to a certain point."

"What point?" Wiri swallowed, knowing what came next.

"He says someone cracked him on the back of the head."

"Ah." Wiri's chest deflated. "Right."

Tane's torso jerked back, and he peered at Wiri sideways. "You don't sound surprised."

"I'm not." Wiri closed his eyes and conjured up the scene. "I spoke to Larry yesterday. He helped me to get things into order, but there are parts missing. I heard Vaughan grunt, and the ladder fell almost on top of me. But when I looked up at the hatch, I saw someone staring down at me. They unhooked my safety rope from the back of the truck and threw it into the tank. Then, they closed the inspection hatch over me."

"What?" Tane's eyes widened, and he propelled off the mattress hard enough to cause Wiri to bounce. He faced him, an imposing figure with his hands over his hips. "And you said nothing!"

"I need to speak to Vaughan." Wiri willed Tane to hear his determination. "I want to know what he saw." He realised as he spoke the words that he also wanted to ensure Vaughan hadn't been part of some mysterious plot to bury him alive. The fear rose again into his throat and he quelled it with a sheer act of will. If Seline hadn't come, he would have drowned.

Tane shrugged and turned to face the window. "He remembers nothing after the blow to the back of his head. He remained unconscious until he reached the hospital and then went straight into surgery."

"Why did he need that?" Wiri scratched around for the missing pieces, desperate to find relevance in each tiny detail.

Tane tutted. "It's personal and his story." He turned to leave, halting in the doorway. "Do you think someone followed you here? When they didn't manage to bury you in the tank, they killed Hendricks and planted evidence to at least get you put away?"

Wiri gaped at him. "Someone from my family?" A croak entered his voice at the same time as a dark thread of dread entered his veins. It floated around his body, tainting every organ it touched. He swallowed down the denial, picking apart the difference between possible and probable.

"It's just a thought. You are a Du Rose, after all." Tane held two fingers to his temple in a mock salute and stepped through the doorway. "I'll see myself out," he said. "I need that statement, but later will do."

Wiri lay back on the mattress, letting each muscle tense and relax in turn as he made the long journey backwards to a flat position. He listened to Tane close the front door behind him and waited for the patrol car's diesel engine to fire up and bear him away. When it scrunched over the gravel and the hum grew quieter, he allowed himself to relax.

His phone buzzed next to him on the bed and he swatted his hand around without moving his head. His fingers closed around the device and he pulled it up in front of his face to read Leilah's text.

'*Vaughan is home now. We'd appreciate it if you could feed the stock again today. The health and safety inspector would like to interview you soon.*' She'd added a sad face to the end of the message.

He groaned. "Yeah, I bet." He dropped the phone onto his chest, where it rose and fell in line with his breathing. With farm injuries on the increase, the government had tightened the investigation process and nothing escaped the ministry's interest any more. Logan rarely referred to the local inspector without interjecting a cuss word into the sentence.

The problem remained. He couldn't talk to the inspector until he'd spoken to Vaughan. He pictured himself making the walk across the adjoining paddock and finding himself faced with Seline's glare. Too many loose ends cascaded through his mind like a waterfall of confusion. "Maybe you should just ask her," he said out loud. "Why did she come to our house and? Had she done it before last night? Did she go through my stuff and nick my shirt? Who did she speak to on the phone?"

He knew she wouldn't answer any of his questions. She didn't have to, and the knowledge left him powerless. He sensed she'd arrived with a clear agenda. She'd made no secret of her disdain for Vaughan, and the sentiment seemed mutual. "Bloody small towns," he sighed.

He watched his phone rise and fall before grasping it in the fingers of his right hand. He pulled up a recent new contact and dialled, lifting the device to his ear to wait for the connection.

"Is this a hatch, match or a despatch?" A chuckle punctuated the question.

"None of the above," Wiri replied, picturing the gentle pastor's affable grin. "But I need your help. Are you free this evening?"

35

TANG SAFETY

After another day of working alone on the farm, Wiri used the supplies he bought from the local supermarket to fix avocado on toast for dinner. Every movement caused him pain, the cacophony of internal groans dulling into the buzz of white noise. He'd spent over an hour herding the cattle away from the paddock surrounding the water tank. They'd tasted the lush grass and no sooner than he'd closed the gate, four of the steers broke through the wire fence. He cursed whoever had let them in there in the first place.

His stomach growled as he sliced up the avocado and laid it on top of the lashings of margarine. Phoenix called him mid-way through his preparation and he put her on speaker. Her voice echoed in the kitchen, reverberating off the cupboards and stainless steel fridge. "What are you eating?" she demanded as his knife clattered onto the breadboard.

"Avo on toast." He licked his index finger and closed his eyes against the comfort of the familiar taste.

Phoenix giggled. "We had spaghetti carbonara. It's Mac's turn, and he burned the spaghetti and ate most of the bacon. Mama made the cheese sauce, and it was the only decent part."

Wiri snickered and imagined the scene. He'd thought he craved freedom, but discovered he missed the routine and familiar boundaries of the Du Rose household. Mac hated cooking, but Hana insisted all the children learn simple meals. The teenager could run a muster with his eyes closed and his hands tied behind his back. But he couldn't cook to save his life. The kid could burn water.

"Your ma's cheese sauce is nice," Wiri admitted, frowning at the green gunk staining the gauze on his left middle finger. "What did your pa say?"

Phoenix's sigh whistled through the speaker. "You can still call her Ma, you know," she said, her tone soft and filled with regret. "Don't lose everything because of me."

"But she's not my ma." He swallowed, thinking of Anahera incarcerated for her crime and for her own safety. "My real ma doesn't want to see me."

"Well, mine does!" Phoenix's voice rose. "I can't watch you just burn everything so we can be together. We're not brother and sister, but she raised you as though we were. It's not incest just because we grew up in the same house, Wiri! For that, you'd need to share a parent, which we don't." She sighed and continued the well-worn arguments he'd used a million times on her. "Your father and mine didn't even have the same mother. They're half siblings and we're half cousins." Her voice faded as she ground to a halt. The difficulty of their situation chased away the humour in the conversation. Wiri's fingers twitched, and he ached to touch her, to brush her curls aside and press his lips to her cheek. He needed to act, to retrieve the call from the dark side it had strayed into, but the words wouldn't formulate in his aching head.

Like the left shoe in a tattered pair, Phoenix did it for him. "How are you liking the farm you're working at?" she asked. "Are they actually part of our family or just friends of Papa's?"

Wiri faltered. He wished she'd picked a different topic for her segue. "Not sure." He eyed the green slices of avocado slipping sideways off the toast and regretted his choice. The boulder matched its movement, compressing his stomach and chasing away his appetite. He stared through the kitchen window at the mountain rising like a forbidding spectre behind the house. His view should encompass a seascape and gentle rolling hills.

But he hadn't gone where he'd claimed.

"How is school?" The question popped into his head, and he gulped in relief.

"Good." Phoenix sighed, and he imagined her stretching out on her bed, her tanned toes nestled against the bedspread Nonie quilted for her last birthday. "I think I disappointed Papa because I don't want to follow in his footsteps. Can you imagine anything worse than teaching a group of sweaty teenagers?"

Wiri snorted. "Not really. What happened to your dream of becoming a vicar?"

Her voice held a wistfulness. "It died in summer camp. I think I still like God, but his followers suck."

"Yeah." Wiri lifted a section of the toast between finger and thumb. He glanced at the digital clock on the microwave and estimated he had another hour before Jet returned home from work. He took a bite and his stomach growled as though not able to wait for him to finish chewing and swallow.

"What about you?" She turned the conversation towards his future and he winced. He couldn't see a way forward beyond making enough money to return for her on her sixteenth birthday. He'd made the promise but realised he didn't even know if she'd go with him.

"Phoe?" He gulped as he swallowed. "I meant what I said. I'm coming back for you." He remembered her kiss at the edge of the graveyard. She'd stepped from the sacred space of her own free will and stood on tiptoe to press her lips over his. It felt as though she'd traversed barbed wire in her bare feet to reach him. He recalled the sense of weightlessness it induced in his chest. He stumbled over the sentence. "Is that what you want?"

"Yes." She sounded so sure. A flame flickered and burned in the space beneath his ribs and Wiri dropped the toast onto the plate. "It's always been you and me, Wiri. I don't want to fight it any more. I should have let you speak to Papa, and things would have been different for both of us."

He grunted, not able to affirm her statement. Logan Du Rose held his family in a vice like grip, not through dominance but care. His own awful history meant he'd never accept Wiremu for his daughter.

Not Phoenix.

Not in a million years.

"That wasn't my question, anyway." Her voice grew muffled, and he frowned before realising she'd held her hand over the speaker. "Please don't, Edin!" she growled. "Put my jeans back right now or I'll tell Mama."

Wiri didn't hear his half-sister's argumentative reply. She was the family magpie, helping herself to whatever shiny thing took her fancy. He shook his head and distanced himself from her influence. The Du Roses had given her a home as they had him, but he doubted Edin felt any loyalty or gratitude.

A sense of judgement bit into his psyche.

The Plan made him appear no different to her.

From tainted stock.

Hana should have walked away from them both.

A door slammed in the background and Phoenix sighed. "I meant, have you given any thought to your future? You're clever, Wiri. You could be anything you wanted. We were so proud when you won first place in the school awards at the end of last year. I thought Mama would burst. You're in the top one percent of all students in Australia and New Zealand."

He pursed his lips and buried his own dreams in favour of The Plan. The words came with practised ease. "Farming is fine for now. I'll make enough to set us both up somewhere and then we can think about our future. You should go to university and do whatever makes you happy."

"What if I don't know what that is?" Her voice sounded so small and faint, it caused Wiri physical pain. He wanted to hold her, to offer comfort and reassurance. The distance between them seemed more than just kilometres, but a spiritual and conventional void of pitfalls and hazards.

"You have time." He infused confidence into his voice. "We both have plenty of time to make choices."

"You're right." She exhaled, but her tone grew tight. "Papa is home. I wish you were here, Wiri. There's so much to talk about and you left before I could say any of the things in my head."

"It's okay," he promised, making himself believe his own words. "We'll sort everything out once I have the money to support us both."

"Wiri!" her voice rose in an agonised hiss. "We won't need to hide, though, will we?"

"Hide?" He eyed the soggy yellow puddle spreading out from beneath his toast. "What do you mean?"

"Hide from Mama and the family. You're going to make them understand, aren't you?"

"Right. Yep." He kept his answer brief, not wanting to descend into yet another lie. Their conversation had revealed to him the utter cruelty and selfishness of The Plan. He knew then beyond any shadow of a doubt that Phoenix Du Rose, in her innocence, didn't understand its far-reaching ramifications.

36

Monobloc

Wiri texted Vaughan and received no reply, which didn't surprise him. So, he tried Leilah. Instead of countering his request over text, she phoned him.

"He's too tired for visitors," she said, her tone soft. "Maybe tomorrow."

Wiri ended the call with an angry stab of his finger. His chest ached with the burden of the boulder and the murder accusation which rested on top of it. He abandoned his dinner after picking the avocado off the toast and slinging the rest into the waste disposal.

Another dose of the doctor's pills took the edge off his aches and pains and he locked up the house and left. On the front deck, he inspected his work boots. A tentative sniff revealed the floral scent of washing powder, but they needed another night in which to become dry enough to wear. He sat on the bench and ensured his trainers slid onto the correct feet, again tucking the laces behind the tongues to avoid the effort of tying them. Then he rose, all six feet of him towering over the loaded tassels of grass seed blowing in the breeze. He clambered over the fence and into the paddock between his house and Vaughan's.

The walk and his steady gait loosened the muscles in his spine and alleviated the headache. Two stints of coma-like sleep had given his body time to ease the various ailments, and he rolled his shoulders as he walked. The man who arrived on Leilah's doorstep resembled a powerful mix of Kane Du Rose's notorious temper and Logan's calculating and often manipulative negotiator.

"Oh. Hi." Leilah pulled the ranch slider open, and it creaked and groaned beneath her tugging. "Is there a problem?"

"Yes." Wiri stared at her, his gaze impassive. He stood close enough to the door for her to have reached out and touched his chest. If she had wanted to. Anger blazed in rigid stance and flickered in his irises. He cocked his head, sensing the thrill of dominance and intimidation. It should have bothered him more that he enjoyed it. "I can talk to you now, or I can call your cop friend. The choice is yours." He turned his right palm to face upward in a flourish, as though offering her options in a game show.

Leilah's shoulders drooped, and she took a step backwards. Naked fear flickered in her eyes and Wiri held his breath, regret dousing his flame in seconds. He'd seen it before, the cowering of an abused woman. But not for a long time.

"Okay." She sighed and recovered herself, forcing a mental rod into her spine and straightening her spine. "Come in." She retook control, and he allowed it, channelling his anger towards the one he believed deserved it. And it wasn't Leilah.

"What's happening?"

Wiri stepped over the threshold and turned to close the ranch slider. He heard Vaughan's enquiry and used his feet to change his view instead of twisting at the hip. Pain still shot from his spine to his head as he stepped around to face him. "I need to talk to you both before I make my statement to the police. And to the health and safety investigator," he added, his tone laden with the weight of responsibility. "I can talk and you can listen, or we can have a conversation. Either way, it needs to happen. Right now."

Vaughan's hunched stance made him appear smaller as he clung to the door frame and lurched across the kitchen to prop himself against the counter. "Okay." He licked his cracked lips and glanced at Leilah.

Wiri stared at her and she refused to meet his gaze. Vaughan shuffled towards the dining table and hauled out a chair. The back legs tangled with the frayed tassels of a nearby rug and he lost the fight in the first movement. Leilah rushed to his assistance, waiting for him to take a measured step backwards before flattening the rug and setting the chair on top of it. Wiri watched her, observing the care in each deft movement and recognising true love for the second time in his brief life. They reminded him of Logan and Hana, swimming in the ebb and flow of a fast river and still managing to remain together. He sighed, and the fight left him.

"Sit. Have you eaten?" Leilah pulled out the chair opposite as Vaughan hefted himself to a seated position with a laboured groan. She patted the seat Wiri had taken only a few days earlier. It seemed a lifetime ago.

"I had avocado on toast," he replied. He didn't add that he'd wasted all but the avocado.

Leilah smiled and her expression altered to reveal her hidden beauty. "That's why the young people in this country are so poor," she joked. "Because they live on avocado on toast."

"We have a tree at home," he said. He sank into the chair, facing Vaughan. The time for honesty had arrived and relief made his fingers twitch. He'd never been a great liar, anyway. "My uncle is Logan Du Rose." He focused his attention on Vaughan. The man's lips twitched, but he didn't react. "Yeah, that Du Rose family." Wiri exhaled, truth a welcome catharsis. He leaned back against the hard wooden prongs of the chair. He'd denied his whakapapa for long enough. Pride in the name replaced the shame which had dominated it and he pushed his shoulders back, dwarfing the taller man in his cowed state.

"Right." Vaughan pursed his lips.

"I thought your name was Kingii." Leilah frowned as she pottered in the kitchen. "Why did you say that?"

Wiri watched a flush creep from Vaughan's neck and into his cheeks. "Vaughan knows," he replied.

"Doesn't matter to me." Vaughan lifted an abandoned teaspoon from the table and used his middle and index finger to turn it. It dropped with a clang. He exhaled and leaned forward, his left forearm cradling his stomach. "I'm sorry for what happened to you," he said, his voice a low hush. "And you're right to come here. We need to sort it out."

"Before the health and safety inspector arrives?" Sarcasm added an extra load to Wiri's tone.

Vaughan shook his head, his forehead creasing into lines of concern. "No. Not just because of them. We need to sort it for ourselves."

Leilah made a pot of tea, her concentration focused on her task but her mind across the room with her husband. Wiri leaned forward and rested his forearms on the table. "I told your cop friend what I thought," he said.

"Tane?" Vaughan nodded. "Me too. Someone cracked me over the head and then closed the hatch." He turned to glance at Leilah, a frown deepening to flatten his features. "I think Hendricks did it."

Wiri jerked backwards, clattering his spine against the chair. Vaughan's conclusion headed in a different direction from his own, and it took him by surprise. "The guy who died?" His jaw dropped and his rapid blinking made his vision swim. "Wow. Okay. What makes you think that?"

Vaughan inhaled. He ran a hand through his fringe, momentarily releasing his hold on his painful stomach. But Leilah interrupted, the clunk of the teapot landing on the table forcing a pause. Her fingers shook as she withdrew her hand.

"This is all my fault," she said. Her voice wavered and tears caused her irises to sparkle. She rested her hand on Vaughan's shoulder. "I need to tell you both something."

37

TOP LEVER

Vaughan spread his hands in a silent indication of his bemusement. Wiri responded with a shrug. Leilah fetched mugs, sugar and milk before settling at the table next to her husband. She produced a tissue from her sleeve and laid it in her lap as though expecting to need it.

Wiri breathed out a long breath and stared at them both. When neither spoke, he glanced at the digital clock on the oven behind Leilah and shook his head. "Okay, so what's the deal. I'm guessing Hendricks had something on you." He looked at Vaughan and tipped his head. He thought back to his arrival at the farm and his employer using a shotgun to emphasise his point. Vaughan pursed his lips, but Leilah interrupted. She rested her wrists on the table.

"This is so hard," she said, her voice wavering. "I've lied to everyone."

Vaughan's brows shot into his black fringe and he screwed his head round to face his wife. Wiri spotted the bald patch in his hair and a jagged line of stitches, each one knotted individually.

"What?" His voice held a hoarse quality, as though he didn't want to hear her reply.

Leilah knotted her fingers and stared at a crumb next to the teapot. "Mari's cafe is failing," she began. "She couldn't make the rent two months in a row." She sighed. "None of this would have happened if she'd just borrowed the money from me. I might have helped her turn things around."

Vaughan snorted, the sound jarring and unexpected. "Her cafe is going under because her coffee has sucked for the last thirty years. Times are hard and the ambiance of Ted's sweat and burnt milk can't cut it anymore." The comment drew a glare from his wife.

"It's failing because Hendricks was her landlord. He made four rent rises in the last year and she started ploughing her profit into his pockets."

"Since when?" Vaughan drew backwards and winced. His right arm moved to protect his stomach again. "Dan Clough owns all those buildings in the middle of town."

Leilah shook her head. "Not anymore. Hendricks bought the lot in a private sale. He didn't want to earthquake proof the buildings. The regional council gave him permission to raze them to the ground."

Vaughan gaped at her. "But that's our town centre." A reverential whisper displayed his shock at the travesty. "It's been like that forever."

Leilah shrugged. "Hendricks wanted Mari to leave, but he didn't want to give her notice. He's done the same to the florist and the hairdresser. Like you said, things have been that way for our lifetime and before that. He didn't want to take responsibility for kicking them out and then building an ugly mall. The development focused on drawing people from Hamilton to shop."

"The developers are from Hamilton?"

"Yes." Leilah nodded. "They didn't want any trouble with local people. Protests and public meetings might damage their brand. Mari overheard Hendricks talking to a surveyor a few weeks ago."

Wiri waved his hand as though requesting permission to speak. "How does this relate to Hendricks trying to kill me?"

"I don't know," Leilah sighed. "But it's complicated. Mari wouldn't borrow from me, but she took Ted's money."

"Ted doesn't have any money!" Vaughan snorted. "He lost all the profit from the sale of his business in the last financial crisis. Or was it the one before that?" He frowned as he searched his memory for facts, deciding halfway through that he didn't care. "Where would he get what she needed?" He blinked at his wife and groaned. "Oh Lei! You gave Ted the money to bail her out, didn't you?"

"No." Leilah ran a hand over her face. "Believe me when I say that would have been simpler. Ted went to someone else for a loan. He told Mari he had savings, and she paid her rent."

"I wonder who Ted borrowed from." Vaughan leaned closer, his gaze boring into the side of her cheek.

Leilah pursed her lips. "I should have made her take it from me."

"Does Mari know?" Vaughan reached beneath the table, and Leilah pursed her lips as he took her hand.

"She does now." Leilah sighed. "I told her when she popped up here to see Seline. She's devastated he got into debt for her. He just wanted her to like him."

"How did you find out Ted borrowed it?" Vaughan gripped his stomach, glancing across at his wife to see if she'd noticed.

Leilah sighed. "Mari told me he'd lent it to her. He lives in a house with holes in the roof and survives on what she feeds him in the cafe. It didn't sit right, so I visited him and asked if he was interested in investing in the farm."

"My farm?" Vaughan's irises flashed. "Ted?"

Leilah shook her head. "I wasn't serious. He got upset and admitted he'd borrowed the money for Mari. At first, he wouldn't tell me who lent it, but I saw his fear. He wanted me to promise not to tell Mari, but she deserved the truth. She needed to understand what he'd done for her."

"I think I know where he got the cash." Wiri sat back in his chair and shook his head. "Hendricks inferred he needed to pay for something. He said he had one more day before he'd tell Ted's lady-love."

The heightened colour drained from Leilah's cheeks. Wiri's question had the opposite effect on Vaughan, raising a heady flush which bloomed up his neck and consumed his Adam's apple. "You think Ted borrowed from Hendricks so that Mari could pay Hendricks?"

Wiri nodded, not enjoying the discomfort radiating from Vaughan's side of the table.

"It gets worse." Leilah spoke from behind her fingers as though it might take the sting from her words. "Ted told me everything when I pressed him. He's exhausted with the weight of the debt and feeling blackmailed. So, I offered Hendricks the money to pay the debt, and he refused. He said Ted borrowed it and Ted needed to pay him." When she dropped her hand, her lips twisted into a grimace.

Vaughan exhaled. He shook his head. "You should have told me," he growled. "We're meant to be in this together."

Wiri stared at him from across the table. When Vaughan caught his eye, he tilted his head and raised an eyebrow.

"What?" Vaughan snapped.

Wiri tutted and turned to Leilah. "The first time I met Hendricks, he piled through your door face first with a shotgun hot on his heels."

"He what?" Leilah's expression clouded, morphing from distress to shock. She rounded on Vaughan, causing the teapot to shudder against her jolting of the table. Liquid trickled down the spout and pooled beneath the trim. "What did you do?" Her tone held the hint of a wail. The fingers of her right hand fluttered up to touch her left shoulder, and Wiri frowned. He'd seen the movement before and recognised the remnant of a remembered trauma.

"I didn't shoot him!" Vaughan glared at Wiri, his tone brimming with indignation. He exhaled, and a weight pressed his body lower as he curled in on himself. "Mari isn't the only one going under." His lashes fluttered closed to shutter his eyes and shelter his agony from view. "I've maxed out all my credit cards and used everything I had to keep this place afloat. I went to the bank for a loan last year and they turned me down flat. Hendricks worked for the farm management company who underwrites the loans and he saw the paperwork." Vaughan turned to face Leilah. "It's the reason I wouldn't let you invest. I couldn't take your money knowing it would go into a never-ending pit of credit."

"Oh, Vaughan." Leilah groaned and reached out to touch his wrist. "And why you didn't file the paperwork for our marriage." She sighed. "You didn't want anyone coming after my divorce settlement."

Vaughan started, jerking backwards and then wincing. "You know about that?"

Leilah rolled her eyes. "Yes. I found it last week. You need better hiding places."

The hardness of Vaughan's jaw relaxed enough to offer her a hangdog smile. "I wanted to marry you and I intended to post it, but I didn't want to take you down with me financially. When it came to it, I couldn't do that to you." He looked around him at the peeling wallpaper and soot-stained fireplace. "I stopped you renovating this place because I need to sell it. Soon." He exhaled and resignation caused the black cloud which shrouded him to become more transparent. "Please don't tell Mari. She doesn't need any more excuses to heckle me." He ran his palm across the table, pausing to touch the dents which represented a legacy of age. "Whoever inherits Hendrick's estate will need to recover my debt. His death doesn't make it easier. It means they'll still come, but it'll be through the courts."

"You signed an agreement?" Wiri cocked his head. "A legal document?"

"Yep." Vaughan nodded. He lifted his hand to pre-empt Wiri's next question. "No, I couldn't afford a lawyer to look over it. I just had to risk it."

"Fair enough." Wiri sighed. "Let me have a copy, anyway. I know someone who can look at it for you. If there's a loophole, she'll find it."

"Who do you know?" The strain played in a shadow across Leilah's expression. She spoke for speaking sake and to give her husband a moment to collect himself into a semblance of control.

Wiri licked his lips. "Judge Eliza Du Rose is my uncle's sister."

He heard himself say Liza's name and realised he'd misjudged her. In all his ducking and diving from the bad associations with the Du Rose name, he'd rejected the notable connotations. His reluctant spine straightened, and warmth flooded his stomach. He needed his family. "She's badass," he said with pride. "I'll ask her to look at it."

"Thank you," Leilah whispered. She glanced at her watch and Wiri saw the hour mirrored by the oven clock. "I wonder where Seline got to," she murmured. "Mari was desperate to see her. Maybe she went to the cafe and helped her to close for the night."

Vaughan fixed his glance on the teapot and said nothing. Wiri sensed him tense even before his formidable biceps flexed beneath his tee shirt. He imagined Seline stacking crates of vegetables in the chiller and pursed his lips to avoid commenting. The image jarred with what he already knew about the woman and he deemed it unlikely she'd help anyone without recompense.

Vaughan blinked before turning to his wife. "Why would Hendricks bash me over the head and shut the hatch on Wiremu?" he asked her. "It's too complicated. I bust my stitches and was already face down in the dirt. If he wanted this place, why wipe me out and force it to go through probate after my death?" He drew his lips into a thin line. "If we tell Tane all this, he'll arrest us both."

Leilah tutted. "He won't."

Wiri exhaled through his nose. "Is it possible he wanted to sabotage your business?" He directed his question to Vaughan. "Maybe the intention wasn't to kill you, but to make you unable to work. Wouldn't that force you to face bankruptcy earlier if you couldn't limp along like you were?"

Vaughan winced. "Yeah, true. And shutting you in the tank would cause enough disruption for the emergency services to attend."

"Which automatically flags an incident for the Health and Safety department to get involved." Leilah shook her head. "It makes sense if Hendricks wanted his pound of flesh."

"We need to keep this between ourselves." Wiri raised his hand to quell Leilah's gasp of protest. "If we tell the cops any of this, you're both in the frame for killing Hendricks. You each have a powerful motive. It doesn't matter how much of a friend Tane is, Vaughan's right, he'll have to arrest you."

38

Forearm Take-down Lever

J et arrived home to find Wiri busy in the kitchen. He fiddled around with his flatmate's coffee machine and had tipped two boxes of the expensive capsules onto the counter. Jet stood in the doorway and frowned as Wiri sifted through the flavours for one he fancied. "Oh." Jet's tone held irritation. "What's mine is yours, then." He didn't frame it as a question, so Wiri didn't offer him anything other than a nod.

Jet's footsteps padded to the end of the hall. Wiri heard the laundry door open and something drop into the washing machine. The house vibrated as an outside door shut with a click. He appeared in the kitchen, his tanned brow creased and his jaw set hard. "Why did you leave the back door unlocked?" he demanded.

Wiri selected a strong Colombian blend and dropped it into the capsule holder, ignoring the question. He set the machine working and loaded milk into the frother. Seline's easy access to the house bothered him. In his mind, it all led back to Jet.

Wiri had unlocked the back door after arriving home from Vaughan's and left it ajar as Seline had done the night before. He wanted to assess Jet's reaction to the security breach.

"You didn't even close it properly." Jet's voice rose, and Wiri smiled to himself. He'd found Logan's psychology lessons intriguing. His uncle taught him early that the best way to get the truth from a reluctant opponent was to antagonise them until they made a mistake. *'Anger breeds stupidity,'* Logan had said. He'd repeated that particular phrase often to Wiri because he'd been the angriest of all the children and always cracked first.

He turned aside to choose a mug from the cupboard. The action hid his grin as the fingers of his good hand closed around one with the word *'Son'* scrawled across the front in a cursive blue font.

"Not that one!" Jet spoke through gritted teeth and Wiri stuck his chin in the air and set it on the counter. The coffee machine finished its cycle and produced a passable espresso. He lifted the jug and poured the black liquid into the mug. His injuries ached as he forced his muscles to maintain a relaxed stance. Waves of fury rolled off Jet and enveloped him from the other side of the room. "What's your problem?" Jet ground out the words as though dragging them through broken glass. "Or are you just trying to get yourself evicted?"

Wiri snorted. He lifted the mug and sniffed the coffee. Wrinkling his nose, he tipped it and poured the contents into the waste disposal.

"What the hell is wrong with you?" Jet shouted. "They cost a dollar each!"

"Do they?" Wiri turned and planted his feet on the tiled floor. He'd kept his trainers on to provide another source of rule breaking annoyance. Concentrating on the angry patches of colour creating bursts of pink on Jet's neck, he picked the right moment to launch himself at him. Anger made the other man blind. Wiri had him around the throat and up against the pantry cupboard before he realised what was happening.

Army and police trained, Jet made a formidable opponent. He aimed his knee at Wiri's groin but overbalanced as he dodged sideways out of range. Wiri ground the heel of his trainer into the toes of Jet's right foot just as the other man attempted to peel back the index finger on his good hand. They were evenly matched, but Wiri had the element of surprise and capitalised on it. Jet hadn't expected to find himself under attack in his own home.

Wiri curled the reluctant fingers of his left hand and dug his knuckles into Jet's solar plexus with force. The police officer bent double at the waist with a gasp. "Stop!" he begged. "Just stop!"

Wiri backed away from him, taking up his original position on the other side of the kitchen. Jet collapsed onto his hands and knees and gulped air as he waited to catch his breath. Wiri expected him to come out fighting and remained loose limbed and able to defend himself.

"What's your problem?" Jet eased himself back against the pantry door and drew his knees into his chest. "Have the bloody coffee. I don't care. Just ask me next time."

Wiri snorted, but the sound contained more scorn than mirth. "You touched my stuff, so I'm doing what I want with yours." His eyes narrowed to slits, and he glared at the man still rubbing a spot below his ribs. Satisfied that Jet would need a minute's grace before he could clamber upright for another round, Wiri folded his arms. He winced as the action tugged at the muscles on either side of his spine.

"So, that's why you searched my room last night?" Wincing, Jet looked up at him through his lashes.

"What do you think I am?" Wiri sneered at him. "I don't go through people's gear. Unlike you." And Seline. So, she'd searched Jet's room during her visit but been less careful about it. She and Jet were as bad as each other. He took a calculated punt, levelling the accusation. Hendricks, Jet or Seline. One of them had looked through his meagre possessions and knocked the bracelet onto the floor beneath his bed.

"How did you know?" Jet didn't even try to deny it.

Wiri humoured him. He tugged Phoenix's bracelet from his back pocket and held it up where the gaudy beads caught the light from the overhead spots. "You knocked this onto the floor. Why did you search my bed?"

"Weapons." Jet blew out a heavy breath. "I just needed to know if you had any."

Wiri sniffed. "Why did you throw my shirt in the tank to incriminate me? Did you do it before or after you killed Hendricks?"

"Wait! What?" Jet's eyes widened. "I didn't do either of those things! I'm a cop!"

Wiri watched his expression change from horror to shock. His jaw dropped open, and he oozed injustice in the way he blinked up at him and dropped his palms to the floor. He grunted as he tried to push himself upright.

"But Hendricks had something on you, didn't he? I heard him hint at it when he came to ask me to make a statement against Vaughan."

Jet groaned and bent in half. He placed his palms over his knees and drew in a ragged breath. "It's not my secret to tell," he pleaded. "It's someone else's and you can do what you like to me, but it'll make no difference. I won't tell you."

"Whose secret is it?" Wiri dropped his arms and Jet winced. "Tell me that and I'll leave it."

"Tane's." The revelation cost him and Jet seemed to visibly deflate. His head dropped lower, and he shook it from side to side.

"What do you think?" Wiri asked, his voice calm. "Do you believe him?"

Jet gaped in surprise as Larry stepped beneath the arch leading to the lounge. The darkness had concealed his black shirt and trousers. He leaned his shoulder against the wall. "Yeah. I think he's telling the truth." Larry stared at Jet and lifted his lips into a sad, flattened smile. "About that, but not about everything."

39

Barrel Selector

"You're ganging up on me. You can't do this." Jet limped to the dining table and hauled out a chair. The legs dragged on the tiles, creating an ear-splitting screech.

"You owed him money, didn't you?" Wiri persisted, remembering Hendricks' comment about roulette. "You're a gambler."

"I'm not a gambler!" Jet rolled his eyes and Wiri caught Larry's gaze and shrugged.

"I don't know what to believe anymore." He ran his right hand through his fringe and sighed.

Jet sat down with a heavy grunt. "Hendricks got most of his information by snooping. My father arrested him once for getting caught around the back of the schoolteacher's house. He'd climbed onto a flat roof to peer in a bedroom window at her daughters. The magistrates refused to convict him, which means he probably knew something damaging about them, too. He got smarter after that and made sure he didn't get caught."

"So?" Wiri shrugged.

Larry exhaled. "So, he walked into the church and overheard me chatting to my alcohol sponsor on the phone."

"And he knew I'd had mental health problems because he caught me playing Russian roulette not long after I moved here. He threatened to tell Tane and held it over me when I stopped him for speeding."

Wiri blinked and glanced from Larry to Jet. "Real Russian roulette?" he demanded, his tone hushed. "With live ammo and a one in six chance of death."

"Yes!" Jet fixed his gaze on the fridge and kept it there. "What other sort is there?"

Wiri frowned and considered the question. "Well, did you spin the barrel after firing or not? The odds change if you do that."

Jet gaped at him. "Thanks to the mathematician in the corner! I warned you I had issues when you moved in. That's why I wanted to live alone."

"How do you catch someone playing a dumb-ass game like that?"

Jet's colour intensified, creeping up his neck and flaring in his cheeks. "He wandered around all the time. Snooping. I had a bad day and decided I didn't want to keep going. He found me sitting on the deck with my gun." He glared at Wiri. "I wouldn't have pulled the trigger."

Larry frowned. "That's a contradiction. You wanted to die but wouldn't have pulled the trigger." Pain made his irises sparkle. "What about Leilah? Or Vaughan?"

"What about them?" Jet swallowed and stared at his hands.

"Who do you think would clear up the mess? And poor Tane. Can you imagine his distress?"

"You don't need to guilt trip me!" Jet's voice rose.

"Where do you keep the gun?"

"It's hidden." Jet narrowed his eyes at him. "And don't search for it!"

The men stood for a while, considering their own problems. Larry spoke first. "This doesn't solve the issue of who wanted to hurt Vaughan and Wiremu."

"Or who killed Hendricks and threw my shirt into the crime scene."

"You beat me up for nothing." Jet rubbed his ribs and winced. He glared at Larry. "And you conspired with the local vicar. I might arrest both of you for assault and conspiracy."

"If you want." Wiri shrugged. "For an army guy, you're rubbish at keeping the bro' code. I quite like your brother. He'd be interested to hear Hendricks kept a secret for him." He grinned at Jet. "Which you actually didn't need to mention. You could have just told us about the roulette and that would have explained his barbed comment."

Jet grimaced. "You took me by surprise. I panicked. And anyway, Tane's thing is way worse than mine." He raised an eyebrow at Wiri. "Don't stare at me like that. I'm not spilling my guts any more than I already did."

Larry hissed through his teeth. "Is it something illegal?" he probed. "Or something unconscionable? I couldn't lie straight in bed if he was a serial killer or worse."

Wiri wondered what could be worse than a serial killer, but there were crimes beyond his understanding which ranked in that category. He joined his concern with Larry's. "It's not kids, is it?"

"No!" Jet rose and blew out a breath. He reached in the freezer section for an ice pack and pressed it against his ribs where Wiri had punched him. "It relates to his marriage and I'll take it to my grave." He winced as the ice numbed the ache from Wiri's jab to his solar plexus.

"I didn't realise we had that," Wiri commented, eyeing the ice pack. "That would have been handy for my back. Or my head. Maybe even my finger."

"We don't have it," Jet growled. "I do. Just like I own the coffee machine and the capsule you wasted."

Wiri cocked his head. "You were the cop at the hospital, weren't you? Why did you lie?"

"I dunno." Jet exhaled and pressed the ice harder against his stomach. "My warrant card gets me into most places."

Wiri shrugged. "My uncle Logan goes anywhere he likes. People let him." He pictured his intimidating uncle and imagined someone trying to stop him.

"I didn't mean to lie. It just slipped out."

"Like my shirt kinda slipped from my bag and landed in the water tank with a dead body?" Wiri narrowed his eyes.

"I didn't do that." Jet sat back in the chair with a sigh. "I promise I didn't kill anyone, and I didn't frame you. Check the logs at work. Tane picked me up at seven-thirty and we went to work together. I stayed at the station doing paperwork until after Tane brought you in for questioning. The morning disappeared with statements and interviews. I didn't hear about the body until I finished lodging that missing person's report for Mrs Hubert's son."

"The woman with the magnifying glasses over her eyes?" Wiri frowned.

"The very same." Jet shook his head.

"Is Dan Hubert missing?" Larry took a step forward, a frown creasing the corners of his eyes.

"Not any more. I'd loaded his description into the system about two minutes before she popped back in to tell me he'd arrived home after three weeks in Melbourne. He told her he'd left a note on the mantelpiece to say work had sent him there and he expected he'd be too busy to phone her. She says she didn't remember the conversation. She'd also thrown away the four postcards he sent her because she couldn't make out the signature." Jet frowned and clicked his fingers. "Oh, I also helped Mari change her tyre. She picked up a nail and didn't have a wrench." He exhaled. "Why did I come back here? I could have gone anywhere."

Wiri's phone vibrated in his pocket and he ignored it.

"Why did you come here?" Larry took the seat opposite and Jet fixed his gaze on a knot on the edge of the table. He traced its outline with his index finger.

"I thought I'd feel safe here," he said, his voice little more than a whisper. "I hoped I'd find peace."

Wiri barked out a laugh. "And then people started dying."

40

Sears

Wiri made coffee for all of them. Jet offered no comment, but he sipped from the mug set before him. They sat together at the table, heads bowed in silent thought.

"So, why the roulette?" Larry asked with a sigh. "Did things get so bad?"

Jet nodded. "Yeah. The force rejected my first application. It felt like the end of the world. I joined the army to make a difference and left when I realised my actions had no impact. It cost me a marriage and a daughter. The squadrons were faceless pawns in a game where we became the victims. Numbers on a page. Collateral damage. Tane is a third-generation local cop. I wanted to be like him, so I applied. They turned me down flat."

"But you still became a cop, didn't you?" Wiri frowned. "How come?"

"I applied again and my father spoke for me. He pulled some strings, and I got in. But then I felt I needed to prove myself because I didn't win it fair and square." He stared at the ceiling and gave a slow blink. "This is messed up, isn't it?"

"Na, I get it. I really do." Wiri smoothed the fingers of his right hand around the rim of the mug. He'd kept the *'Son'* one just to enforce his dominance, but it seemed like overkill. Jet had lost all his fight, his head bowed and the intimate confessions tumbling over his lips like an excess. "My Uncle Logan had it all mapped out for me. University, a good job somewhere." He flexed his jaw as he ran his tongue around the inside of his lip. "Somewhere far away from his daughter." He exhaled. "Don't get me wrong, he's a good man. He's been kind and generous to me and treated me like one of his own. My father caused him nothing but trouble, so he didn't have to take me in when my ma got locked away by the state." He tapped the bottom of the mug as though to punctuate his thoughts. "I wanted to prove something to him. He spoke to family in the north about a job for me, but I needed to strike out alone. That's why I'm here." His low chuckle held no humour. "Now, I'm in debt worse than when I arrived, and the local cop fancies me for a murder charge. So much for my big plans, hey?"

Larry's eyelashes fluttered, and he stared into his empty mug. He sighed. "I wish there was a tot of whisky in this," he murmured. He flapped his hand in front of his face in denial as Jet's lips parted. "I know, I know," he replied to the unasked question. He pushed the mug away, and it skittered across the table to leave a darker line of damp wood in its wake. "Right men. What can we do about this situation?" He slapped the table with both palms, his clerical ring rapping against the surface. "We are officially the three musketeers and we need to fight for truth!"

Wiri smiled across at him, warmth blossoming in his chest. The boulder's painful weight lessened as the pastor took some of the burden. Perhaps The Plan wasn't completely lost after all. "Thanks," he said.

He meant it.

Jet rose and stuffed the ice pack back in the freezer compartment. He seemed lighter of spirit as he pulled a bottle of beer from the fridge, glanced at Larry, and then replaced it. "Who wants more coffee?" he asked, clapping his hands. He shot a slanted glance at Wiri and smiled. "I'll show this northern chump what real coffee tastes like."

Jet turned investigator, issuing instructions as he loaded the machine with another capsule and spoke over the hiss of the milk frother. "We've established none of us killed Hendricks."

Larry nodded. "I can vouch for Wiremu." He patted the table in front of Wiri. "I spoke to Tane this afternoon. He agreed the timing is rather tight between you leaving my place and when he thinks Donovan Hendricks died. He's waiting for an exact time of death but is most concerned about the period you spent here alone sleeping. You have no alibi for that time, but your truck is visible from the road. Perhaps a nosy local saw it parked there." He offered an encouraging smile. "Tane acknowledged the state of your health makes it unlikely you went on foot to kill Hendricks, even if you can't establish an alibi. And he checked your tyre tread and found nothing like it at the scene."

"Thanks." The chair scraped on the tiles as Wiri rose and walked to his bedroom. He pushed the door, and it startled him as it hit the wardrobe parked behind it. "Oops," he whispered. He winced and pulled the door away from it, crossing the room to flick on the lamp. The foil packet on his bedside table reflected the light, and he lifted it, frowning at the name of a tranquilliser printed in tiny writing on the reverse side. After stuffing it into his pocket, he found the Panadol given to him by the doctor and popped two from the foil. He stood in the centre of the room, acknowledging that something bothered him. But he couldn't place the sense of unease. He walked back to the kitchen, bouncing the loose pills in his right palm.

"I just needed these," he said, throwing them into his mouth and taking a slug of the fresh coffee Jet placed in front of him. It burned, and he coughed. Jet had swapped out the *'Son'* mug for another. Tugging the foil packet from his pocket, Wiri dropped it onto the table. "What if I provided Tane with a blood sample?

I didn't realise these were tranquillisers. They wiped me out cold. Would that help with an alibi?" His phone vibrated, and he pulled it from his pocket and read the name flashing on the screen. Wincing, he killed the call from his uncle.

"Where did you get these?" Larry's eyes crinkled at the corners as he read the writing on the back of the packet.

Jet groaned. "I lifted them from the nurses' station when Wonder Boy here discharged himself. Tane will go nuts." He tilted his head back on his neck and stared at the ceiling. His torso seemed to fold in on itself with his sigh of resignation.

"Are they illegal?" Larry waggled the packet.

Jet shook his head. "No. But stealing them was."

Both men stared at Wiri and he shrugged. "I'm rubbish at lying."

Larry recoiled. "I'm not advocating telling untruths." His fingers tapped the cross which hung around his neck and nestled against the buttons of his black shirt. He'd abandoned the white collar which poked from the top pocket of the jacket he'd hung around the chair.

"I don't think it matters." Wiri eyed the packet. "If they're not illegal, it's irrelevant where I got them. Do you think Tane will agree to a blood test? We'll need to do it tonight, won't we?"

Jet dumped his reclaimed mug on the table and sank into his chair. He pushed his fingers through the handle and clasped it in both hands. The word *'Son'* showed between his index and middle fingers and Wiri envied him its importance. He'd grown up as no one's son and it pained him, despite Hana and Logan's stellar efforts to integrate him into their family. He understood why Jet had confiscated and washed it. Sipping his coffee, he tried to put aside the sense of emptiness and filled it instead with a vision of Phoenix's serene smile.

"It might be too late." Jet spoke over the lip of the mug, wanting Wiri to look up and understand he'd reclaimed the prize and the status.

"Sorry, what?" Wiri leaned forward. "Too late for what?"

"Blood tests. It was hours ago. I'm not sure how long the drug stays in your system." He dug his phone from his pocket and tapped a message on the screen. It beeped as it sent and he laid the device on the table. "Tane will know."

Wiri's mind took him back to his bedroom, and he frowned, staring at Jet without seeing him. "Something is wrong," he said. The chair skittered backwards as he rose and strode to his room, keeping his steps light against the laminate flooring of the hallway. His back ached, but the pain had spread further through his torso and lost its horrible intensity. Footsteps padded behind him, and Larry and Jet joined him in the centre of the room. Larry spun on the spot as he looked around him. Wiri's phone buzzed again, and he pulled it free and pressed keys to silence it. He couldn't face his uncle's questioning about the farm and his job. Logan could detect a lie within seconds.

"Looks okay to me." Jet narrowed his eyes and frowned as he studied the heavy renovated furniture with an investigator's eyes. Then he swept his gaze towards the doorway and snapped his fingers. "You're right. I know what it is." He swallowed, his Adam's apple bouncing in his throat, and despite the gentle light of the bedside lamp, Wiri watched the colour fade from his complexion.

41

Grip Cap

Jet rushed towards the doorway, deviating left at the last minute and slamming the door shut. Wiri jumped and shot a glance at Larry, twisting his lips in question. They watched as Jet squatted to examine the stripped and varnished rimu floorboards. "Oh, no!" he hissed. "Please, no!"

"What?" Wiri joined him, casting the boards into shadow as he peered over his shoulder. "I can't see anything."

"Move out of the way." Jet waved his hand and hit Wiri in the thigh. He took a step backwards and clattered with Larry.

"What's the matter?" Larry demanded. "This is getting freaky now. What are we looking at?"

Jet spun to face them, his complexion ashen. He raised his hands as though measuring the distance between them. It emphasised his panic as he licked his lips. "This was originally my room," he began, a swallow bisecting his sentence. He winced and exhaled, shooting a nervous glance from Larry to Wiri. "It's complicated, but something happened here last year." He cleared his throat. "Leilah got shot and someone else died."

Wiri recoiled in horror. "In my bedroom?"

"No!" Larry patted his shoulder in an effort at reassurance. "In the lounge next door. It's why she refuses to live here."

"I moved into the house while the builders were still renovating. They replaced some of the floorboards in the lounge to get rid of the blood. While they did that, they took out some dry rot in here, so I shifted next door. I stayed there because it has an ensuite bathroom." Jet inhaled. "But Leilah's father had an old safe hidden behind one of the dry walls. The house changed hands after he died and Leilah bought it back when she returned to the town. They found the safe when they ripped out the wall in my new room to create the adjoining bathroom." Jet jabbed his finger at the space behind the bedroom door. "This is what's wrong."

Wiri cocked his head and realised what seemed different. "The door doesn't usually hit the wardrobe," he said, his brow furrowing. He tilted sideways to study the gap between the heavy wooden piece of furniture and the back of the door. "So that whole thing has moved." He pointed at the wardrobe and then glared at Jet. "Did you come in here again?"

"No." Jet touched his chest to emphasise his sincerity. "Not me. But someone did."

Larry shrugged. "And? What's the problem?"

"Oh." Wiri groaned. He bent his right knee and dropped his hip. The action hurt, but it seemed irrelevant against the thing Jet hadn't said. "Did you hide your weapon in here somewhere?"

Jet nodded, the motion almost imperceptible. "Yes." He pursed his lips and his eyes held a frenzied light. "The builder moved the safe in here and dropped it below the floor. He's Leilah's friend. She got so messed up after the shooting, he never got around to telling her what he'd done. It belonged to Hector, and Claus knew she'd regret getting rid of it one day. He thought it might prove useful."

"And he told you what he'd done?" Larry exhaled. "Did you tell Leilah?"

"No." Jet winced. "She won't talk about it. She doesn't even stay very long over here when she visits. It never seemed the right time."

"Let's check if it's still there." Larry brushed past Wiri as he grabbed a corner of the heavy wardrobe. "Not you." He jerked his head at Wiri. "You're already a mess."

"Thanks." He took a step back as Jet grabbed the other corner.

"Gee, it's heavy." They edged it forwards by only a few degrees after a lot of grunting.

"Use the rug." Wiri fetched the rag rug from next to his bed and bent as they tilted the wardrobe onto its rear edge. He pushed the expensive, chunky fabric beneath the front corners, his tail bone complaining at the compression as he tried to rescue his fingers before the men dropped the wardrobe onto them.

They stepped back and observed the heavy piece of furniture. The original armoire had been reinforced and brushed with pale chalk paint. Crackle glaze around the edges offered a weathered appearance. Wiri shook his head. "How did you move this by yourself to use the safe underneath?" He fixed his hands over his hips. "It's not possible. Even two of you can't move it out of the way."

"I didn't." Jet wiped sweat from his brow onto his forearm. "This wardrobe used to sit over there. It belonged to Leilah's dad. She found it at the back of the equipment shed and paid someone to renovate it." He pointed towards the left of the window. "The builder put it there after the floor varnish dried." Then Jet stilled, his mind straying elsewhere as he winced. "Seline broke the catch on the door when she stored a saddle in there. It didn't fit, but she forced it closed and broke it." His fingers smoothed a ridge in the left door where the wood had split and been repaired. The paint hid the wound but couldn't mask the shallow dip where a smaller piece of wood filled the gap. "She doesn't take care of anything." The observation held a depth which alerted Wiri to something brewing beneath the surface.

"Seline?" He stiffened. "She stayed in here?"

Jet nodded. "Yeah. During the summer. She didn't want to stay at the house because she hates Vaughan. She blames him for everything that's wrong in her life. The builder came out after she left and repaired the damage." He ran his finger over the join. "It took Claus and another guy to get it this far. In the end, he unscrewed the door and took it back to his workshop."

Wiri began nodding, the action growing in impetus as the pieces fell into place in his mind. "She has keys."

Jet shrugged. "Dunno. I guess so."

"To the back door."

"Why?" Jet leaned back against the wardrobe and the doors creaked as he rested against the join. Larry kept one hand on his hip, the other pressed against the front corner and his fingers twitching against the painted surface. "What's the relevance?"

"She left the back door unlocked last night." He licked his lips. "Tane dropped me at the bottom of the driveway when he got called to a job. I walked up here, and she didn't hear me arrive. She'd ridden over and tied her horse to the rail on the back porch. It shied and left a crack where it joins the struts. I heard her speaking to someone on the phone. She mentioned furniture being moved around so she couldn't get to something she needed." He closed his eyes and poked through the mind-fog which had hung over him, seeking to isolate the important portions of the overheard conversation.

"She came into the house?" Jet stepped towards Wiri as though proximity gave him more understanding.

Wiri nodded and opened his eyes. "Yes. I sat on the porch and heard her. She went into the lounge, but when the horse freaked out, she walked through the back door and left. I guess she forgot to close it."

"I thought you did that. Figured you walked through the laundry for some reason and put the Yale on the catch." He shrugged. "Or came home that way."

Wiri shook his head. "I only have a front door key. There's been no reason to go out through that door." He took a step back and eased his bottom into an armchair he'd not yet used. "I did it tonight to see if it bothered you. It seemed a logical way of assessing if you allowed Seline to come and go as she pleased, or if she has a key. By your reaction, I'm guessing she has a key."

Jet glared at him. "You could have just asked!"

Wiri snorted. "Oh, yeah. Hey Jet, are you shagging Leilah's daughter?" He sighed. "That reminds me, I need to empty the washing machine. Is it okay if I use your airer to hang my stuff?" He wiggled his bottom against the chair. Harder than he expected, it provided a surprising amount of support.

Jet nodded to his question about the airer, waving off the trivia with a flick of his wrist. "Whatever." He frowned. "How did your mind go from Seline to dirty laundry?"

Wiri observed him as he shrugged. He imagined Jet's fragile ego withstanding Seline's determined flirting in her child-sized tee shirt. He realised he'd had a lucky escape as his mind veered from wondering if it shrank in the wash, to his own damp clothing sequestered in the washing machine. Ignoring Jet's confusion, he pushed his conclusion. "So, you are shagging her then? You knew she had a key and didn't try to take it back from her."

"It's irrelevant. Let's assume Leilah's daughter knows about the safe under the floor." Larry pressed a finger and thumb on either side of his nose and squeezed the bridge. "How would she know it contained a gun?"

"And what does she want it for?" Wiri gave an involuntary shiver. "She already hates me. I don't like the idea of her having a door key and a weapon."

Jet swallowed and folded his arms. His biceps flexed as he created the barrier between him and the other men. "Okay, I might have kind-of-accidentally slept with her. And I let her keep the key because I hoped she'd be interested in another sweet night of bliss with me." He couldn't look at them. "In my defence, it wasn't a great time in my life and things got very messy with her living here for those few weeks." He studied the rumpled rug wedged beneath the front of the wardrobe. "She knew I kept the gun and suggested I put it into the safe."

Larry winked at Wiri. "How can you kind-of-accidentally sleep with someone?" he asked, his tone soft.

"I knew it!" Wiri's mind turned to Phoenix. He held her in too much regard to defile their relationship with a quick tryst. Not that he didn't want to. Very much. He turned his attention to Jet, focusing on the stricken cop to help banish the other thoughts which rampaged through his teenage mind.

"It just happened." Jet lifted his gaze to meet Larry's. "Do you need to tell Leilah or Vaughan?" His colour morphed from pale to the hue of a tomato. Wiri saw a pulse tapping above his collar. "Please, don't tell Vaughan."

Larry shrugged. "I'm a priest. We're society's secret keepers." He dipped his chin and observed Jet through the tops of his eyes. "Unless someone is likely to get hurt." He turned his head to include Wiri in his gaze. "So, let's stop that happening," he said, his tone severe.

42

INTERCHANGEABLE CHOKE TUBE

It took three of them to move the wardrobe. The rug helped, assisting them in sliding the front forward and preventing the sharp edges from creating grooves in the floorboards. Jet dashed to his room to retrieve his own rug, jamming it beneath the back edges as the others tilted the whole thing forward. Empty coat hangers clanged inside it, hammering on the doors as though demanding release. The men huffed and puffed until the wardrobe journeyed as far as the door, blocking their exit but revealing the slight colour change in the floorboards in its wake.

"We can't get out now," Larry commented. He stood back to unbutton his shirt. Sweat darkened the fabric beneath his armpits and coursed in a line along his spine. Without the fitness demanded by his volunteer fire rescue role, they would have failed in their mission. Jet and the injured Wiri couldn't have moved it without his help. Larry removed his shirt and hung it by the collar over the door handle. "I need to use the bathroom," he commented.

"Bad luck." Jet squatted down in the vacant space where the wardrobe had sat. "We've damaged the floor a bit," he said, wincing up at them. "Hopefully we can move this back and nobody will notice."

"Are you worried about getting your bond returned from Leilah?" Wiri leaned over to inspect the light scratches in the varnish.

"I didn't pay one." Jet dug his index fingernail through a wider point between two of the floorboards. "Tane and Leilah were best friends at school. She just let me move in on a handshake."

Light bloomed in the bedroom as Larry flicked the switch for the main light. He stood next to Wiri and peered over Jet's shoulder. "Oh yeah, there's a join," he said, the thrill of discovery lifting his voice. "Claus is a genius. I wouldn't know that existed if you hadn't pointed it out."

Jet cocked his head as he moved his fingernail a few millimetres towards the door. Wiri heard the faintest of clicks and the boards shifted as one. He blinked as it messed with his vision, the panel lifting as a single piece. Larry clapped his hands. "That's awesome," he gushed. "He fixed the boards to a piece of plexiglass."

Jet lifted the panel until it hinged at right angles to the rest of the floor. He smiled up at him, sharing his appreciation for the hiding space. "Yeah. He didn't want it visible from above, so he disguised it. He couldn't seal the space totally between the boards because there's a slight gap in the old ones. It would cause it to stand out. The glass holds it all together but prevents it looking so solid." Jet tapped the wooden struts on the back of the panel, which held it all rigid enough to walk across. "He can build me a house any time."

Larry nodded, his head bobbing hard enough to detach from his neck. "I'll ask the church council to put him on the list for our repairs," he said with enthusiasm. He clapped his hands together again before pointing at the panel. "That is truly marvellous."

Jet leant into the dark hole and Wiri frowned at the sound of his fingers bumping against a metal object. "How do you know the code for the safe?" he asked.

"There isn't one." Jet screwed his head around, but his immersion in the gap prevented him from meeting eye contact. He wobbled his head from side to side. "Well, there is. Leilah knows it because her father set it years ago. Claus said he didn't want to lock it until she knew about it, just in case. I put the gun in here and dropped the door."

"Can I see?" Wiri tapped Jet's shoulder as curiosity got the better of him.

"Yeah." Jet rose with a grunt and eased himself between the narrow space flanked by the wardrobe and the lid to the hiding place. Wiri planted his feet and tipped his torso to peer into the shadowy depths of the old house's footings. "Get closer." Jet's voice muffled as he wiped his sweating face with his discarded tee shirt. He exhaled. "It's hot in here. Can I open the window?"

"I don't want to get any closer," Wiri grumbled. "I've had enough of dark holes in the ground."

A metal catch scraped as Jet threw open the window and breathed in the fresh air on the other side of the room. He called over his shoulder to Larry. "You can pee out the window if you're desperate. I won't tell." He cackled at his own humour, but Larry didn't join in with him.

"It's not that kind of bathroom break," he murmured. He raised an eyebrow in horror and turned his body to face Jet. "Oh. I don't take drugs either. It's a genuine poo break."

Jet snorted as Wiri edged forward to look at the safe. The builder had installed it on its back so the dial faced uppermost. He twisted his lips and frowned. "A safe works with cogs and tumblers. Gravity plays a huge part in its functionality. Will it work on its back? If you lock it, it might not open again."

Jet returned from the window. He balled up his tee shirt and threw it onto the floor near Wiri's bed. "I didn't think about that," he admitted. "It's not locked, anyway. Claus tried standing it upright, but then we couldn't reach the dial or open the door." He took a giant inhale and tapped Wiri's shoulder. "Give me some room. I need to get this over with. Hopefully, the gun is still there."

Wiri exhaled and took a step backwards, shuffling out of his way. Larry moved to the window and leaned his forearms on the sill, the bones in his spine cracking as he bent forwards to stretch. Jet returned to his knees and reached into the gap, tugging on the dial to lift the door. "That's how you damage it," Wiri complained, intrigued by the age of the safe and not wanting the mechanism affected by rough treatment.

"It's not like there's a handle!" Jet growled. Both arms disappeared into the hole as he hauled the door against the force of gravity. A hinge creaked, and he got it open, catching hold of the metal and forcing it into an upright position. "Take the weight of this," he demanded, glancing up at Wiri.

"I'm not touching that." He shook his head and stepped back, clattering with the armchair. It tipped before righting itself. "I don't want my fingerprints on that, thanks." He imagined confessing to Logan that the police had evidence that he'd touched a safe containing a missing gun and shivered. "You put it in there for your stupid game. You get it out."

"Larry!" Jet called to the vicar, who gulped fresh air through the narrow aperture of the open window. "Can you help me?"

Larry turned and Wiri saw the denial in his expression. His lips turned down, and he shook his head. "I'm with Wiremu. Sorry."

Jet groaned. He held the door upright with one hand and dug into the space with the other. His head and shoulders dropped beneath the level of the floorboards and his voice echoed. "It's still here." Relief lightened his tone. "Thank goodness for that."

"But Seline wants it for something." Curiosity drove Wiri nearer, and Larry followed. With their shoulders touching, they watched Jet's head bob as he grappled in the safe to retrieve something which clanked against the metal. "She talked about furniture moving and it being too heavy for her." He glanced at Larry. "She has a key and she'll come back for it."

"I wonder why she wants it," Larry mused. "Is she planning to kill someone?"

"Or frame them." Wiri jerked his head towards Jet's arched spine. The cop knelt on the floor with the toes of his socks sticking out from beneath his backside. He popped upright and the safe door dropped with a clang, the sound filling the room with its tinny cry.

"Got it." Jet waved a gun in his left hand. He turned on his knees and lifted his other hand, displaying a single .44 Magnum round. "The bullet is here."

"Where did you get that gun?" Wiri frowned. "That's a Smith and Wesson." He cocked his head to admire the neat wooden handle and the alloy frame. Jet spun the titanium cylinder. "Didn't you have to hand everything back in before you received your discharge papers?"

"It's not from the army." Jet twisted his lips. "It belonged to my grandfather."

"You need to hand that in," Larry said, his voice a low growl. "Tell the truth."

Wiri glanced sideways at him and caught his eye. He half expected him to add, 'For the first time in your life.' But he didn't.

Jet shook his head and began backtracking. He used the corner of the wardrobe to haul himself to a standing position. The presence of the gun changed the dynamic in the room, causing the air to crackle. Larry tensed next to Wiri.

"How?" Jet said, his tone urgent. "Tane doesn't know I have it."

"I don't care." Larry's voice held authority. "Give it to your brother. Tell him the truth and he can help you." He raised his right hand with the palm open, warding off Jet's instant protest. "I'm not interested. You hid it. You fix it." He levered his wrist forward and used his pointed index finger to jab at the gun. "If that falls into the wrong hands, you're in deep trouble anyway. The truth will come out because it always does. Give it to Tane and let him dispose of it legally."

The gun rested in Jet's open hand, covering his thumb and all his fingers. Its matte surface seemed to consume all the light in the room, but it also held a disturbing sway over its owner. A strange craving showed in Jet's eyes, the pupils dark and cavernous as he stared up at Larry. Wiri had seen the same mania in his mother, the self-destruct button always so near the surface of her existence. His shoulders slumped, and he knew he had to take it. Or find Jet dead in the morning.

He opened his mouth to speak, but Larry beat him to it. "Fine!" he growled. "But you speak to Tane as soon as you can reach him." He lowered his chin and glared at Jet from beneath his bushy eyebrows. "You speak to him or I will. If I do it, he'll have no choice but to suspend you."

"Okay, okay." The hunger remained in Jet's eyes and Wiri gnawed on his lower lip as he watched Larry deal with the situation. The priest instructed Jet to wrap the gun and ammunition in his own discarded tee shirt and set the bundle on the floor near the skirting board. Gratitude flooded Wiri as he watched him supervise Jet. Left to his own devices, Wiri felt sure Jet would have demanded something of his to wrap the gun and introduced his DNA into the mix. He wasn't sure he could have refused.

Jet dropped the trap door, and they moved the wardrobe back into place. Larry stepped back before they'd quite finished. "Should we move it back where it was originally, or where Seline left it?" he asked, cocking his head. Sweat dripped down the side of his cheek and pooled above his eyebrows. "Are we assuming she'll return?"

"I don't know." The lateness of the hour and the growing pain in his injuries left Wiri without energy for thinking.

"Put it back where it was." Jet made the decision. "She'll assume Wiremu moved it because it kept hitting the door. It might put her off if she needs to start all over again."

Both men looked at Wiri and he shrugged. "I don't care anymore," he replied with a sigh. "I just want my bed."

"Okay." Larry braced himself against the wardrobe and prepared to heave it through the last few centimetres to the wall. "Let's get it back in place and then whip out those rugs."

Jet wedged himself between the wardrobe and the door, readying himself to slide the wardrobe into the corner. "I'll need to leave a bigger gap," he grunted as he squeezed himself into position. "Don't squash me."

"Tempting," Wiri grumbled. Grinning at Larry, he pushed one hand behind the back left corner. He rested the other over the side and prepared to guide the huge robe into place. He winced as he straightened his index finger, which forced the sore one to extend. With another glance at Larry, he noticed something move in his peripheral vision. The net curtain had slithered through the open window and flapped against the frame. Wiri groaned. "Larry, before you get settled, please, can you pull the curtain back inside and close the window a bit more? They look brand new and I don't want them to tear against the frame."

Larry dropped his arms and turned on the spot. He padded towards the window and pulled the fabric back in like a fisherman hauling in a weighted line.

"Why do we even need net curtains?" Jet grumbled from the narrow gap. His voice sounded hollow as it reached Wiri.

"Flies," he replied. "Hana had them everywhere at our place until Uncle Logan paid for proper fly screens. It drove him mental. He built a multi-million-dollar house at the top of the mountain overlooking the Tasman Sea, and she covered every window with voile or lace." He paused and licked his lips, hating how he'd sounded both boastful and feminine. What did it matter if he knew the names of window coverings? Jet's low snort told him it mattered a great deal in their masculine world.

"It's all gone out." Larry buried himself beneath the draping cream tresses to close the windows. "The wind is picking up tonight. She's made them full length and weighted the hem, but the wind sucked out the whole thing." He moved between the curtain and the window, resembling a veiled bride with a headdress. The length kept coming until it covered his whole body and only his feet showed beneath it. Wiri noticed Jet didn't laugh at Larry for knowing the finer manufacturing details of net curtaining. "Got it!" His voice held satisfaction, and the window banged as he pulled it almost closed and put it on the catch to allow a little ventilation.

Larry eased himself from beneath the curtain, holding his arms out on either side of his torso. The lace rode up his back until the hem hung level with the waistband of his slacks. Then he froze in place, his body bent in half and the curtain still shrouding him. "Who the hell is that?" he demanded.

"What?" Jet squeezed from his position and wiped his forehead on the back of his hairy arm. "Can we just get on with this now?" He glanced at his watch and sighed. "It's after midnight. Tane's picking me up at seven."

"Someone's out there." Larry lowered his voice. He remained frozen beneath the curtain. "I saw a face."

Wiri dropped his arms and stared at Jet. "Seline?" he hissed. His shoulders slumped. "Damn. We should have closed the curtains when we turned on the light."

Jet spun and smacked his palm over the light switch, plunging the room into darkness. Three jogged steps took him to the bedside lamp, and he fumbled with it, looking for the off button.

"It's near the bulb." Wiri began walking towards him, but Jet reached forward and a pop signified the socket coming out of the wall. All light winked out with such suddenness, Wiri found it difficult to focus his eyes. He waited a few seconds and discerned Larry as a ghostlike figure still shrouded beneath the curtain fabric. Footsteps told him Jet was on the move.

Larry grunted as the police officer joined him at the window. Jet fought his way beneath the cloth to see through the glass. "There's no moon," he complained.

"You're steaming up the glass!" Larry hissed. "Step back a bit. Ouch! Not on my foot."

Wiri heaved out a breath and sank onto his mattress. If he closed his eyes and put his hands over his ears, it felt like any other night. He laid back against his pillow, edging his spine flat by slow degrees. The pounding in his head lessened and if he kept very still, his back ceased its relentless ache. He laid his injured hand on his stomach and released a grateful sigh.

Larry and Jet continued to argue beneath the curtain. A whoosh of static told Wiri they'd extracted themselves. He groaned as the overhead bulb bloomed to life from its position over the bed. "Go away!" he demanded. "I need to sleep."

"We can't get out until we've moved this wardrobe." Jet's voice altered as he squeezed back into position. "Come on, help. I want to check round outside and see if our little peeping Tom touched the cars or tried to get into the house."

"He doesn't look so good." Larry's voice rumbled from nearer the bed and Wiri opened one eye and stared up at him. "We can move the wardrobe without him."

Jet objected, his voice muffled again. "He needs to pull the rugs free. Get up, Wiremu. Stop being a princess."

Wiri held his arm out to Larry and he hauled him upright, keeping his hand beneath Wiri's elbow while the teenager forced his feet onto the floor. "Who did you see?" Wiri broke the sentence with a yawn, which made his jaw ache.

"Just a face." Larry's forehead creased into frown lines. The harsh overhead bulb cast them into pits of shadow. "They hid in the flowerbed beneath the window while I closed it. But I opened it again to place it on the ventilation setting and I don't think they expected that to happen. He stepped out and looked back at me just as I looked up."

"He?" Wiri frowned. "So, not Seline then?"

"Maybe a she, it's hard to say." Larry shook his head from side to side. He offered Wiri his hand and he accepted the assistance to stand. "I'm not sure."

"Come on, you two!" Jet complained. Only his left arm and one foot peeked from the side of the wardrobe.

"Vaughan?" Wiri cocked his head and lowered his voice. "Or Tane?"

"I don't know." Larry's answer held certainty. "I'm sorry. Something sparkled on one of their arms as they ran away. But it's too dark out there."

"Great." Wiri released a sigh which would have held exasperation if he'd had any energy to spare. Instead, it held despair. "So, an unknown person just watched me and two naked dudes shift a wardrobe?"

Jet popped his head from the gap and his expression held worry in the lines around his mouth. "Do you think they saw the gun?" he demanded. He screwed his eyes closed and rested his forehead against the wardrobe's wooden corner. "Do you think they heard everything we said?"

Wiri exhaled. "I don't know. Maybe they heard, but I doubt they saw much. The house is raised onto high piles, so the window sills are above my head height. I only ducked a little when I didn't want Seline to see me creeping past your bedroom window." Wiri jerked his head towards Jet. He turned his gaze to Larry. "Did they appear really tall?"

"No." Larry licked his lips. "Just average." He sighed. "It's hard because there's no light outside. Do you think we should look around in the flowerbed for footprints?" He stepped across to the window and drew the heavy taupe drapes across the aperture.

Wiri groaned and flapped his right hand. "Help yourself." He shook his head and winced at the darts of pain which tunnelled through his skull. "As soon as this wardrobe is back in place, I'm going to bed. You can do what you like. Just make sure you take that gun with you. I want nothing to do with it."

He helped to guide the wardrobe back into its corner as Larry and Jet heaved it into place. Bending to retrieve the rugs made his back muscles go into paroxysms of agony and he laid on the floor on his side. Jet sank into the armchair, and Larry replaced his clerical shirt and sat on the end of Wiri's bed.

"Is it okay if I stay here tonight?" Larry asked.

Wiri grunted his assent and Jet agreed. "Yeah. But there's only the sofa or the floor. Leilah made the other room into an office when she expected to live here. There's no bed."

Wiri turned onto his back and struggled to control his breathing. "What's happening to the gun for tonight?" he asked, his voice hoarse. "It's not staying in my room."

Jet blew out a ragged breath. "Larry should keep it," he said. His tone wavered. "I feel heaps better in myself, but just looking at it takes me right back to when things were at their worse."

"I could put it into Wiri's truck and lock it," Larry suggested.

Wiri turned his head to watch Jet as he exclaimed, "Oh yeah, where's your car?"

"Wiri fetched me earlier," he replied. "I left my car at the vicarage."

Jet leaned forward and placed his elbows on his knees. "Why?" he demanded. "Why jump me the second I walked through the door and then set Larry up as a witness?" He directed his question to Wiri.

"Because I suspected you went through my gear." Wiri rolled over onto his other side, finding the pain lessened. He made a mental note to sleep on his left once he got into bed. If he ever made it that far. "If you did it once, you could have also taken the shirt and framed me after you killed Hendricks. I also couldn't be sure you didn't whack Vaughan on the head and close the lid on the tank with me still in it."

"Oh." Jet shot back in the armchair hard enough to pitch it onto its rear legs. "You believed I did all that?"

"You had the opportunity." Wiri rolled onto his hands and knees and crawled towards the bed. He kept the motion going and Larry stood to allow him to rise onto his toes and push himself face first into his pillow.

Jet's voice continued to rumble as he expressed his dismay. "What motive do I have for hurting Vaughan and trying to kill you?" he demanded.

"Dunno," Wiri growled, his pillow absorbing his words.

"Okay, so you said you got caught up at the station when Hendricks died. But where were you when Wiri became stuck in the tank?" Larry demanded.

"Not stuck," Wiri grumbled. His next sentence caused his tongue to get trapped against the pillow's cover and it rendered it unintelligible. He hated the description which made him sound like a child who had suffered an accident through naivety, like getting its head stuck between metal railings.

"That's easy." Jet released a long sigh. "I gave evidence in court against a drug dealer."

43

SHELL LIFTER

The next day didn't start well.

"Oh, I'm glad you finally bothered to show up today!" Seline's voice issued from the darkness of the shed. She emerged from the open doorway and a security light flicked on overhead, spotlighting her in a warm, yellow glow. Again, her clothing left little to the imagination. Tight jodhpurs hugged her hips and thighs like a second skin. Her shirt gaped to just below the front of her bra. The light kissed the rounded arcs of her breasts and threw the shirt beneath them into shadow. Wiri tensed and fought the groan back behind his teeth.

"I'm not late." He kept his tone even, resenting her implication when he'd worked through his pain to show up on time. Tane had arrived with questions after Jet's attempt to contact him the previous night. He'd dismissed any notion of testing for tranquillisers in Wiri's system after the time lapse.

He gave Larry a ride to town on his way to the police station. Wiri imagined Larry would hold on to the gun until Jet confessed to Tane. He'd hand it over once Tane calmed down enough to take and dispose of it.

Seline shrugged and turned back towards the shed, beckoning him to follow. Her finger curved in a lazy arc, and her lips morphed into a seductive smile. She peeked at him through her lashes and tossed her auburn hair. The yellow glow set it ablaze over her head and shoulders like a river of flame.

Wiri stood his ground. Logan had coached him about women who tried to turn his head. He hadn't needed to tell him anything that Tama's behaviour didn't already demonstrate. His cousin led with the contents of his underpants. Always had, always would. Tama would die at the hands of an angry husband, probably shot while climbing a garden fence naked. It ran in the family genes, passed down from his biological father in his DNA.

"I need to see Vaughan first," he said, turning his boots in the direction of the porch. "I'll take my jobs from him."

"But I'm working with you today." She pouted and shadows grew under the frown lines between her eyes. "He already gave the job list to me."

Wiri shook his head. "I need to see Vaughan," he reiterated. "Won't take a second." He clumped up the porch steps, making enough noise to communicate his presence before knocking. The ranch slider yawned to reveal Leilah.

"Vaughan's still not great," she said, her tone apologetic. She jerked her head towards the shed. "Seline offered to help you today. Just feed out again and check the fencing as you move around the property. Take my truck." She lifted her hand and dangled the vintage keys in front of him. "Seline can drive it if you're not familiar with a stick shift."

Wiri took the keys with a nod. He didn't want to correct her. It seemed easier just to follow her instructions. "How's Vaughan?" he asked, glancing through a gap in the net curtains to the lit lounge beyond her. The scent of toast drifted in the air and mingled with the damp scent of morning.

Leilah sighed. "Sore and tired." She cocked her head and smiled. "Grumpy. How are your injuries?"

"They'll mend." Wiri offered what he hoped was a reassuring smile. But his back tweaked at every opportunity, and the banging hadn't diminished in his head. He turned to leave and then stopped. "What's happening about the health and safety inspector? When does he want to speak to me?"

Leilah exhaled. "I don't know, Wiremu. Keep your phone on and I'll shoot you a text when he gets here. We expected him sooner than this, but it's possible the police investigation delayed him."

"Right." He turned away with a frown.

"Oh, stay away from the hay barn and the water tank." Leilah pursed her lips and took a giant inhale. "The police want it kept clear in case they need to search for more evidence."

"Thanks." Wiri nodded and his chest burned as he faced the orange sliver of sunrise. "My credit card bill is due in a few days." He swallowed, awkwardness descending over his shoulders like a jacket.

"I'll sort it," Leilah promised, her tone earnest. "Send me a text with your bank details and I'll make it right."

Wiri kept his back to her and closed his eyes. Relief washed through his body, lightening the weight of the boulder. The Plan revived in his mind, causing him to shiver with anticipation in the cool dawn air.

Seline waited for him in the shed, her shoulder leaned against the rotting corner post. Wiri knew she'd heard the conversation as her lips parted in a sneer. "So," she said, her tone bitter, "My mother is bailing out Daddy Dearest, is she?"

"It's none of my business," Wiri commented. "As long as I do my job and get paid."

Seline snorted. "Well, it is my business," she replied. She held out her hand and glared at him. "I'll drive the truck."

"I can manage." Wiri stuffed the keys into his pocket. "Let's get this hay loaded and out to the animals."

His body complained as he clambered over the hay bales and lowered down the ones closest to the shed's vaulted roof. He'd forgotten the gloves and his finger joints smarted against the tension of the string as he slipped them beneath it. Wiry and strong, Seline's slight body belied her strength, and she piled the bales next to the truck's high wheel arches. She carried their weight with ease, her breasts bulging over the top of her lacy bra and her biceps flexing beneath the soft fabric of her blouse.

Wiri estimated the number of bales required and added an extra one for good measure. A gap between the wall and the tower of hay meant Vaughan's winter stocks were less than he'd imagined. He pursed his lips and tried not to worry about the animals and the farm as the weather bit harder and the grass ceased growing. The Plan demanded he remain at work until at least next spring. Then would come Phoenix's birthday and their escape.

He clambered down from the stack and heaved in a breath as his boot soles touched the solid concrete floor. His watch lit up as he turned his wrist, the screen less bright after its bath and the numbers speckled by dark stripes. But it told him they needed to move faster in order to feed the stock at first light.

It seemed like too much double handling to load Seline's pile into the truck. But the height of the tail gate made it impossible for one person to lift and load without another standing in the flat bed. Sweat dribbled along Wiri's spine after the effort required to haul the highest bales across the top level of the stack and lower them to Seline.

It took the two of them long enough to mean the sun had already crept above the horizon as Wiri started the truck's engine. He waited for Seline to haul open the roll door wide enough to let him drive into the waning dawn. She appeared in the passenger seat with a grunt, brushing hay from her long hair. "I'm leaving it open," she said, her voice containing a growl of irritation. "It's knackered. I can't close it." She shrugged and stared over the seats to view the shed through the back windscreen. "The entire structure is on its last legs, anyway. It needs tearing down."

Wiri made no comment. He depressed the clutch and shifted into first gear, bumping the truck half way down the rutted driveway to the first of many gates. He held it on the brake and glanced sideways at Seline. She sneered at him. "I'm not your assistant," she snarled. "I'm the daughter of your boss. If you want the gates opening, do it yourself."

Wiri heaved out a breath of exasperation. He pulled on the handbrake and pushed the gear lever into neutral before descending from the driver's seat. As his fingers closed around the gate catch, a roar of the truck's engine disturbed the quiet air waves still humming over the landscape. He whipped around and saw Seline's face through the windscreen. She'd used his diversion to hop across and into the driver's seat. "Don't let her get to you," he coached himself, keeping his back turned as he pushed the gate wide. "She'll get bored and leave as soon as she gets the chance. This is all for show."

He climbed into the passenger seat without making a comment, determined not to let her control his mood. She glared across at him. "You need to close the gate after me," she snarled. "The driver doesn't open and close gates."

"Well, this driver just did. So, I'll open and you close them. Sounds fair to me."

Seline turned in her seat. Her boot caught the gas pedal, and the truck growled. "Who the hell do you think you are?" she demanded, her irises flashing in the dull sunlight sparkling off the windscreen. A pink hue crawled from between her breasts and blossomed in her cheeks.

Wiri shrugged and ignored her, turning his face to stare through the side window. He folded his arms to emphasise his point and leaned back in the seat with a sigh. The stalemate continued for over a minute. Wiri infused himself with calm, mimicking his Uncle Logan's unflappable spirit and enjoying the way his body obeyed. He pictured himself riding with Phoenix and picked out the details of her long black curls from memory. They flew back over her shoulders as she raced off into the distance on a borrowed mare. She looked back at him and laughed, and he smiled into the past with longing.

But Seline fidgeted beside him. His nonchalant stance infuriated her. After a minute, she released the handbrake and cranked the gear lever into first. The truck bunny hopped through the gateway with too much gas, fighting against the bite of the clutch. Wiri clamped his lips closed over the laugh bubbling in his chest. He released an exaggerated sigh and stretched out his arms over his thighs. His long legs occupied all the space in front of his seat and he lounged just to annoy her. "Thanks for driving," he said, his sincere tone making a mockery of her petty stand. "I still ache from where you locked me in the water tank."

44

Dust Cover

S eline jerked on the wheel and the front bumper of the truck clanged against the metal gate. Wiri raised an eyebrow in question. "Oops," he said, a smile creasing his lips.

Her mouth opened and closed, but she said nothing. She hauled on the hand brake with a hideous ratcheting sound, forgetting to first depress the button. The truck lurched forward and stalled as she removed her feet from the pedals without taking it out of gear. Another clang sounded as the shock of the stall sent the bumper into the gate for a second time. He hadn't expected his accusation to cause her such distress. He'd issued it as a lucky guess and hit pay dirt.

Seline pushed open the driver's door and jumped to the ground. Cool air rushed into the cab, and Wiri inhaled the scent of a nearby pine forest. It reminded him of home and the steep slope he'd helped his uncle to turn over to forestry. Back breaking work, Logan engaged all the children to help. Even Edin, though with great reluctance. 'This is your start-up fund,' he'd told them. 'Look after it and you can cash in on it when you need the money in your forties.'

Wiri wasn't sure what kind of emergency would require a cash injection in the next few decades years. But he understood taking Phoenix would forfeit him to any of the rights and gifts bestowed on him by the Du Roses. He expected Logan would cut him off forever, and he didn't blame him. He deserved it. Hana would prevent her husband from killing him, if Wiri was lucky.

Seline slammed the truck door and jammed her feet back over the pedals. She ground her teeth in her jaw and Wiri glanced in the mirror to see the gate opened wider. He shook his head but bit down on the rebuke. If she'd driven with more care, the truck would have slipped through the gap he'd left without an issue.

"Your turn!" Seline didn't look at him as she ground out the sentence.

Wiri smirked. "How is it my fault you messed up the entrance? I open and you close. Remember?" He leaned sideways and saw her recoil at the intensity of his stormy irises. "Did you mess up killing me too? Or did you just get scared?"

"Get out!" Her laugh changed to something verging on maniacal as it pealed around the truck's interior. "You're nothing to me, Wiremu Kingii. I wouldn't waste my time on you. Get out and shut the gate, little boy!"

He got out.

It galled him to let her win, but the rage in her face and the sound of her laugh reminded him of his mother. The same spark of unhinged emotion lurked in Seline's expression, repelling him like the scent of death. It hung around her, cloying and sickly, tainting everything she touched.

The truck moved into the paddock at a slower speed, and Wiri closed the gate behind it. It didn't surprise him when Seline didn't stop to pick him up, and he dug his hands into his jeans pockets and rounded his shoulders against the uphill climb. The fresh air outside seemed preferable to Seline's unpredictability. Wiri used the time to wrangle his thoughts into some kind of order. He forced his mind back to the incident with the water tank and let his feet guide their own steps.

The grating of the lid dragging across the concrete tank sounded the same as when Seline removed it. He hadn't given it much thought until then, but realised the same person might have carried out both actions. Her hefting of the hay bales proved her capability. "But why?" he breathed. White condensation blew back into his face from his breath and he turned his head to let it move past him. His boots darkened across the toes from the damp grass and the bite of autumn nibbled at his cheeks. The truck rumbled ahead and stopped in front of the next gate. Pirongia's third peak darkened against the sky line like a pointed head.

Wiri steered a wide berth around the rear of the truck. He didn't trust Seline not to drop it back and roll right over him. She'd almost killed him once. He unlatched the gate and pushed it wide, pausing for the truck to pass through before closing it again. Seline waited, the engine idling, but he no longer wanted to share a ride with her. He kept walking, heading for the first mob of cattle crowded near a concrete water trough. A group of them lay on the damp grass, their enormous heads turned to create an arc with their body. Poppa Alfie always said that heralded rain. Wiri stared up at the sky, acknowledging a gathering of black, ugly clouds beyond the mountain. The hammering in his head continued.

"Get out of the truck." He moved to the driver's side and spoke to Seline through her open window. Her brow narrowed in confusion before her lips curved up at the edges.

"Who's Fiona?" She leaned her right elbow on the windowsill and peered down at him. "It's nice to think you'd fall in love with me after only two meetings, but then you called out a girl's name. Who is she?"

"Mind your own business." Wiri left enough distance between himself and the truck to dive out of the way if required. "Now, get out of the truck. This mob needs feeding, and I'm not in the mood for you to reverse over me, or whatever other plan you're cooking up in that twisted head of yours."

Seline's eyes narrowed, and she pushed open the driver's door. Wiri saw her slender fingers tug the keys from the ignition, wincing as she slipped them into the front of her bra. Her irises glittered with promise and she used the runner board to glide from the vehicle as though descending a cat walk. Her hips swayed as she put effort into the seductive walk to his side.

Wiri shook his head and dropped the tail gate before clambering into the back of the truck. The corrugated steel scraped beneath his boots as he hefted the first three bales from nearest the cab. Laying cattle rose, digging their front hooves into the ground and lurching upright on tottering feet. The mob crowded around the truck and headed for the hay. Wiri paused, waiting to see if Seline produced a knife to cut the bailing twine. When she continued to stand and watch, he ticked off the possibility of her possessing a weapon. He dropped from the truck bed and withdrew his penknife from his back pocket. The cattle nudged and bumped against him as he dipped to cut the twine and wind it into a ball. He stuffed it into his front pocket with his phone and the bracelet before turning and walking away from the truck.

And from Seline.

45

RECOIL SPRING

He didn't get back into the truck. Every passing kilometre competed with the aching of his muscles. The banging inside his head grew no louder, maintaining its irritating white noise hum of distraction. Wiri made sure Seline drove ahead of him and climbed out at every stop. On a long downhill slope during which every footstep jarred his spine, he compiled a file of notes as a Google document on his phone. He set it to share to his cousin's email address as soon as he got a decent enough Internet connection. He imagined Mac's confusion when he opened it and discovered notes about a group of people he'd never met. The lock screen displayed six missed calls. Guilt prickled at the back of his neck at ignoring both Logan's and Hana's attempts to contact him. They loved him and wanted the best for him. "But I'm a rubbish liar," he whispered, and stuffed his phone back into his pocket.

Having the document as an insurance policy made him feel better. He'd added a message for Mac to contact a local cop named Tane and give him the information if anything happened to Wiri. He sighed and continued his long trudge towards the final paddock containing the horses.

Seline waited for him by the fence. She'd unfastened another button and added lip gloss to her winning smile. "This is ridiculous," she said, her tone soft. "You look like death warmed up. Just get into the truck. I can finish feeding the horses."

Wiri glared at her and dropped the tail gate. He hauled himself onto the flat bed and tossed the remaining bales over the side, where they scattered strands of hay into the scrubby grass. Skirting around her, he pushed them over the fence and watched the horses jockey for pole position. He leaned through the gap between the panels and popped the twine with his knife, sliding it from around each of the bales and adding it to the growing ball in his pocket.

"You missed one." Seline pointed to the stray bale which had landed on its short end and leaned up against the back tyre. Wiri kept her in his peripheral vision while he dug the fingers of his right hand under the orange twine and hefted the bale to the paddock gate. He let himself in and closed it behind him. Hay tumbled like snowflakes as he carried the bale a distance from the gathered crowd of horses. He laid it on the ground and cut the twine before approaching the row of swishing tails and stamping hooves.

The pregnant mare didn't object to Wiri's gentle tugging on her mane as he shed her from the melee. She followed him, subdued, as he led her over to the loose bale. "Here you go, girl," he whispered, patting her neck as she stretched her muzzle towards the feast. "Let them fight over there while you eat all you need." He ran his right palm over her strong plates of muscle and lifted her feet one at a time. Vaughan's faith in the mare seemed so tenuous and risky. He'd funnelled his hope into the tiny foal whose weight caused the mare's belly to hang low and distended. Wiri ran his hand over the lumps and bumps which designated a hoof or a muzzle and wished for a good outcome.

For all of them.

Despite her advanced pregnancy, the mare proved feisty. She defended her slices of hay against marauders by turning her backside on any who dared to approach her feast. Wiri patted her neck and left her alternately spinning her rear and gorging on the hay. He returned to the gate, opening and closing it with relief.

"Mum wanted us to check the fences." Seline's manicured brows curved in towards the bridge of her nose. "Get back in the truck."

Wiri snorted. "Did you drive blind? I checked all the fences on our way around the property. Same as I did yesterday." His energy levels depleted by degrees, the sands sliding through the narrow neck of the hourglass to leave him with only enough to get back to the house.

"Just get in the truck." Seline's soft tone lulled him, promising him a few minutes to catch his breath and assess his aches and pains. She walked towards him and he lacked the momentum to shift out of her way. Her fingers curved around his right elbow. "Come on. I'll drive you back to your place." She lifted her wrist to check an expensive analogue watch. "We need to talk. And you need to sit down for a minute."

Her pressure against his arm guided Wiri towards the truck. "I need to keep going," he said, digging his heels in and halting their progress. The long list of jobs which Vaughan had reeled off on Monday morning seemed endless. And a lifetime ago. He shuddered at the memory of the second item on the list beneath the fencing repairs.

Patch up the water tank.

"Why?" He rounded on Seline and dragged his arm from her grip. "What did I ever do to you?" He staggered backwards, shaking his head and sensing his brain rocking on its stem. A raging thirst sprang up in his throat, sucking the moisture from his mouth and causing his tongue to stick to its roof.

Resignation flooded Seline's expression. She pursed her lips and sadness swept over her features. "It's not personal," she said.

A toss of her red hair seemed to send the responsibility for his misery over her shoulder and into the dirt. "Come on. I'll drive you back to the house."

The driver's door clicked shut and Wiri watched the truck shudder as the engine fired. The horses nearest the fence stopped fighting over the hay and shied backwards in fear. Food won over anxiety and within seconds, they'd buried their muzzles back into the tufty mounds. Wiri turned to contemplate the distance remaining until he'd walked home. The downhill slope proved more painful, the impact of each step jarring his spine and his head. The brake lights flashed on the back of the truck as Seline engaged the gear lever and he sighed. He knew what she wanted.

And it wasn't him.

46

GUIDE ROD

He got it wrong.

Seline drove them both to the rental house and squeezed the truck next to Wiri's vehicle.

"Thanks." He slid from the passenger seat and called to her through the open door. "Please, can you let your mum know I'll walk back over in about an hour? I just need to take more painkillers."

"No need." Seline removed the key from the ignition and this time, pushed it into a pocket at the front of her jodhpurs. She slammed the door behind her. Wiri followed her as she skipped up the porch steps and halted in front of the shelf containing male shoes. Wiri's stained trainers occupied a rung near the top. Seline wrinkled her nose before unzipping her ankle boots. "I forget how much Mum hates mess," she commented. Bending made her words sound breathy. She raised an eyebrow at Wiri. "It's hard to believe when she cohabits a pigsty with that idiot."

Wiri made it as far as the bottom step. He didn't want Seline inside the house, but a sadistic voice in his head urged him to see what stunt she pulled to access the safe below the floorboards in his room. Part of him wished he had the strength to move the wardrobe for her under a guise of innocence. He would have liked to watch her face crease into lines of dismay at seeing the gun no longer there.

"I don't think this is a good idea," he said. She waved off his protest. Against his better judgement, he unlocked the front door and kicked off his boots. He reasoned her possession of keys meant she could return any time she liked. With or without his help.

"It's so much nicer over here," she said, performing an elegant twirl in the hallway. She spread out her arms and touched both walls at once. "I stayed here last time." Her eyelashes fluttered. "With Jet."

Wiri nodded and waited for her to go into the lounge before proceeding to the bathroom. He heard her moving around the house and forced himself to relax, safe in the knowledge that the object of her interest no longer rested where she thought. But she had already proved dangerous. His time in the water tank acted as a constant reminder, his injuries hindering his reason and his ability to make good choices.

He used the toilet and washed his face and hands, careful to pick the pieces of hay from his hair. Jet had left toothpaste on the sink and a streak of green mouthwash in a trail across the counter. Wiri used a wad of toilet paper to clear up the mess. Slipping the bracelet from his jeans pocket, he untangled it from the ball of twine. He slipped it onto his wrist. It had taken him far too long to perform the feeding task, which he could have done in his sleep just a few days earlier. He rolled his shoulders and twisted his body from side to side at the waist. The tight muscles complained.

"Get some pills and then leave," he told his reflection in a low voice. "That girl is nothing but trouble." The beads of Phoenix's creation jangled together on his brown wrist. He peered down at it with a smile. It honoured their relationship with its simplicity, and he wore it like a talisman, believing it could ward off Leilah's unpredictable daughter.

Wiri searched for Seline in the lounge and kitchen, finding the space empty. The front door stood ajar and for one glorious moment, he imagined she'd gone back to the truck. He trudged down to his bedroom in search of the painkillers and stopped in the doorway.

Seline lay naked beneath his sheets. She'd scattered her clothing in a wide arc from the door to the bed, her bra and panties nestled together on top of her jodhpurs. She peeled back the duvet to reveal her tanned breasts and the side of one pointed hip. The skin curved over the bone and dipped to a space hidden by the fabric of the sheets. Her nipples gave a tantalising bounce as she flipped backwards onto the mattress. She patted the pillow next to her with fluttering fingers. "Come on," she said, her tone wheedling. "I know you want to."

Wiri closed his eyes, but the sight of her nakedness remained burned into his retinas. His conscience went to war with temptation, both turning him into collateral damage. Damned if he did and damned if he didn't.

A draft moved the hair at the back of his neck as he remained frozen in the doorway. He opened his eyes and Seline still lay sprawled on his mattress. She tugged on the duvet until it moved aside to display her wares to their fullest. A wary voice in Wiri's head told him she just wanted the gun.

Disappointment coursed through his veins as she rolled away from him, landing on her stomach and pushing her tender ass higher. The duvet stroked her thighs as she spun in its folds and his imagination tortured him with images of its softness against her skin. His conscience began to lose the battle as hormones flooded his body until he shook. Temptation urged him to take what was on offer, to purge himself of his desire and keep it a secret.

'No!' the inner voice cried out, warning him of regret and lost dreams and endless, all-encompassing pain. 'Wasn't that the story of your conception?' it reminded him.

Seline pushed her fingers beneath her and released a soft moan. Wiri swallowed.

She might still be interested in the gun. But she definitely wanted him.

47

SLIDE

P anic set up a furious beat in Wiri's chest as his heart raced. It didn't help his headache and his finger throbbed. Seline rolled onto her back again and invited him to enjoy her, a beckoning finger moving in an enticing stroke of the air between them. "You're really hot," she purred. "And you have no idea how gorgeous you are." The low chuckle in her throat heightened the tension.

Wiri gulped and tried to speak, his mouth dry and his words stuck somewhere between his brain and his throat. A stutter emerged. "I don't need your objectification," he managed. "This isn't a period romance. Besides, it's not your interest I want." Thoughts of Phoenix consumed his mind. He wanted her to look at him in that hungry way, as though a moment devouring his company was all she needed.

A sigh passed through Seline's pink lips and she shuttered her eyelids. "Come on, big boy," she whispered. "No one needs to know. Just you and me satisfying an itch."

The air moved around him and something brushed against his arm. He held his breath and forced his body to turn. A sharp inhale held a woman's lightness, the pitch higher than a man's guttural gasp of shock. Wiri floundered, expecting to see Leilah joining the audience to her daughter's debauchery.

Instead, Phoenix gazed up at him, her jaw fixed and her eyes filled with dark swirls of accusation.

He opened his mouth to speak, but she was Logan Du Rose's daughter.

Hit first and ask questions later.

She shifted onto her back foot with a natural grace born of practice, raising her fists in self-defence. He knew what was coming, but injury and exhaustion turned his feet into blocks of concrete and he listed backwards instead of getting out of her way.

Phoenix nailed him first in the stomach and then in the groin with the jagged knuckles of her balled right fist. Air locked in Wiri's lungs and as the pain reached his solar plexus, he bent double and collapsed face first onto the floorboards.

Pure agony radiated out from the centre of Wiri's body as he writhed on the floor. He drew his knees up to his chest and the bloom reached out to conspire with all the other sites of pain to create one giant throb. Closing his eyes, he prayed for it to pass, one pulse-beat at a time.

He felt the draught as Phoenix stepped over him, but lacked the ability to track her movements. Seline's seductive chuckle sent dread into the remaining functional corners of his brain.

"Ah, is it little Fiona?" Her voice held an annoying, sing-song quality, guaranteed to stoke Phoenix's ire. Wiri groaned, but both women ignored him, locked into their moment of truth.

"Fiona?" Phoenix spat the name, her voice wavering and her control gone. "There's more of you?" Seline shrieked, a pained sound backed by shock. A thud betrayed her naked body hitting the floor in a jumble of bones. "Get up!" Phoenix snarled. "You filthy skank!" Seline wailed, and Wiri uncurled his body enough to screw his head backwards on his neck.

Phoenix held Seline by her auburn curls, hauling her onto her knees. Her expression held a darkness he'd seen when she returned from the fated summer camp. It seethed from her flashing irises and the furious set of her jaw. She dragged Seline across the room by her hair and forced her to step over Wiri before releasing her with a violent push. With quick, stabbing movements, she gathered Seline's discarded clothing and threw it at her as she stood in the hall. The zipper of her jodhpurs caught Seline in the eye and she raised her hands to cover her face. Her nakedness acted as a flame for Phoenix, lighting the touch paper and sending her completely beyond her limits. Wiri covered his head as she leapt over him and cannoned into Seline, her fists flying like a lightweight boxer.

"Stop!" Wiri forced himself onto his knees and extended an arm towards the scrapping women. A bump signified Seline's head hitting the wall. "Phoe, stop!" His spine gave a vicious twinge as he used the corner of the wardrobe to pull himself to a standing position. Seline had raised her bundle of clothing to protect her face. The nakedness she'd displayed with such divisiveness appeared jarring and vulnerable against Phoenix's fury. She tore and punched with abandon, unleashing a pit of ugliness from somewhere deep in her soul. With her back towards Wiri, it seemed she'd forgotten him in her pursuit of Seline.

Wiri lurched for her and closed his arms around her torso in a pincer movement. She used everything she'd ever learned from her father, jerking her head back and aiming to break his nose. At the same time, she dragged the heel of her boot down his shin and dug it into the top of his instep. He held on, tightening his arms and closing his mind to the pain she meted out to his already battered body. "Stop," he whispered into her ear. "I did nothing, Phoe. Just stop."

She smelled of soap and hair conditioner. The floral haze rose from her clothing, underscored by the faint odour of sweat and dust. Her hair had escaped its ponytail, tendrils hanging across her shoulders with a layer of frizz she always hated. He wondered where she'd been to have missed her morning shower. Then he recognised the haze of cigarette smoke and beer hanging around her. He tightened his grip and felt her body lose its edge. A low sound in her throat mewed desperation and tiredness. "Let me go right now or I'll really hurt you."

"I know you can." He kept his tone level, reasonable, a thread of pleading underscoring it. "But please don't."

"She's crazy!" Seline found her voice, hauling her shirt over her head and pulling it down to cover her breasts. Her nipples poked through the fabric and Wiri closed his eyes, resting his chin over Phoenix's shoulder.

"Just get out," he growled.

"Oh, I'll go!" she snarled, pressing her feet through the legs of her skimpy underwear. "I'll make sure you're not far behind me."

"What does that mean?" Phoenix lurched forward and Wiri increased his grip, feeling her collarbone pressing against his forearm as he crossed his wrists.

"I'll get him fired." Seline jutted her chin forward and wiggled into her jodhpurs. "You can help him pack." She retrieved her forgotten bra from the handle of Jet's bedroom door and her body dipped in anger as she faced Phoenix. "Did you know he's wanted for murder?" She jabbed her finger at Wiri. "He's been here less than a week and he's already behaved to type." Her cackle echoed in the narrow hallway, and she turned on her heel. She strode from the house barefoot and slammed the front door behind her.

Wiri groaned and rested his chest against Phoenix's back. "Yeah, because I'm brown," he said with a sigh. Phoenix bowed beneath his weight. He hoped she didn't go to work on breaking his fingers or use her heel to score his other shin.

48

REAR SIGHT

"Can I release you now?" A hoarseness entered Wiri's voice, and he lacked the energy to defend himself against her. He preferred to punch once, punch hard and leave, but it wasn't an option.

"I'll think about it." She ground out the words, her tone tight and filled with foreboding.

Wiri exhaled and stood up straight, a hiss escaping his lips as he lurched backwards and pressed his right shoulder against the door frame. Phoenix whirled to face him. Her lips turned down at the corners and tears sparkled across her irises. He held up his left hand in placation, displaying his palm in a sign of truce. She saw the bandaged middle fingers and frowned.

"What happened?" She stared at it before lifting her gaze to his face.

He shook his head. "It's a long and complicated story." His other hand strayed to his stomach, and he pressed it against the ache. The beads of her bracelet tinkled on their elastic. "Nice punch, by the way. Especially the one to the nuts."

"You deserved it!" She fixed her hands over her hips and put her weight on her forward leg. "You told me you loved me, and that you'd wait for me." Her index finger jabbed toward his rumpled bed beyond the doorway. "It didn't take long for you to change your mind, did it?"

Wiri groaned and bent double. His voice gained a muffled quality. "I didn't forget. She invited herself into my bed." He turned his head to look at Phoenix. "I walked in here and found her like that. Did it look to you like I had anything to do with taking her clothes off?"

Phoenix shrugged and her stance lost its rigidity. "I don't know. How long does it take for one person to undress another?"

Wiri exhaled. "I think I'd need to actually be in the room for a start. My arms aren't four metres long, Phoe. Isn't it obvious she made a play for me and then you arrived?"

Phoenix took a step backwards and leaned against the hall wall. She splayed her hands on either side of her and smoothed her palms along the wallpaper. "Who is she?" A sulkiness entered her tone. "Your boss' daughter? What made her think you wanted to sleep with her?"

"No idea." Wiri rose, using his hands against his thighs to push himself upright. "But she's poisonous." He forced a smile onto his lips. "You did good, Miss Du Rose. You're a battler. Uncle Logan would be proud."

He groaned as his phone vibrated in his pocket. Pressing his body against the door frame and straightening his spine, he reached for it. Phoenix took a step forward, her eyes wide and her hand reaching for his. "Don't answer it," she pleaded. "Please. Let it go to voicemail."

"So, this is why Logan and Hana keep calling me, is it? Because you're missing."

Wiri stood in the kitchen and fired up Jet's coffee machine. It wasn't his intention to upset him again, and he hoped the police officer didn't pay an unexpected visit home.

Phoenix roamed around the kitchen behind him, picking up the washed '*Son*' mug and placing it back on the draining board. "Do you live with a girl?" she asked.

"No." Wiri shook his head. "A cop rents the other room. Jet." He raised his eyebrow and glanced sideways at her. "He also slept with Seline, possibly on multiple occasions." He poured milk into the jug and slipped it beneath the frother. "Another reason I wouldn't be interested."

"Another reason?" Phoenix pulled open the cutlery drawer, inspected its contents, and closed it again. Her movements conveyed distress, her fingers jabbing and snatching as she drifted around the room.

Wiri blew out a breath and paused his activity. "Yeah. There are many reasons, Phoe. The first is you. The second is I don't fancy her." He set the jug on the counter and crossed his arms over his torso, seizing the hem of his tee shirt. He hauled it upwards and over his head, leaving his hair sticking up like a cockerel's plume. "This is a good enough reason for a reluctant third."

Phoenix turned to face him and gasped. She clapped a hand over her mouth. "What happened?" Pique and confusion left her in a rush, replaced by alarm. She pressed a gentle palm over the bruising which snaked up his spine as a black line before turning purple and blue on its journey through the muscles. "That looks terrible!"

"Thanks." Wiri turned to face her, embarrassment causing his cheeks to flush a heady pink. They'd grown up as family, their physical distance becoming more appropriate under Hana's watchful eye. He smiled, his lips flattening with his awkwardness.

Phoenix giggled. "I've seen your boobs before, Wiri," she said, her eyelashes fluttering.

"I don't have boobs." Wiri peered down at his chest, wincing as the bruising around his spine and ribs restricted his neck movements. He stuck out his bottom lip and admired his defined pectoral muscles. "No boobs here."

Phoenix snorted. She threw herself onto the lounge sofa and peered at him over the back of it. "Make coffee for me then," she demanded. "And I might just hear you out."

49

LOCKING SURFACES

"How did you find me?" Wiri eased onto the sofa next to her after passing her the coffee. He held his breath as his backside dropped onto the cushion. He exhaled and waved a hand at her. "Don't bother. Mac told you, didn't he?"

Phoenix shrugged. "I might have guessed the code for his phone whilst looking for something else and discovered a whole raft of texts between you and him."

Wiri squinted in pain as he bent his left leg and put his weight into his hip. He turned his body and stretched out his left arm along the back of the sofa behind her. "So, Miss Du Rose, what did Mac have on his phone that you needed?"

"It doesn't matter." Phoenix sipped her coffee, wrinkling her nose as she burned her top lip.

"No. Tell me." Wiri tapped her shoulder and then left his hand there, the bandaged fingers hanging at a strange angle across her sleeve.

Phoenix's eyelashes fluttered, and she stared through the window at the scene beyond. Blurred by the net curtain, it gained the appearance of a foggy day. "He kept looking at something with great interest. You know what he's like with tech. But it felt different, like he was monitoring something. Even at school." She raised an eyebrow and studied Wiri with practised perception.

He frowned. "What was it?" When Phoenix moved her head, a lock of hair tumbled over his hand and he caught it, frowning as he tried to keep hold of it between his bandaged index finger and his thumb.

"You." She narrowed her eyes. "He's watching you."

"What?" Wiri sat up straight and looked around him at the sterile room with the showcased furniture. "How?"

Phoenix giggled. "You shared your location data with him."

"No." Wiri straightened his legs and dug in his pocket for his phone. "I didn't. He just has the address in case of emergencies."

Phoenix twisted her lips into a pout. She laid her coffee mug on the table, which Leilah had placed artfully in front of the sofa before walking away from her childhood home. "He's got real-time data for you. I know you spent a long time in a paddock without moving the other day. Perhaps that's why he kept checking every few minutes. He got worried about you. It's a pin on a map. I followed it here." She rose and walked across the room towards the hallway. Wiri used the pause to examine the location settings on his phone. Mac had called him numerous times the afternoon he'd spent interred in the tank. He'd left no message.

Wiri held his phone up to face her when she returned. "He's got into my Google account and added a backup email address. All notifications get sent to him." He blew out a low whistle. "What a hacker!" He dropped his phone onto the sofa cushion and gnawed on his lower lip. "That means any notifications about location sharing in future will go to him. He'll confirm it's fine and I'll be no wiser."

"Until you need to enter your email and password for some reason." Phoenix sat on the couch next to him. He noticed she took more care not to rock the seat and cause him pain. "It doesn't matter anyway," she said, holding up a device in her right hand. "I stole his phone and left mine turned off and hidden at home."

"Wow!" Wiri feigned shock and his irises sparkled with humour. "You're not the person I thought you were, Phoenix Du Rose."

She lifted her chin and grinned at him. "Well, now he can't track either of us."

"I've missed you." Wiri's tone grew serious, and he slipped his arm around her shoulders. She scooted nearer, their hips touching as she leaned her cheek against his collarbone. It felt new and yet so ancient, as though someone had knitted them together before either of them were born.

"I missed you too." Phoenix blinked up at him. "You've been a constant in my life." She gulped. "Until I went to that awful summer camp."

Wiri placed his index finger over her lips. "Let's not talk about that," he said, his tone soft. "Just sit here with me while I close my eyes. Then you can tell me how you made a two-and-a-half-hour journey south without a vehicle."

Phoenix yawned, covering her mouth with her hand. "But I want to know how you got all those bruises," she said. Her eyelashes fluttered as Wiri drew her against his side. He ran his index finger across the bridge of her nose and in less than a minute, he'd soothed her to sleep. Just like when she was a toddler.

They snoozed together on the sofa like collapsed dominoes. Phoenix woke first, rising from beneath Wiri's arm with her hair in tangles over her face. She sighed and rubbed her eyes. "Where's that noise coming from?" Her voice sounded over loud in the quiet house.

"What noise?" Wiri forced himself to a sitting position and groaned. He ran a tentative hand along his ribs. "I never got those painkillers. That's why I went into the bedroom." He shifted to the edge of the cushion and Phoenix rose. Her soft steps padded across the rug and into the hall.

"That girl left her socks." Her voice echoed in the narrow space. A ball of pink fabric pinged against the lounge doorway and bounced into the centre of the rug. A second joined it, hitting the door frame and flying back in the opposite direction.

It took three attempts for Wiri to stand, the ultimate effort involving the coffee table. He winced as Phoenix's abandoned coffee slopped over the side of the mug.

"Is this hers?" She appeared in the room without warning, holding a phone out in front of her. "I found it on your bedside table."

Wiri took it and peered at the screen. Black and lifeless, it gave no indication of its owner. Turning it over, he examined the floral pattern on the case and nodded. "Seline's I guess. Perhaps she's phoning it to see if she left it here."

Phoenix's pupils flared, and she set her jaw in a hard line. She took it from Wiri's open palm. "Good. Then I'll answer it next time she calls." She twitched her shoulders up to meet her ears and grinned at him. "I'll teach her to get naked with my boyfriend."

Wiri smiled. He leaned forward and stroked her cheek with his right hand, smoothing his thumb over her top lip. "I've missed your sass," he whispered.

Phoenix wrinkled her nose. "I've missed it too," she admitted. "I lost myself for a while there after summer camp. A black cloud descended over my head and when it lifted, you'd gone."

"Well, we're both here now." Wiri dipped his head and his lips covered hers. Only their third kiss ever. It packed a punch and Phoenix stepped closer to him, wrapping her arms around his waist and lifting her face for more. She held the phone in her left hand and it bumped the waistband of his jeans as she pressed herself against him, their mutual craving threatening to move into dangerous territory.

Wiri pulled away first, making his best decision of the day. "You're only fifteen." He kissed the end of her nose. "You might change your mind, and I need you to be able to do that."

Phoenix pouted and wrapped herself around him, causing him to wince as he tried to pull away from her. "I'm ready," she whispered, her eyes sparkling with danger and mischief.

The phone rang in her left hand and she jerked backwards and dropped it. The rug absorbed the impact, and she bent to retrieve it, scrabbling to lift it to her ear. "Hello," she said, her tone biting. When no one spoke, she frowned and looked back at the screen. "Oh, oops." She pressed the green flashing icon of a telephone and waited.

"I told you to be ready!" a male voice snarled into Phoenix's ear. Wiri heard it as a muffled echo. Her jaw dropped, and she drew it away from her face, holding the device out between them. Wiri shook his head, not wanting responsibility for it. She pressed another icon to activate the speaker, and the voice boomed into the lounge. "Do you think it's easy for me? I can't just use the phone when I want to. You know that. Answer next time I call you!" His voice rose to a shout, and Phoenix inhaled. "Are you there?" he demanded.

"Yes." The answer came from a reflex, drawn from her lips with great reluctance.

Wiri spread his hands in question, mouthing, "Keep him talking."

"What do you want?" Phoenix swallowed, the hand holding the phone shaking between them.

"You know what I want," the voice snarled. "I want both of them dead. Stop mucking around and get it done." The call ended, and the screen flared before morphing back to black. Phoenix dropped the phone onto the rug and Wiri snatched it up again. The fingers of his uninjured hand moved fast, pressing the buttons on the side of the phone to activate the screen. The security settings had allowed them to take the call, but required a code for any other function.

"What do we do now?" Phoenix's eyes filled with fear, wide and unblinking, as she looked at Wiri for all her answers.

"I don't know," he whispered, realising he'd already failed to protect her. "Logan's gonna kill me," he breathed.

50

BACK STRAP

Wiri sank onto the sofa, his body folding like crumpled paper. The fight left him as he contemplated the growing mess his life had become. He ran a shaking hand over his face. Phoenix's presence added a clarity he didn't want. It hit him afresh that he'd almost died in the water tank. Now he understood why. A random stranger wanted him and Vaughan dead.

Phoenix sat next to him. She slipped an arm around his bowed shoulders and laid her cheek against his biceps. "It'll be okay," she promised, sounding just like her formidable father. "We can fix this. Tell me what happened to you."

Wiri snuffled a soft laugh, which died on his lips. He turned to face her and wrapped his arms around her shaking body. Her courage was an illusion, a borrowed facade demanded by their shared genetics. Reuben Du Rose's blood coursed through their veins, both a blessing and a curse. "I accused Seline of trying to kill me," he whispered. "It was a long shot, a comment I just chucked out there." He sighed and his chest hurt. "It was true. She tried to kill me."

"Why?" Phoenix drew back to stare up into his eyes. "Why you? How does this man even know you?"

Wiri shook his head, and it ached. "I don't know, Phoe. Do you think Uncle Logan could have anything to do with it? Did he find out about us?"

Phoenix's lips parted in protest, but the shake of her head lacked energy. She shrugged. "No. I don't think so." She exhaled and her breath stirred his fringe. "The man seems to want her to get rid of more than one person. You arrived alone. I think you've got caught up in something accidentally." She reached up and kissed him, lingering as his arms tightened around her. "Let's get you some painkillers and think about everything that's happened in the last few days." Her lips flattened. "If we can't fix it, Wiri, we need to call Papa. You understand that, don't you?"

He nodded, every movement of his head shifting the boulder. It grew heavier, more tiresome in its efforts to stop him breathing, functioning, moving, living. "Yeah," he replied, his tone lacklustre. "To keep you safe. Yeah."

Phoenix heated her discarded coffee in the microwave and fetched pills for Wiri. She handed both items to him as he sat on the sofa. Circumstance pinned him in place, the mystery whirling around his head without coherence. He felt utterly defeated. The Plan had imploded around him and he had nothing to offer.

"You're a mess." Phoenix sank down next to him, lifting her hand to brush his hair from his eyes. She sighed. "I love this."

"What?" Wiri gulped three of the tablets with a mouthful of coffee, staring up at her in surprise. He shook his head. "You love taking calls from a maniac and beating up a hired killer?"

Phoenix threw her head back and laughed. "Not quite. I love being able to touch you and kiss you without thinking we're doing something wrong. The other stuff is incidental."

"You're so badass." Wiri swallowed another slug of the coffee with the last white pill. "You totally laid into her."

Phoenix narrowed her eyes. "If the last few weeks have taught me anything, it's not to let life walk all over me." She shrugged. "You and I are inevitable." Her fingers rested on his knee and stilled. "I'll kill or be killed for you, Wiremu Du Rose. Get used to it." Her expression clouded. "And don't mess with me unless you want to spend life as a eunuch."

The laugh exploded from his chest. It seemed years since he'd enjoyed any humour and it caused happy endorphins to release in his brain. A lightness of being shrouded him and his vision blurred. "Which pills did you give me?" he asked.

Phoenix shrugged. "Two of them are from the foil wrapper on the dining table. I found the others in your flatmate's room." She frowned. "I stripped off your bedsheets and dumped them on the floor. I don't want that skank's skin cells anywhere near my boyfriend."

Wiri shuddered. "That's beyond gross, Phoe." He exhaled and a familiar mist descended over his thoughts. "I think you gave me the wrong pills," he said. A blessed numbness snaked through his muscles and sinews, making him feel invincible. "This might not be good," he sighed. He pushed his phone across the sofa cushion towards her. "Can you search for a contact named Larry and call him?" He blew out a ragged breath as the room tilted. "Why did you give me four?"

Phoenix shrugged. "Two of the ibuprofen and two paracetamol. You can do that because they're different types of medication." She smiled at him and winked. "I learned that on a first aid course."

Wiri's head moved up and down in a disjointed nod. "They weren't ibuprofen," he said with a sigh. "They were something else."

Phoenix leaned back in her seat. "Why would you have anything stronger in your possession? Papa hates drugs." She added Logan's stance as though to punctuate her disgust. Wiri waved his hand in an ineffectual flapping motion.

"I don't know what they are. The ones on the table came from the hospital after the fire brigade got me out of the water tank. If the others came from Jet, I could be in trouble."

Phoenix gave a sharp inhale. "Fire brigade? Water tank?" She shook her head. "You have some explaining to do, young man." She sounded just like Hana, her emphasis precise and comforting. She rose, her steps staccato against the floorboards. Wiri flopped back onto the sofa and watched the ceiling rose dive bomb him.

She returned, a worried look on her face. "I pulled the empty foil wrapper from the dustbin. Sorry, but the others from your flatmate's room aren't ibuprofen, Wiri. The outer cardboard said they were." She swallowed, pushing her index finger between her lips and nibbling on the nail. "I'm sorry. I should have checked." She closed her eyes and her body stiffened as she berated herself for her stupidity. "What should I do, Wiri? Can I phone for an ambulance?"

"No." He turned sideways on the sofa. "I'll be fine. Let me sleep for a minute. Call Larry."

"Larry. Larry." Phoenix retrieved his phone and unlocked the screen using the first four digits of her birthday. She scrolled through the list of contacts and found Larry's. He answered after the fourth ring, his voice jovial and bouncy.

"Ah, Mr Kingii," he said. Something clanged in the background and he sighed. "Sorry. Mrs Ropata just dropped her flower decoration. Can I call you back in a moment?"

"No!" Phoenix gushed. "I think someone tried to kill Wiri and now I've drugged him. Please, can you come?"

"Who's this?" A business-like quality entered Larry's tone, the humour banished.

"Phoenix. Phoenix Du Rose. He was in pain, so I gave him some pills from his flatmate's room. I found some others in the kitchen and doubled up." Her voice cracked. "He's gone really groggy. What should I do? He doesn't want an ambulance."

"I'll come now." Breaths issued through the phone as Larry started moving. A door slammed, loud enough to be close. "I'll be twenty minutes at the most. Try to read the packets and call me back when you have the names of the pills. What's he doing now?"

Phoenix groaned and pressed her shaking fingers to Wiri's forehead. "Sleeping," she replied. "He looks peaceful. He's smiling."

"I bet he is," Larry said with a sigh. "Okay. Find the names of the tablets and we'll take it from there. See you soon." He killed the call. Phoenix left Wiri and rounded up the various foil wrappers she'd purged in her bungled attempt to relieve his pain.

"Alprazolam," she breathed, using Mac's phone to Google the name on the foil packet from Jet's room. She groaned as the Google search found its mark. "Sleeping tablets." She gnawed on the inside of her cheek as she read the contraindications, trying to gauge if she'd given him enough to fell an elephant or not. "Please don't die," she whispered into the empty kitchen. "Please don't let me kill you after only three kisses."

51

Grip Frame

Larry's tyres ground against the driveway as he screeched his old car to a halt next to Wiri's truck. He leapt from the vehicle, becoming tangled in his seat belt during his haphazard exit. It took a wasted moment for him to extract himself, and the front door opened as he pounded up the porch steps.

He screeched to a halt at the sight of the slight teenager facing him. Phoenix observed him from beneath a cloud of dark curls which hung lopsided from a ponytail. Grey eyes just like Wiri's stared at him from her elfin face. Her mouth opened but nothing came out, and she closed her lips again.

"Where is he?" Larry demanded. His clerical cassock swished as he walked and he didn't stop to remove his shoes. The white dog collar at his neck seemed to give him additional power, and Phoenix stepped aside to allow him to pass. She pointed towards the lounge sofa.

Larry dropped to his knees and placed a hand over Wiri's chest. "Still breathing," he remarked.

"I know." A sullenness entered Phoenix's tone. "I've checked him every few minutes." She pursed her lips. "He's snoring."

Larry placed his ear over Wiri's mouth and gave a definitive nod. "Did you find the pill packets?"

"Yes." Phoenix indicated the packets laid on the coffee table. Larry snatched them up and inspected the labels. His shoulders lost their rigidity, and he bowed his head.

"Thank God," he breathed. He exhaled and spun on the soles of his shoes, his knees bent beneath his cassock as he squatted next to the sofa. "A derivative of diazepam and diclophenac. I don't think there are contraindications between them, but he might be out for a while." He rose and his cassock rustled. "The kid's been riding around all week on the diazepam. He might feel better after a decent sleep but he mustn't take any more." He yawned and stretched his arms above his head. The cassock rode up to reveal sensible black shoes.

Phoenix pursed her lips. "The packet is empty. I don't think he has another."

Larry jerked his head towards the kitchen. "How about we share a cuppa and introduce ourselves?" His face creased into a smile and he stretched out his right hand. "Larry Hendricks. Nice to meet you."

52

LINK

Wiri woke after an hour, his head listed to one side and a line of dribble snaking from his open mouth to his ear. He stirred and pushed himself upright, which involved a crablike crawl using the back of the sofa.

His eyelids blinked, scratchy sand scraping against his eyeballs. It proved a mistake to rub them. He poked himself in the face with his bandaged finger and made his eyes sting with the pressure of the rubbing action. Looking around the lounge, he frowned, confused about the unfamiliar location. He recognised Leilah's expensive furniture and the dreaded net curtains across the picture window. The bone deep sense of isolation shrouded him and he reached for the mobile phone next to him on the coffee table.

"Phoenix." He said her name and forced himself to rouse with more energy. The isolation retreated, nipping at the fringes of his consciousness but wary of his newfound courage. He fumbled the phone into his fingers and stared around the room, seeking her essence but not finding it. "Phoe!" He called louder, expecting her to appear from the bathroom or bedroom, her hair neatened and her grey eyes sparkling with affection.

Nothing.

Wiri rose and shuffled through to the kitchen. The coffee mug sat in the sink, half filled with water and a layer of silty scum covering its surface. He rubbed at his eyes again before dropping his hand. "Maybe I dreamed it," he said with a sigh. He ran his index finger over his lips and frowned. "It felt so real."

Defeat shrouded him like a veil and the sense of isolation joined in to bow his shoulders and cause his head to hang. The passion and her declaration of possession, the fight with Seline and Phoenix's care, dissipated on the wind as a false memory. "It didn't happen," he murmured. "She isn't here."

He turned back to the lounge, entering through the wide archway before halting, his brow furrowed. A pink sock nestled near the coffee table, balled as though tugged off a wriggling foot. Wiri swallowed and his reason stuttered over the presence of the alien thing. Seline's sock. Kicked there by a petulant Phoenix.

He searched the house. Splashes of product on the mirror showed where she'd tried to tame her curls. Wiri spun, finding the lid ajar on his hair gel. He jogged to his bedroom and found the mattress bare. She said she'd stripped the sheets.

"Phoenix!" He lifted his voice and pulled open the back door leading from the laundry. Unlocked and ajar, it filled him with trepidation.

She turned to face him, her features aglow from the high sun and her hair damp. She sat on the top rung of the post and rail fence, swinging her feet beneath her. "Hey. You didn't sleep for long."

Relief coursed through Wiri's veins and he struggled to stem the flood of adrenaline. He leaned against the balustrade and it wobbled, still damaged from its fight with Seline's gelding. Dipping his body, he rested his forehead on his arms.

Phoenix's feet tapped as she hopped down from her perch and walked up the steps. She arrived next to him and slipped an arm around his shoulders. "Larry visited," she said, resting her temple against his biceps. "He checked you out, but then someone from the church called, needing him to sort out a crisis."

"I thought you'd gone," he whispered. His chest hitched with the effort of regaining control. "Or that you'd never been here at all."

"Funny boy." She used her mother's expression for him and rose on tiptoes to place a kiss against his cheek. Drawing back, she traced a line along his jaw with her index finger. "You always shaved at home," she said, eking out the thought. "I've never seen you so stubbly. I like your rugged look."

Wiri laughed, the sound a muted snuffle. "How did you get here?" he asked, her lack of an explanation troubling him. "You never told me."

"Ah." Phoenix chewed her lower lip. "Perhaps it's best you don't know."

"Tell me you didn't hitchhike?" Wiri narrowed his eyes, tilting his head sideways on his forearms to glare at her.

Phoenix shifted on her feet. "It wasn't quite hitching, but it also kinda was." She stumbled over the sentence, creating more curiosity than she dispelled. Wiri rose and stared at her.

"You need to tell me now," he demanded.

Phoenix inhaled. "I got a ride with David Allen."

Wiri cocked his head. "Wait. What?"

She shrugged. "He doesn't know. I used the bush path to get from home to the hotel. He parked in front of the main entrance and ran inside, but he left his truck open. I hid in the boot and hopped out when he stopped at the service station on the Bombay Hills. The hardest part was making it across all four carriages of the motorway in the dark and then finding a bus heading south. I had to wait until seven o'clock this morning for one to stop at the services."

"You ran across the motorway?" Wiri jerked his head back in horror. "Not only is that dangerous, you'll show up on CCTV." He ran a hand through his hair. "Don't you understand how vulnerable you made yourself just sitting alone at a service station at night?"

Phoenix wrinkled her nose. "I didn't think about that." She shrugged. "I'm here now, anyway. The bus didn't have many people on it, so the driver let me pay cash, seeing as I only needed to stay on for a couple of hours."

"You caught the night bus?"

"Yeah." She smiled up at him. "I sat near the driver and he chatted to me. He also did a minor detour off the main highway, so I didn't have so far to walk to get here."

Wiri exhaled and bent to place a kiss over her lips. He closed his eyes, grateful she'd proved more than a figment of his imagination. Pulling away with great reluctance, he slipped his arm around her shoulders and tugged her closer. "Why were you sitting on top of the fence?" he asked, his voice a low rumble in her damp hair.

"Watching that horse." Phoenix lifted her left arm and pointed up the slope to the paddock beyond the house. "She keeps going down and getting up again." Her brow furrowed. "Pastor Hendricks came out to look at her, but he said he doesn't know much about cattle or horses."

"Hendricks?" Wiri's body stiffened. "As in, Hendricks like the one who drowned in the water tank?" A picture painted itself in his mind. Donovan Hendricks knew things about people, things perhaps only a vicar would know.

"Drowned? But they pulled you out again. Larry told me about it." She stared up at him, sunshine kissing her loose fringe and casting her features into highlights of glow and shadow. "What are you talking about?"

Wiri blew out a sharp breath and fidgeted, opening and closing the fingers of his right hand over the balustrade. He shook his head, unable to order his thoughts into anything which might help him formulate a plan.

A plan.

The Plan.

"We need to leave," he said, his tone brusque. "Right now."

Phoenix tilted her face to observe his panic, her irises paling through tiredness to the colour of a cloudy sky. "I don't want to run," she replied, her tone firm. "We're never running, Wiri. I want to face things and take the consequences. But I'm not running."

53

BARREL BUSHING

"But you've already run. So, why are you really here?" Wiri dropped his arm and took a step away from her. The boulder lodged in his throat and stopped him from swallowing.

"I didn't run away, I came to see you." Serenity settled over Phoenix, a confidence and a peace older than her years. "I'm here because I miss you. We didn't get the chance to talk because of everything that happened over the summer." Her gaze slid to his wrist, and she smiled at the beads clinging to the weak elastic. "I love you, Wiri. But we're going to make Mama and Papa listen to us." She turned with a sigh and stared up the mountain, at the paddocks dotted across the landscape. They resembled a patchwork of green, bisected by lines of fencing. The cattle grazed in groups, always a few stragglers littered about the hillside.

Her gaze settled on the mare as the horse lay down again, collapsing first onto her knees before sinking her rump into the grass. "Papa hates lies and divisiveness more than anything. You were right before when you wanted to tell them the truth. I should have listened."

She reached for his hand, clasping her fingers around it and bringing the bandage to her lips. "He's afraid we'll be like the others," she whispered. "Like our ancestors. He believes we'll mess everything up and ruin what he's built. But we won't, will we?"

Wiri groaned. "It's too late for that, Phoe. I've already lied. He thinks I went north to the cousins and instead, I came south to a job I got on my own." He shook his head and licked his lips. "Look how that turned out!"

"It's too late for a lot of things!" Phoenix rounded on him, her eyes flashing and her teeth gritted. "But it's not too late for us."

"How do you know what Logan thinks?" Wiri slapped his palm on the balustrade and the impact sent pain through his torn finger. He shook his head and glared at her. "You told them, didn't you?" It hurt more than he imagined it would. The Plan meant he'd be cut off, but he pictured himself getting ready for the moment, preparing for his future as a Kingii and not a Du Rose. "It's too early," he said, his tone laden with regret. "I'm not ready. You're not sixteen." He turned back to her, sensing her trepidation as she faced him with defiance and fear. She looked so tiny and fragile, a twenty-year-old woman in a fifteen-year-old's body. But it didn't make it right. Or legal.

He wrapped his arms around her and held her tight, as though waiting for the world to crash down on their shoulders and bury them together in the loamy soil. "What happened?" He asked without wanting to know the answer.

"Nothing." She spoke the word into his chest. Even muffled, it communicated her sadness. "He got up and walked out of the house. Mum ran after him. I don't know where they went. Mac avoided trouble by going in the shower, so I stole his phone. The later it got, the more I realised I couldn't face them, so I left."

Wiri arched his spine so he could study her expression. His muscles felt less rigid. The heady mix of Phoenix and pain pills had given him a temporary reprieve from his ailments. The headache seemed less angry. "Didn't you bring anything with you?" he asked.

Phoenix shook her head. "Just Mac's phone. I turned mine off and hid it at the bottom of my wardrobe. I didn't want Papa to track it. You can bet your life Mac's blocked the GPS app on his." She slid her lower jaw to one side, twisting her face and giving her a quizzical expression. "I want to face them, but I need you with me. We understand what they're afraid of, Wiri. We can prove we're different."

He exhaled and looked around him at the craggy mountain, wondering what it thought to their shared dilemma. He guessed it had seen many others, worse or couched in more hopelessness. "This place is a bust," he admitted. "I doubt I'll get paid, although I've spent more time damaging myself than actually working." He tutted and watched the mare stagger to her feet. She walked a few paces before lying down again and rolling onto her side. Phoenix followed his gaze and pursed her lips.

"We need to go up and see what's happening," she said. Her fingers twitched as she lifted them to push her fringe from her eyes. "I have a bad feeling."

"Me too." Wiri winced and heaved in a breath filled with conviction. "We can take my truck, but you should drive."

54

MAINSPRING

Vaughan and Leilah didn't answer either of his texts. Wiri imagined Seline spreading her bile and their silence didn't surprise him. He locked up the house and followed Phoenix outside, handing her the keys to the truck. She hopped into the driver's seat and grumbled about the distance between the seat and the steering wheel. It took her a moment to work out the controls and get herself into position.

"Do we need to go on a public road?" She winced with her finger over the ignition and her right foot resting on the brake pedal. "I don't even have my learner's licence."

"No." Wiri shook his head and hauled the seatbelt over his torso. "We'll go across country." His lips flattened into a smile. "You're a skilled driver. We all drove off-road as soon as we could reach the pedals." He thought of Poppa Alfie's patient lessons. The old man had enjoyed teaching all of them. Except Edin. He refused to take her again after she drove into the stable wall.

Phoenix drove with competence. Unlike Seline, she took one look at Wiri and got out to open the first gate. The door slammed as she climbed back into the truck. He watched her pursed lips as she steered the vehicle through the gap and pulled on the handbrake. "No." He leaned across and squeezed her wrist as she dropped her hands from the steering wheel. "Let me do it." He raised a quizzical eyebrow and smirked back at her as his other hand rested on the door handle. "Hopefully you won't drive off and leave me to walk."

Phoenix's eyes narrowed to slits, and her jaw hardened. "Is that what she did?" She released a tut in response to Wiri's nod. "Bitch! I should have hit her harder." She leaned sideways to peer through the driver's window. "Hurry, babe. She's down again."

Wiri hustled to the gate and closed it behind her. Between them, they made quick work of the distance. They eased into a well-worn pattern of shared labour and arrived at the paddock containing the horses.

The mare lay near the furthest fence where she'd shed herself away from the herd. A gelding had stepped up to take charge, exercising his ineffectual masculinity as he nipped at the hocks of the mares and drove them into the corners of the paddock. Wiri slammed the passenger door and surveyed the scene. "Vaughan intended to move her into the field nearest the house," he mused. "She's gone into labour early."

"Where can I put the others?" Phoenix stood next to him, the shoulder of her light jacket brushing against his biceps.

He shook his head and heaved out a breath of relief. "I love you so much," he said with a sigh. "You just know what to do. I don't need to explain anything."

She gave him the side eye, but her lips raised at the corners. "Good," she said. "Just keep telling me that." She didn't wait for his reply, but clambered over the fence and into the path of the group cantering towards her. The gelding drove them into a lazy arc and covered her in dust.

"Hang on!" Wiri limped around to the back of the truck and lifted the tailgate. Reaching in, he grabbed the handle of a lunge whip and tugged it free. He passed it over the fence to Phoenix, and she nodded in thanks, winding up the long lash and keeping it in her left hand.

"I'll put them in with the mob in that one!" she called over her shoulder. Wiri waved in response and steeled his nerves before clambering over the fence. He dropped to the hard ground on the other side and winced at the impact, which shot through his muscles and lapped at the back of his head.

"Come on Du Rose," he coached himself, striding across the paddock. He wrapped his arms around himself once before flexing his shoulders. "You've done this before. You know what to do."

Phoenix reached the gate on the other side and Wiri saw her fling it open. The grazing cows lifted their heads and watched with interest as they considered their potential exit. The mare lay on the ground as though dead. Only the heaving of her rounded belly showed any life.

Wiri hissed through his teeth as the horses passed him too close for comfort. He swiped at the gelding but missed, intending to distract it from its dangerous mission. Circumstance pressed him between the proverbial rock and the hard place. He needed to check on the mare, but his practical, strategic mind had already worked out that Phoenix couldn't hold back the steers at the same time as driving the horses through the gate. The impossibility of being in two places at once nipped at his sense of duty at the same moment as the mare thrashed her head against the ground. She tried to get enough momentum to sit, her distended stomach turning her into a rolling beach ball.

"Sorry," Wiri called to her. He altered his trajectory, heading for the gate and hoping he could get the horses through the gap while Phoenix controlled the cows. "I'm coming back," he promised.

The gelding drove the group in a tight circle, not thinking through his trajectory as the thrill governed his mania. His eyes rolled back in his head as the herd responded, twisting and flowing at his direction.

The steers gathered, edging together to form a mob. They eyed the gate, driven by the genuine belief that the grass was always greener on the other side.

"I'm good!" Phoenix waved her right hand at him as she saw him heading towards her. Wiri's steps slowed, doubt stopping him from trusting her and turning back to his original mission. But he shouldn't have worried.

Phoenix crossed the paddock containing the cows at a sprint, covering ground as though racing. Her feet flew across the grass and her dark curls streamed behind her like an air current in her wake. Wiri watched, his body paralysed as he drank in the phenomenon that was Phoenix Du Rose. She stopped with such sharpness, she almost overbalanced at the next gate. Fumbling with the catch, she threw it open and walked backwards for two strides before turning and retracing her steps. Wiri sighed, wishing he'd thought of the tactic first. Move the cows into a different paddock before herding the horses.

Phoenix halted and turned once she reached the space between the curious mob and the gate back to the horses. She unfurled the whip and lifted it in a single, fluid motion. An expert flick of the wrist jerked the lash, and it cracked, the sound reaching Wiri's ears a fraction of a second after the action. The steers jerked backwards as one and their feet moved, like a ship beginning its slow turn after a warning. One bucked and ran, and it was all it took to shift the others. She kept the whip cracking left and right as she moved towards them. Wiri licked his lips and turned back to the mare. She hadn't got up. He hissed through his teeth and made the tough decision to leave the tiny girl facing down a mob of cattle alone. "Just trust her," he told himself out loud.

He hustled across the paddock to the mare. His bandaged finger struggled to haul his phone from his pocket and he cursed at the stupidity of shoving it into that one instead of the other.

He dropped it twice before closing his right hand around it and checking the screen. Pulling up Vaughan's number and calling, he left it ringing, shoved it back into his pocket, and ran to the mare.

He slowed to a walk before approaching her. "Hey girl." He spoke to her, making sure she knew of his presence before startling her. "You need some help?" Squatting in front of her, he stroked her long muzzle and looked into her eyes. Her wide, staring pupils communicated her fear, and she blinked and snorted as though pleading with him. He pursed his lips as her eyes rolled back in her head and she thrashed again.

Wiri kept speaking to her as he moved his palm along her body. She strained and her stomach muscles flexed, squeezing to little effect. Her head lifted with each contraction before crashing onto the ground. Dust coated her eyelashes and dulled her mane. "It's all gonna be okay," Wiri promised, the words acting as a fuel for his courage. He dropped to his hands and knees, avoiding her hooves as she straightened her legs with the pain. "I know how you feel," he soothed before correcting himself. "Well, not exactly. I know what pain feels like, though." He glanced up to check on Phoenix, glad she couldn't hear his nervous prattling.

She didn't look at him, cracking the whip and driving the cattle towards the open gate. A bulky Holstein-Friesian dodged sideways and ducked from the mob, steering a course away from Phoenix. She ignored it, holding her nerve as she continued to focus on the mob. She cracked the whip towards the back of the group as another contemplated following the escapee. They picked up speed and the bunch of bobbing heads began to move as one.

55

CYLINDER GAP

Wiri's palm coasted over the mare's flank as he dipped to look under her tail. He brushed away loose hair from the grass and she obliged by flicking it aside. A hoof protruded from her swollen birth canal, but the heel faced upwards instead of towards the ground. The amniotic sac bulged from around it, dangling towards the scrubby grass like a white latex bag hanging from a peg. "I'm gonna help you." Wiri stroked her flank, communicating his position through touch. He rose onto his knees and wiped his hands on his jeans, giving him a moment to mentally prepare. Then he wrapped the fingers of both hands around the hoof and waited, ensuring he worked with the mare and didn't rush her.

Her head rose again as she strained. Wiri pulled gently at first as he found the rhythm of her contractions. "Come on, girl," he called to her. "I don't want to hurt your baby." His muscles flexed, but he avoided the temptation to yank too hard and damage both the mare and the foal. "It's the wrong way around," he said with a tut. "And I can't see the other hoof."

The ground rumbled as the horses made another pass. Dust rose in a choking haze, and Wiri coughed and dipped his head to wipe his eyes on the sleeve of his tee shirt. He didn't let go of the hoof, maintaining the pressure and glancing across at the mare. "I don't even know your name," he told her. "Come on, girl. We can do this."

Thrilled with himself, the gelding drove the group back towards him and Wiri shouted at it, his cussing drowned out by the drumming of their combined hooves. The dust fell again like sheet rain over his head. The mare closed her eyes as the contraction ended, but her brow rested against the fence rail. She lacked the energy to move it forward a fraction and drop her muzzle to the ground.

Unnamed fears whizzed through Wiri's mind as he fretted about Phoenix facing down the curious mob of cows alone. The gelding made another pass with the group, enjoying their frenzied kicks of protest. Devilment glinted in his eyes as he shook his mane and preened himself. Tail high and his gait stiff, he carried his front hooves in a high trot of pure enjoyment. As he drew close to Wiri, he bucked. Hooves arced like missiles, metres away but moving the air waves as though just missing his head. He could do nothing to change his situation. The gelding had tasted leadership and become drunk on the herd's acceptance. It tested its dominance with every beat of its hooves, straying closer to the man tending the stricken mare.

Wiri clung to the motionless hoof as each contraction pushed it mere centimetres from the mare's body. But with each droop of her exhausted head, it slipped back inside and Wiri struggled to hold on to it.

The hooves pounded behind him and he stopped looking, feeling the air shift alongside the thunderous vibration of their impact. He decided it was best he couldn't see how close they came. Logan always told him horses didn't intend to cause injury. They'd jump if they could and he kept the faith of the statement, choosing to believe it in that moment.

The mare groaned from deep in her chest and her ears twitched as she lifted her head away from the fence rail. Wiri strengthened his grip on the hoof and leaned into the motion, pulling to bolster her efforts like a tug-of-war team.

The herd of horses rebelled behind him. One tired mare decided she no longer wanted to run in the direction of a gelding acting above his station. She kicked out at him, dividing the group in Wiri's peripheral vision and releasing a high, antagonised squeal which echoed off the mountain's craggy ridge. It made the situation worse.

Like children in a playground, the others went along with the rebel, squabbling and kicking. Steam rose from their bodies, foaming white sweat collecting in the grooves between their chest muscles and along their necks. They milled around Wiri, close enough to send tingles of anticipation snaking along his spine. His shoulders stiffened, expecting an accidental kick to knock him into oblivion. They circled, shedding and isolating the gelding and turning their flanks and threatening hooves in his direction.

As the mare collapsed with exhaustion, Wiri popped his head up and tried to see Phoenix between the rails of the fence. He realised he hadn't heard the whip crack in the last few minutes. His heart set up an increased throbbing in his chest. "We're all good!" he called to the mare, hearing the exhaustion in his voice. "We can do this. Ignore these idiots."

A tail swished against his face. The whipping action caught his right eye, setting up a blaze of burning, which made him blink. He couldn't release the foal's hoof and wipe it, too afraid of losing the battle. His eye streamed, tears coursing through the dust on his cheek and soaking his tee shirt with streaks of watery grey filth. "Go away! Get on with you!" he shouted at the milling herd. He turned his head, squinting and blind in his weeping eye. They reacted as one, jerking aside, but not far enough for his comfort.

Wiri turned back towards the mare, lifting to peer over her rounded belly. Her tongue lolled through the side of her open mouth, touching the dust beneath her. "Phoenix!" Wiri lifted his voice and bellowed for her, panic ticking in the back of his skull. "Phoenix?"

"I'm here." Her gentle confidence swept over him like cool water. "The cows are in that empty paddock next to them. Sorry if you were keeping the grass for winter." He glanced up to see her wipe her nose across her jacket sleeve. Dirt streaked her cheeks, and she grinned down at him. "One stroppy bugger decided to take me on, but I left him next door. If he comes back through here, I'll muster him with the horses." She frowned at the sight of him hanging onto the hoof and her lips parted as she studied his face. "What happened to your eye?" She dropped to her haunches.

"Tail." He blew out a tired breath and gave a long blink. "This foal is stuck. Vaughan isn't answering his phone. I can't see the other hoof and the foal is meant to come out with its spine aligned with hers."

"Okay." Phoenix squeezed his left shoulder with a dirty hand. "You're sure it's not breach?"

"No." Wiri shook his head. "I'm sure."

Phoenix glanced around at the gathered horses. "I'll get these through the gate. Then I'll come back and we'll get her standing. Even a second might turn the baby."

"Okay." Sweat ran down Wiri's temples and joined with the tears from his eye. "Don't use the whip. Not near me, anyway."

"Yes, sir!" Phoenix gave a mock salute and rose. She spun in the dirt and sent up another cloying cloud of dust. "Sorry," she murmured, already moving towards the horses.

In the end, it proved as simple as catching the gelding. She stroked his muzzle and gripped the hard bone at the bottom of his nostrils between her finger and thumb. He followed her with such placid obedience, Wiri shook his head in disbelief. The gentle plod of his hooves vibrated through the ground into

Wiri's knees as Phoenix led him towards the gate. She kept the whip curled around the fingers of her left hand.

After a moment's hesitation, the other horses followed. Their heads drooped, and the air rang with the sound of their heavy breaths blowing out loose grass seed and condensation. They followed Phoenix and the gelding without question, resembling riding school ponies in an arena.

The gate clanged and Phoenix jogged back to him, careful to slow and greet the mare on arrival. "Hey girlie," she said, her tone bright. She stroked the wide cheek and pushed the matted forelock back through her twitching ears. "Let's get you up, shall we? This is taking too long already. Your baby needs to hurry and meet the world." She took a step back and walked around behind Wiri, brushing her fingers across his shoulders. "Keep a gentle grip on the hoof and see if it turns. If another one appears, grab it. Getting her upright will make everything start moving again." She observed the mare from behind. "Pity she doesn't have a head collar," she remarked. "I could have used it to make her stand."

Wiri exhaled. The protruding amniotic membrane had lost its fluid and become sticky. It welded to his fingers and wrists like glue. "Okay," he said, his words puffing from his lips. "Go."

Phoenix set to work rousing the mare. She pushed on her neck from behind, speaking to her and projecting urgency into the tired, equine brain. "Up you get!" she called, her tone level and confident. "Come on girl. Get on with you!" She pushed and cajoled, patted and persuaded. The mare's ears twitched and her front legs straightened.

Wiri closed his eyes and let his head fall back on his shoulders. The stream of tears from his right eye ceased as though a well ran dry, leaving a sting in their wake. He hung onto the tiny hoof as though his life depended on it. But a steady hum of dread began deep in his chest. "I wish Logan was here," he admitted, his voice louder than he intended. The words emerged as a cry of defeat, as hope for the foal and the mare ebbed into the cracked ground like a futile drizzle in a long drought.

"You don't need him!" Heaving breaths punctuated her ragged sentence as Phoenix shoved against the mare's shoulder. Dust raked up beneath the toes of her boots as she heaved, forming a dense cloud around her head. She dropped onto her knees and forced her fingers beneath the stricken horse's head. "You have me instead!" she yelled. "Up! Up! Your baby needs you to stand!"

The mare lifted her head. She rocked once and then twice, attempting to gain momentum. Then her head hit the fence again and her eyes closed.

56

Centre Pin

"No! We're not doing this!" Phoenix's voice caught as despair infected her. She snatched the coiled whip from the ground and unfurled it, moving away from Wiri far enough to release it with a resounding crack. The mare twitched and her eyes opened. Phoenix cracked it again. The mare strained, diverting the energy from her stomach to her legs. Nature wired her to avoid danger at all costs. A cracking whip constituted a potential threat, even though it didn't touch her.

She swayed as she lifted, balancing her weight on her huge abdomen. Wiri clung to the fragile hoof, and it moved as the mare's centre of gravity shifted. "That's it!" Phoenix yelled. "Wiri, watch out for her feet."

The mare drew her legs beneath her. Fresh hope surged through Wiri as she twitched her front hooves, preparing to dig in and stand. She dragged them one at a time into position, her body swaying as she threatened to lie flat and give up the fight.

"No, you don't!" Phoenix dropped the whip and pressed the advantage, slapping the exposed side of the mare's neck and shoulders. "Up! Come on," she pleaded. "Just stand once. Come on!"

The mare's muzzle dipped to the ground, and she rested, her chin pivoting in the dirt like a digger balanced against the counterweight of its bulk. "Up!" Phoenix demanded. She worried at the mare's neck and shoulders, moving her palm over the newly exposed side of her stomach. "Come on, do it for your baby," she pleaded. "Again!"

The front hooves gained purchase in the dirt and the tendons tightened. She lifted her chest from the floor and the hoof shifted again, twisting beneath Wiri's fingers.

"She's going up!" Elation filled Phoenix's cry. The mare caught hold of her energy and dug in hard. "Get ready, Wiri!"

He tried to stand, alarmed, when he realised he couldn't feel his knees. Numbness had spread through his legs and switched off contact with his brain. He swore, a vile swearword dragged from the annals of the school's changing rooms. Phoenix glanced back at him as the mare's spine arched inwards and she funnelled power into her haunches. Wiri saw the moment Phoenix realised he was in difficulty, his jaw hanging slack and wordless as he saw into the future. The mare would finally rise, batting him aside with her rump. He'd let go of the hoof and be unable to stand, his legs filling with the venom of a hive of tingling bee stings.

Phoenix disappeared from his view and he sensed her hands grip beneath his armpits. "I've got you," she breathed into his ear. His arm muscles ached and his spine had moved beyond the point of pain to a searing, all-consuming agony. He couldn't thank her, the words inaccessible to his tired brain as he hung onto the single hoof as the mare's flanks rose in his vision.

Phoenix grunted as she hoisted Wiri's weight. His brain commanded his feet, trying to place them as they rose as one. The tingling began in his calves as the blood flooded his muscles, gripping every nerve ending in an unforgiving vice. Phoenix extended her arms around his torso, linking her fingers together at his sternum. The hoof twisted in his fingers and he inhaled with enough force to break Phoenix's grip. The mare's tail swished in his face, blinding him with a mass of wiry hair which left stray threads across his sweating cheeks.

"She's up!" Phoenix squeaked in his ear and he couldn't reply. The wide flank arced around as the mare shifted her hooves. They went with her, Phoenix holding Wiri and his feet moving like drums filled with concrete. Every step sent another flutter of agony through his legs until nothing but pain and white noise occupied every corner of his mind.

Then the mare went down again, bending her front legs and plummeting to earth hard. Wiri kept hold of the hoof, but the force threw him sideways until his body twisted and he landed on his knees, his left foot trapped beneath Phoenix's fallen body. His right hand slipped, his fingers opening in an unauthorised release and he cried out in rage. The fingers of his left hand clung to the knotty hoof as though glued to it. The twist in his spine filled his mind with nothing but the sound of his own agony.

"It's okay, it's okay!" Phoenix staggered up behind him and ran to his right side. "Look, look!" she urged. "It worked."

Wiri hacked on the dust in his lungs. He peered through the murk of dirt and tears to see the hoof now joined to a fetlock and a long, wiry shin. Another had joined it. The movement had caused a release, and the mare strained again. Amniotic fluid flooded from her pelvic canal, running up Wiri's forearm and making his bandage slick. He clasped his right hand around the ridges of bone and set his jaw.

Phoenix's hair fluttered against his cheek as she fixed both hands around the exposed shin. Her black curls blocked his view and smothered him with a ticklish cloud of dust and the remnants of his borrowed hair gel. He closed his eyes, focusing on the sensation of her shoulder touching his as they worked in tandem.

"Now!" Phoenix cried. They pulled together, allying with the mare as she dug deep to push her foal into the world. When the contraction stopped, they halted, Wiri relying on Phoenix's direction. "Gentle, gentle," she instructed, turning her head so her cheek brushed his eyebrow.

Wiri nodded his head, unable to speak. A combination of exhaustion, tranquillisers and stress had depleted his energy reserves. He had nothing left, clinging to the protruding hooves because Phoenix hadn't told him yet to let go.

The mare rested for less than ten seconds, her chest heaving and her body rocking from front to back like a tidal swell. The foal's hooves bobbed like a loose catamaran and the teenagers hung on together. With a last heave, something gave deep inside the mare's body and the foal rushed towards them. A tangle of bones hit Wiri in the chest, knocking him backwards onto the dry earth. Phoenix gasped and collapsed across his legs with a groan. "It's out," she breathed. "It's out."

Winded, Wiri stared up at the sky. Fluffy white clouds scudded in front of his face, blurred by his right eye. Laden black ones chased them, rounding them up and spreading them across the mountain like a blanket. "Rain's coming," he murmured, the words sticking in his throat.

"Help me, quick!" Phoenix sounded breathless, her words rimmed with panic. "Get up, Wiri. Help me with this foal."

Wiri rolled onto his side and forced his left arm to take his weight. It took three gargantuan heaves to get himself onto his knees. Phoenix fought the amniotic sac, peeling swathes of it from the foal's body as though trying to order stretchy, uncooperative wool. "I don't think it's breathing," she whispered. "This is bad. This is terrible."

The mare remained on her stomach, her front legs curled around her as though resting. Her muzzle sank to the ground and stayed there, her eyes closed. But she was alive. Wiri scrabbled across the dirt on his knees to reach Phoenix. She cradled the foal's head in her lap and a tear leaked from her left eye and bounced off her cheek.

"Don't give up," Wiri huffed, his ribs painful and his head thudding. "We've come too far." He took the weight of the foal's heavy skull and nudged her to move aside. "Rub its body. Get the circulation going." She obeyed, shifting aside and rubbing her hands over his matted fur. The fluid dried and left his coat spiky and dull.

Wiri lifted the slender muzzle and pulled open the foal's mouth. He scooped out the fluid with his left hand and flattened the lolling tongue to check behind it. "Rub its chest." He turned his head to direct Phoenix, and she obeyed, slipping her hand between the spindly front legs and rocking the tiny body with the rhythmic action. Sharp teeth clamped down over Wiri's sore finger and he yelped. The foal jerked as he withdrew his hand, the bandage an unsightly grey. "Come on!" Wiri pleaded. "I'm not giving mouth to mouth to a dude!"

Phoenix's sudden giggle startled him. "It's a girl," she said. Relief sparkled in her eyes as she met his gaze. "She's good. She's moving."

The mare remained still. Phoenix ran around behind Wiri and dropped to her knees to stroke the wide forehead. The mare's head bounced, but she didn't open her eyes. "I think she's just exhausted." Phoenix blew out a breath.

"She needs to get up soon, though." Wiri kept hold of the long skull, stroking the stubby hairs across the foal's ears. "Help me drag this baby towards her face. I need her out of the way in case she stands and kicks her."

Phoenix returned and together they dragged the foal towards the mare's muzzle. The slender legs gave a feckless thrash as the infant fought against an unknown foe without energy. The mare looked spent, her eyes closed and her ears splayed on either side of her head as though she'd relinquished all natural sense of alertness. A nearby snort signified the watchfulness of the herd as they waited on the other side of the fence. The stamp of a hoof made the mare open her eyes.

"Look at your baby." Phoenix leaned across the foal to stroke the mother's ridged nose. "She's beautiful." The fluffy white foal bobbed her weighty head as though in answer and the mare's ears flicked forward.

Wiri extracted himself from beneath the white body and dragged himself backwards using his arms. When he lost his balance and tipped, he didn't bother to right himself but laid on his back, his arms and legs splayed.

"High five." Phoenix slumped down next to him and gave a light slap to his cheek. She rested her head on his shoulder. "That's what Mac would do."

"Hmmm." Wiri kept his eyes closed. "And I wouldn't have the energy to slap him back."

Phoenix shot upright, placing her hands against his ribs. "Oh, look. She's sniffing her baby."

"Yep." Wiri didn't attempt to open his eyes or rise to a sitting position. "I feel like a steam roller ran over me," he murmured.

Phoenix twisted on her bottom. "You've ripped the stitches in your finger. It's bleeding." She lifted his hand and cradled it in hers. He grunted in response, no longer caring. "We should call your boss again." She wrinkled her nose. "I can't use Mac's phone unless you know the number off by heart."

"It's in my phone." Wiri swallowed, his Adam's apple giving a lazy bob in his scratchy, parched throat. "Back pocket. I left it ringing, but it probably went to voicemail. All he'll hear is grunting."

Phoenix laid his hand on the ground with care. She dug behind him, biting her lip as he groaned in pain. "Sorry. Which back pocket? This one or the other side?"

His eyeballs moved beneath his lids as he tried to remember. "Other one," he replied with a sigh. His lips stretched into a smile. "Front one, actually. Both. Have a good poke around."

Phoenix snorted. "In your dreams. At least I know you're fine." She crawled around his head and shoved at his waist to lift his body enough to dig into his pocket. The phone slid free, bumping against his aching muscles on its way past. Phoenix sat back in the dirt and crossed her legs. "You've broken the screen." She cocked her head, and he opened one eye to see her expression of pity.

He exhaled, his chest falling. "Story of my life," he sighed. "Four steps forward and five steps backwards."

Phoenix nudged his arm with the back of her hand. She frowned at the screen as the first spot of rain left a splat in the centre. "You have me," she concluded without looking up at him. "You need nothing else."

Wiri smiled and forced himself to study the rain clouds gathering above his face. Not only had he hurt his eye and his back, bust his stitches and ruined another set of clothes, he'd also broken his phone. Pay day loomed, and he didn't expect cash to flood his bank account. He sighed as a rabbit shaped black cloud overtook and demolished a streak of white. "I'm so screwed," he breathed.

"Hello?" Phoenix had connected with someone and Wiri heard the one-sided conversation. "Is that Wiri's boss?" She paused while he answered. "Yes, he tried to call earlier, but he couldn't get through to you. The pregnant mare got into difficulty and became cast. We drove up because we thought we could help her. I'm sorry, but I needed to move your cattle and horses, and then we stayed with the mare and helped her to foal." She bit her lower lip and Wiri turned his head to find her staring at him. "I've got a bit of a problem now."

He lifted his hand to tell her he was just resting. A flash of lightning flickered overhead, forking and leaving its imprint on his eyeballs. He lifted his left hand to cover his eyes and noticed the blood staining his middle and index fingers. "Oh, great!" he whispered to the angry God he felt sure hated him.

57

Loading Gate

Wiri rolled onto his stomach and studied the first spots of rain slapping against the earth. They formed craters ringed by dust, reminiscent of the ones he'd seen in a picture book about the moon. His back ached, his head throbbed, his finger bled, and his myriad cuts and bruises smarted in individual waves of pain, which created a general hum. "Ouch," he said with a sigh, seeing how his breaths stirred the grass beneath his face.

"We're okay." Phoenix's hand landed on his shoulder and gave it a gentle pat. "Help is coming."

"I don't care." He closed his eyes and allowed his dire thoughts to sink into the pit of despair, which beckoned him with soft whispers of peace. Then he remembered his mother and released a painful sob. "It's okay, Wiri." Phoenix brushed his hair back from his cheek and peered down at him. "You need a doctor."

"No." He pushed himself up onto his elbows and tried to formulate his next sentence. "Logan doesn't use a doctor," he grumbled.

Phoenix snorted. "Oh goody. Let's be Logan Du Rose, shall we? Hand me a sewing needle and I'll stitch you up in the bathroom with purple tapestry thread. Then we can wonder together why it gets infected and almost needs amputating."

Wiri groaned. "Help me up." Rain spattered his eyelashes, the spots landing heavy on his forehead as he glared at her.

"No." Phoenix narrowed her eyes. "Look." She smiled, and he turned his body with a sigh until he rested on his right elbow.

The mare nuzzled her foal. The baby reached her face upward, eager to make her acquaintance. She dug her tiny front heels into the dirt and rocked as though trying to stand. Phoenix had tied the arms of her jacket around the foal's neck. The hood flapped over the twitching ears and protected her from the rain. The back panel stretched only as far as the slim shoulders and dangled either side of her spine to cover the protruding ribs. She shook her body and the zipper of the jacket tinkled, causing the mare to prick up her ears and peer closer at her jangling offspring.

The rain increased in strength, tipping from the severe clouds like emptying a bucket over their heads. Droplets sparkled in Phoenix's hair and on her eyelashes as she smiled at the foal, satisfaction lifting her shoulders. Wiri rested his cheek against his right hand and watched her enjoyment, his heart swelling enough in his chest to displace the weight of the boulder. "I love you, Phoenix Du Rose," he whispered.

She smiled down at him, her grey irises matching the hue of the storm clouds overhead. In answer, she dipped her body and pressed her lips over his. "I'm glad," she replied. "Because I've loved you forever."

The fingers of her right hand tore at the raggedy grass as though afraid to be still. Wiri covered their dance with his firm grip. He lifted them to his lips and kissed the knuckles. She'd grown cold, and he held her hand against his cheek and tried to infuse her with warmth.

The mare made her first attempt to stand. Phoenix rose to pull the remnants of the white sac from her tail. The last of it contained mucus and placenta, and she let it drop onto the grass like a discarded water balloon. The mare shook herself with a vibration which began at her ears and ended at the tip of her tail. She dropped her muzzle to the foal, encouraging her to follow. The front hooves gained purchase on the slippery ground and for a worrying moment, the foal teetered like a coffee table with the legs kicked out from beneath it.

Wiri rocked back and utilised the momentum to sit up, using his stomach muscles. The relentless downpour welded his shirt to his stomach and chest, exposing the brass belt buckle inherited from his father. Logan had retrieved it from the gully when he searched for his body.

The only thing left of Kane Du Rose.

Phoenix glanced across at it and frowned, but she said nothing. "Help me get her up?" she asked. He nodded and flipped onto his hands and knees, overbalancing as he pushed himself upright. The landscape tilted, and he threw out his hands in front of him to compensate.

"I'm okay," he said, replying to Phoenix's unanswered question. The dirt seemed to jump up to meet him and he only realised he'd listed when Phoenix grabbed his elbow and leaned her weight against him. "I'm good," he said again, not sure whether he intended to reassure her or himself.

"You're not okay," she muttered. "You have a concussion."

"Na." He staggered and trod on her foot. She tutted and caught him as he tried to lift his boot from her instep. Raising his right index finger, he pointed towards the foal.

"I don't think so." Phoenix turned her back on him. "She doesn't want her first human contact to be you face planting her into the dirt."

He blinked and lifted his hand to rub the rain from his eyes. The right one smarted, and he hissed. "Wearing a girl's jacket was her first contact," he mumbled. The words slurred, and he tutted at his ineptness. "Phoe. I don't feel so good."

"Sit down," she instructed. "Before you fall down."

Wiri staggered sideways, before deciding to follow her advice. He dipped his knees and tried to sit, underestimating the distance and dropping straight onto his tail bone. Crying out in agony, he rolled onto his side and straightened his legs. His left hand scrabbled behind him, pressing against the bloom of pain working its way up his spine to his head. "Not again!" he gasped.

In his peripheral vision, he saw Phoenix straddle the jacket-wearing foal. She stuck her hands beneath the furry chest and hauled. The foal's head bobbed four times between Phoenix's chest and chin before finding the spring in her back legs. She shot upright, her poll banging Phoenix in the mouth and her legs wobbling as she tested them.

"You okay?" Wiri grunted, drawing his knees into his stomach.

Phoenix nodded and rose. She let the foal totter from between her legs before turning towards him. "Bit my tongue." She wiped blood from her mouth with the back of her hand.

The mare made an affectionate rumble deep in her chest and nuzzled her daughter's skimpy mane. She pushed her lips over the baby's withers and rubbed her opposite shoulder with her chin. The foal scented the let-down of her milk and went in search of it, wobbling like a Saturday night drunk in heels too high for her.

The engine of Leilah's truck arrived as a vibration through the ground which reached Wiri's ear. He didn't need to announce them. Phoenix brushed her soaked fringe from her eyes and licked the rain from her lips. "A dark haired, furious looking giant is running towards us," she said, keeping her voice low. "Is that okay, or should I punch him?"

Wiri sighed. "Just punch him," he said, pushing a blade of yellowing grass from his mouth. "Make it count."

"He's waving to us." Phoenix wiped her mouth again, spreading blood across her chin. "Should I still punch him?"

"Yep." Wiri breathed out a gush of painful air and felt grateful that Logan Du Rose's stock men couldn't see him rolling around in the paddock like a stunned mullet. "I hate my life," he grumbled to no one in particular.

58

HAND NOTCH

Leilah remained on the mountainside with the mare and foal. "I'll walk them back to the house as soon as she's ready," she said, her eyes bright and shining. "I'll put them in the paddock we set aside for foaling." She reached across to squeeze Phoenix's shoulder. "I'm so grateful," she gushed. "You've done an amazing job."

"Seline needs to move her horse." Vaughan's words contained an edge, and he jerked his head at his wife. "I've asked her twice. Maybe she'll do it for you."

Leilah winced and nodded. She tugged her mobile phone from her jacket pocket and her fingers moved across the screen.

Vaughan leaned down to offer Wiri his hand. "I'll get the doctor to meet us at your place," he said, his tone gruff. He grazed his upper lip with his lower teeth as he considered Phoenix's presence. "You coming with us?"

"Yep." Phoenix grabbed Wiri's elbow and helped to haul him to a standing position. She tucked his arm beneath hers and clasped his filthy hand in her fingers. The stiffness of her stance conveyed her anxiety at the looming explanation for Vaughan's benefit. Wiri smiled at her, telling her not to worry.

They traversed the paddocks in silence, the truck bumping over the rough ground. Phoenix took the outer seat, leaving Wiri trapped next to Vaughan's muscular body. She hopped in and out to deal with the gates. As they lurched across the final swathe of grass, Wiri noticed the water tank in the distance. Yellow crime scene tape fluttered in the breeze, the rain causing portions of it to weld together as it twisted and arced. A shiver ran through him, and Vaughan frowned and glanced sideways to observe his discomfort.

Phoenix jumped from the truck and slammed the door behind her again. Vaughan cleared his throat. "Thanks for what you did for the mare," he said. He rested his hands on the top of the steering wheel and leaned forward to rub his eye sockets with his blunt thumbs. "We met with the Health and Safety inspector. Had to put my phone on silent."

"Right." Wiri turned his body to face him, but the minuscule space between their thighs made the moment too intimate. He turned back to the windscreen. The wiper blades shuddered across the glass and, through their ritualised dance, he watched Phoenix struggling with the final gate catch. "Does he want to see me?"

"She." Vaughan corrected him. "And yes. She does." He exhaled and ran a hand over his forehead. "She's liaising with the police. Who knew a simple job like fixing up a water tank would cost one life and almost another?"

"Two others." Wiri frowned. "You got hurt too." He filtered the question before he asked it, forcing out the judgement and the rushed conclusion and keeping his tone level. "Was Pastor Larry related to Donovan Hendricks?"

"Yeah." Vaughan nodded. "Brothers. Estranged. I don't think Larry realised he lived here until after he accepted the parish."

"Right." Wiri cleared his throat. "He never mentioned it."

Vaughan shrugged. "He probably thought everyone knew. Donovan moved here twenty years ago. He had a wife and a couple of kids back then. She shifted out and took the kids with her."

Wiri closed his eyes and leaned back against the worn leather. Larry never mentioned his connection with the dead man, and it struck him as odd. Yet he'd laboured the issue of his alcoholism and the fact that Donovan Hendricks knew about it. Wiri sighed. He would know if Mac developed a drinking problem, so what was Larry's angle? Why keep the link a secret from him when the rest of the town knew?

Phoenix got the gate open and Vaughan nodded to her as he drove through the gap. She closed it behind them and walked the short distance into the driveway. Vaughan eased the truck around the front of the house and the brakes squealed as he pulled up next to the porch steps. "Doctor is on his way," he said, knocking the gear lever into neutral. "Tell him I don't mind paying for his visit." He exhaled. "Or Leilah will, seeing as she's bailing me out nowadays."

"How's that going?" Wiri stared at the rivulets running down the windscreen. Like a landscape of tributaries, they continued their journey without regard for anyone else's drama. He wrinkled his nose and gave a shudder. "Sorry. None of my business."

"Na, it's fine. You were just the catalyst, really." Vaughan pulled on the handbrake and turned the key to silence the engine. "It's good. Leilah wants to take an active role. She had big plans when we married, and I didn't let her do any of it. Failure kind of froze me in place. I'd lost control worse than she believed and I thought I'd lose her if I came clean."

"But you didn't."

"No." Vaughan shook his head and his lips rose in a smile which appeared genuine. He glanced at Wiri sideways. "I bred that mare from a second generation stallion out of one of Hector's. Red belonged to Leilah's father. You live in Hector's house." His lips twisted in thought. "Leilah thinks we should turn both farms back into a horse stud. You just saved our first foal."

Wiri winced. "Wow," he said with a sigh. "Not much responsibility then. That had all the hallmarks of being a disaster. You know that, don't you?"

"Yeah." Vaughan swallowed. "Her death would have cursed it from the start." He shrugged. "I'm more grateful to you than you know. I won't forget it." Phoenix popped up on to the porch, her boots clicking against the wood. She dived beneath the overhang and wrapped her arms around herself. "Who's the girl?" Vaughan raised a speculative eyebrow. "She looks young."

"Yeah, she's my cousin," Wiri replied. "She's fifteen." He raised his good hand and flapped it between them. "Don't worry. I'll sort everything out. You won't need to intervene."

"Okay." Vaughan gave a definitive nod. "I'll have to trust you. The last thing I need right now is an angry father showing up here with the police in tow."

Both turned towards the sound of car tyres crunching over the driveway. A sedan pulled up in the space usually occupied by Wiri's truck. Through the rain spatter on the windscreen, he saw the doctor emerge. The man sat his briefcase sideways on his head and dashed towards the porch.

"Call me," Vaughan instructed, as Wiri shifted across to the passenger seat and pushed open the door. "Let me know how you're doing."

"I'll be fine," Wiri promised. He turned to face Vaughan. "Maybe we could get back to normal tomorrow?"

"Deal." Vaughan sighed and lifted his hand to touch the stitches at his crown. "I'll think of some jobs that won't kill both of us."

"Thanks." Wiri dropped from the truck and hustled towards the porch steps. He stopped and turned to face the driver's window. Vaughan obliged by winding it down using the handle.

"I'll text Aunty Liza about your contract with Hendricks. Email it through to me."

Vaughan nodded and when Wiri laboured up the porch steps, he found Phoenix already chatting with the doctor.

She paused to catch his hand. "Keys," she demanded, holding out her palm.

The doctor ambled inside, ignoring the shoe shelf and exempting himself wordlessly from removing his boots. He followed Wiri to the kitchen. Phoenix disappeared along the hallway after kicking off her boots outside. Wiri heard the click of the airing cupboard door and she reappeared with a towel. "Dry yourself with this," she instructed. "You're shivering." She frowned at the damp footprints dotted over the floorboards and tiles and then at her socks. "Is it okay if I get a shower?" she asked. "Can I borrow some stuff?"

Wiri nodded and gave her a smile of gratitude. He used the towel to dry his hair and face as the doctor opened his briefcase on the kitchen counter. Then he stood back and observed Wiri with his arms folded. "Well, Mr Kingii. You're certainly in the wars, aren't you?"

"It was nothing," he replied. "I'm wasting your time and Vaughan's money."

The doctor jerked his head towards Wiri's filthy hands and arms. "I'm not sure which is yours and which is equine, to be honest," he said. A frown bisected his dark features. "And it's pointless me bandaging you up just for you to take a shower and soak it all." He dug in his bag and smiled to himself as his fingers emerged, clasping two white packets. "Good thinking, Gareth," he mused. He waggled them between him and Wiri. "My last two waterproof plasters." He glanced at his watch and then swivelled his head to admire Jet's coffee machine. "How easy is it to work that thing?"

"I'll do it." Wiri pushed away from the counter and trod a wavering route towards the sink. "I'll wash my hands first."

"I'd like you to wash more than that!" Gareth's eyes widened. He pointed to the front of Wiri's tee shirt. "You look like you've danced with an axe murderer."

"Afterbirth." He blew out a breath and pinched the hem between the fingers and thumb of his right hand. "I'm destined to lose all my clothes in this God forsaken place."

Gareth chuckled. "It most definitely isn't God forsaken, my friend. This is where he puts his very special subjects."

Wiri grunted. "It doesn't feel like it." He jerked his head towards the pantry. "The capsules are in there unless Jet got fed up and hid them somewhere else. Phoe can make you a coffee as soon as she's dressed." He glanced at the wall clock, blinking in surprise to discover day had already marched into mid-afternoon. "Are you sure you have time to stay?"

"I'm taking a break." Gareth pulled out a dining chair and sank into it. "I've seen eleven patients at the surgery, visited the police station twice and done three laps of the town on home visits." He sighed and pulled his phone from his pocket. "I'll just text my receptionist and ask her not to make any appointments for the next hour." His fingers worked a crazy formation across the screen before stilling. "How's the head?" he asked Wiri.

"Sore." Wiri sighed. "I just get real tired.

"What about your back? Did the activator help with the pain at all?"

"I'm sure it did." Wiri rested his palm on the counter and then jerked it away at the sight of his stained fingers. "The whole incident was a nightmare. I can't wait until it's over."

"Oh." Gareth winced. "So, it's not over then? Tane still thinks you killed Donovan Hendricks?"

Wiri shrugged. "I don't know. He found my shirt in there with him, so I guess I'll remain a suspect until he finds someone different to blame. But for what it's worth, he agreed with you. It's unlikely I somehow fitted Hendricks through that little hole in the top of the tank. Not with my injuries. Especially if he was still alive when it happened. I'm struggling to heft the bales at the moment." His fingers opened and closed at the memory of his difficulty holding onto the tiny hoof. He shook his head in disgust at himself.

"He wasn't alive when he went into the tank." Gareth cocked his head. "But you didn't hear that from me."

The water pipes overhead clunked as Phoenix turned off the shower. Wiri stared at the doctor. "Someone killed him and then put him in the tank?"

"I can neither confirm nor deny your surmising." His lips flattened into a line. "I just pronounced him dead. The Hamilton crowd determines the rest of the details.

Wiri blew out a breath and chewed his lower lip. "So, he could have died somewhere else altogether?"

Gareth shrugged. "Or next to the tank. But as far as I'm aware, a colleague at the coroner's office says he didn't drown. He had a nasty cut over his left eye and someone imprinted their foot in his back too."

Wiri stared at the ceiling and attempted to order his thoughts. "I remember there being water up to my knees when they pulled me out of the tank." He closed his eyes, and the experience returned as water flowing down his face and soaking through to his underwear. When he opened them again, he found Gareth observing him like a man watching interesting bacteria through a microscope lens. He exhaled, forcing out the pent up breath and encouraging his shoulders to relax. "I've known a twenty-five thousand litre tank fill overnight with a decent rain." He cocked his head and frowned at Gareth. "Did Tane call you out to the scene?"

"Yes. I didn't go down into the tank, but I looked inside. The deceased floated face down in the water and a volunteer fireman went in after him."

"Which fireman?" Wiri swallowed, imagining forcing himself to enter the dark concrete cave for a second time and finding Mac or Phoenix. "Not Larry?"

"Pastor Larry? No. The mechanic from the local garage. I think his name is Neil."

"How much water did you see?" Wiri narrowed his eyes and cocked his head. "When they brought me out, I remember hearing someone say they'd disconnected the spouting from the barn roof. The level should have remained the same." He dipped forward to draw a line across his knee. "About this high. No one would have reconnected it. We still need to get Vaughan's ladder out somehow. It can't stay in there or it'll rust and pollute the water."

Gareth turned his head and viewed Wiri sideways, as though testing his thoughts before he said them out loud. "That's interesting," he mused. "Because I'm positive the fire officers measured the depth, and it was over half full. No one could stand up in it. They winched the deceased out of the water. The aperture was so narrow, they had to pass the body up first while the fireman waited on the line beneath him. It was too deep to stand."

59

Steel Ears

Wiri blew out a ragged breath and considered the doctor's words. "Then someone reconnected the spouting after my accident." He licked his lips. "Why would they do that?"

Gareth shook his head. "It makes no sense. Unless they didn't want anyone to look into it and figured no one would mess around with a full tank."

A door closed in the distance and Wiri sensed the vibration of Phoenix moving around the other end of the house. A mental calculation revealed he had two remaining sets of clothes in his duffel bag. He wondered which one she'd borrow as she'd arrived with nothing.

He turned his mind back to the mystery. "Bodies rise, don't they?" he asked the doctor. "They fill with gas and water and other stuff and rise to the surface?"

Gareth stared hopefully at the coffee machine. "Yes. But what difference would it make whether the tank contained a little water or a lot of it?"

Wiri blew out a breath. "You can only see into the tank through the inspection manhole unless you actually go down into it. But it is possible to see most of the water surface by leaning in and directing a torch beam around the area."

"Oh." Gareth waggled his eyebrows. "I see where you're going with this. If the tank filled right up to the lip of the inspection hole, it would cut down the visibility. The lower the water, the better the view."

"Yup." Wiri put a hand up to the back of his head and released a sigh. "There's still the possibility that the body might float to just beneath the hatch, but it's a one in a few thousand chance." He shrugged. "My uncle could work out the odds mathematically, but I suspect it would be a long shot."

"The roof is pitched. Would that matter?" Gareth's attention switched to Phoenix as she padded into the kitchen. She wore one of Wiri's shirts and a pair of his jeans clung to her hips. She'd turned up the cuffs to stop the legs dragging along the floor.

"No." Wiri sent his mind to the water tanks at his uncle's farm and the hotel he owned in the valley. He lifted his right hand, gesticulating as he worked through the problem. "With our tanks at home, they set the inspection hatch into the roof, which had a very slight pitch to it. You pull off the hatch and slide it sideways. It's easy to stick your head inside the tank and shine a torch around the surface of the water. You'd see most of it. But Vaughan's tanks are different."

Phoenix gave a shudder and smiled at the doctor. "I hate those tanks," she admitted. "Papa went to work once and Mama said the water smelled stinky. My brother pulled off the lid and found a dead rat floating on the surface."

Wiri smiled at the memory. Mac tried to retrieve it using a fishing net. He'd almost fallen through the hole and accidentally dropped his net. Logan later removed the rat and put chemical tablets in the water, but they'd needed to wait until the next drought to retrieve the net. He jerked as Phoenix nudged his arm. "The doctor would like coffee. Should I make you one as well?" She wrinkled her nose. "You smell. Maybe get a shower?"

Wiri nodded, but his tongue remained still as he pondered Vaughan's water tank. "The inspection funnel looks like a safety feature. You can't get into the tank without going down deliberately. I doubt you could just fall into one of those. It sticks about a metre above the roof. But it also stops you from seeing most of the water surface from above, unless you can somehow dangle half your body into it and get past the lip at the end of the tunnel."

"Rather you than me, thanks." Gareth cheered as Phoenix presented Jet's container of coffee capsules and waited while he selected a strong Colombian blend. With the sound of the machine firing to life, he pointed at Wiri. "Grab a shower, my friend. I'll drink my coffee and then inspect your injuries." He waggled his eyebrows. "Again. Your eye is watering. Be careful not to irritate it with soap."

Wiri went for a shower. He stripped off his filthy clothes and shoved them into the washing machine. Phoenix had already loaded in hers and added powder and fabric softener. He stood in his boxer shorts and pressed his nose to the glass in the rear door. The tiny pieces of the puzzle nudged at his tired brain. His breath fogged up the glass. "Someone reconnected the tank to make it fill," he sighed. Lifting his right hand, he drew a circle in the condensation and added a rectangular barn with an apex roof. After the addition of a stick man, he ran a line from the barn to the image of the tank. Another stick man laid on the ground with his legs in the air. Wiri wrinkled his nose. "Who are you?" he breathed. "And are you the same person who wanted me dead?"

Phoenix had run off the cold water from the system, so when Wiri stepped beneath the shower flow he enjoyed the instant heat. The tray beneath his feet filled with grass clippings, dust, and the orange clay which covered the mountainside. His finger smarted as he used shower gel to wash his body and hair. Tentative fingers against his skull revealed the unfortunate bald patch and the sutures. He grimaced and wondered how long it would take for the hair to grow back again. Phoenix had seen him in almost every humiliating position possible during their time in the Du Rose household, but their changed status made things different. He worried about what she thought and quailed against her judgement. As he towelled dry on the damp mat outside the shower, he recognised the seed of rejection he unwittingly nurtured in his soul. He wished he knew how to banish it.

After cleaning up the bathroom one handed, Wiri padded to his bedroom with a towel wrapped around his waist. Phoenix had stripped his bed and bundled the sheets next to the door. He felt reluctant to touch them, as though they might bear the contamination of Seline's intent to seduce him. He retrieved the last set of clothes from his duffel bag and sat on the mattress to push his feet into his socks. His body aches had settled into a low hum and he couldn't imagine life without them, even though experience promised time would banish them eventually. "Good job I'm not like my father," he whispered to himself, listing one of the few positives from his genetics. He hadn't inherited the haemophilia which the female line had carried to many of their men. A stab of pain in the back of his head made him catch his breath, and then he remembered Phoenix. She carried it too, and the reminder sobered him.

Chatter drifted from the other end of the house and forced Wiri to hurry. He arrived in the kitchen wearing a tee shirt and jeans. Phoenix looked up from her coffee and smiled at him. The doctor tucked into a plate of biscuits with his drink. "I hope these were yours," she said, jerking her head towards the open packet. "I found them on the middle shelf of the pantry."

Wiri smiled without commitment. They belonged to Jet. Somehow, without meaning to, Wiremu Du Rose had turned into the worst flatmate imaginable. He'd never wanted to be that person, but had eased into the role with such effortlessness that it bothered him. Leilah's refund for the credit card bill had hit his account while he slept. He consoled himself that at least now he could replace Jet's coffee capsules and his biscuits.

Gareth rose after shoving a biscuit into his mouth whole. He spoke around it as though in a rush. His gulping swallow sounded painful. "Head first," he ordered, tapping Wiri's shoulder to make him turn. He parted the damp black curls and made a series of low grunts and murmurs. "You've hit it again," he concluded. "The bleeding has stopped, and the stitches held. You're fortunate."

Phoenix stared up at them, her eyes wide. "He fell backwards while we were helping the mare."

Gareth grunted and tugged at the hem of Wiri's shirt. "Lift this up so I can see your back."

Wiri shot a frown towards Phoenix and her eyes glinted. He pursed his lips and willed her not to say that she'd seen it all before. It mattered to him what Gareth thought, and the sudden realisation intrigued him. He was building acquaintances of his own from a stock of people not influenced by his surname or his uncle's power. A flush of warmth flared in his chest at the notion of him creating his own independence. He smiled and looked up to find Phoenix still watching him.

"The bruise is spreading, but it's also changing colour."

"That's good, isn't it?" Wiri infused the question with hope.

"Where exactly does it begin?" the doctor mused. "I should probably look at the site."

"No thanks." Wiri shook off his gentle pressing of the muscle around his spine. "I'm not dropping my undies again."

Phoenix snorted and opened her mouth to speak. His glare in her direction stopped her. She wore his last pair of boxer shorts and she knew it because she'd taken them from the duffel bag. The rest were swishing around in the washing machine or still damp over the clothes airer in the laundry.

"Fingers." Gareth waited while Wiri lifted his left hand. He'd stripped off the disgusting tape before taking his shower. The doctor stepped back with a sigh. "I'll dress your hand," he said, turning to lift one of the white wrappers from the table. "You need to keep it dry or it'll get infected. I'll leave your head alone, as that's healing well. You might benefit from some more chiropractic work on your back before I leave." Wiri imagined himself prostrate across the kitchen table and winced. Gareth cocked his head. "You don't want it?"

"No, I do. Can you do it while I stand up, like last time?"

"Definitely." Gareth fought the paper sleeve for the plaster, using his fingernails to lever up the flap. "At some point, see a professional. I can recommend a lady in Hamilton. Bones and muscles get crushed and move out of alignment. Not fixing them leads to long term health issues." He used his strange clicker to press the sorest spots along Wiri's spine.

Then he got to work on Wiri's other ills, instructing him to lift his finger while he wrapped the bandage around the stitches. He used tape from his briefcase to strap the middle finger to the index to stop it bending. He inspected Wiri's sore eye and concluded it hadn't suffered any long term damage.

Slurping the last of his coffee, the doctor closed his bag with a snap. "Oh, you might need a test for giardia along the line," he said. "Tank water is hazardous. Rural families don't know they're drinking a bacterial and parasitic soup when they don't install a proper filter."

Phoenix frowned. "Oh, yuk. Papa has a UV filter at home." Her gaze strayed to Wiri's face. "But I guess you accidentally drank it while you waited for rescue." She gave a shudder. "Bird poop off the roof and all the crap in the pipes."

"Thanks for that." Wiri shrugged. "It's not like I have any other medical problems to worry about."

"You'll be fine." Gareth snagged another biscuit and kept it in his hand as he headed towards the hallway and the front door. "Some people in this town have worse problems. I hospitalised a man last month who'd picked up a giardia bug in his stomach. He'd had symptoms for over twenty years and never linked it to the water. A course of antibiotics and he's finally making less trips to the bathroom." His eyebrows waggled as he tugged on the handle of the front door. "He should have known better, too."

"Why?" Phoenix followed them, her natural curiosity demanding all the details. "Why should he know better? Is he a doctor?"

Gareth stepped out onto the deck and grimaced at the wet sheen on his car. Rain fell in sheets like a curtain shaken out by a divine hand. "No," he replied. "He made water tanks for a living. You can't do that for over fifty years and not know the risks."

"Who is he?" The thought sprang into Wiri's mind like a sunburst. If he could speak to a tank maker, he could test his theory about the motive of whoever reconnected the pipe after Hendricks died. They would know the answer.

Gareth chuckled and waved his hand behind him. "Sorry, my friend. Patient confidentiality. I've already said too much." He turned and gave Phoenix a mock salute. "Thanks for the hospitality. I hope you stick around. Perhaps we'll meet again."

Wiri closed the door behind him and leaned against it. "Damn," he breathed. "I could have asked the tank maker about the water pipe." His brow furrowed, and he stared at the slender girl in front of him. "What did he mean about you sticking around?"

60

Front Strap

"**N**o! No! No!" Wiri defended his stance as he found fresh linen in the airing cupboard and remade his bed.

Phoenix tucked the bottom sheet under the mattress and protested. "I can't go back now! Papa will kill me and then he'll come for you! We'll talk to them together, but afterwards I'll stay here with you."

Wiri snorted. He stuffed the fluffy duvet into a clean cover and shook it out flat. "I'm not ready, Phoe! I need to earn enough money to sustain us before we go off grid."

"You're not listening!" Phoenix sank onto the bed, preventing him from fastening the buttons at the edge of the quilt cover. "I don't want to go off grid. You wanted to speak to Papa, and I should have let you. I want everything out in the open so we can plan our lives together. We can't live in secret forever."

"Not forever." Wiri sank down next to her and slipped an arm around her shoulders. He pressed his lips to her temple as she sagged against him. "Just for long enough for his anger to settle."

Phoenix snorted. "Are we still talking about Logan Du Rose?" She tipped her face up and her grey irises glinted like the stormy sky beyond the bedroom window. "After his anger settles is the dangerous part. That's when he works out how to get even."

Wiri groaned. His failing courage refused the call to arms in the face of his uncle's might. Guilt still lapped at the edges of his soul, reminding him of the debt he owed both Hana and Logan. He closed his eyes and squeezed the bridge of his nose between his finger and thumb. The doctor had left without giving him any more pain pills. Only Phoenix seemed to care that he had the symptoms of concussion. "This is a mess," he whispered.

"I'm sorry." Phoenix leaned her head against his shoulder. "It's because I'm here, isn't it?"

"No. It's your age. He won't believe we love each other. Even if he did, he'll hate it because of my father. And I'm older than you, so he'll assume I've manipulated you." Wiri sighed, wondering how he ever convinced himself The Plan had any merit or hope of succeeding.

"I think you're judging him too harshly." A defensive tone entered Phoenix's voice. A daddy's girl, she'd protect Logan despite her earlier statement to the contrary.

"Not where you're concerned." Defeat rounded his shoulders. "What are we doing, Phoe? This is crazy."

"I'm not giving up, so get used to it." She tossed her head and her damp curls whipped against his arm. "I've had the worse summer of my life and still didn't quit. I refuse to do it now, because things are difficult."

Wiri closed his eyes against the realisation that his perception of difficulty and Phoenix's didn't align. His future contained a world of pain at her expense and he didn't think she fully comprehended it. Logan Du Rose would not allow the illegitimate offspring of his most hated family member to waltz away with his most prized possession. His first born.

"I need to buy some stuff in town." Wiri rubbed his eyes with his right hand. He blinked to clear the scratchiness from the injured one.

"Okay. I'll come with you." Phoenix wrinkled her nose. "Is there a shop that sells clothes?" She patted the jeans with her palms. "Do I look weird? Should I stay here?"

An image of Leilah's daughter rose into his mind and he tensed. "No, I don't want to leave you here alone. Seline might come back for her phone. Or that man could call again."

"About that." Phoenix shifted her palm from her own thigh to his. "What was that sound in the background? And what did he mean about not being able to just phone her whenever he wanted? Why does she have to answer his calls when he says she must?"

Wiri blew out a breath. "I don't know. Grab the phone and I'll drive us into town. The tranquillisers have worn off, but I'll take some paracetamol before we leave. There's a cafe in the main street and a supermarket. We can work it out while we get some food and afterwards, you can go clothes shopping."

His phone vibrated on the bedside table where he'd plugged it in to charge. He picked it up and inspected the screen. "It's your mum," he said, his tone laden with foreboding. "This isn't fair to Hana, Phoe. She doesn't deserve this."

Phoenix blew out a sad breath and nodded. "Okay. Let's drive into town and I'll call her on Mac's phone. Help me think of something to say."

Wiri forced a smile onto his lips. "Deal. Let's enjoy our last supper together before Armageddon." He held out his good hand to her and helped her to rise. She wrapped her arms around his waist and pressed her cheek against his chest. A stopwatch hung over their heads, the minutes ticking past until their worlds imploded. The Plan lost its idealism but none of its hope.

The rain pounded against the glass outside, melting away the footprints beneath the window which they'd all meant to search for at first light.

61

Sight Blade

T hey retrieved Wiri's truck from the horse paddock and he drove into town. The main street buzzed with activity.

Farmers strode through the rain wearing shorts and gumboots, camouflage jackets hanging to the backs of their knees. The rural uniform meant Phoenix didn't stand out in Wiri's oversized clothing. He left the truck in the angled parking outside the cafe and led Phoenix through the front door. The place resembled an ant's nest, with bodies moving around and almost every table filled. The bell jangled and Ted looked up from his corner.

"Ah, have you come to make me decent coffee?" he demanded. All conversation ceased and knives and forks stilled, as though waiting for the response.

Wiri winced as Mari appeared through the archway from the kitchen. She carried two plates filled with toast and scrambled eggs to a table of men talking in lowered voices. "Shut up, old man!" she barked across at Ted. Her gaze coasted from Wiri to Phoenix and back again before she smiled. "What can I get you?" she asked.

"Same as them, please?" Wiri eyed the fluffiness of the eggs as the men unwrapped cutlery from folded napkins. His stomach growled.

"And me." Phoenix smiled at Mari, offering encouragement after Ted's cruel jibe. She slipped her arm around Wiri's waist and tucked her fingers into the back pocket of his jeans. Mari's lips quirked up at the edges as Phoenix staked her possession. Wiri's cheeks flushed as he dug in his front pocket for his wallet. He tried and failed to fathom the undercurrent of feminine communication, no wiser when he gave up than when he started.

Phoenix released him and they wandered to the only free table. She pulled out a chair, her arm brushing the back of Ted's jacket. The old man spun on his stool to eye her with a frown. He jerked his head towards Mari. "She's in a snit because she got stopped by the cops. The postman just bought the ticket." His lips parted to reveal his pink gums.

"Shut up!" Mari appeared and snatched the mug from in front of him. "Don't be telling everyone my business, old man!" She bore the mug away to the kitchen and Ted turned back to the newspaper laid out before him. The world continued through the window in front of him and he ignored it.

"What was all that about at the cash register?" Wiri dipped forward. "Cuddling up to me in public." He jerked his head in Ted's direction to indicate the eavesdropper.

Phoenix nodded and replied in a whisper. "There's a photo on the wall behind the counter. Didn't you see it?"

Wiri shifted his gaze in a casual arc and took in the wall she referred to, noticing the picture of Leilah and Seline on horseback. He pursed his lips and stared at the knots in the table's grain. "Ah. You think Mari might be related?"

Phoenix shrugged. "I don't care. That skank isn't coming anywhere near you again." Her eyes flashed and her jaw tightened. "It's another reason I don't want to leave you here alone."

"You don't trust me?" The words caught in his throat. "If I'd been interested, do you think you'd have found me still standing in the doorway?"

She crinkled her face into a sneer. "Maybe I should have hung around and waited to find out what you'd do," she bit. Her tone rose to a hiss. "Then it would all be over."

"What would?" Wiri demanded. He jumped as Mari placed two mugs between them.

"On the house," she said. She grinned to reveal black spaces from missing front teeth. They stared at the floating scum on top of the coffee and floundered.

"Thanks," Wiri managed, his tone faltering. "You didn't need to do that."

Mari shrugged and spun away, her steps lighter than her years dictated.

Phoenix leaned forward and lowered her voice to a hiss. "Do you think she heard what I said about her skank relative?"

"No." Wiri sighed. He studied Phoenix's flushed cheeks and reached across the table to take her hand. She'd pressed her fingers through the handle of the mug and he pried them free. "Do you want this to all be over, Phoe?"

"No." Her eyes sparkled with unshed tears. A gulp punctuated the sentence. "It's all too hard. I didn't think this through properly. I've abandoned everything on the strength of a kiss and it seems so stupid and yet so right." She appealed to him for understanding. "I left Mikaere for you." Wiri watched her swallow and knew she thought of her prized horse waiting for her in his paddock. He'd been her only genuine friend at the disastrous summer camp and she'd abandoned him at a moment's notice.

For him.

For his promises.

Wiri exhaled. "We need to eat and then talk about what we're going to do next." His hand shook as he clasped her fingers. "I can't come home with you until the police sort out who tried to hurt me and who killed Hendricks."

"I think that girl hit Vaughan over the head and closed the lid on you." Phoenix lifted the mug with her free hand and sipped the liquid. She recoiled. "Do you think that lady reuses washing up water to make the coffee?" she whispered.

Wiri's mind filled with bigger issues than Mari's beverage making skills. He gnawed on the inside of his cheek. "I accused Seline of locking me in the tank," he said. He spoke so quietly, Phoenix bobbed her head to lip read. Ted shifted behind them and she glanced up at him. Then her expression brightened, and she shook off his grasp of her hand.

"Sign." She performed the action with her fingers and he grinned. Mac's deafness demanded they all learn the rudiments of sign language for his benefit. His cochlear implants had given him some hearing, but he still relied on lip reading and signing, especially in crowded, confusing situations.

Wiri nodded and lifted his right hand. He curled his fingers into a ball, raising his index finger to signify his agreement. They continued their discussion in silence, safe in the knowledge Ted couldn't overhear their business.

"Why would Seline try to hurt you?" Phoenix asked. She spread her hands in question, forced to spell out the letters of Seline's name against her palm. She blinked as Mari set their plates in front of them. "Thank you," she said out loud, but her widening eyes towards Wiri communicated her gratitude they'd switched to sign.

"She hates Vaughan," Wiri replied. "His farm is in trouble and she wants it to fail. Hurting him and trapping me attracted interest from the wrong quarters."

The bell over the door jangled as the group of men left. They waved to Mari and shrugged hoods over their heads as they dashed from the safety of the overhang to their waiting utility vehicles. Table by table, the cafe emptied until just a few die hards remained.

Phoenix rolled her eyes. "It's too hard to sign while eating," she said with a sigh. Her black lashes fluttered and when she looked up, Wiri met her gaze with a smile.

"This is nice," he agreed, swallowing before speaking. He swivelled in his chair and looked around the cafe before dipping to peer at Ted. The old man snoozed on his stool, his body listing and his eyes closed. His cap had slipped to one side to make him look like a cutesy shelf ornament. The newspaper lay open on the counter in front of him, a brown ring covering the headline where he'd rested his mug. He'd propped his elbow on the counter and his chin balanced on the heel of his hand. Wiri caught Phoenix's eye and jerked his head towards him. She turned and winced.

"That looks precarious," she whispered. Her fringe tangled with her eyelashes and she lifted her shoulders and shook with silent laughter.

Wiri bit his lip and enjoyed the moment of levity. "Wonder how many times he's fallen off his stool," he remarked, keeping his voice low.

Phoenix shrugged and stabbed a piece of toast onto her fork. She used the knife to add a fluffy ball of scrambled egg and closed her eyes as she popped it into her mouth. "I'm so hungry," she admitted. "It seems ages since yesterday's lunch."

62

REPEATING

"Tell me about your conversation with Ma and Uncle Logan." Wiri savoured his toast, disappointed to look down and realise he'd eaten it all. He watched as Phoenix slid a diagonally cut section of hers onto his plate. "No, you need it."

"I just want the egg."

He jumped as something touched his calf beneath the table. Then he smiled. She hooked her toes around the back of his leg and continued eating. "I missed you, but it wasn't just that. You sounded odd on the phone." She tilted her head sideways to glare at him. "Now I know why, having seen your injuries. I wanted to buy something and post it to you, so I went to see Mac yesterday after school. I asked if he knew your address." She waved her fork in the air. "He acted odd about it. Made excuses, which got me thinking."

"Right." Wiri exhaled. He lifted the donated triangle of toast in his fingers and bit into it. "And Phoenix Du Rose doesn't like mysteries, so she started hunting."

She shrugged, but didn't dismiss his observation. "I waited until he took a shower and borrowed his phone." Her lips twitched. "I don't imagine my brother will leave such a simple code on his devices in the future." She lifted her fork and peered at the cloud of egg pressed over the prongs. "I read your texts to Mac, got the address, and realised things weren't as you made us believe. I tried to speak to Mama and Papa about it, but foolishly led with how I felt about you. That's when it all turned to custard. So, I left. I used the GPS tracker once I got off the bus." She gave a light shrug. "And here I am."

Wiri couldn't help the grin which spread across his lips. "And here you are," he repeated.

They both jumped as Ted snorted and shifted on his elbow. He listed sideways as though about to pitch off his stool before righting himself with a grunt. Phoenix pressed her lips together to prevent the laugh escaping. Wiri glanced across at Mari and saw her shake her head, an irritated frown pulling her brows together. He exhaled and dipped forward to speak to Phoenix. "What do you think we should do?"

"About me, or about the man who died?"

A dimple appeared in Wiri's left cheek as he tilted his head at her. "We both know what we have to do about you. No, I meant about Hendricks. How do I prove my innocence?"

"Can you leave town?" Phoenix pushed the fork between her teeth.

"Yeah." Wiri turned down his lips into a nonchalant expression. "The cops only say that in the movies. They have no legislative power to prevent you from going anywhere unless they detain or charge you with a crime. If you're under serious investigation, they might ask for custody of your passport to stop you from running abroad."

"Do you have your passport with you?" Phoenix quirked her left eyebrow in surprise.

"No." The curls of Wiri's fringe bounced as he shook his head. "What's the point? I'm not leaving you." He winced and drew his phone from his pocket. "I promised Vaughan I'd contact Aunty Liza for him. He's emailed through the contract, so I'll forward it to her." He finished the message and pushed his phone back into his pocket. "Hopefully she won't contact Uncle Logan. I've asked her not to."

Phoenix blew out a long breath and surveyed the cafe. Another group of farmers finished their lunch and departed. They'd left their gumboots under the porch outside and they chased them around with woollen socks on their feet before clumping away up the street. She turned to face Wiri. "We need to locate the tank maker," she said, bouncing her fork above the plate. A bobble of egg tumbled onto the table. "Let's start there. Didn't Gareth say he lived locally? Perhaps someone here knows him."

"Okay." Wiri winced with discomfort.

"Are you in pain?" Concern darkened her features, and her stormy irises flashed.

"Yes, but it's not that." He drew his phone from his jeans pocket again and peered at the screen. His fingers shook as he turned it to face her.

"Oh." She sat back in her seat and let her fork slide onto the plate with a clang. "They're all calling you, aren't they?"

"Yeah." Wiri sighed. He examined the long list of calls and texts. "Logan, Hana, Nonie." He frowned. "I've ignored three from David Allen." His long fingers scrolled through the litany of messages, his shoulders rounding. "They've called the police, Phoenix." He looked up at her and saw the fear in her eyes.

"Now I'm really in trouble, aren't I?" She drew her elbows to her sides as though to make herself less visible. "Mac won't hold out forever."

Wiri shook his head. "He's loyal, and he approves of us. Logan can't read him like he can everyone else." He blew out a breath. "At least they can't demand his phone because you have it. But it also means I can't tell him you're okay." He pushed the last corner of toast into his mouth and swallowed before speaking. "We need to protect him from the Wrath of Logan once we make contact."

"Plausible deniability?" Phoenix grinned. "No one plays dumb with as much skill as my brother." She inhaled. "I'll face the music, apologise to Mac in front of everyone for borrowing his phone, and accept being grounded for the rest of my foreseeable future."

Wiri's complexion paled, and he set his cutlery on his plate. "They'll get into your phone," he whispered, "the one you left at home to stop Logan tracking you. What if they read the texts or find we've called each other?"

Phoenix shrugged. "I'm not stupid, Wiri. You only left last weekend, and I deleted the texts in both the sent and received folders. It doesn't matter if they see we called each other because it's not possible for them to get transcripts. What's the problem, anyway? Aren't we coming clean about everything?"

Wiri nodded. "Yes, but you've jumped the gun and I'm expecting Logan to march down here and take my head off without asking questions." He cocked his head and frowned. "That reminds me, Larry took the gun back to his place. I need to find out what he did with it."

"And to ask him about his dead brother." Phoenix wrinkled her nose and squeezed his ankle between her feet beneath the table. "We can go there soon if you like?" She tugged at the hem of the borrowed tee shirt. "Can I go clothes shopping first, please? I'm struggling to keep my pants up." She giggled. "Make that your pants. Either way, they're going to end up around my ankles."

"Hold on to them then." Wiri grinned and pushed his chair back from the table. Ted jerked on his stool and woke at the screech of wood against tile. He turned and glared at them before shoving his newspaper across his counter towards the window.

Phoenix rose and tucked her chair beneath the table. She gathered their used crockery together and carried it in a pile towards the front of the cafe. Mari took it from her with a nod of gratitude. "You want a job?" she asked, dumping the stack in front of the cash register.

"Maybe." Phoenix shot Wiri a sideways glance. For a moment of bliss, he imagined setting up home in the rental house, him working on the farm and Phoenix making coffee for Mari. And then reality reminded him she was still only fifteen, clever, and destined for greater things than he could offer. Dismay shrouded him as The Plan faded into the background of the looming fight with Logan. He closed his eyes against the thought of facing Hana and witnessing her disappointment. Focussing on his inner pain, he missed Phoenix's next sentence and struggled to understand Mari's reply.

"Oh, you need to see Ted," she said. "He knows everything." She dipped her frail body to see between them, her gaze raking the vacant corner where they'd left Ted sitting. "Oh. Where'd he go?"

Phoenix spun on her heel, staring up at the bell over the front door. "I didn't hear him leave."

Mari wrinkled her nose. "He's gone to the bathroom," she said, as though following him in there engendered painful memories. She widened her eyes and wafted her hand in front of her nose. "I'd leave him for now. If you need the bathroom, there's a public one near the police watch house. No one blocks my toilet as regularly as that old man."

They left the cafe, surveying the sheets of rain covering the main street. It formed rivulets of order, each drip building with a universal purpose to reach the storm drain and the river beyond it. Like a mission.

"Here." Wiri called over the sound of the deluge hitting the roof of the overhang. He slipped his arm around Phoenix and tucked her against him, guiding her to a nearby clothing store. The wind attacked them, darting around the parked vehicles to snatch at their legs and buffet them against one another. They entered the store giggling and flustered.

Phoenix took longer than Wiri anticipated. She leafed through the racks, growing more discomfited with every turn of a coat hanger. He checked his text messages again, following behind her as though tethered but paying no attention to her choosing. A desperate plea from Hana begged him to get in contact. A threat from Logan made the blood run cold in his veins.

'*Call me or we'll have a problem.*'

'*Please contact us,*' Hana begged in the text which followed Logan's. '*We need to talk.*' He quailed against his betrayal. He needed to put her mind at rest about Phoenix's safety. It would at first cause her extreme relief.

And then devastation.

Wiri shoved his phone into his pocket, his expression pained and tight. Phoenix moved to another rack of clothing and he glanced at his watch, realising yet another day had passed beneath him. "What's wrong?" he whispered. "Just grab some jeans and a tee shirt. I'll use my credit card."

Phoenix leaned sideways to whisper to his biceps. He dipped his head to catch the last of her sentence. "Old people."

"What?"

Footsteps sounded on the wooden floor as the elderly shop assistant moved towards them. "Can I help you?" She kept her tone level, although her gaze raked Phoenix's haphazard attire.

"I just wanted jeans and tee shirts." Phoenix's voice lowered to an almost inaudible depth. "I don't think any of these will fit me."

The assistant sized her up and pouted. "We don't have petite sizes," she admitted. Two enormous bosoms wobbled behind an old-fashioned house coat, which bulged to reveal ordinary clothes beneath. She tucked a stray grey curl behind her ear and jabbed her index finger towards the back of the shop. "Let's try the children's section."

Phoenix shot Wiri a look of disgust and he tapped his watch to tell her to hurry. She emerged from the changing room ten minutes later, wearing a set of clothes more suitable for a ten-year-old. The pink sweatshirt gripped her breasts in a vice, splatting a distorted kitten across her chest. The jeans hugged her figure hard enough to cut off the circulation.

"Perfect," the shop assistant declared. "I'll get the till ready to take your payment." She made the comment sound like a threat with just the right inflection.

Phoenix carried Wiri's borrowed clothes over her left arm. She moved towards him with difficulty, appearing unable to bend her legs from the knees down. "What shall I do?" she hissed. "She won't take no for an answer."

Wiri withdrew his wallet from his jeans pocket and pulled out his credit card. He struggled not to laugh as Phoenix spun in a circle to remove the seam from between her buttocks. He paid the shop assistant and hustled Phoenix outside into the rain. "It doesn't matter," he told her. "You'd look sexy in a sack."

"I could sit down in a sack!" she grumbled.

Wiri ran into the rain to open the passenger door and Phoenix limped past him. She climbed onto the runner board and took her time sitting down on the seat. She kept her eyes closed as Wiri slumped into the driver's seat and brushed his soaked fringe back from his brow. "It's raining cats and dogs out there," he said, borrowing one of Hana's English phrases. He shook his head. "Larry only lives around the corner but we can't walk in this weather." He tugged on his lower lip with his finger and thumb. "I wonder what made Seline look inside the water tank. If she hadn't, Hendricks' body might have stayed there for months. Why her?"

Phoenix made a gagging sound. "Don't. That's disgusting. If that tank feeds your house, you'd have drunk eau de dead man for months." She clapped her hand over her mouth. "Stop talking about it."

Wiri's finger played over the ignition button. "It doesn't. Our water comes from our roof. That tank sends a trickle feed to the water troughs in the lower paddocks. The water would smell horrible, but the gasses would disperse outside in the open air. We might never have noticed." He exhaled. "What if Seline thought the man on the phone killed Hendricks? She said something odd to him in the conversation I overheard. She thanked him for sorting out a problem. What if he left something behind and she rode up there to find it? She has a back door key to our place. What if she put my shirt in the tank to implicate me?"

Phoenix groaned. "I don't know, Wiri. Can we hurry to Larry's so I can stand up straight again?" She tugged the kitten away from her breasts and inspected it. "This is animal cruelty."

"Nice shirt." Wiri opened the wadded receipt in his hand. "You should treasure it forever. That old lady stung me for almost a hundred dollars for those two items."

Phoenix blew out a breath. "Three items. I bought some knickers." She raised her gaze to stare at the truck's ceiling. "You think the jeans are hurting me, but you can't imagine what havoc the underwear is wreaking."

Wiri bit his lip as indecent images passed through his mind. Phoenix narrowed her eyes as she folded his discarded boxer shorts on her knee. "Underage girl here, buddy. Keep it decent."

Wiri fired up the truck's engine and backed onto the street. Headlights danced behind his vehicle, spraying up water as he waited for the other cars to pass him. Phoenix squirmed in her seat. "How far is Pastor Larry's place?" she asked. "Give me exact minutes to hold on to. I need something to take my mind off my discomfort."

"He lives next to the church." Wiri made the necessary turn, driving less than a hundred metres from the cafe. "We're here." He pulled up next to the house and parked on the street. Then he turned to Phoenix with a frown. "I think you should stay in the car."

Her face crumpled. "No! Why?"

Wiri shrugged. "I'm not sure. Instinct?" He second guessed himself, sifting through his concerns and finding them only marginally sound. "I don't know," he admitted, cocking his head. "He's a Hendricks. Could you maybe do as you're told for once?"

"Hell no!" Phoenix pushed open the passenger door.

Wiri shook his head. "You're definitely your mother's daughter," he mused as she covered her head with her arms to avoid another soaking. He climbed from the truck and locked it behind him before following her up the porch steps and under cover.

"Will I need to take off my shoes?" she whispered as he rapped on the front door. Wiri cocked his head in confusion, not sure why the concept caused a dent to form between her brows. She jabbed a finger at her tight jeans. "I can't bend down again," she confessed. "I'll puke up my breakfast."

"Just let me do the talking," Wiri advised. When no one answered, he turned to face the church. "He must be next door," he said. "What does Pastor Sam do when he's not at the church?"

"I don't know." Phoenix's lips tightened and her terse reaction took Wiri by surprise. Phoenix had idolised Sam since she learned to walk and talk. He opened his mouth to question her, but jumped as the front door flew open to reveal Larry.

"Mr Kingii!" he said, throwing out his arms in welcome. "It must be my afternoon for guests." His gaze turned to Phoenix and his lips parted in a wide smile. "And your delightful young lady."

"Hi, Pastor Hendricks." She held out her hand, and he engulfed it in his wide palm. Wiri looked for any sign of discomfort and saw none. His confusion grew.

"Why didn't you tell me you and Donovan Hendricks were brothers?" Hostility entered his tone and Larry lifted his left hand and placed it behind his neck as though nursing a headache.

"Foster brothers," he said. His tone saddened. "The same kind couple took us in and tried to raise us. They adopted me and gave me their name but Donovan didn't give them the chance. He caused them much grief before running away. I didn't realise until I arrived in town that Donovan changed his name by deed poll and just took theirs. He wasn't my brother, but I should have mentioned it. I figured everyone knew about our connection."

"I didn't." Wiri exhaled. He spun on the deck and surveyed the black clouds gathering overhead. He turned to face the pastor. "What did Tane say about Jet's gun?"

Larry winced. He clapped a hand across his mouth. "Sorry. I've spent all day sorting out a crisis with the ladies of our parish." He raised an eyebrow and appealed to Phoenix as Wiri glared holes in the side of his face. "It took most of the morning to soothe ruffled feathers after a mistake on the service roster." He pursed his lips. "Then I married three happy couples, took two funerals and counselled a dying parishioner." The back of his right hand strayed to his face, and he scrubbed at his eyes and stifled a yawn.

Wiri dipped forward, his chest bumping Phoenix's shoulder. "But where did you leave the gun? Please tell me you locked it away somewhere safe."

Larry flapped his hand. "I'll do it right now." He opened the door wider and beckoned them across the threshold. "Leave your shoes on. Perhaps you can show me how to make it safe."

"What do you mean, make it safe?" Wiri's shoulders tensed. "Jet made it safe before you took it."

63

RECEIVER

Larry winced. He cleared his throat and his chest swelled to create gaps between the black buttons of his clerical shirt. The dog collar looked as though it tried to throttle him. "I know nothing about guns," he admitted. "You shouldn't point them at people, but that's about my limit."

Phoenix exhaled. As though sensing Wiri's concern, she placed gentle fingers against his forearm and followed Larry as he turned. "I can secure it," she said, her tone level. She shot Wiri a warning look over her shoulder. "My papa made sure all of us knew how to use guns."

Wiri shook his head and clamped his teeth down over his tongue. The pastor's ineptitude sent a flare of angst from his brain to his chest. "You put it somewhere safe though, didn't you?" he demanded, despite Phoenix glaring back at him. "You locked it away?"

"It's on my desk," Larry said, no urgency in his tone. "It's quite safe. You go in there and I'll grab a glass of water from the kitchen."

Wiri's phone vibrated in his pocket. He pulled it free and winced at the screen. His phone recognised the one he'd linked his Bluetooth with once before. "I should get this," he said, turning aside as he activated the device.

Tane's voice rumbled through the speaker and into his ear. "Forensic examiners went through Hendricks' vehicle. They found two tyre wrenches. One belonged to his Mercedes, but the other didn't."

"Right." Wiri glanced towards Larry's office door at the end of the hallway, cocking his head to listen for Phoenix. He wondered if she needed help with the gun, but doubted it. Jet removed the only bullet. A glass clinked in the kitchen and water gushed from a tap.

Tane cleared his throat. "The other one contained traces of Vaughan's blood. We think Hendricks hit him and shut you inside the tank."

Wiri exhaled in a whoosh. He'd expected relief, but found none. Seline's involvement swirled like an uncaptured thought above his head. Tane's conclusion created more questions than answers. "So, do I have more of a motive for killing Hendricks or less?" he demanded.

Tane tutted. "I don't know, mate. Sorry it doesn't help. We'll work it out."

Wiri shook his head. "Why would he have two tyre wrenches in his car? Or did he keep one for hitting people? Why not use his own and clean it?"

"Who knows?" Tane released a breath laden with exhaustion. "We might never find out the truth."

"Hendricks liked to have bargaining power," Wiri mused. "Maybe he took it from someone else."

"I thought I'd let you know, anyway." Tane seemed keen to disconnect. "Have a good afternoon." He killed the call before Wiri could respond.

He shoved his phone back into his pocket and traced Phoenix's footsteps along the hallway. Someone had mounted an office sign on a bedroom door. Hearing no sound from inside, Wiri paused before pushing at the door. It revealed a room containing office furniture.

A desk, a computer monitor, a chair on casters.

And an old man pointing a gun at Phoenix.

Wiri ran into Phoenix's spine, unable to stem his forward trajectory. She locked her hips, and he caused her to dip at the waist. He wrapped his arms around her torso to stop them both from hitting the floor. Hindsight would be a wonderful thing. They should have dropped like stones while they had the opportunity.

But they didn't.

"Get over there." Ted jerked the barrel of the Smith and Wesson towards Phoenix, using it to indicate the path he wanted her to take. She edged sideways, clamping her fingers over Wiri's hands as he held her around the waist. "Not him." Ted jabbed the gun towards Wiri's head. "I want him in the opposite corner."

Larry cannoned into the room as they divided, a tsunami squeezing itself through the narrow aperture between buildings. He met the barrel's dark void with a grunt of disbelief. A glass of water wavered in his right hand. "No, Ted," he said, his tone loaded with dismay. "What are you doing?"

"Get over there with her." He jabbed the gun at Phoenix again and Wiri held his breath. He raised his hands, palms facing outwards.

"Ted, the gun's not loaded," he said. "Jet took out the ammunition." His tone held authority, and Ted shifted his feet on the rug covering the floor of Larry's office. Instead of complying, he waved the gun at Wiri.

"I don't need your advice, kid," he growled. "I know it's loaded."

Wiri bit down on his denial. He ached to spin the barrel and check for himself. He glanced at Phoenix, reassured by the air of calm which surrounded her. Larry's brown eyes held a manic quality as his quarrelling ladies took on an extra attraction. Better them than this. Ever the peacemaker, he drew Ted's attention to himself as he sought to smooth more wildly ruffled feathers than earlier that day. "Just put the gun down, Ted," he advised. "You're a good man. I know how much it would plague you if someone got hurt."

"You think you know everything about me." Ted's voice rose an octave, betraying his extreme distress. "But you know nothing. I sit at the back of your church every Sunday and I attend your Matins and your Evensong and every mass you hold, but what do I get for it?"

Larry frowned. "What do you want from it, Ted?" he asked, maintaining the sense of calm. "What is it you're not receiving?"

Wiri blinked as Larry edged forward until he almost obscured Phoenix from Ted's view. Almost, but not quite. She looked so tiny wedged into the corner. The bookshelf filled with hardback biblical commentaries dwarfed her.

Wiri relaxed as he calculated the trajectory of a discharge.

Larry continued to close the aperture between her and Ted. Wiri blew out a slow, controlled breath and with it went all his suspicions about the pastor.

Ted swiped his left hand across his eyes, his body contorting with an internal agony. Wiri tensed, looking for an opportune moment to rush him and reclaim the gun. He allowed Larry to occupy his attention and forced his painful muscles to move him closer to Ted at a rate of a few centimetres at a time. He kept the shift invisible, trying not to cause a movement in the old man's peripheral vision.

Ted gulped. "I borrowed the money because I wanted Mari to love me," he said. "But now she's angry. Says she's disappointed in me." A disgusting sniff landed phlegm in the back of his throat. "I made everything worse. She said she'll never love me the way she loved Hector."

"She's always upset with you, Ted. Why is she even angrier now?" Larry cocked his head and offered a serene smile. He clasped his hands before him, the fingers gentle as they brushed the heavy cross which rose and fell as he breathed. "Perhaps we can talk to her."

Ted shook his head. The gun wobbled in his hand. "There's no talking to her. I didn't realise Donovan Hendricks bought the building. She didn't tell me she owed the back rent to him. I'd never have borrowed from him just to see her put it right back into his filthy hands. And the interest kept compounding. He cleaned me out and I couldn't keep up with it. And then he said she owed even more. The cost went higher than either of us could ever afford."

"I'm sure Mari is grateful." Larry blinked at Ted and Wiri shot a look at Phoenix. She tilted backwards to catch his eye, and he eased his chin in a motion, which indicated the door. She frowned as though refusing and he glared at her, willing her to use Ted's distraction to escape. Then Larry scuppered his plan. "Just let the kids go, Ted," he soothed. "You and I can sort this out together. There's no need for them to stay." He turned towards Wiri and Ted followed his gaze. Larry's hands whipped behind him and he grappled for Phoenix, seizing a clump of her tee shirt and sliding her behind him. He smiled at Wiri. "Please fetch Mari from the cafe?" he asked. He made it sound as though he'd asked him to retrieve something innocuous, like a bible or a pencil.

"No." Ted pointed the gun at Wiri's face.

One .44 Magnum round, unless Ted walked around with his own ammunition in his pocket. A one in six chance, decreasing if he didn't spin the barrel after each shot. The chrome rimmed eye aimed at Wiri's forehead, the short distance guaranteeing maximum damage.

Phoenix released a gasp of realisation as she dipped sideways to see past Larry. She followed the trajectory of the barrel to Wiri and he heard her audible gulp. "No," she gushed, her tone ragged. "Don't you dare hurt him!" She grappled against Larry's grip and he lurched forward as she forced her way through the narrow gap between the bookshelf and his body.

"Phoenix, no," Wiri hissed, seeing the struggle in his peripheral vision but keeping his focus on Ted's fingers. He wanted to tell her it was okay. Jet had emptied the chambers the previous night. He'd seen him do it.

The knuckles moved beneath Ted's skin and Wiri saw the moment his finger tightened over the trigger.

Ted grunted. "Stay there, little girl. You both know too much, so it doesn't matter which of you dies first." He tilted his head sideways. "Sorry Pastor."

"I don't quite understand why we're here." Larry released Phoenix and spread his hands before him. "Why does anyone need to die?"

"Because they know!" Ted lifted his voice to a shout filled with misery. "I heard them. They're looking for me!"

The pieces dropped into place like the panels of a slot machine to create a winning line. One lemon, two lemons, three.

Wiri inhaled as Phoenix scurried the remaining distance to his side. She wrapped her arms around his waist. Her strength infused him with courage and he held her, wanting their combined will to be the last thing he remembered. Logan had taught them to use weapons and to defend themselves.

But not like this.

Not when the stakes were so unimaginably high.

"Why do you think they're looking for you?" Curiosity edged the calm of Larry's voice with an undertone of bewilderment. "They're just kids."

"I heard them." Ted kept the barrel trained on Wiri's head. The slightest of tremors turned its single black pupil into a blur. "They want the tank maker." He jabbed the gun in a forward motion. "He knows why I reconnected the down pipe." Hysteria entered his voice. "It's only a matter of time before they tell."

Larry cleared his throat, his tone level. "This is my sanctuary, Ted," he persisted. "I took an oath to keep confidences and I'll extend that to you. But you must hand the gun to Wiri or Phoenix so they can make it safe. Otherwise, I can't help you. My oath only extends so far."

He didn't get it. Wiri heard his lack of understanding and relaxed his grip around Phoenix's shoulders. His mind filled with the blue buzz of concentration as he filtered out all other sounds. He pictured himself jettisoning her backwards through the open door. A sideways glance calculated the angle he'd require, and he worried that she'd resist his push. It needed to be hard, but if he got it wrong, she'd tangle with the door frame and become injured despite his efforts.

But she wouldn't die.

He dropped his arms from around her and sensed her grip become harder. The fingers of his left hand strayed to the small of her back and he balled the hem of her tee shirt into his hand. The stitches in his finger smarted, and he ignored the warning as his right hand moved across his stomach. He needed to spin her and push, hoping Ted's reactions proved slower than hers.

"Let's call Mari now." Larry dipped at the waist and his fingers fluttered towards the telephone at the far edge of the desk. "What's the number for the cafe?"

64

Automatic

"It's too late!" Ted turned his head enough to send the barrel of the gun notching to the right. Larry's fingers reached out, stretching towards the curved receiver. "No!" Ted screamed.

Wiri seized the moment and dragged at Phoenix's tee shirt. He powered his right arm with everything he possessed, sending all his weight into his fingers as he drove her sideways towards the door. But he hadn't factored into his equation that she was Logan Du Rose's daughter. Or that she'd spotted the same moment of weakness that he had and made her own contingency. She'd already dropped her weight back into her right foot by the time Wiri launched and she resisted, toppling sideways but not going where he'd intended.

The black void of the barrel's interior moved as though time had stalled and Ted aimed at Phoenix.

And fired.

Ted's hand recoiled even though the gun gave a gentle click, as though he'd manufactured the actual effect in his mind.

But he'd pulled the trigger and prepared to live with the consequences.

Wiri held his breath and in his peripheral vision saw Larry raise his arms to cover his head. The sleeves of his cassock sagged by his sides like a washing line of garments attacked by the wind. Phoenix kept falling as Wiri watched, her eyes closed and her lips pursed. Shock and rage imbued him with strength and an unhinged desire to mete out revenge before Ted fired again. Phoenix hit the ground hard, driven there by the force of Wiri's misplaced push. She rolled onto her side and Larry dropped to his knees, his body shielding her from further harm.

Wiri spun to face Ted, his fingers balling into fists of steel. But Ted lifted the gun and pointed it at his temple. "Sorry," he breathed, before pressing the trigger again.

Wiri jerked backwards in shock, blinking as Ted remained standing. Jet's game of roulette returned as a laughing spectre and he faced the old man with venom in his flashing irises. Jet's next foray into depression may well have been his last.

"You're dead!" Wiri ground out the words through gritted teeth, seeing just an outline of Ted's blurred shape through a lifetime's compounded grief and rage. He bounced forward, determined to send the old man into the afterlife with his bare hands. All reason abandoned him, and Logan's self-defence tactics paled to nothing. Kane Du Rose whispered to him from the depths of his soul, a gentle voice urging him to destroy because he could. It reeked of revenge and the filth of a life ill spent. Wiri listened, saturated by the swirling emotions he couldn't even name. Ted had fired at Phoenix, intending to take her away from him. Wiri's reasoning abandoned him and left him with a pervading hollowness in his gut.

He crossed the distance in one gigantic stride and his fingers closed around Ted's throat. The old man's eyes bulged in his grizzled face and his cap slid sideways to reveal a bald head.

Then the gun discharged a third time, and a deafening tinkle of glass accompanied it. But the burning was nothing like Wiri had ever experienced before.

T hird time unlucky.

Wiri lay on the tasselled rug in Larry's office while Phoenix tried to stop the bleeding. Her lips moved, but he struggled to hear the words she spoke over him. Perhaps they were prayers. Perhaps admonishments.

The gun's report still echoed in his ears, ricocheting around the room and bouncing off the framed, crucified Jesus over the mantelpiece.

Ted dropped the gun next to the fireplace, and it spun and clattered against the brick hearth. Larry lurched for the phone and dialled the emergency services. He didn't stop Ted from leaving, placing the receiver on the desk and leaning over Phoenix's shoulder. "What do you need?" he demanded, his voice husky.

"Something to stop the bleeding," Phoenix replied. She leaned hard against Wiri's left thigh, putting all her weight into the action. The fingers of her right hand snatched at his belt buckle and he felt his lips slide into a smile as indecent thoughts crowded into his conscious mind. A clank and a thud followed the sense of something running along his spine. It curled around his waist and he saw Phoenix holding up his belt. His father's buckle drooped from the end, the brass head of a horse there and then gone as she dropped her hand beyond his vision. Phoenix's lips pursed hard enough to make them pale. "Kane did nothing else for him," she said through gritted teeth. "Maybe now he'll help to save his life."

Pressure dug into his thigh, eking through the blaze of pain which burned like a bush fire. It throbbed and ached, the heat backed by a peculiar chill which attacked the rest of his body.

Phoenix's face appeared above him. He grunted as the pressure tightened in his thigh, an ache consuming his knee and everything beyond it. His fingers scrabbled against the rug, fighting the way its threadbare surface curled and bunched beneath his grip. "What's happening?" he demanded, his words slurring.

"Larry's tightening the belt." Phoenix's curls draped across his face, tickling and sticking to the sweat beading on his brow and running along his neck. "I think the bullet went straight through and broke the picture leaned up against the wall behind you." Shaking fingers brushed her hair from his cheek. "An ambulance is on its way."

"Yes, I'm a trained first aider, but my friend is doing a grand job." A thud signified Larry laying the receiver on the desk again. He rose and disappeared, but his voice continued from a distant corner of the room as he gave Phoenix instructions. A heavy blanket landed over Wiri's body, pressing him down into the floorboards and forcing him to acknowledge the ridged lumps in the rug. One ran behind his tail bone and he wanted to move away from the pain. He squirmed and Larry knelt beside him and forced him back with a hand to his right shoulder. "Keep still," he advised, authority in his voice. "You're going into shock. Keep the blanket over you."

Wiri swore and Phoenix raised a smile. "I think you're okay then," she said, masking her fear behind humour. But he recognised the hugeness of her pupils and the trembling of her chin as she looked down at him.

"Ted didn't load it." He inhaled and controlled the breath as it left his lungs, letting it out by degrees so he could focus on it. "And he didn't know it had only one round in the chamber."

Larry uttered what sounded like a prayer. He tutted and peered down at Wiri. "I put it in there for safe keeping," he admitted. "I just needed to keep them both together. Ted noticed the gun, asked if it was loaded and I said yes. I never expected him to pick it up when I went to answer the door and fetch him a glass of water."

Wiri groaned. "You loaded a gun to avoid losing the bullet?" He whimpered and tried to contain the laugh bubbling in his chest. "That's hilarious."

"It actually isn't." Larry's eyelids shuttered to hide the dismay radiating from his eyes. "It was stupid. I knew better and now I'll need to explain myself to the authorities." He exhaled. "I wish I'd never taken possession of it."

"Not as much as I do," Wiri replied. His teeth chattered. He focussed on the rhythm of them clicking together as another sound added to the melody. The siren wailed in peaks and troughs of a tinny cry. Wiri lost count as he tried to match the two noises together. Instead, he concentrated on the shaking fingers clutching his between the blanket. "Larry?" he said, his voice cracking. "I got you all wrong. When Phoe called you Pastor Hendricks, I figured you told Donovan all the town gossip. But you didn't, did you?"

"No." Larry shook his head and sighed. He glanced over his shoulder and into the hallway, shifting on his knees as he prepared to admit the paramedics clattering onto the porch. "Ted did. He knew everything about everyone."

65

BOLT ACTION

Phoenix travelled with him in the ambulance. She sat on the bench opposite, leaning right and left as the paramedic moved around her. He fixed a bag of fluid onto a peg and pumped it through a vein in the crook of Wiri's elbow. "Nice job with the tourniquet," he told Phoenix as he released the belt and handed it back to her. "Where'd you learn to do that?"

Phoenix reached for Wiri, pressing her fingers over his hand and slipping her thumb into the warm cave beneath his palm. He groaned as the paramedic parted the fabric of his jeans with curved scissors. "My father has haemophilia," she said, the statement loaded with meaning. The man nodded, and she relaxed when he made no further comment. As a female child of a haemophiliac, she had a fifty-fifty chance of becoming a carrier. The odds weren't in her favour. Unlike Edin, who got away Scot free. Life just wasn't fair sometimes. Wiri folded his fingers around her hand. The pain medication pumping through his veins made everything blurry, but he found her face and offered her a smile of solidarity.

Wiri closed his eyes, and the paramedic nudged his shoulder with sharp fingers. "Keep talking," he insisted. "No sleeping. We're almost at the hospital."

He turned his head to observe Phoenix as she wiped a stray tear from her cheek. The way she struggled to swallow told him more than words, and he tapped the top of her hand with his thumb. She pursed her lips, a flare of alarm in her slate grey irises as he lifted it and held out his arm to her instead.

Phoenix unclipped her seat belt and dropped to her knees on the hard corrugated floor of the ambulance. She wrapped her arms around his chest and buried her face against his neck. Her genteel sniffs stopped the paramedic's objections as the vehicle turned right into the main entrance for the hospital. It ran with lights but no sirens and Wiri took that as a good sign.

"Will I need surgery?" he asked as the man swayed with the motion of the vehicle and pushed liquid from a syringe into a port on the drip.

"Yeah." He wrinkled his nose and gave a definitive nod. "But you're lucky it ripped right through and did its worst to the furniture behind you. Nobody wants a 44 Magnum exploding in their leg." The ambulance lurched to the left, and he placed his palm against an overhead cupboard, shifting his weight without concern like a pro surfer. He leaned forward and tapped Phoenix's shoulder. "We're here now, miss."

Wiri stared up at various ceilings as hospital staff wheeled him through vast kilometres of faceless corridors. The strip lights blinded him, but every time he tried to close his eyes, someone shook him awake. The pain in his tail bone paled into significance against the fire in his left thigh. They let Phoenix stay with him, and he sensed her quiet presence. A nurse pushed a pen into his hand and helped him make a slanted signature. Her lips moved, and he smiled and nodded, concerned only with making her go away and leave him alone.

Sleep came fast and hard. A man leaned over him, a disembodied head wearing a surgical mask. "Count backwards from ten," he ordered.

Wiri blinked up at him, confusion swirling around his brain and mixing with the powerful burn which snaked up his leg and into his stomach. "Uncle Mark," he managed. Hana's brother tugged the mask from his face, hiding his concern with his usual good humour.

"The very same." He gave him a wink before speaking to someone on the other side of the gurney. "Let's get this open and take a look," he said with the authority of a surgeon speaking to a junior. Wiri tilted his head, finding another man to his right. The eyes watching him from above the mask looked only a little older than his own. Gloved hands wielded a needle, and he sighed with resignation.

"Ten," he began, hearing his voice as though it began to someone else. "Nine." He stumbled over eight and seven before forgetting all about six. As his lips struggled to form a coherent five, he heard Mark say something about saline. Then a giant vacuum cleaner snatched at his frozen limbs and sucked him into a brightly lit tunnel of peace.

66

BOLT RELEASE

Wiri wasn't sure when he woke. He made several attempts to lift himself from the void, which reminded him too much of the water tank. It seemed so difficult to connect himself with the world around him. He was there and then, not there. Cursory explorations of his body discovered pain emanating from somewhere south of his stomach, but he couldn't isolate it from the general hum of discomfort. He sighed and a cool hand appeared over his right wrist. "Phoe?" His tongue stuck to the roof of his mouth and the sound of his own voice seemed to hurt his head.

The cool hand moved to rest over his warm forehead, gentle, reassuring and familiar. "Ma?" Her scent washed over him, orchid, jasmine and sunny meadows. His recent crimes fled in the face of the comfort she brought with her. He craved it like oxygen. "I'm sorry," he whispered.

"We'll talk about it later," she promised, her tone level.

"Phoe?"

"She's safe. Logan took her to the cafe for something to do while we waited." Soft lips pressed a kiss to his forehead. Her breath held the scent of coffee. It reminded him of Jet and how he hadn't reached the supermarket to replace what he'd used. "Everything will be okay, sweetheart." Her English accent picked out the gentle lilt of her vowels. His hair swished against the pillow as he made a silent denial.

Nothing would ever be okay again.

"Sleep now." Hana stroked his hair back from his forehead in a rhythmic, soothing motion. The movement of her hand across his vision made his eyes cross over and he closed them.

"Sorry," he murmured again, wanting her to know how much he regretted hurting her. But it changed nothing. Their disapproval couldn't stamp out his adoration for their daughter. He remembered Logan calling another of Hana's waifs a cuckoo many years ago. The boy had brought a raft of misery into their home with him, igniting a terrible chain of events which ended in disaster. He hadn't meant Wiri to overhear, but he had, applying the image to his own existence within their family. Edin's appearance hadn't helped.

She hadn't helped.

He couldn't see her as his half-sister, but as yet another cuckoo in the Du Rose nest.

They were buried land mines in a decent family.

Just waiting to detonate.

Now he'd done it too and there would be consequences. He squeezed his eyes closed and tried not to think about Logan's arrival. At least if Uncle Mark was still on duty, he could pick out yet more shrapnel from Wiri's broken body.

A clattering woke him with a start.

"Sorry." A nurse smiled down at him. She switched a bag hanging next to him, taking away the empty one. Pink stains covered its sagging bottom, and he frowned. "You needed a little transfusion." She said the sentence with an air of dismissal, as though every patient required a litre of someone else's blood to survive. Perhaps they did. "Nothing to worry about." She closed her fingers around his wrist and lifted a watch face attached to her pocket. He focussed on his pulse racing past the pressure of her fingers over his artery. It registered as strong and regular as his heart pumped someone else's blood around his body.

He cleared his throat, the sound scratchy and cracked. She placed his hand gently on the mattress and lifted a beaker. A straw protruded over the lip, swinging left and right as it moved through the air.

"Let's sit you up a bit," the nurse said. She lifted a control unit and whirring vibrated beneath Wiri's spine. He groaned, and she pursed her lips in sympathy. "Sorry. You fractured your coccyx," she said, her tone matter of fact.

Wiri's mind chased the remnants of a biology class he hadn't enjoyed. He couldn't place the bone she named and frowned in confusion. "Femur?" he asked, assuming she'd made a mistake. "I got shot in the leg."

"Yes." She placed the straw between his lips. "But you came in a few days ago after a fall. Remember? Another radiologist looked at your x-ray and discovered a fracture in your tail bone. I don't know why they didn't contact you." She cocked her head and winked at him. "Maybe it's because you used a different name." He remembered her then and winced in guilt. He'd removed her careful bandages without a second thought.

Wiri sipped water and avoided her gaze. Apologising again seemed too difficult when he couldn't string a sensible sentence together. Instead, he nodded and caused himself to choke on the tepid water. He blew out a ragged breath and waited for the air to whoosh back into his lungs. "Where did my family go?" he asked. He imagined Logan storming from the hospital and sweeping Hana and Phoenix up with him. The picture didn't fit with what he knew of the Du Rose women.

But would Hana fight for him after what he'd done? What he'd caused?

Phoenix appeared first. She barrelled into the room at speed, her eyes widening at the sight of Wiri propped up in the bed. "Oh, you're awake!" She clutched a cardboard coffee cup in her left hand. She'd dripped brown liquid in a line across the face of the kitten on her tee shirt. The too-tight jeans had slipped down over her hips and formed wrinkles at the junction with her thighs. She dumped the coffee cup on the wheeled table next to him and dodged the nurse to wrap her arms around his neck.

He returned her embrace, grounding himself in the solidity of everything that she offered. His arms reached around her slender body and he buried his face in her hair, closing his eyes and breathing in the scent of his borrowed shampoo. The future rolled out before him, containing images of their shared lives amid bright spots of hope. The pipe taking fluid into his vein smarted in his right hand as it trailed across the bed. He gripped his fingers over her spine and held on as though his life depended on it.

"Careful." The nurse's voice lifted, but only a fraction.

Phoenix's dark curls obscured his vision as she lifted her head and rose with reluctance. "Oh," she said, her tone serious. "Sorry."

Wiri glanced down to see the needle protruding from the back of his hand. His stomach lurched, and he closed his eyes against the pink stained fluid spilling from the vein onto the sheets.

"Let's fix that," the nurse said. The soles of her shoes squeaked against the linoleum as she moved around the bed and took charge of the disaster in her unflappable manner. She switched equipment and set up another cannula, pressing the clear plastic plaster over the back of his hand. "That's better," she said, standing back to admire her work. She raised her gaze to Phoenix.

"How long have you been together?" she asked, making conversation to distract them.

Phoenix looked at Wiri and her irises changed to the colour of granite. She smiled, and they replied at the same time.

"Forever."

67

Stock Retaining Screw

Wiri sensed Logan's presence before he saw him.

The air in the room seemed to crackle and fizz as his ethereal mana connected with Wiri's. Phoenix stiffened. She'd been talking about Ted's arrest, but the words faded on her lips and she hung her head. "He's coming," she whispered. Her eyelashes fluttered. "Do you want me to stay?"

He shook his head to mean no, although a sliver of cowardice craved her solidarity.

Logan appeared in the doorway within seconds. His aura occupied the room without entering, sucking out all the oxygen and leaving Wiri breathless. He looked up to find his uncle observing him. He tried to gauge his mood, anticipating and mitigating, his brain performing cartwheels as it searched for excuses and reasons. Perhaps even the odd lie.

Wiri swallowed as Phoenix rose. She leaned forward in her father's eye line and placed a gentle kiss over Wiri's lips. He held his breath and tensed. "It'll be okay," she whispered.

Logan dipped his head to enter the room, more through habit than necessity. Wiri clasped his fingers over his stomach and fixed his gaze on the ragged stitches poking from his middle finger. He'd hated every second of his time in the water tank, but it was nothing compared to facing Logan. Disjointed sentences piled through his mind, all of them pleading and none of them helpful. He swallowed and waited for Logan to speak.

He didn't.

Wiri looked up to find him leaning against the wall, arms folded and watching him. He'd been here before and his heart pounded, rebelling against the sickness of familiarity. A litany of childhood mischief rose into the forefront of his mind. Logan never raised a hand to his children.

He didn't need to.

His disappointment was more than enough to reduce the worse offender to tears.

Logan Du Rose saved his violence for those outside his family. He never shat on his own doorstep.

Wiri cleared his throat. "Please, can you pass me the water?" he asked. His voice sounded raspy, as though he'd swallowed a million razor blades.

Logan settled his weight back onto his feet. The heels of his worn cowboy boots clicked across the floor. Scarred hands lifted the flimsy mug, hands capable of wringing a man's neck.

If he wanted.

He held out the drink and Wiri took it. "Thanks," he managed. His head ached as he moved it from side to side to track the straw as it evaded his lips. Finally, he sipped the water, buying himself time as it slid down into his stomach.

Logan waited and took it back from him, his fingers brushing Wiri's as he accepted it into his hand and placed it back on the table. Then he dug his thumbs into his jeans pockets and stood next to the bed, waiting with the effortless patience of someone who had a lifetime to waste.

Wiri caved.

He didn't want to, but he'd been here before. Too many times to count. He possessed enough of Kane's genetics to have spent his childhood sailing very close to the wind. His redeeming factor was the lack of cruelty which drove his father; eventually to his own death, just when his life had finally become wholesome and worthwhile. "I know you're angry with me." He mumbled the words, hearing the self-defeat in their echo. Shaking his head, he forced himself to face Logan like a man worthy of taking away his first born. "I love Phoenix." The sentence held a crystal clarity which seemed to ring in the air like a gong.

Logan pursed his lips and said nothing. His silence offered Wiri enough rope to hang himself. But exhaustion and morphine nipped at the fringes of his energy, sapping the frayed remnants he still possessed. Wiri sighed and picked at the raggedy stitches on his middle finger. To his surprise, Logan hauled a visitor's chair across the floor with a hiss of its plastic feet on the linoleum. He sank into it with a sigh. "Hana always warned me," he admitted. He ran a hand across his eyes. "It's not like I don't know how you feel. I met Hana when I was fourteen. We didn't even speak, but I knew I wanted to spend the rest of my life with her." He folded his arms and stared at Wiri. His grey irises sparkled, as dark as the inside of the water tank. "Why didn't you come to me or to Hana? Why run?"

Wiri let his head fall back against the pillows. He'd asked himself the same questions many times. He formulated the words into a sensible sentence, hindered by his foggy, anaesthetic addled brain. "Scared," he admitted. "We didn't want to acknowledge it at first. I dated other girls, and we skirted around it. Then we ended up right back where we started." He blew out a ragged breath and remembered the kiss on the edge of the graveyard. Their ancestors had watched them step across a hidden line in the whenua. He'd sensed their elation. Wiri pushed himself up with one hand. "Phoe gave me a bracelet."

Panic seized him as he searched his wrist and found it gone. "Where is it?"

Logan leaned forward and his firm grip on Wiri's shoulder pressed him back against the bed. "The nurse gave Hana a bag of your stuff. It's probably in there." When he felt Wiri acquiesce, he sat back against the chair with a bump. He gnawed on his lower lip. "We've been worried sick about Phoenix."

Wiri exhaled. He nodded against the pillow. "I know. She meant to call you, but then everything went wrong." He lifted the sheet to peer at his thigh. The hospital gown ended at his knee and he yanked it up high enough to discover a transparent plastic plaster. A gaping hole showed beneath it. Blood seeped against the plastic as though trying to escape. He frowned and his stomach churned. "They didn't stitch it closed?" His voice wavered. Someone had shaved the hairs from his leg and myriad raised lumps of skin surrounded the entrance of the bullet like a crater rim. A black bruise began at the site and snaked outwards like mountain tributaries. Wiri followed the curvature of his thigh to the back and his fingers probed a matching covering on the other side. He winced at the realisation he'd arrived at the hospital without undies.

"You were lucky." Logan sniffed as though containing his emotion despite his expression remaining blank. "The bullet missed the bone and major artery. Mark got another surgeon in to repair a tendon and some cartilage." He jerked his head towards Wiri's midriff. "Apparently you broke a bone a few days ago, but left before they could let you know."

Wiri nodded and thought back to the night in the hospital. Jet had smuggled him out at his own request. "Is there a cop here?" he asked. "A blond guy."

Logan nodded. "He's wandering around with a bloke dressed as a vicar. It looks like a fancy dress parade."

Wiri smirked. He imagined Jet's dismay at Logan's easy dismissal of his ego. Logan swallowed and Wiri forced himself to meet his eye. "The cop says it wasn't your fault. They got the guy who shot you."

Wiri gave a slow blink and smothered a yawn with his hand. "What do you want from me?" he asked. The question gave him relief, even though he hadn't yet heard the answer. But there arrived a sense of clarity with everything coming out into the open. Bearing the secret for most of his life had been a weight he wasn't equipped to carry. He flattened his lips and stuck his chin in the air. "As long as Phoenix wants me, I'm not going anywhere."

Logan exhaled. He lay back in the chair and stretched his legs out in front of him. "I don't like it." He spoke the words Wiri had always known. They cut deep, just like he expected. The emotional wound burned more than the bullet hole.

"Because it's me? Because you hated my dad?" Wiri's voice wavered. He started as Logan recoiled.

"No!" His head jerked back in shock. "No, Wiri. We've raised you like our own." Doubt crept across his face like a returning tide. "Haven't we?"

"Yes." Wiri nodded, the action laboured. He couldn't raise the accusation of being a cuckoo, because Logan had never levelled it at him.

Only at the other boy.

The one who almost got Hana killed.

He shrugged. "You raised us as brother and sister. We figured you'd hate it."

"I do hate it." Logan ran a hand across his chin. He dipped forward and leaned his forearms along the length of his thighs. "But not for the reasons you believe. It's because of the past."

"The haemophilia?" Wiri said it out loud, although they rarely did within the Du Rose household. The disease occupied air space alongside them, lurking at family gatherings and threatening every outing with its opportunistic blood loss and misery.

"Maybe." Logan sounded unsure. "I don't know. Hana says it's my hang up and I shouldn't place it onto you. Our family spent centuries being insular, and it destroyed them in the end. My father and mother were first cousins, and it became a tangled mess."

"Not because of their blood!" Wiri's voice rose with more power as he protested the tainting of his ancestors. "Because of their behaviour. They blurred the lines. We won't."

Logan dipped his head and stared at the linoleum between his boots. The grey pinpricks in his hair created a salt and pepper effect against its black origins. Handsome and imposing, he lost nothing with age. He represented the best of the line, the kaumatua of his family. Wiri ached for the fracture he'd caused in their relationship. "Perhaps," he acknowledged. Though he didn't give the answer the certainty, which Wiri craved.

68

Flush Nut

Phoenix clattered back into the room. The guilty pout told Wiri she'd listened to every word from outside the door. But she lifted a phone in her hand, the floral cover gaudy in the dour hospital. The screen strobed with an incoming call, and she gnawed on her lip and appealed for help. "What should I do?" she demanded. "He told her to kill two people. One is dead and then you got shot." She gulped and her gaze moved from Wiri to her father.

"What?" Logan's pupils bloomed to create unfathomable black pits within his grey irises. He held out his hand for the phone. "Who told who what?" Taking the device, he swiped the green phone icon across the screen and lifted it to his ear. "Who is this?" he demanded, his voice loaded with authority.

Silence.

"Hello?" The phone gave a tiny vibration in his hand as the call ended. He glanced up to find Wiri and Phoenix watching him. "Who the hell was that?" He handed the phone back to his daughter.

"We don't know." Phoenix pursed her lips and sent Wiri a silent appeal for help. She pushed the device into her pocket. Her dark lashes grazed the top of her cheek as she looked down at the floor. Wiri rallied to her call, using his arms to push himself higher up the bed, the pillows bunched behind him. He opened his mouth to speak, but a male voice cut across him.

"Knock knock." He followed the action with an actual knock on the open door, a gentle rap of acknowledgment. Vaughan stepped into the room, his gaze fixed on Wiri. He took in the hospital gown and the drip feeding fluids into his arm. "I came to see how you are." He smiled at Phoenix before his attention fell to Logan. "Leilah's parking the truck." He gave an upward jerk of his head before turning to face him.

Vaughan raised his right hand and stretched his long arm towards Logan. Wiri held his breath in the pause, which seemed to last forever. He heard Phoenix's audible gulp from next to him and flinched as she rested her hand on his shoulder. "It's been a while," Vaughan said.

Wiri frowned and glanced up at Phoenix, the creases in her forehead mirroring his. Logan's face relaxed into a genuine smile, and he took the offered hand. Phoenix blinked as they touched foreheads and noses in a traditional hongi. "It's been too long, cousin." They separated, and the air fizzed between them like the ignition of a dormant spark of familial connection. "Thanks for the call," Logan said.

Wiri stiffened. "Call. What call?" He narrowed his eyes and studied Logan. "I thought Phoenix called you after I got shot."

Her hand wobbled on his shoulder and he glanced up to find her shaking her head. Her long curls flicked his right ear. "I didn't call them." She shrugged. "I assumed the hospital did it. Or Uncle Mark."

Wiri pointed from Vaughan to Logan. "You're cousins?"

"Yup." Logan resumed his station against the wall. He bent his right knee and placed the sole of his boot against the plaster.

Vaughan dug his fingers into the front pockets of his jeans. He shrugged. "Same whakapapa until the French man. Maternal line."

"Right." Wiri frowned at the irony. He'd avoided availing himself of Logan's family contacts and stumbled across them, anyway. He sighed, acknowledging the throbbing in his thigh.

"You gonna be okay?" A line appeared between Vaughan's eyes. "Ted shot you?"

"Yeah." Phoenix answered for him. Her thigh touched the bed frame as she edged closer, as though to protect him.

"Where'd he get the gun?"

Wiri swallowed, but Logan got there first. "Are you missing one, cousin?" he asked.

Vaughan nodded. "Yup. My rifle."

Wiri inhaled. He closed his eyes and let his head fall back against the pillow. He didn't want to see Vaughan's expression as he smashed up his family. "Ted killed Hendricks, but Seline locked me in the water tank." He swallowed.

"Someone's giving her orders over the phone." Phoenix picked up the tale. "A man. I have her phone and he thinks I'm Seline." She pursed her lips and drew the floral case from inside the back pocket of her jeans. She winced at the discomfort of the action. From the other side came Mac's phone, and she stepped forward to hand both to Logan. "I stole Mac's, Papa. He knows nothing."

Logan took it from her without comment, pushing it into an inside pocket in his leather jacket. He jerked his head towards the other phone. "Call the number," he ordered, his tone raising only slightly in concern.

Phoenix shook her head. She ran her fingers over the screen and it lit up to demand a code. "I can't," she admitted. "I can answer calls, but to do anything else, I need the code."

Vaughan wrinkled his nose. "Leilah might know it. What did the guy sound like?"

Phoenix shrugged. "Gruff, angry. He sounded white." She squeezed her eyes tight shut and shook her head. "I know that sounds weird. Also very sure of himself, like someone used to giving orders." She stared at the screen as though willing another call into existence. "He thinks she's going to kill someone for him."

"There's a sound in the background." Wiri stared at the ceiling until the overhead strip lights blurred his vision. "I've heard it before somewhere. It reminds me of my ma."

His lips twitched as he remembered Anahera as she'd been in the early days.

Before Rueben's fire.

Before Asher started copying Kane and their world detonated. His mind's eye produced a memory of her laughing as she showed him how to make a daisy chain. Her dark hair swung in a ponytail, tapping her shoulder as she leaned forward to tweak the reluctant stems. She'd known happiness for a while. He swallowed and forced himself to acknowledge that he needed to see her again. Hana had offered many times to drive him to the prison for a visit. Next time, he'd say yes.

"Prison!" His tongue tripped over the word as though not wanting to release it into the ether. "He's calling from a prison. It's the same buzzing of the security doors as they open." He clicked the fingers of his left hand and hissed at the pain it caused his finger. "Ouch! That's why he needs Seline to take his calls. He's either queuing for the communal phone or renting a mobile."

Logan cocked his head as though seeing Wiri in a different light. He'd sheltered his children from much of the world's horrors. Yet so many had come to his own doorstep, he should have realised they'd already seen too much. He wrinkled his nose and Wiri saw regret in his eyes as he ran a hand over his face.

Vaughan released a breath which seemed to hurt. He splayed the fingers of his left hand over his stomach as though to protect himself. "I know who that is," he admitted. His jaw ground hard enough to make the bone press through his cheek. "I need to speak to Leilah."

Leilah and Hana arrived together, converging in the doorway of the small hospital room. They bumped shoulders before apologising. An eerie warmth started in the pit of Wiri's stomach at the sight of Hana again, guilt and shame rising into his throat to restrict his airway. He coughed, and Phoenix leaned across him to retrieve the cup of water.

Leilah introduced herself as Wiri chased the straw with his mouth, finally resorting to using his fingers to fix it in place. He sipped, buying himself time before he witnessed Hana's disappointment first hand. He wished he'd had more presence of mind when she'd sat with him earlier.

A missed opportunity.

His imagination had supplied endless iterations of the scene over the years. But he hadn't been naked beneath a flimsy hospital gown, especially with an audience. He choked on the water and Phoenix drew it away. With her other hand, she rubbed the back of his neck.

"Wiri." Hana's voice sounded soft and filled with tenderness. He stared down at the starched sheets to avoid the moment, not wanting to see the undeserved pain he'd caused a woman who'd given him nothing but love.

"I'm sorry," he whispered. The fingers of his right hand strayed to worry at the stitches over the seam of his middle finger. Redness bloomed along the join and it prickled as though needing him to scratch it.

He smelled her perfume and the familiar scent of her shampoo as she wrapped her arms around his neck. She rested her cheek on the top of his head. "I told you before, it's okay," she whispered. "It's okay."

His arms lifted of their own volition and he held her around the waist. Slender like the stem of a daisy, Hana had been bowled over by circumstance many times but never broken under pressure. She'd formed the lighthouse in the child-Wiri's world. So many of his kin orbited her like boats adrift at sea. She pressed her lips to his forehead before releasing him. His gaze strayed towards Logan, seeing only love written there.

"And as for you, miss!" Hana met her daughter at the end of the bed. She wrapped her arms around her and held on as though reluctant to release her back into the world. Her palms cupped Phoenix's cheeks as she studied her. "I'm not letting you out of my sight again. You'd better get used to it."

"We've got bigger problems." Logan called a halt to the threatening emotional scene. He drew Seline's phone from his pocket and showed Leilah the cover. "Your daughter's phone." He stated it as a fact. "She's taking calls from a man who's telling her to kill someone."

The colour drained from Leilah's cheeks. Her eyes darkened and though her lips moved, nothing emerged. Vaughan's steady hand landed on her shoulder. He drew her back to him and out of Logan's range. A protective move, though unnecessary. "What are you saying?" A whisper filled with denial and regret. She jabbed a finger towards Wiri. "Ted did this. Larry, the police, they all said Ted did it."

Hana and Phoenix had turned to face the drama. They blocked Wiri's view of Leilah as though shielding him from an unseen horror. He pressed his right palm against the mattress and dipped his body to see around them. Vaughan's calm expression belied the fury and confusion bubbling in his irises. His boots scraped against the floor as he turned to face his wife. Wiri almost missed the muttered words. "It's me he wants dead, Lei. Revenge. Your ex-husband wants me gone, and he's using our daughter to do it. It's perfect justice, isn't it, if you think about it?"

Hana slunk towards Logan, keeping hold of Phoenix's hand. She mouthed something to him, and he nodded. A sense of isolation built as Wiri remained trapped in the high bed. Vaughan and Leilah formed a perfect circle, and he recognised a spark of empathy for Seline. Vaughan had referred to her as *our daughter*, yet he shared no emotional or parental connection with her. Wiri's heart sank. He and Seline were from the same corrupt mould. They'd both had another man passed off as their father. He'd found Hana but Seline had become feral, following a criminal's bidding like an automaton and seeking something denied to her. He hated that shared thread of commonality between them. It made her easier to understand and he didn't want to tap into any part of Seline's twisted psyche.

But he'd been right. She'd wanted to ruin Vaughan's business and incapacitate him.

For someone else.

Wiri was nothing more than collateral damage in her dangerous scheme. She'd wanted Jet's gun to kill Vaughan.

"We need to call Tane." Vaughan's baritone rumbled through the room.

69

GARAND ROTATING BOLT

"No!" Leilah's hiss of dismay accompanied her jerking upright. She caught hold of Vaughan's arm. "He'll arrest her! She'll go to prison."

"Ah, you're out of surgery. Good, good." Larry poked his face through the open doorway and everyone froze. Then Leilah ran towards him and gripped his hand.

"We think Seline has Vaughan's gun," she gushed. Her head wobbled in a series of jerky movements. "I don't want Tane to know." Her voice broke, and Vaughan winced behind her.

"What sort of gun is it?" Logan spoke, his commanding tone causing Leilah to pause and wrap her arms around herself.

Vaughan sniffed. "Shotgun, Iver Johnson, break action twelve gauge. Belonged to my Uncle Horse. I keep it locked in a gun cupboard in the laundry." He exhaled. "I'm assuming she's taken it, but it might not be the case."

"We're jumping to conclusions!" Leilah's eyes gained a wild quality, the irises sparkling like gems against her pale features.

"I asked her to move the horse so we could put the mare in the paddock. She did it. Maybe she went for a ride in the bush."

"The police have the gun that shot Wiremu." Larry wrinkled his nose. "I think they might charge me for my stupidity."

Jet appeared behind Larry, nudging him to move aside. "This is all my fault," he admitted.

"And you are?" Logan cocked his head and narrowed his eyes. Jet introduced himself, offering an outstretched hand. His shoulders rounded with guilt beneath his uniform shirt as Logan shook hands with him. Phoenix used the opportunity to edge her way closer to Wiri. She eased herself onto the bed next to him, their elbows touching. The residue of the anaesthetic, combined with the pain medication, removed all sense of anxiety. It made him feel bomb proof. He slipped an arm around her waist despite the proximity of her father.

Wiri laid his head back against the pillows and closed his eyes as the adults argued in hushed voices. Phoenix rested her head against his shoulder. No one asked their opinion or sought their wisdom. Hana protested in favour of calling her son to seek advice. Jet got upset when he discovered Bodie's rank, maintaining he could answer anything she needed to know. Self-preservation guided every syllable and at one point, Phoenix nudged him and shook her head in disgust.

When Hana glanced back and recognised Wiri's defeated posture, she resumed her maternal authority and ushered everyone outside into the corridor. Larry offered him a feckless wave, and a mouthed apology as he followed the crowd. Hana closed the door after them and pulled the visitor's chair closer to the bed. She sat with a sigh, pulling her red curls into a bundle at her right shoulder and performing a plait without looking. It hung down over her breast, faint lines of ash grey creating detail beneath the harsh hospital lighting. "Right," she said, her tone gentle. "What do you want to do?"

Phoenix sighed. She reached for Wiri's hand, the action natural because she'd done it for most of her life. He sensed the familiar flicker of rightness which he'd run from and then craved. "You're the first person to ask us that, Mama," she acknowledged. "All they want to do is save themselves."

"Except your father." Hana winced. "I could hear the cogs turning in his brain. We don't want him making plans, do we?"

Wiri snorted. "He can take Seline out, I don't mind. Save us all the bother."

They explained their sorry tale to Hana, and she listened, beginning with Wiri's arrival in the town and stretching beyond Phoenix's appearance to their current predicament. She said nothing, absorbing the information in her measured way.

"I don't want Jet to get into trouble for keeping the gun that shot me," Wiri stressed. "He's an idiot, but he needs help. And Larry knows nothing about guns. He took it for safe keeping and didn't expect Ted to use it on me."

Hana frowned. Her lips flattened into a bow. "The police are already interested," she said. "They'll trace the gun, reprimand Jet for not registering it and then press charges against your vicar for leaving it lying around on his desk. Short of concocting an elaborate tissue of lies, I don't see how you can change any of that."

Wiri groaned and tilted his head back to stare at the ceiling. "I don't know then." His voice croaked with exhaustion. Phoenix gripped his hand harder.

"I'm not lying," she stated. She studied him, her eyes round and fearful. "Lies got me into a gigantic mess in the summer. It's wrong. I'm not doing it."

The weight of responsibility bore down on Wiri. Their fate rested in his hands and it left him powerless to steer the best course of action.

"What about the girl with the other gun?" Hana asked. "Is she really planning to take out her father with a shotgun?"

Wiri blew out a breath. "I wouldn't put it past her."

Phoenix narrowed her eyes. "And yet she removed the lid from the tank and called for help?" She frowned. "Why would she do that if she wanted Vaughan dead? Bashing him over the head is quite hit and miss. His wife would have searched for him eventually, wouldn't she? Unless Seline brained him, he was always going to survive." Phoenix tucked a curl behind her ear and exhaled through her nose. "Why look for the gun after she'd hurt Vaughan? She knew it was there."

"Maybe hurting him wasn't enough. She wanted to finish the job."

"It makes little sense." Hana sat back in the chair, wincing as the plastic creaked. "Not when her father had an accessible shotgun. What if she felt under threat herself? Could she have needed the smaller gun for her own protection?"

"The face at the window!" Wiri shot upright with a groan. He almost pitched Phoenix off the side of the bed. "Larry saw them. We need to find out who watched us take the gun from under the floorboards."

70

HAND GUARD

Tane arrived anyway. Vaughan's summons only caused him to press his foot harder on the gas pedal. Already on his way, he barrelled into Wiri's room with a frown bisecting his forehead.

Logan appeared behind him, closing the door on the worried faces of Wiri's other visitors. "He's not speaking to you without a lawyer," he growled, his tone threatening.

Wiri's jaw clenched at Tane's jerk of surprise. He hoped the cop didn't tell his uncle about their lengthy chats at the police station. Tane ran a hand through his blond hair and loosened the collar of his uniform. "I'll keep it off the record," he promised. "I just want to understand."

Still mistrustful, Logan set up a video call with a minion at Liza's former office. A lawyer in an expensive suit jumped at the chance to beat aside his cut throat colleagues and impress Judge Du Rose's brother. They began the conference with an understanding that nothing Wiri said would be admissible in criminal proceedings. Tane's colour paled as the tale unfolded.

"So, the gun belongs to Jet," he concluded. He exhaled and leaned back in the chair. "I suspected he'd gained some dodgy habits, but never anticipated that."

"It's not his fault." Wiri defended him, swayed by a guilt reflex which reminded him he'd abused the flatmate code of conduct in every way.

"Can you make it disappear?" Logan asked the question, and Wiri watched the lawyer's eyebrows disappear into the creases of his forehead. He spluttered and remained silent as though trapped inside the pixels of the tiny phone screen. Logan shrugged and caught the trolley wheels with his foot. The lawyer bounced against the box of tissues supporting the phone. "They got it from a safe hidden under the floor," Logan continued. "No one told the homeowner about the new location of the safe. The builder didn't know about the gun. Can you palm ownership onto Leilah's father?"

Tane nodded. "Maybe." He closed his eyes and blew out his lips. "What a mess."

"Go back to when the vicar saw the face in the window." Hana spoke, and the men turned to stare at her. "I'm sure it has relevance. Perhaps Pastor Larry has something more to share."

"I assumed he'd seen Seline. She knew where Jet kept the gun." Wiri picked at the stitches on his finger.

"Hendricks was the only Peeping Tom around town," Tane concluded. "He died before this happened."

"What about Ted?" Phoenix raised her eyebrows and glanced at Wiri, searching for solidarity. "He shot you with the same gun."

Tane shook his head. "He doesn't own a vehicle. How would he get to your place from town?"

"Wait." Logan held up an index finger. His grey irises misted as his strategic brain sifted through the facts. "He doesn't own a vehicle and yet he killed a guy on their property." His eyes narrowed. "How does that work?"

Tane sighed. "Good point. Perhaps Hendricks drove him out there?"

"To extort money from him. Miles away from town while trespassing? That makes no sense." Wiri leaned his head back against the pillow with a sigh. "Everything is jumbled."

Tane's jaw flexed, and he rose. "I'll interview Ted again tomorrow. But he's not talking." He glanced at the back of the phone screen and lowered his voice so the lawyer couldn't hear him. "I'll get Leilah to agree that the gun belonged to Hector. I've got officers looking for Seline." He slapped his thighs with fingers, which remained loose. "Look, Hendricks' car contained the wrench stained with Vaughan's blood. It's obvious he hit Vaughan and sealed Wiremu into the tank. And Ted admitted to killing Hendricks the next day. Everything else is circumstantial. I'll go back to the station and get it all wrapped up for today." He offered Wiri a feckless wave as he turned towards the door. "Sorry for dragging you into all this, son," he said. His blue irises flickered. "Thanks for your help."

The door clicked shut behind him, and Logan thanked the lawyer before disconnecting the call. He pushed the phone into his pocket and frowned at Hana. "If it looks like roke and smells like roke," he began.

She raised her hand in protest. "Don't swear in front of the children," she rebuked. "But I know what you mean." She flattened her lips as Wiri hid a yawn behind his injured hand. "My boy needs to rest," she said, rising from the chair and facing her husband. "We'll come back tomorrow and talk about it more." Leaning sideways, she pressed a kiss to Wiri's temple. "Get some sleep, sweetheart."

"Thanks Ma." Another yawn nipped at the corners of his lips.

Phoenix wrapped her arms around his neck and her kiss made a popping sound in his ear. "We'll get your truck from Larry's in the morning," she promised. "Don't worry about anything."

Wiri tilted his face towards her, surprised when she planted a kiss on his mouth. He didn't look at Logan, but sensed the vibes of antagonism pulsing across the room. "Where will you stay?" he whispered.

"Papa booked rooms in a motel in Hamilton," she replied. Her irises flickered with a strange grey light. "I hope I can stay awake during his lecture."

Wiri shook his head. "Not his style," he replied, his voice low. Logan loved words, but didn't waste them. That was one of his more unnerving qualities, alongside his ability to make his expression and body language unreadable. He squeezed her fingers with his good hand and watched his family file from the room, taking the mystery with them.

The nurse returned, nodding with approval because she didn't need to chase them away. She checked Wiri's pulse and blood pressure before unhooking the empty transfusion bag from the drip. "The doctor wants to keep you here for two nights. He'll visit early tomorrow to check the wounds. You're stuck with the fractured coccyx, though."

Wiri groaned. "How long does it take to heal?"

"Between two and three months."

He shifted on the mattress and frowned. "It doesn't hurt as much. I guess that's because of the anaesthetic."

She disconnected the pipe from the cannula in his right hand and shook her head. "Your surgeon brought in an orthopaedic registrar to give you a steroid injection while you were still unconscious." She waggled her manicured eyebrows. "Lucky you."

Wiri blew out a relieved breath. "Thank you, Uncle Mark," he whispered.

The nurse helped him onto his side and altered the pillows behind him. Then she dimmed the lights and left him to settle for the night. Wiri's fitful sleep took him back to the water tank, and as he stared up at the hatch closing the aperture to the outside world, he remembered something.

71

SAFETY SELECTOR LEVER

"What? No! I don't want to hear any more!" Wiri pressed his hands over his ears. Daylight slid between the slats of the blinds to cast scattered patterns across the linoleum floor. Jet had appeared before dawn, uniformed in case of opposition from the nursing staff. Larry had driven him and hung around outside.

"We didn't mean it to happen. It was an accident." Jet pursed his lips and glanced towards the door. "Larry said I had to tell you."

Wiri closed his eyes and blew out a whoosh of disgust. Jet dipped forward in the visitor's chair and dug his fingers into his fringe. The heavy silence closed around them until Wiri spoke. "You're corrupt."

"What?" Jet jerked upright, his irises flashing like diamonds. "I am not!"

"Yeah, you are." Wiri shook his head. "A bent cop, bent brother, bent tenant, bent everything. You just take what you want no matter who it hurts. The gun. Seline. Your brother's wife. My gear."

Jet lifted a hand in placation, though the lines of his jaw showed his veiled anger. "I searched your bag, but I took nothing from you." He snorted. "Yet you've helped yourself to all my stuff back at the house."

"Yes, coffee, biscuits and laundry powder." Wiri glared at him. "I intended to replace all of it at the supermarket yesterday afternoon, but got shot by your gun on my way there."

Jet ran a hand across his eyes. "She's pregnant. Miriama, Tane's wife. It's mine. That's why I've avoided going around there."

Sickness roiled in Wiri's stomach. His mother had coupled with his father in a gesture of defiance to his brother. The sordid act of revenge unleashed years of poison on his family.

And soiled him from his inception.

"Get out." He issued the command from behind clenched teeth. His heart ached for the unwanted child growing within its shocked and disappointed mother. He couldn't look at Jet. "Just go," he breathed.

Jet rose. "You can't tell anyone," he bit, his tone terse. His eyes danced a desperate jig as his gaze bounced around the room. "Not Tane."

Wiri squeezed his eyes shut and leaned his head back against the pillows. He searched for peace within himself, sending out tendrils of his consciousness to connect with Phoenix. An image of her appeared in his inner vision, smiling and rising onto her tiptoes. The kitten tee shirt pulled tight across her breasts and exposed the soft curve of her waist. He ached to touch her. But he wasn't like Jet.

The click of the door closing brought him extreme relief, and his shoulders sagged against the pillows. He couldn't live with Jet anymore. The Plan had no room for loose cannons in its carefully crafted schedule.

The Plan.

It had provided solidity and grounding as he'd struggled to find his way in life. Formulated months ago, after a single moment of passion and elation, it had lasted until yesterday. He'd kissed Phoenix in the barn and birthed The Plan. But did it make him as selfish and manipulative as Jet? The realisation hit him like a king tide. "I don't want to be like him," he murmured. He needed to set Phoenix free.

T he clatter of trolley wheels woke him from a fitful slumber. He groaned as his tailbone complained at his awkward position. Shifting on the mattress set up a bloom of heat in his thigh.

"Steady." The gentle male voice offered reassurance and firm hands clasped his shoulder. "What do you need?"

Wiri stared up through a fog of pain to find Larry smiling down at him. "I don't know," he whispered. "Help me time-walk to before last weekend."

Larry chuckled, a low rumble issuing from his chest. "I can't count the number of times I've woken with the same thought." He dipped sideways and retrieved a remote control from the bed rail. The cable swung as he lifted it and inspected the buttons. "Let's get you more comfortable. You're laying like a fallen rag-doll."

"Thanks." Wiri grumbled as he shifted on the mattress. He used his hands to support himself while Larry fluffed the pillows and raised the angle of the bed.

The remote control gave a metallic clang as he replaced it on the rail. He wagged his index finger at Wiri. "Did you send Jet packing while I ate breakfast in the cafeteria?" He cocked his head. "I should have ordered it to take away. Are you a grumpy patient, my friend?"

Wiri exhaled. "He got his sister-in-law pregnant," he said with a sigh. "I can't live with him anymore. He makes me sick!"

Larry tutted. "Watch your words, young padawan. If you overuse that expression, you will indeed become sick."

"You think?" Wiri rolled his eyes and spread his hands to encompass his various injuries. He thudded his head against the pillow and groaned at the tug of the stitches in the back of his head. "Is this not sick enough?"

Larry pursed his lips and sank back into the visitor's chair. Then he rose as if electrocuted. "You'd rather I leave? I wanted to check on you before Matins, but I don't mean to make things worse." He cleared his throat. "Your current predicament is my fault."

"No," Wiri sighed, dragging out the word. "Your involvement was a fluke, but at least you've owned it. Jet seems to think he's made of Teflon and nothing will stick to him."

Larry nodded and sank back into the chair. "I told Tane the truth, but he intends to perjure himself for his brother, despite my advice."

Wiri snorted. "Until he finds out what Jet's done behind his back!"

Larry flattened his lips into a sad smile. "Perhaps he won't find out."

Wiri swallowed and blinked away unexpected tears of regret. "The truth always comes out," he whispered. "Lying is like trying to hold back the tide with your hands."

Larry nodded. "What will you do?" he asked. He silenced as an orderly knocked before pushing open Jet's door.

"Tea or coffee?" she sang, her rounded pink cheeks and wide smile lightening the atmosphere.

Both men settled on tea and sipped in silence, waiting for the trolley wheels to squeak along the corridor. When Larry repeated his question, Wiri shrugged. "What will I do about what?" he asked. "About my job, my relationship, or Jet?"

"All the above." Larry wrinkled his nose and peered into his cup. "I should have asked for sugar."

Wiri stared at the ceiling, creating a blank canvas for his mind to sift through his issues. "I could go home," he mused. "Ma and Logan know everything now. I could work on the property and wait for Phoenix to reach sixteen."

"Is that what you want?" Larry cocked his head and studied him.

Wiri sighed. "Yes and no. I'd love to, but proximity drives the temptation to jump further into our relationship than we should. It needs to be her choice. And living under the same roof might make things awkward for the family. Logan will grow tired of watching me and eventually bury me somewhere remote." He shrugged. "It's safer to stay away and return for visits. I've waited for Phoenix since just before my fifth birthday. At least I have more hope now than I did then." His lips twisted into a grimace. "But first, I need to offer her the chance to just be friends. I'd hate to feel she fell into this through some misguided sense of obligation." He sighed. "I also refuse to live with a corrupt cop, so if I stay here, I'll need to find somewhere else."

"Move in with me." Larry's gentle smile flickered as though he feared rejection. "I could use the company."

"Thanks." The word caught in Wiri's throat and he bit down on his lower lip. "I'd like that." Larry's sparkling irises contained kindness, but Wiri feared guilt lurked beneath the offer. It was impossible for him to live like that again, always watching for another's hidden motives. He decided to test the friendship by moving in with the vicar, promising himself he could always leave again if necessary. He changed the subject. "Where's Jet? Outside?" He glanced towards the door.

Larry's grey curls bounced as he shook his head. "No. He has another day of giving evidence. A colleague picked him up in a patrol car and drove him to the courthouse."

"Another drug dealer?" Wiri's eyes narrowed. Logan Du Rose tolerated no such organisations to stain their small township with their poison. He'd run the last group out of town, using broken bones and threats to reinforce his message. Wiri twisted his lips. "Your town is a hotbed of vice."

Larry chuckled. "It's not so bad. A few gamblers, weed smokers, and the odd alcoholic." He patted the dog collar at his throat with tentative fingers. He sighed. "Today's case is a gentleman who believes the highway rules don't apply to him. He met Jet while driving on the wrong side of the road. At speed."

Wiri winced. "Right. So, he'll lose his licence then."

Larry waggled his eyebrows. "More than that. He wrecked Jet's personal vehicle and then picked a fight with him next to the remnants of a rather nice Mustang. I believe he's defending himself against a few charges."

Wiri's gaze strayed to the ceiling tiles. "So that's why Jet has no car. I wondered." Speaking about the law gave him a strange sense of security. "Please, can you pass my phone?" He jerked his head towards the side table where Hana left his bag of belongings. Tane had taken his jeans and tee shirt as evidence against Ted.

Larry rose and dug in the bag before handing over his phone. Wiri wrinkled his nose and tutted. "Damn," he breathed. "I only have twenty percent of the charge left." He unlocked the screen and opened Vaughan's email containing a wonky scan of his contract with Hendricks. His lips parted in a smile. "I didn't need Aunty Liza," he mused. Larry looked up from his teacup, one eyebrow raised in question. Wiri shook his head. "The interest rate is extortionate. It's a loan shark agreement. There's anti-profiteering legislation against this type of lending now. Whoever inherits Hendricks' estate will struggle to enforce this. They'll need to come to an arrangement through mediation. But Vaughan's actual debt is a fraction of the total."

"I don't know what you're talking about." Larry shrugged.

"It doesn't matter." Wiri leaned back against the pillows. "I'll let Aunty Liza's interns rip it to pieces just for fun. But it's void.

No wonder Vaughan couldn't keep up the repayments. I bet Mari has something similar." He sighed, the irony painful. "And Ted."

Larry wrinkled his nose and took another sip of his tea. "I'm not great with money things." He cocked his head. "Or legal things either. You obviously are."

Wiri pursed his lips. "Yeah." He let his phone fall onto the mattress next to him. "I love it. It's like tracking something through the bush. It offers the same thrill of success when I find it. The signs are there in the legislation and the case law. It's a hunt." His irises glittered, and then the light faded. He shrugged. "Anyway, the agreements weren't enforceable. I got shot for nothing." He closed his eyes and his hair shuffled against the pillow as he relaxed. Regret bore his shoulders lower. "I wish I'd thought about it earlier. I saw Vaughan throw Hendricks out on my first night at the farm and sensed it related to money. None of this needed to happen."

"I'm sorry, my friend." Larry sighed. "I wish I could help you."

"You can." Wiri winced as he shifted in the bed. "I remembered something in the early hours. Did you tell Tane about the face you saw at the window the night we moved the gun?"

"Yes." Larry nodded. "But the darkness stopped me from recognising them."

Wiri tapped his left wrist with his right index finger. "You mentioned something sparkling on their arm. What was it?"

"A watch, a bracelet." Larry shrugged. "I don't know. Maybe they carried their car keys in their hand."

"Fair enough." Wiri inhaled. "But we assumed you saw Seline."

"You guys did." Larry shook his head. "I never identified the person."

Wiri sipped his cooling tea and mused over the important nugget of memory. "The thing which convinced me Seline closed the tank was the dragging of the lid across the roof. It took time for her to lift it up over the inspection tunnel. It's heavy concrete and needs muscle to raise it the full distance to sit over the hole. She had as much difficulty getting it off later." Wiri tapped his teeth with his fingernail. "I know she opened it, but I'm no longer convinced she shut me in there and closed the lid."

"Leilah?" Larry's eyes widened, and the cup tilted in his hand. Wiri noticed tea leaves forming a pattern against the white ceramic where the bag had split.

Wiri shrugged. "Why not? Having a threatening ex-husband in prison seems convenient." He stared around the clinical room as another puzzle piece dropped into place. "Oh, wow," he whispered. His eyes widened as he gaped at Larry. "I need to go back to town."

72

GAS PISTON

"This is ridiculous!" Larry grumbled as he pushed the wheelchair through the corridors at speed. "I just stole hospital property! I'm a vicar, in case you hadn't noticed."

Wiri heard his tone change as an oncoming group smiled and waved to him. A frail woman in their midst kept her gaze fixed on the blue stripe on the linoleum. She stared at it as though unable to focus on anything more than following its path to the cancer treatment centre it denoted. Wiri pursed his lips and cast his gaze at the pressed edges of his hospital gown. Larry's fake brightness irritated him as they barrelled towards the external doors. "Hello everyone," he chimed. The chair jerked sideways and headed for the wall as he became distracted. "I'll pop back later to see you, Mrs Macalister."

Wiri inhaled as the wall grew nearer before Larry righted his trajectory. Freedom beckoned from beyond the glass doors and another rainy day. He clasped his hand over the flapping hem of his gown. "Slow down!" he hissed. "You almost killed me! I've made it this far in this bloody town. Don't add indecent exposure to my list of problems."

"Tetchy, tetchy." Larry breezed through the automatic doors and nodded to a security guard standing sentry by the sign for the emergency department. Smoke curled from behind his back, suggesting he'd indulged in a crafty cigarette break. Larry's sensible shoes squeaked against the flagstones. "Now, where did I leave my car?"

"I'm freezing." Wiri's teeth set up a furious chatter reminiscent of the water tank. He revisited the trauma in flashes of memory as rain spattered his face and neck. The wind attacked the hem of his gown, threatening to flash his wares at another group of inbound patients. He held his hand down over it, noticing the bruise from the cannula he'd pulled from the vein.

"Well, you wanted to do this." Larry's tone held little sympathy. Wiri found it disappointing, considering his vocation.

He gripped his phone in his right hand and used the remaining battery life to send Phoenix a text. *Stall the parents,'* he demanded. *'I need two hours.'*

Larry located his car and watched as, barefoot, Wiri manoeuvred himself into the passenger seat. He checked for the watchful eye of the security guard before collapsing the wheelchair and bundling it into the boot of his car. The transparent bag containing Wiri's remaining possessions went in next to it, but Larry retrieved the truck keys and dropped them into Wiri's lap.

"Ouch!" Wiri complained as they jangled against his wound. "Thanks for that."

Larry blew out an exasperated breath as he started the engine. "We shouldn't be doing this," he commented. "I should call Tane right now!"

Wiri snorted. "What, so he and Jet can hush everything up and make it go away? No thanks. Didn't you notice how quickly they arrested the new kid for murder?"

Larry groaned. "I'm a new kid." He pursed his lips and navigated the ticket machine at the entrance. The barrier arm rose without demanding cash after he presented an all-access pass. He growled deep in his throat. "I was a new person in town." He slapped his thigh. "Jet was a new kid, for goodness' sake! This isn't about status. Tane isn't like that!"

"Whatever." Wiri licked his lips and stared through the windscreen as the wipers left streaks across the glass. "I don't see him rushing up to Leilah's and arresting Seline."

"Maybe she isn't guilty."

They travelled in silence through the smaller townships as Wiri stared at his phone. His shoulders dropped with relief as Phoenix sent him a thumbs-up reply to indicate she'd understood. He glanced up with a sigh as Larry navigated the bends north of Pirongia village.

"Are you okay?" The vicar gave him a sideways smile and then concentrated on the road. "Hamilton is eating the surrounding townships. It's like an insatiable monster, gobbling up farmland for housing and development."

Wiri nodded. "Like Auckland." He shifted in discomfort on the seat. "Why are you helping me, Larry?"

A tight smile lit the vicar's lips. "Because someone other than the town's vicar needs to bring it justice."

Wiri narrowed his eyes. "You know, don't you? When did you work it out?"

Larry exhaled and lifted his left hand to run it through his grey curls. "Perhaps at the same moment you did. His own secrets clouded Tane's judgement. The weight of minding his brother hasn't helped either of them. It made Jet sloppy and Tane blind."

Wiri hauled on the hem of his gown. "This would seem so much better coming from you," he said. He liked him, but the vicar's lack of courage seemed to diminish him.

Larry shook his head in an instant denial. "No. You know what I think about your plan."

Pirongia mountain blocked out the sky as they diverted from the main road and drove a more circuitous route around its western side. The three distinctive peaks seemed to bow their heads with regret at the tumultuous news the men carried.

Larry helped Wiri from the vehicle after parking in front of the vicarage. He shuffled to his truck and used the key fob to unlock it.

"I'll grab it." Larry pulled open the rear door and retrieved the paper bag containing Wiri's remaining set of clothing. He scrabbled on the floor until discovering where Phoenix had left it after swapping into the kitten tee shirt and too small jeans. Then he helped him climb the steps to his front door.

"Thank goodness Logan didn't decide to drive back here last night to fetch my truck." Wiri leaned against the wall just inside the hallway to catch his breath. The strings of the paper bag dug into his fingers. "I can't confront a murderer wearing no undies."

"Should I retrieve the wheelchair?" Larry asked. He paused, unsure of his next role in the sad mission.

Wiri nodded and limped towards the bathroom. "In a second, please. I'll pull these clothes on and meet you at the bottom of the steps. "

In the bathroom, he slipped out of the hospital gown and stood naked in front of the tarnished mirror. Little of his body retained its usual healthy glow. Raised weals littered his torso, the bruises spreading to join as a rainbow of black, purple and yellow. He lifted his fingers to touch the back of his head, wrinkling his nose at the bald patch surrounding the stitches. With a sad exhale, he tugged the jeans and tee shirt from the paper bag. Phoenix's perfumed scent rose from the fabric, and he pressed them to his nose and breathed in her essence. He didn't want her here for this.

It took longer than he imagined to drag the clothing onto his body. He winced as he slipped his injured leg into the jeans and shrugged them over the wound. Every part of him ached, from his crown to the tips of his toes, but he sent a silent thank you to his uncle Mark for the steroid injection which had eased the pain in his tailbone. Phoenix had discarded everything except the socks and he stared down at his bare feet. His reflection smiled back at him in the mirror. "At least you're wearing undies," he told it.

Tane hadn't kept his boots and Wiri retrieved them from the hospital bag in the hallway. He bent to shove them onto his feet, but didn't linger to tie the laces. Larry's dark shape appeared in the glass of the front door as he pushed it open. "Want some help?" he asked, jerking his head towards Wiri's feet. "I left the wheelchair at the bottom of the steps."

"Na, I'm good." He ran a hand over his face, irritated by the burgeoning bristles and wishing he'd had time to shower and shave. He exhaled and faced the vicar, dread snaking through his heart. "I'm ready, he said," though his wavering voice betrayed him.

Larry nodded. "Push you there and then leave you? Are you sure?"

Wiri gave a slow shrug. Conflict prickled the skin at the back of his neck. "It's what my kaumatua and kuia expect," he replied.

And they would.

His forebears had instilled him with respect for his elders.

He intended to make them proud.

73

FRONT TRUNNION

Leilah met them at the door of the cafe, hauling it wide to allow room for Larry to push the wheelchair into the warmth. An apron snuggled around her hips to hide her gentle curves. "Hey," she said, a smile creasing the skin on either side of her eyes. "I'm glad you're well enough to leave the hospital." She stood aside as Larry parked the chair next to the nearest table. "We're not quite open yet, but you're welcome to wait here." The bell tinkled again as the door closed with a click. Wiri's hand shook as he raised it in thanks to the vicar.

"Did you find Seline and the gun?" Larry cocked his head at Leilah.

She winced and ran her wrist across her forehead. "Yes. Silly misunderstanding. She took her gelding to the riding school in Hamilton and called me when she'd finished." A frown crossed her forehead. "We still haven't found the gun." A series of rapid blinks communicated her distress, and she lowered her voice. "Tane is dealing with the other matter." She glanced at the entrance to the kitchen and wrinkled her nose. "My ex-husband will get an unexpected visit from the authorities soon."

"Right. I'm sorry you had to go through that." Larry said, avoiding Wiri's gaze. He jangled his car keys in his pocket. "I need to nip across town on an errand." Raindrops speckled his hair, laid there during the short walk from the vicarage to the cafe. He checked his watch and pursed his lips. "Won't be long," he said to Wiri. Strain pulled his eyes into narrow slits and he breezed from the cafe with too much energy. It wouldn't take long for him to pick up Wiri's scant belongings and move them into the spare bedroom of the vicarage.

Leilah locked the door behind him and waved to a farmer who'd slowed his truck on the main street. His hope of an earlier than usual coffee faded in his eyes as he stomped on the gas pedal. Leilah glanced towards the kitchen, where a metal pot clattered against the sink. "I can make you a sneaky drink," she said, devilment sparking behind her eyes. "Mari doesn't pay me, so she also can't fire me for breaking the rules."

"Thanks." Wiri's voice caught in his throat. Sadness cascaded over his head like a waterfall. His fingers twitched over the phone in his jeans pocket before dropping into his lap. He regretted not calling Vaughan. Larry had suggested it, but he'd dismissed the vicar's common sense with a hasty ease. Larry had used part of the drive to relay the tale of Leilah's traumatic life and the state she'd arrived back in the town. He'd wanted to stay. For her.

Leilah busied herself behind the coffee machine and Wiri used her diversion to gather his thoughts. He formulated the sentences in his head, planning his arguments like a barrister. His phone buzzed against his thigh and he winced as pain bloomed from his wound. He wiped his damp fingers against the rain-soaked fabric of his jeans and tugged the device free. "Yeah," he answered, his tone lacklustre.

"Wiremu?" Tane cleared his throat. "I'm glad I caught you. How are you faring?"

"Yeah, good," Wiri lied. The coffee machine whooshed in the background as Leilah steamed milk. Tane faltered, wrong-footed by the assumption he'd called Wiri in hospital but found him elsewhere. "Where are you?" he demanded.

"What do you want?"

He sighed. Wiri imagined his mission contained an element of unpleasantness and envied him. It couldn't be worse than the course he'd chosen. His knees bumped against the table as he turned the wheelchair one-handed. Tane cleared his throat again. "The coroner released Hendricks' body. He died of a haemorrhagic stroke. Could have happened anytime. All his injuries were post mortem."

Wiri snuffed out a laugh devoid of mirth. "Right," he managed. He shook his head and stared at the ceiling. "So, you hounded me for nothing? Just an easy stranger to pin all the bad stuff on as it suited you."

"It wasn't like that!" Tane's voice rose in protest. Then he groaned. "Maybe you're right. You were the unknown quantity in the equation. I know you think it's personal, but I promise it isn't."

Wiri ground his teeth and conceded the point. "Yeah, Larry said the same." He smoothed his hand over the raindrops poised as perfect circles on the arm of the wheelchair. They exploded beneath the pressure, dampening his hands and spreading darker streaks across the faux leather. Many hands had touched the arms of the chair, some relaxed and others gripping in claws of fear. He wiped his fingers on his jeans again and wished he could rid himself of the electrical current which hard wired him into the fate of others.

He'd never managed it yet.

But at least now he knew how he'd use it to make a future for himself and Phoenix.

"Thanks for letting me know," he told Tane. "Will you release Ted now?"

Tane tutted. "He still bundled a dead body into a water tank to hide it. And shot you. I'm talking to the prosecution lawyer about what to do next."

"Right." Wiri forced a smile onto his lips in acknowledgement of Leilah as she placed a brimming mug of hot coffee on the table next to him. He disconnected the call and laid his phone beside the mug. Steam rose from the surface of the milk like rolling fog. It made him ache for Logan's mountain and the unpredictability of its natural environment.

Mari appeared from the kitchen, wiping her fingers on a cloth dangling from her apron pocket. She glanced at Wiri and then at Leilah. "We don't open for another ten minutes," she said, her forehead drawing into frown lines. She noticed the wheelchair and wrinkled her nose. Wiri sensed the moment she decided to edge around the counter and face him, her gnarled fingers wringing the cloth.

"Sit down, Aunty." He jerked his head towards the chair opposite him.

"I'll leave you to it." Leilah smiled at him and jerked into action, turning towards the kitchen and the myriad jobs awaiting her.

"No, stay." Wiri's fingers knotted in his lap. The stitches in his left hand tugged, the pain less than before but enough to ground him.

Mari tugged out the chair with agonising slowness. Her gaze strayed to Ted's corner, the stool tucked beneath the kauri counter. Another, less battered companion had joined it as though to make up for his absence. "I'm sorry he did that to you," she whispered, unable to look Wiri in the eyes. "Stupid old man."

"He did it for you."

Leilah froze as Wiri said the words, her lips parting and her head already shaking. She took a step back towards them and stopped again, her irises sparkling with hidden emotion.

74

DETENT PLUNGER

Wiri kept his steady gaze fixed on Mari. She rose and shoved the chair with the backs of her knees. It continued its journey across the floor until it crashed into another. "You're mistaken." Her wooden tone cast him out of her proximity, her cafe and her life.

"What?" Leilah blinked and looked from one to the other. "Why? What are you talking about?"

Wiri sighed. He hated how the women towered over his wheelchair as though to reduce him and his conclusions to nothing more than an inconvenient speck in their busy lives. He'd always struggled to know which of his forebears to channel. His mind vied between Reuben and Kane. Ridiculous really when neither life ended in victory.

So, he changed the pattern and sought to channel a different authority from the failed men in his lineage. His blood soared in his ears as he traced his whakapapa back to Kuia Phoenix Du Rose, detouring down through Alfred to Eliza.

Judge Eliza Du Rose.

Her perpetual fury gave him courage. Enough to straighten his painful spine in the wheelchair and force energy into his knees. He rose, taller than the women and heard her powerful voice project from his soul. Command and energy flooded his chest. "You hit Vaughan over the head with your tyre wrench," he said, pointing at Mari. "You don't believe he's good enough for Leilah. They didn't invite you to the wedding. You ask Leilah to do minor jobs for you to keep her close, but Vaughan threatened that. I don't know why you went up to speak to him that day, but you'd forgotten about me. You looked into the tank and weren't sure if I'd seen you. So, you shut me in there."

The colour drained from Mari's face. It left her with a skeletal appearance. She blinked and swallowed.

"Mari?" Leilah edged closer. Her eyes performed a ragged dance of disbelief as she glanced at one and then the other, striving to comprehend Wiri's accusation. "You brought lunch to the house for everyone. It's why I texted Vaughan to see if they were still at the tank." Her pupils dilated as though a great darkness had descended around her head. "You said you couldn't find him. It's why I asked Seline to walk up and check."

Wiri sighed. "Hendricks made an art form out of snooping. Your tyre needed changing and I remember hearing you couldn't find your wrench. Jet helped you to do it. Hendricks would have heard about that on the town's grapevine. I think he found the wrench and tried to blackmail you with it. The police found two in his Mercedes, one which fitted the vehicle's specifications. And one which didn't. Yours. Covered in Vaughan's blood. Hendricks must have wiped his fingerprints but left the blood. Removing his also removed yours, but you didn't think about that."

Leilah pressed her hands over her eyes. Mari twitched as though wanting to comfort her. She let the cloth fall back against the apron and her fingers patted the air. But she didn't move her feet nearer to Leilah.

Dizziness blurred Wiri's vision and nagged at his brain, muddling his prepared sentences. He needed to sit, but couldn't. He caught his breath and powered through his speech like a queen's counsel, giving his closing arguments. "I'm not sure why you met Hendricks at the tank. Maybe he wanted to present his case at the site of the crime." He cocked his head and surveyed the tremble in Mari's fingers. "Tane stopped you for speeding on the main road. He gave you a ticket, which places you in the vicinity of Vaughan's farm and the water tank. Ted laughed about it a few days later when the penalty notice arrived in the mail. That means he wasn't with you when Tane stopped you. I don't believe he had anything to do with Hendricks' death. Tane just phoned me to say they're releasing the body. Hendricks died of a heart attack."

"What?" Leilah dragged her hands away from her eyes. "So, nobody killed him?"

"Nope." Wiri shrugged. His gaze strayed to Mari. "You could have left him lying there. Or waited for him to die and then called for an ambulance. But you didn't. You bundled him into the tank and tried to cover up his death."

Tears filled Mari's eyes. She left them to cascade down her face without wiping them away. Her chest hitched. "Hector died like that. So sudden." Her face creased into cruel lines which crisscrossed her features at random. It changed her appearance. "It reminded me. I panicked." She used the edge of her sleeve to wipe her nose.

"But she didn't kill him?" Positivity entered Leilah's tone as she spied a glimmer of hope on the horizon. "She just hid the body." She reached for Mari's hand. "We'll talk to Tane. Explain everything. He'll understand."

"Will your husband?" Wiri frowned at her. "She could have killed him."

Leilah's hands dropped to her sides. Her already divided loyalties split into smaller fragments.

Her father and Vaughan.

Seline and Vaughan.

Mari and Vaughan.

Always Vaughan.

She stared at the worn pattern on the floor. She closed her eyes, but her lips moved as she fought old life choices she couldn't resolve.

Mari's chest hitched. Leilah's withdrawal shook her with more intensity than any of the week's poor decisions had. "I'm sorry, Lei," she pleaded. "I'll apologise to Horse's boy."

Leilah's chest heaved. "Horse's boy," she murmured. "That's who he is to you, isn't it? Horse's boy. The foster kid no one wanted. A pawn on a chess board." She shook her head. "This town kept us apart for two decades. I can't let you do it again." She stepped back and her fingers scrabbled at the ties of her apron.

"No, no! Don't leave me." Mari took flight, hurling herself around the counter and disappearing through the archway into the kitchen.

Leilah blinked in confusion, dragging the apron over her head. She dropped it onto the table. The ties trailed to the floor like escaping eels. "I'm so sorry," she breathed. "What a mess."

Wiri tilted sideways and the fingers of his right hand formed an anchor against the table top. His voice rasped as his remaining energy fled. "She wanted the wrench. I'm guessing she tipped Hendricks into the tank before realising he'd taken his car keys with him."

"Oh, gosh!" Leilah pressed her fingers over her lips. Her hand shook. "Let me drive you home. I'm so sorry for everything you've been through, Wiremu. I really am."

"Don't leave me." Mari's voice wavered.

Wiri closed his eyes in resignation at the distinctive click of a hinge pin closing. Leilah gasped as she stopped her gushing apology. Wiri looked up to find a stock and barrel already joined in his peripheral vision. Mari peered over the top of Vaughan's missing break action shotgun. She supported its weight like a professional, her deceptively thin arms stronger than they looked. Years of shifting heavy crates of supplies had honed her into a woman capable of anything physical.

Including lifting a solid lid a metre into the air and closing an innocent man into a concrete tomb.

Leilah's lips moved, but no words emerged. Her right hand moved to her left shoulder and Wiri saw again the memory scored into her muscle reflex by trauma. He lifted his right hand and yanked the back of her shirt, edging her between him and the table. Her feet clattered with the wheelchair and she stumbled. But Mari's gaze and the yawning mouth of the barrel didn't stray from the centre of Wiri's chest.

One shot. At close range.

He wouldn't survive this one. Jet's roulette had caught him in its tricksy twists and turns. Odds of a hundred to zero.

'*Speak, boy!*' Liza's voice urged him from his past. '*Open your mouth, child!*' With her black curls scraped into an unforgiving bun behind her neck, she'd terrified him.

Until the moment he'd plugged into her whakapapa.

And understood.

They were cut from the same lineage.

The Du Rose's ancestor had served as a lawyer in post revolution France. Disillusioned by the limitations of the resulting *Declaration of the Rights of Man and of the Citizen*, he'd emigrated to the new land. He'd never ceased arguing for the autonomy of mankind and rarely lost a verbal battle.

To occupy the land he'd paid for.

For the hand of the chief's daughter.

For the right of his family to live in peace.

After that, he'd progressed to arguing for Māori rights and even hidden the stricken king as he'd fled the English troops at Rangiriri Pa.

Wiri straightened his shoulders and faced the desperate woman as her finger closed over the trigger. He drowned out Leilah's sobbing as she clambered over the wheelchair and ran towards the front door. Her fingers scrabbled with the lock and cool air flooded the cafe as she flung the door wide. He heard her screaming in the street for help.

"You shouldn't have involved Ted." His voice surprised him. It maintained a steady cadence, calm and unruffled. "You took advantage of his affection."

Mari's eyelashes fluttered closed, but not for long enough for Wiri to risk a physical challenge. He ran through the choreographed movements in his mind, but sensed his body might fail to obey him with the speed and strength required. She shook off his accusation. "You're smarter than you look, kid. But I'm telling you nothing."

"Okay." Wiri shrugged. Movement in his peripheral vision showed Leilah intercepting a pedestrian on the other side of the street. She jabbed her finger towards the cafe. He turned his attention back to Mari. "Why did you come up to our place the other night?" He jerked his head towards her right hand where the silver bracelet clanked against her bony wrist. "Larry saw you." Just the glitter of metal in the eerie glow of dusk. Enough to trigger a memory in a night filled with pain.

Mari's lips flattened into a thin line. "Shut up!" she demanded. "I need to think."

Wiri made a sound low in his throat. "Can I at least sit down?" His knees set up a furious tremor, which made his backside sag.

"No." Mari's gaze tracked to the open doorway and back again. She kept the shotgun trained on Wiri as she sidestepped and closed it. The lock clicked, and she dropped the blind. She fumbled with the string, and it hung at a jaunty angle, half up and half down. The enormous glass window displayed her crime, but she seemed not to notice as she worried about the door. Her index finger clasped the trigger before Wiri could consider his escape.

He exhaled. His fingers steepled against the table as he leaned sideways to displace his weight. "I wanted to show you respect," he said, blinking up at Mari. "As a kuia. I can help you speak to Tane, but not if you shoot me."

Mari groaned, and the shotgun butt shuddered against her shoulder. But she adopted a firmer stance and Wiri stared down the barrel and wished he'd taken Larry's advice. His phone vibrated in his pocket and he ignored it. "Ted took the blame," she said, her tone harsh. "Let's leave it that way, shall we?"

Wiri shook his head. "Sorry. I can't do that. It's not justice, Aunty. It's wrong. I'm sure you didn't ask him to reconnect the pipes from the barn, but he did it for you. Did he borrow your vehicle or hitch a ride? I'm sure Tane will work out the details." He cocked his head. "One question though. Did he overhear me and Phoenix asking for the tank maker in the cafe, or did you warn him?"

Mari swallowed. "It doesn't matter," she whispered.

Wiri stared down at his trembling thigh. "It does to me. I took a bullet either way." He jumped as someone rattled the door handle. Unable to gain access, they knocked on the glass. The steady rapping of a caffeine addict denied their fix. Voices sounded in the street. The measured hum of thwarted customers. Mari turned, her trainers squeaking against the tiles until she'd cut out the distraction from outside. The gun barrel remained rock steady in her capable hands.

The cafe vibrated with the gentle click of an outer door. Mari's ears twitched, and she hissed with irritation. "Delivery man," she whispered. Conflict flared in her eyes as her attention split. She shook her head, perhaps chastising herself for forgetting about the back door and the imminent arrival of the day's supplies. Wiri tensed, waiting for his opportunity and praying his battered body stood up to the coming demands on it. The open maw of the gun's barrel shifted enough to his right to guarantee a shoulder strike and possible survival.

"Hey, Aunty." The familiar click of heels seemed deafening in the silent cafe. Wiri held his breath as Logan Du Rose eased around the counter and smiled down at Mari. "Give me the gun,

Whāea," he said, his tone gentle but resonating with authority. "I won't let you kill my boy. That's my job."

75

MAGAZINE FLOOR PLATE

Wiri didn't appreciate Logan's veiled threat. His phone vibrated in his pocket again. He imagined Phoenix trying to warn him of her father's imminent arrival. Too late. He twisted his lips in regret. Larry wanted him to call Vaughan, and he'd resisted. No longer sure of what he'd expected to achieve, he observed Logan edge closer to Mari.

"It's okay, Uncle." He lifted his left hand to halt the inevitable catastrophe.

Logan cocked his head, humour lighting his grey irises and causing them to sparkle with his ready sarcasm. "Really?" His lips flattened into a line. "I hadn't noticed. My mistake." His voice held a gritty, threatening quality. His cowboy boots continued to gain ground.

Wiri winced. He turned his attention to Mari. "The big guns will come from Hamilton, Aunty. You don't want that, do you?" An even bigger gun edged closer to her, and he sensed she'd vastly underestimated Logan's presence. Wiri had seen his uncle in action. Logan Du Rose showed no mercy, but for once, his reputation hadn't preceded him.

She wavered, mania glinting in her eyes. "I've lost Leilah," she whispered. "Nothing else matters." Her tendons showed as she strengthened her grip on the forearm of the shotgun. Logan rounded the end of the counter.

"One shot, Aunty." Wiri's jaw showed against his cheek as he ground the words through his teeth. "There's no contingency in that. You need to be sure where you're putting that cartridge, because it'll be the last thing you do."

Logan's eyes widened, and he shook his head in disgust. He wanted to disarm her, not encourage her to shoot. The pursing of his lips told Wiri to shut up as he edged closer.

The wheelchair pressed against the backs of Wiri's knees, offering relief on its uncomfortable seat. He longed to sink into it and wheel himself away from the tragedy unfolding before him. A siren echoed off the buildings in the main street, its wail of alarm ceasing as though killed by an anxious hand. Car doors slammed beyond the wide swathe of glass through which Ted usually surveyed his narrow, empty world. A police car blocked the thoroughfare, and he saw Tane waving his arms at the pedestrians gathered across the road.

Time slowed.

Wiri studied Mari's calm expression with an experienced eye. He recognised his mother's resignation in the steadiness of her finger on the trigger. "Don't do it," he whispered, his tone dull. "I know what you're doing. Don't wait for them to end it for you."

A frown creased Logan's forehead, and he narrowed his brows. He darted a glance through the window at the police car. In the street, Jet slipped a Kevlar vest over his head and secured the ties with an expert hand. He reached into the cavernous vehicle and withdrew a Bushmaster XM-15 rifle. Logan's eyes widened at Wiri's groan of dismay.

"I don't believe it," Wiri hissed. He shook his head. "He played Russian roulette with a stolen gun when he had access to that kind of firepower." Anger clouded his rational thought, causing his knees to tremble as he struggled to remain upright. He glared at Mari. "Did you know he was a member of the Armed Offenders Squad?"

Mari swallowed, distracted by his tangent. Her lips moved, but she didn't reply.

"I'm sick of that dude!" Wiri snarled.

Mari tilted her view to take in the rifle, which Jet slung diagonally across his body and the lethal thirty-round magazine he clipped beneath it. Her shoulder relaxed and the eye of the barrel shifted a fraction to the left. A chest shot then. Resignation flooded her eyes. She wanted Jet to finish it for her. To put an end to a lifetime of sadness. Wiri saw it written in the lowering of her heavy lids as the skin tightened over the knuckles of her index finger.

Logan moved with surprising speed and agility. He shoved the barrel to the left with enough force to knock Mari off balance. She gasped in a heady mixture of rage and dismay.

And pulled the trigger.

76

REAR SIGHT LEAF

Wiri's knees failed him and he collapsed into the wheelchair's waiting embrace. His vision blurred as the force gave the wheels momentum. He coasted backwards as though seeing the scene in reverse, ploughing through chairs and a table which skittered sideways. Myriad tiny cuts stung his left cheek.

Victory flared in Logan's eyes as he held the gun aloft, fading as the rest of Jet's crew burst in through the kitchen and screamed at him to surrender. Wiri fought the urge to laugh at the fury in Logan's face as they forced him onto the ground and confiscated the shotgun. His lips parted in a grin he could never blame on the painkillers. It drooped with guilt as Logan lifted his chin and gave him a withering glare from between the officer's heavy boots.

Mari sobbed on the floor of her cafe. She drew her knees to her chest, resembling a tiny bundle of discarded clothing as she wrapped her arms around herself. With the build of a child, she seemed easy enough to overlook.

To underestimate.

Glass covered Ted's counter like early snow. It had cascaded across the pair of stools and lay scattered over the floor. Wiri's ears still rang with the shock of the report. It reverberated around the inside of his skull like a tinkling refrain soaring on a loop. The discarded shell cartridge had ejected in the seconds after Logan knocked Mari to the ground. It rolled from side to side in the breeze from beneath the door, its plastic housing split like a distended belly. Black powder spewed from between the slit, having missed its one true purpose.

A black shape appeared in front of him. It obscured the rage boiling in Logan's eyes as the armed police officer kept his weapon trained on him. "You okay, mate? You're bleeding." Jet bent at the waist to peer into his face. His lips curved on one side into a sardonic smile. "I figure you have a death wish. Want me just to shoot you and have done with it?" He jerked in surprise at the vile expletive Wiri released. "Oh," he said, his tone hurt. "Too soon?"

Wiri shook his head and stared past him through the broken window. "Get away from me," he hissed. "You're the biggest fake I've ever met." He lifted his damaged hand and jabbed his index finger at the cop. "Never speak to me again." His eyes narrowed to angry slits. "One day," he snarled, "one day, I'll take you down and I'll enjoy every second." His jaw ached with the pressure of his grinding teeth. "See you in court, officer!" The pledge gave him courage and a purpose. He knew he'd do it, or die trying.

Jet's jaw dropped, and he took a step backwards, propelled there by the force of Wiri's declaration. He glanced down at the weapon slung across his body with such casual abandon. A Glock nestled in a holster at his hip. He knew nothing else but violence. Cause and effect.

Wiri raged inside his own head.

Bent cop and probably bent soldier.

"Let my uncle go," he snarled. His eyes flashed and his fingers balled into fists on the arms of the wheelchair. His voice held authority. "Fetch the Senior Sergeant. Now."

Tane appeared, arriving through the kitchen on tentative steps. Rain plastered his blond hair to his forehead and left it in a cockerel's plume at the crown. He swore beneath his breath at the scene before him. Paramedics followed at a safe distance, brushing past the armed officers as though used to such weaponry.

Tane's lips tightened as he approached Wiri. The wheelchair gave the sergeant a height advantage over the teenager. His head shook as he arrived before him. "What the hell, man?" he hissed through his teeth. "Why didn't you call me first?" His voice rose to a squeak and he blinked against the sudden interest of the milling officers. "Leilah told me you showed up looking for answers. That's my job."

A paramedic inspected Mari without touching her, an armed officer flanking the activity. Jet stared at Wiri and Tane's interaction. Anxiety budded in his eyes. The index finger of his right hand tapped the barrel of his rifle. Another police officer held Vaughan's liberated shotgun in gloved hands, his grip careful not to smudge fingerprints or disturb evidence. He stood astride the discarded shell case and waited for the forensics team to arrive.

"Is he okay?" The second paramedic pointed towards the wheelchair.

Wiri noticed Jet shrug in his peripheral vision. Then he turned away from the paramedic and directed his command to Logan. "Sir, you need to leave." Jet's head jerked back at the swearword Logan released, and Wiri sighed in resignation. Tane's feet shifted in front of him and Wiri realised he'd tuned out the cop's angry rebuke.

"I'm not leaving without my boy." Logan folded his arms across his chest. "So, shoot me." His lips curved upwards in a familiar and effective defiance.

Wiri closed his eyes and let his chin drop onto his chest. Everything hurt. "Mari dumped Ted's body," he said, his words lacking enthusiasm. "She attacked Vaughan and shut me in the tank. Ted reconnected the pipes to raise the water level and hide the body." He closed his eyes against Tane's shocked expression. "Speak to Leilah. I'm leaving now." He glanced up in time to see the colour fade from the officer's cheeks.

"You can't leave." Tane lifted his left hand and patted the air between them.

Wiri shook his head and set both hands over the chair wheels. "Just watch me," he replied.

77

PISTOL GRIP

The wheelchair crunched across the broken glass as Logan pushed Wiri through the front door. A blast of cold air hit him full in the face. His family reacted from the other side of the road, arguing with the officer maintaining the cordon.

"That's my son!" Hana's voice rose in protest. Phoenix saved her energy, lifting the flapping tape and dipping beneath it. Her boot soles slapped against the wet road as she ran across the empty street. An echo followed her, bouncing off the shop windows and floating like a drumbeat. The officer's voice rose in anger as he lost control of the milling pedestrians.

"Wiri!"

His vision blacked as she wrapped her arms around his head, engulfing him in warmth and a floral scent he didn't recognise. Her hair hung around him like a curtain, filling his senses with motel shampoo and the promise of comfort.

"I'm so tired," he whispered. "I bloody hate this town."

Hana joined them, peppering his head in kisses. Her fist moved in his peripheral vision and he saw her dig Logan in the ribs. "Idiot!" she hissed. "But well done."

With nowhere else to go, Wiri directed them towards Larry's house. Phoenix clasped his uninjured right hand and kept time with the steady spin of the wheels. The pavement shone with the continued downpour and droplets coated Wiri's eyelashes like glitter. Hana took over, pushing the wheelchair after Logan's long legs banged the seat for the third time. They walked in silence, each consumed by their own thoughts. The rain intensified as they made the turn off the main street and Logan slipped off his leather jacket and laid it across Wiri's knees.

Larry pulled his car up to the curb as they arrived at the vicarage. He reversed almost to the bumper of Wiri's truck. A frown bisected his forehead as he clambered out onto the road. "You're here already." He jerked his head towards the intersection where traffic bunched in a rare gridlock. "I got turned around at the end of the main street." He eyed Logan as though he might be a dangerous snake before addressing Wiri. "How'd it go?"

Logan snorted. "How do you think it went?"

Phoenix winced and shot Larry a glance containing sympathy. "Well, we found Vaughan's missing gun," she said. She squeezed Wiri's fingers. "He's freezing and wet. And Mama needs to see if there's glass in his cuts. Please, may we come in?"

"Of course, of course." Larry jogged up the front steps and took shelter beneath the porch. He jammed his key into the lock and the door swung open.

"What about the chair?" Hana pushed Wiri's damp fringe back from his forehead with her palm. She lifted Logan's jacket from his lap. "We could carry it up between us."

"No. I'll walk." Wiri braced his forearms against the seat and pushed himself upright. A bolt of pain shot through his thigh and he collapsed back with a groan. The wheelchair rocked against the force.

"It won't go through the front door, anyway." Phoenix glanced up at her father, looking to him as always for solutions.

But before he could reply, Larry skipped back down the steps and dipped his torso. He slung Wiri over his shoulder in a fireman's lift, the movement fluid and practiced. Wiri had no time to protest about the indignity as Larry clasped the backs of his knees. He disappeared into the vicarage ass first, affording himself a second to observe the startled expression on the faces of the women.

Logan caught his eye, and something passed between them.

Something ethereal and beyond words.

Like a handing over of responsibility to another.

Regret, loss and hope bound up in that single expression.

Wiri closed his eyes against the weight of the moment. Larry carried him into the lounge and set him on the raggedy brown sofa with care. He heard shuffling from the hallway as the family removed their shoes.

"Oh, don't worry about your feet!" Larry hurried away to stop them. "The old floors will mark your socks. Leave them on. Leave them on. It's fine. I promise."

Crockery clattered from another room as he sourced refreshments. Wiri closed his eyes and let his head fall back against the cushions. His body listed as another joined him. He opened one eye. "Hey," he said, his voice a croak.

"Hey yourself." Phoenix pursed her lips and frowned. "I thought she shot you." Petulance entered her tone. "Why did you speak to her without me?"

Wiri blinked and pushed himself upright. His backside slid into a dip and his thigh bumped hers. She snorted and her anger fled. "Ouch!" Wiri pressed his fingers over the wound. A dark stain on his jeans showed where it had leaked from beneath the surgical bandage. He shook his head. "I swear I didn't think it would go that way. Not for a second. I figured I'd tell her I knew she buried me in the tank and killed Hendricks. But it didn't play out like that at all."

"What happened?" Phoenix turned sideways and laid her palm over his hand. "Let Mama look at it. Don't make it bleed even more."

Wiri turned his wrist and their fingers knitted together, perfectly matched. He shifted their joined hands onto the sofa cushion. "She didn't kill Hendricks." He used his other hand to rub his eyes. "Nobody did. Dude died of natural causes. Who knew?"

"Wow!" Phoenix exclaimed. "Then why did she fire the gun?"

He exhaled. "Accident. Death wish. I'm not sure. Uncle Logan flattened her, so maybe just the force of him slamming into her. She's built like a twig. But she also attacked Vaughan and much as Leilah adores her, their relationship can't survive that."

Phoenix wrinkled her nose. "So, that silly old man shot you because he wanted to protect her?"

"Yeah." Wiri shook his head. "Love, greed, and revenge. It's always one of those three. He loved her, but she didn't love him in return."

Crockery clattered against wood, accompanied by the hum of voices. Larry directed Hana towards a first aid box in the pantry. Wiri glanced at the door and estimated only another few seconds remained before the adults entered the room. "About that," he began, his tone serious. He lowered his voice to a whisper. Thoughts of Ted and Mari flitted through Wiri's mind. He'd held onto her, to both their detriments. He shared more with Seline, the bastard child twisted by resentment and misplaced loyalty. He swallowed, not wanting to suck Phoenix into the miasma of confusion which epitomised his existence.

So, he took a deep breath and released her with a litany of gentle platitudes. "We can't keep doing this. We need to just be friends." But as Phoenix's protests grew, he turned up the heat until he didn't recognise his own voice. "I don't want this!" he hissed. "You should go."

He'd wanted to release her but cringed at the hurt which blossomed like a heat rash across her neck. She jerked away from him as though he'd struck her, reeling back in horror. His fingers chilled as she snatched back her hand. Tears speckled her irises as she rose and stepped away from him, her head already shaking. "Still!" she bit, agony dripping from the single word. "And still, even after everything, you don't see me." She stumbled as her feet tripped against the worn rug, her body stiff and unyielding. Wiri watched her leave, wondering if deep down, she felt relieved.

78

Sear Axis Pin

The gunshot wound left a dip in the muscle on either side of Wiri's left thigh when it healed. And a limp which embarrassed him, though few others noticed. Phoenix returned home with her parents and he remained at the vicarage with Larry. As autumn released its grasp on the mountain to the bite of winter, he learned to live with his own choices. And find peace with those made by other people. With the burgeoning spring came hope that he'd make better ones in the future.

Wiri pursed his lips and stared at the battered brown envelope in his left hand. His scarred middle finger refused to bend around it. Hammering on the bathroom door told him Larry had woken late for Matins again. "Get a move on, Du Rose!" he wailed through the keyhole. "I need to shave before I meet the dragons of the parish. They don't appreciate hairy vicars!"

Wiri flicked the lock and stood aside as Larry blasted through the gap. "Morning!" he called, his tone bright as his dog collared flatmate slammed the door in his face. He lifted his right hand and wiped toothpaste residue from around his lips, and returned to his bedroom to neaten his bedding. The envelope tumbled to the rug, and he stared at it nestled against the tufted wool. He debated just leaving it there and forgetting about it for a while.

Water sloshed in the bathroom as Larry shaved. The vicar tumbled through life in a perpetual state of chaos which Wiri struggled to endure. But the man possessed qualities he hoped to emulate. He'd accepted the mantle of responsibility from Logan, though the latter proved loath to relinquish it entirely. Eight months of living with Larry had taught Wiri much about cohabiting with relative strangers and making it work through compromise.

The bathroom door flew open hard enough to hit the wall behind it. Larry scurried into the hallway, pausing to peer at Wiri. "Why are you just standing there?" he demanded. "Isn't Leilah expecting you at the cafe?"

Wiri checked his watch and wrinkled his nose. "Yes. In twenty minutes. Then I'm leading a trek onto the mountain. I might be home late tonight. It depends what time we finish settling the horses."

"Is Leilah hosting another group at Hector's place?" Larry raised an eyebrow.

"Yeah." Wiri sighed and frowned at the envelope. "It's her new package deal idea. She wants to use the property to make money now Jet's moved up to Hamilton. The guests get the house for the weekend, a riding lesson on the Saturday and a trail ride on Sunday. They can muck around on the farm in between times."

Larry crinkled his nose. "Rather you than me having to ride on the mountain." He wrapped his arms around himself. "The weather forecast is good for today, though. It's fresh but clear." His gaze fell on the envelope and he cocked his head. "Didn't that arrive in Friday's post?"

"Yeah." Wiri sighed and touched it with the toe of his sock. "I'm not ready to face it yet."

Larry waggled his bushy grey eyebrows and straightened his cassock. "We're never ready for the important things, my friend," he said. He flicked a fingernail across a ketchup stain over his stomach and groaned. "See you later." His shoes squeaked against the stripped and freshly varnished floorboards of the hallway. The front door slammed and his footsteps continued across the deck and over the low wall surrounding the church.

It had surprised Wiri to learn that Larry owned the villa. He'd assumed it came as a tithe house with the role of vicar. But he'd enjoyed helping with the renovations, although it also highlighted another career he'd rather not pursue. He picked up the envelope, folded it, and stuffed it into his back pocket, putting off the inevitable disappointment until later.

A watery sunshine dappled the pavement as Wiri walked along the main street. Spring nipped at the frayed edges of winter, bringing the promise of freshness and new life. A crowd gathered outside the cafe's front door, farmers grunting at one another clad in weatherproof jackets and gumboots. Wiri turned left down an alley before the florist and skirted the rear of the buildings. He entered the cafe through its rear door.

"Hi, love." Leilah threw a clean apron at him before he could speak. She jerked her chin towards the shop. "The coffee machine is already heating." Her movements appeared frantic as she whisked eggs in a wide bowl. Wiri took a step towards the archway leading to the counter and halted.

"No." He backed away, his head already shaking.

Leilah swallowed and her irises danced with anxiety. She set the bowl on the centre island. "She's my daughter!" she protested. "You don't need to interact with her."

"Nice." Seline's lips drew into a thin line as she stepped beneath the arch and leaned against the chiller door. "Hello, Wiremu."

"Stop it!" Leilah's tone held more bite than usual and Seline blinked. "You owe Wiri an apology." Leilah raised the whisk and pointed it at her daughter. Egg mixed with milk dripped into the bowl.

"Sorry."

Wiri detected no hint of sincerity in Seline's utterance. It held no other purpose than placating her mother. He snorted and narrowed his eyes. His spine twinged as though to advocate mercy for her. She had, after all, brought him rescue from the water tank. "What are you sorry about?" He folded his arms and observed her. Discomfort sent a flush of colour from her chest into her neck. Her gaze flicked to Leilah and, finding no sympathy there, back to Wiri.

She swallowed. "I'm sorry for planting your shirt in the tank with the man who died." She twisted her lips, but her eyes glinted with devilment. Her left hand strayed to a red curl next to her shirt buttons as though she attempted to draw Wiri's attention to something more entertaining. She hinted at her thwarted seduction of him with every subtle movement. But she wouldn't apologise. Her tongue slipped free to run across her lower lip. "I assumed my father took a hit out on the dead man because he'd harassed me. Vaughan owed him money and so Hendricks thought that gave him leverage over me." Her jaw slid sideways to produce a sardonic smile. "In order for that to happen, I'd have to care about the debtor, wouldn't I?"

Wiri heard Leilah give a hiss of impatience behind him. Seline didn't miss a beat. "Anyway, I tried to steer the cops away from the same conclusion." She released a throaty chuckle. "Turns out people have less power in prison than Dad made me believe."

Leilah tutted. The heavy exhale through her nose conveyed her irritation. "Well, your *step-father* won't be trying it again," she concluded, her tone harsh. She emphasised the label as though it pained her. "Because Seline's promised not to visit the prison or take his calls anymore."

Seline's irises glittered like diamonds. Wiri pitied Leilah her blind faith. Her eyelashes fluttered, and she regarded him like a spider imagining the devouring of a mate. "Anything else?" she demanded, fixing an expression of feigned innocence over her face.

Wiri didn't dignify her charade with a reply. A thud against the front door indicated the caffeine addicts grew restless in the street. He blew out an exasperated breath and balled the apron in his right hand. "Fine!" He turned to stare at Leilah. "But keep her away from me."

"Thank you." Her smile revealed the first genuine emotion of the encounter. Gratitude caused her shoulders to relax. She lifted an eyebrow at Seline. "She'll stay out of your way."

"Whatever." Seline picked at a cuticle as Wiri fixed the apron around his waist and tied it behind him. Leilah ran out to her vehicle to retrieve a crate of homegrown vegetables and the rear door slammed closed.

Wiri side stepped Seline on his route through the archway, jerking in shock as her hand slid into his back pocket. "Love letters?" she purred into his ear. She slipped the folded envelope free, her sensuous touch through the coarse fabric of his jeans sending tingles shooting into his stomach. "How is your wee schoolgirl?" She smiled to show her upper teeth as she affected a baby voice. "Did the little child break up with poor Wiremu?" Her fingers closed around the corded muscle of his forearm in an unwanted teasing, stroking action. Lust rose from her in a haze, ugly and misplaced.

Wiri's left arm twisted beneath her grasp, and Seline found her wrist pinned between his strong fingers. The envelope fluttered to the tiled floor, forgotten. It took every fibre of Wiri's being not to press the fragile bones until they broke. Hana wouldn't approve. It wasn't how she'd raised him. He leaned forward, his lips curling into a sneer as he delivered his message. "Never touch me again," he whispered. "You're poisonous. And one day, you'll bite off more than you can chew." He clicked the fingers of his right hand. "I wouldn't screw you, even if my life depended on it." He dropped his arm and stepped away from her. She ran her fingers across her wrist as though surprised at his restraint. He realised in that moment that she'd wanted more violence. Expected it. Disappointment flashed in her eyes.

"I'll tell Mum's good friend, Tane, what just happened," she hissed.

Wiri's laughter made her jump. He retrieved the envelope from the floor and stuffed it into his front pocket. "You do that," he replied, standing up straight. "But I think he's sick of clearing up your mess." He stepped beneath the archway and approached the coffee machine, his mind already switching to the complaints from beyond the front door. "Oh." He turned back with mischief in his eyes. Seline's jaw gritted, forcing her teeth to meet in an attractive overbite. Wiri wagged his index finger. "Next time you visit the prison, ask Michael Hanover how he got the black eye and broken ribs a few months ago." Her eyes widened and her jaw slackened. She took a step towards him.

"How do you know about that?" Urgency entered her tone. "Did you get someone to beat up my dad? Who do you know in the prison?"

Wiri narrowed his eyes and ignored her questions. His lips slid into a satisfied smile as Leilah squeezed past him to unlock the front door.

79

Bullseye

Wiri worked for an hour before he noticed Seline's absence. Leilah slammed the drawer of the cash register and leaned her forearms on the counter next to him with a sigh. His phone vibrated in his pocket and he winced. A glance at Leilah's sagging shoulders told him not to check the message. "I hope you're never disappointed in your children, Wiri," she said, her tone laden with emotion.

He finished wiping spilled grinds from in front of the coffee machine before answering her. "I'm not having kids."

"Oh." Leilah frowned and stood upright. Her features pinched into a concerned expression. "How can you know that already?"

He shrugged and stepped into the kitchen to rinse out the cloth. The sudden lull in customers allowed Leilah to follow him and his shoulders stiffened. Other people didn't understand. It's as though they couldn't see him as complete unless he was prepared to father offspring. She leaned against the chiller and he sensed her preparing arguments he'd heard a million times before. But she didn't pursue the subject. "Sorry about Seline," she said. Her sigh showed she'd uttered one more apology in a growing line of them. There would be more to come, and she knew it.

"No worries." Wiri shook out the cloth and turned towards the archway. The unopened envelope burned through his jeans, scouring the flesh from his thigh. His fingers twitched against the cloth and he ached to find a quiet space and face the contents. He squared his jaw and resisted further confidences with Leilah. "I'll fetch the old boy his coffee and then head up to the farm." His tight smile indicated the end of the conversation.

Ted grunted as Wiri set the cappuccino next to him on the counter. Cinnamon dusted the surface of the frothy milk in a smiley face. Ted snatched at the handle of the mug and inspected Wiri's careful handiwork. "Twat!" he offered as a rebuke.

Wiri laughed. "That's my best art, man!" he protested.

Ted's crabbed fingers dragged the mug beneath his hooked nose. He exhaled and cinnamon dust floated upwards before gravity halted its flight and cast it onto the counter like snow. Or glass. Wiri swallowed at the memory of the window pane speckling the surface. The cuts to his cheek had scarred, creating thin white ridges against his tanned skin. Ted glanced up at him, his lower lip folding over to reveal his pink gums. "You're leaving, ain't ya?"

Wiri's head jerked backwards. He gaped at the old man, unable to source the right words for the moment. "I don't think so," he replied instead.

"Yeah. You are." Ted sighed. He ran a thin hand across the top of his cap and straightened the brim. Remand prison hadn't been kind to him. He'd lost weight. And hope. He swallowed and his hand snaked towards Wiri, the fingers flattening into the offering of a handshake. Wiri accepted it, his wide palm closing around the fragile paw. Ted gulped and turned on his stool. He sat alone at his counter again. The other stool had disappeared soon after his release. Leilah didn't search for it.

"I never thanked you, tama," he said, his voice a scratchy whisper. "I've seen you struggling with that bullet wound and you've never once complained. You sorted out the money stuff with your legal friends. And you spoke for me in court." He nodded, the action a sad bobbing of a too big head on a thin strand of a neck. "You're the reason I got me this ankle bracelet and not a jail term." He bumped his leg against the stool and it gave a metallic clang. His chin wobbled. "Thank you, my friend," he whispered. "I'll miss you." He withdrew his slender fingers like a lizard sliding from a burrow in the ground. Wiri gaped at the side of the old man's head, his chest tight and his knees weak.

"Now, piss off. You've got places to be and it ain't here."

Wiri turned his boots towards the kitchen, but his legs resisted the command to walk. He faltered, licking his lips as he considered his request. Ted glared up at him with his brows drawn low over his eyes. "One thing," Wiri said. "Who gave you the ride up to the water tank?"

"Eh?" Ted grunted. His body scrunched smaller on his stool. "It doesn't matter anymore."

Wiri swallowed. "It does to me. Did Mari give you a ride up there? Did she ask for your help?"

Ted groaned. Few people spoke her name anymore. She'd died alone and afraid in the women's prison in Auckland while awaiting her trial date. Her lawyer argued during the first hearing that she should receive bail, but the judge disagreed. The charges ranged from grievous bodily harm to hiding a body and attempted murder. Unlike Ted, who accidentally discharged a firearm, the judge deemed Mari a greater risk. Death took her that night while she slept. The coroner promised Leilah she'd known no pain. She went to sleep, her heart stopped, and she didn't wake up.

Ted's feet shuffled on the rungs beneath the stool. His Adam's apple bobbed in the stubble coating his scrawny neck. He would have rebuffed anyone else, but he owed Wiri. "That girl," he said, his tone a low growl. "Leilah's daughter."

"Seline?" Wiri's neck jerked back hard enough to make the tendons pop. "But she was at Vaughan's place. I spoke to her."

"Aye." Ted's index finger curled through the handle of his mug. "Then she went somewhere after that." He shrugged. "Mari told me what happened with Hendricks and what she'd done. I started walking towards Vaughan's place in a panic. Hoped one of the farm boys from Pirongia might drive past and give me a ride. A few of them came in here for their lunch. But the girl recognised me and stopped. She dropped me on the main road before turning into her driveway. I got a ride back to town with Roddy, who works for Boston's farm. He didn't remember because he was stoned."

Wiri heaved out a sigh of exasperation. "Where did you tell Seline you were going?"

"Didn't." Ted blew on his coffee and the froth moved. "She didn't ask. Too busy pulling a big trailer with a finicky horse inside it. Mari arrived back here in a terrible state. I thought she might have left some evidence behind." He chuckled. "She left more than that."

Wiri cocked his head. His thigh ached, and he yearned to take the weight off his feet. A twinge from his coccyx deadened his other leg as though in sympathy. But Ted's body relaxed as he found catharsis in the truth. "Bloody Hendricks lay on his back staring up at the sky."

"Wait, what?" Shock obscured Wiri's discomfort. He leaned closer, as though unable to believe Ted's story. "Mari didn't tip him into the tank?"

"Na." Ted dug his crabbed index finger into the mug and obliterated Wiri's smiley face. "She panicked and drove back here. Tane nabbed her for speeding at the end of Hector's old driveway." He raised a bushy eyebrow and stared at Wiri. "I shouldn't have mouthed off about her speeding fine. Didn't realise it was from that time." He gave a solemn shake of his head. "She was always getting them. But that one put her at the scene. Shoulda kept my mouth shut."

Wiri groaned and his shoulders slumped. "You tipped the body into the water tank. Not Mari. And you let the cows out to trample the crime scene."

Ted frowned and licked the froth from his finger. "What does it matter now?" His voice degenerated into a growl. He lifted his right leg to inspect the electronic tag placed over his ankle by a probation officer. "She's gone, anyway. The only wāhine I ever loved. I'd have done anything for her."

Wiri ran a hand through his hair and left his fringe sticking up at the front. "Yeah. Hide a body, lie about it, watch me take the fall, and then shoot me." He slapped his thigh with his palm and gasped at the pain which ricocheted through the muscle. "I'm such an idiot!"

"Na." Ted exhaled with force. "I like ya. Are ya coming back ever?"

"No!" Wiri spat. "Not if my life depends on it!"

80

FIRING WIDE

Wiri grunted to Leilah as he left through the back door. He heard her call after him that she'd help him tack the horses at Vaughan's place soon.

The woman she'd employed to work the rest of the Sunday shift smiled at him as he hurried along the street. He nodded but didn't stop to chat. Her smile drooped. The whole town knew how much she liked him and waited as though holding its breath for a wedding. Wiri shook his head. There wouldn't be one.

Phoenix.

His mind flicked to her as it always did, like a reflex of his soul. The bitter tang of regret flooded his chest and snaked up the back of his neck. He'd pushed her away one time too many, wanting to do the right thing and then living with the consequences. She'd consumed his teenage years with her ready laughter and her irritating habit of slipping Bible scriptures into inappropriate conversations. He adored her and always would. But he'd hurt her, and she'd exited their relationship. Despite the eight months of distance between that moment and this, he still didn't know how to fix it. Or if he could.

Mac helped him to keep tabs on her. His loyal cousin saw off errant hopefuls within their shared mix of friends. He was a Du Rose. A look or a word was enough to make his point. Wiri hadn't asked Mac to do it, but he didn't stop him either.

The envelope made a chuffing sound in his front pocket as he walked. He'd always appreciated his long stride, which helped him cover great distances without effort. He hated it now. The movement of his left leg didn't flow, adding a jarring stutter to that side of his body as his boot sole hit the pavement.

And for what?

He'd borne it because it seemed a noble injury. Administered by a man who'd sacrificed himself for love. He'd empathised with Ted.

But the old man had lied to him.

Wiri made the turn onto Larry's street and his steps slowed. A vehicle bumped into the vicarage's rutted driveway and halted. The signage emblazoned across it culminated in a familiar logo in the centre of the driver's door. "What now?" he hissed. His phone buzzed again in his pocket and he dug it out, peering at the screen and trying not to trip.

Two texts from Mac. Both relayed the same message.

'Incoming.'

His thumb hovered over the keypad as he deliberated his reply. But he didn't have time. The driver had seen him and the truck's heavy door swung wide.

David Allen gave an upward jerk of his chin and folded his arms across his chest. He leaned against the truck and crossed his ankles, observing Wiri's approach with a quizzical gaze. Wiri forced himself to concentrate on his gait, grinding his teeth until his head ached. He hated how the limp weakened him and turned him into the imperfect Du Rose. But David made no comment as he drew level. Not about his leg, anyway. "I'm taking your truck," he declared without preamble.

Wiri swallowed. "Why?" His mind ran into panic mode, calculating a scenario in which he had no transport. It took a second for him to notice the key fob which David held out to him.

"Because apparently it's sending distress signals to the dealer and they want to check it over." He bounced the key fob twice before dropping it into Wiri's palm.

"Is it?" Wiri stared at his truck in disbelief.

David snorted. "No, you clown! But it's missed the six month service. You can have it back next weekend when you visit. Use mine until then."

"Next weekend?" Wiri frowned as someone else moved inside the vehicle. He blinked in shock as Phoenix stepped from the running board of the passenger side and rounded the bonnet. His head emptied of words as though a giant flush had stolen the vocabulary from his brain. She'd grown taller in the intervening months. And become more beautiful than Wiri had imagined. Bouncing black curls tapped the points of her shoulders. She had the ethereal elegance of her elfin mother coupled with the inner strength of a Du Rose. When she studied Wiri from beneath her dark lashes, his heart dropped into his stomach and flapped like a stranded fish.

David groaned and Wiri forced his gaze back to him. "Not much point telling you anything now, is there?" The sentence emerged as a grumble, though humour sparkled in his blue irises. He jerked his head towards Phoenix. "She can fill you in on the details. But the forestry block is overdue its first thinning. Branches need to come off up to four meters and the skinny trees culled."

Wiri glanced at Phoenix and his breath caught in his chest. He found it difficult to concentrate with her staring at him through her intense grey irises. "Culled," he whispered, his tongue tripping over the proclamation of selective mercy killing.

David nodded. "Yes, culled." He silenced as Wiri's mind drifted through time and space to the backbreaking work of planting the tiny saplings. Had it really been six years since they'd stood on the side of the mountain and tried to imagine it as a forest? Edin had been six. She'd complained from morning till dusk for the entire week. Watering them proved even worse during the drought of the trees' first summer. They'd endured weeks of carting watering cans from the tank on the back of the truck to each flailing plant. He sighed and pursed his lips. The trees had become a forgotten legacy, an uncomfortable memory of a promise he'd never appreciated. But he'd known this day would come.

David inclined his head to observe Wiri from beneath bushy eyebrows which ran from blond to white. "Logan always said you needed to do the work yourselves. The girls have completed their chainsaw safety course. And I know yours is up to date because I checked." He rolled his eyes. "You'll just need to keep Macky from felling the bloody lot. Kid's a maniac."

Wiri mustered a smile. Mac loved everything about the farm. Especially the power tools. Hard as he tried, he couldn't imagine Edin breaking a sweat with a chainsaw.

He let his gaze slide back to Phoenix and his heart beat a fast tattoo, causing a dull drumbeat to thud inside his head. He couldn't ask why she'd come. It seemed rude and besides, he didn't want to break the spell. "I have to work," he said, his voice raspy as though something heavy leaned on his windpipe. "But I can text Leilah and make you both a drink." He held his left hand out towards the porch steps, the middle finger sticking out in its permanent protest.

"You're working?" David frowned and cocked his head. "On a Sunday?" Wiri nodded, and his lips parted to reply. But David switched his attention to Phoenix. "I thought you'd checked." His tone held a note of accusation. He shrugged. "What will you do now? Everything is closed."

"I'll be fine." Her voice had lost its girlish quality.

"For eight hours?" David's head bounced as he spoke, disbelief drawing his brows into a bushy line. "I don't think so. You can come with me."

"No!" Wiri cleared his throat and took a step forward. He listed as he trusted his left leg with his weight. "She can come with me. We're hacking onto the mountain for a couple of hours."

Phoenix looked from David to Wiri and back again, uncertainty in the flickering behind her stone-coloured irises. They morphed to a granite hue, and she gave a definitive nod. "Okay."

David snuffed with something suspiciously like relief. He held out his hand for Wiri's car key. Wiri stared blankly at the dirt ingrained along his lifeline before realising what he wanted. "Can I get my gear out?" he asked, the words rushed.

David sighed. "If you're quick. I'm picking up a trailer from near Taupo. It fits the tow ball on your truck, but not mine." He jerked his head towards Larry's villa. "Can I use the bathroom?"

Wiri sorted out the front door key and handed it to him. He waited until David had entered the house before exhaling in a rush. Phoenix stood at the curb, hiding behind her fringe and pretending to inspect an errant cloud hanging over the mountain. Wiri swallowed and took on the role of adult. "Please, can you help me?" he asked. He glanced at the open front door and stepped towards his truck. "I don't want him to see the GPS blocker."

Phoenix nodded and met him by the driver's door. She lifted the hem of her shirt to create a pouch and he unplugged the blocker and placed it inside it. "Thanks," he whispered.

By the time David emerged from the villa, they'd transferred Wiri's belongings into David's truck. Phoenix hid the blocker beneath the passenger seat and rose to face him, her expression devoid of guilt.

"Right kiddywinks," David said. "Meet me here at nineteen hundred hours. No funny business and don't be late." He snapped his fingers in front of Wiri's nose and caused him to jump. "Call Hana about next weekend."

"Okay." Wiri licked his lips and stepped backwards, clattering with Larry's post-box in his haste. It groaned and tipped a little further on its rusting pole. "Seven o'clock and phone Ma." He wasn't sure why he felt the need to repeat David's instructions back to him, other than to busy his whirling brain.

David turned away and clambered into the driver's seat. Phoenix cleared her throat and suppressed a snort as the shorter man adjusted the settings so he could reach the pedals. He fiddled with the mirrors before firing the engine and cranking the gear lever into reverse. The side window hissed as he depressed the switch to open it. "Play nice," he warned with a smirk. He bumped the truck over the rutted driveway and onto the road.

The diesel engine rumbled towards the main street, and Wiri and Phoenix watched it turn right. They stood next to each other, neither one speaking. Wiri blew out a ragged breath and glanced sideways so he could observe Phoenix as she composed herself. He saw her blink and purse her lips.

Larry's front door swayed on its hinges and Wiri noticed the key still nestled in the lock where David left it. He jerked his head towards the house. "Do you need to use the bathroom before we head up to the farm?" The words ground in his throat like needles. In trying to act with politeness, he'd gone straight to something intensely personal. His shoulders slumped and his arms hung by his sides as defeat shrouded him. Every new sentence he sifted for quality sounded ridiculous or inadequate as a follow up.

Phoenix ran her tongue over her lower lip and heat rose from Wiri's groin and frizzed the wiring in his brain. He lost his head.

His arms moved to enfold her without the permission of his rational mind. He crushed her against him and his lips sought hers with a hunger he'd only barely suppressed for eight long months. She didn't resist, lifting her chin and meeting his kiss with shared eagerness. Her lips parted to admit his tongue, and he lost himself, falling into a well of light and abandonment. The old flame revived as he ached to possess her, to connect in a way that life and circumstance couldn't steal.

A car horn sounded on the main street and they jumped. Wiri's nose bumped against her forehead as he took a breath. Phoenix sighed and wrapped her arms around his waist. She pressed her cheek against the hard wall of his chest and her fingers splayed across his spine. "Sorry," he breathed into her hair. "Sorry, I didn't mean to do that."

Phoenix snuffed out a laugh and leaned her chin against his sternum. It sent an ache deep into his chest which felt as though it kick-started his heart. Her irises swam like liquid mercury. "What you said was cruel." Her tone held confidence and clarity. "But I understand now. You were right. I wasn't ready for a relationship with you. What happened last summer ripped me apart, and I needed time to heal. A lot has changed. I'm sixteen in two months, and I expect you to ask me out properly."

Wiri's lips parted, and he swallowed. Her certainty washed over him. Mac said she'd changed, and he saw it for himself in the determined tilt of her head. Phoenix frowned. "Leilah texts me sometimes. She's told me you're not seeing anyone, but there's a girl who likes you." Her grey irises flashed. "I couldn't allow that now, could I?"

Wiri threw his head back and laughed. The jovial sound echoed around the empty street. His lungs seemed to fill for the first time since the shooting. "Ted lied," he said with a sigh. "He tipped Hendricks into the water tank."

Phoenix shrugged. "What does it matter? You're not him and I'm not her. They can only affect us if we let them." She tightened her jaw and pouted her sensuous lips. "We'll be different."

"We'll be different." He repeated her words in a whisper. He brushed his thumb across her lips and revelled in their velvety softness. "I'm coming home," he said with a smile. "I hear there are trees which need taking care of."

She blinked up at him through a fringe which fluttered across her vision. "Good. Because I bought you a new shirt to replace the one the police confiscated. It's at home on your bed." Phoenix sighed. "And you need to call Mama. She spoke to Aunty Liza for hours on the phone last night. Why is Judge Eliza Du Rose interested in you? Do you know what it's about?"

Wiri groaned. He lifted his left arm and checked his watch. "I think so. Let's go up to the farm and I'll tell you everything."

He locked up Larry's house and settled in David Allen's truck. The envelope crinkled against his hip as he sat in the driver's seat. Phoenix leaned sideways as she clicked on her seatbelt. "What's that?" she demanded.

Wiri leaned back in the seat and tugged the letter free. He placed it into her lap as though it contained a priceless diamond. "Something I didn't want to face," he whispered, his tone loaded with disappointment. He turned sideways in the seat and bent his left knee. "Can you open it for me?"

Phoenix shrugged. Her quick fingers tore at the seam. "How's that little foal?" she asked as she tugged a sheet of paper free.

"She's great. Feisty." Wiri watched as she uncreased the folds and pressed it flat against her thigh. "What does it say, Phoe?"

She tutted and stared up at him, her eyelashes fluttering in confusion. "It's from Auckland University." She cocked her head and narrowed her eyes. "But you knew that, anyway, didn't you?"

Wiri nodded and stared at his hands. His fingers knotted together in constant motion. "What does it say?"

Phoenix released a sigh and read the serif font on the expensive cream page. "Following the stellar interview you gave in September, and after having contacted your referees, the Law department wishes to offer you a place for Semester A." She gnawed on her lower lip. "So, you really were leaving?"

Wiri shrugged. "The letter arrived on Friday, but I figured it was a rejection. I didn't think I interviewed well." He wrinkled his nose. "I got halfway through a debate about contract law and noticed horse dung on the side of my boot. Figured they'd dismiss me as a country boy."

Phoenix grinned. "You are. But you're my country boy." She reached across the truck and placed her fingers over his, the pressure of her hand stilling his nervous motion. A jolt of electricity ran through his veins and warmed him. "Congratulations. You'll make a brilliant lawyer."

Wiri shook his head. "I'm a terrible judge of character, so I doubt it. Look at Jet. And Ted! He's out on licence and he hid a body." He rubbed his eyes with the back of his right hand. "Seline gave him a ride up to the farm after she saw me. You know she's still denying that conversation, don't you?" He dropped his hand into his lap. "I bet she got suspicious and rode out to see why he'd gone up there. She thought it involved her step-father."

Phoenix shrugged. "I think it's okay to take someone at face value. I've spent all year forgiving myself for my own mistakes. It makes us wiser for next time." She flattened her lips into a sad smile and her gaze strayed to Pirongia towering over the town. "Anyway, don't we have work to do?" She cocked her head and Wiri nodded. He sensed she meant more than just the holiday makers waiting to ride up the mountain.

The Plan would take a lifetime of hard graft.

But this time, they'd do it together.

Dear Reader

I hope you've enjoyed *Wiremu Du Rose*. I would be grateful if you could take the time to leave a review at your usual retailer. If you'd rather just let me know how you felt, you can email me at admin@ktbowes.com

I often feature snappy review comments on my covers. My work is also ranked on reviews and your comments will allow me to reach a wider audience.

It doesn't have to be an essay - I will be grateful for a few words. Thank you for doing this for me.

About the Author

K T Bowes is a bestselling teen and women's author.
Her novel, *A Trail of Lies*, was the winner of the genre award for Author's Cave in 2014.
Phoenix Du Rose was considered for the prestigious Ngaio Marsh awards for 2021.
K T Bowes is an Englishwoman in exile in New Zealand, swapping rugged cosmopolitan for mountain ranges and terrifying rivers. She loves Māori culture and has learned to weave flax using traditional methods. Her other passion is Rongoa Māori, which involves creating medicines from native plants. She is a student of Te Reo Māori.
You can find her hanging out on social media in the following places.
Check in and say hello. Maybe suggest she gets back to writing and stops watching cat videos.
FACEBOOK
https://www.facebook.com/NZauthorKTBowes/
TWITTER
https://twitter.com/ktboweswrites
INSTAGRAM

https://www.instagram.com/k_t_bowes

Other Books By This Author:

The Hana Du Rose Mysteries in order:
Logan Du Rose
About Hana
Hana Du Rose
Du Rose Legacy
The New Du Rose Matriarch
One Heartbeat
The Du Rose Prophecy
Du Rose Sons
Du Rose Family Ties
Du Rose Vendetta
Phoenix Du Rose

The Calculated Risk Series:
The Actuary
The Actuary's Wife
The Actuary in Trouble
The Heart of The Actuary

Troubled series for teens:
Free from the Tracks
Sophia's Dilemma
A Trail of Lies
Gone Phishing

Escaping the Back Country NZ series:
Pirongia's Secret Free eBook for subscribers
Deleilah

A Keeper's War Fantasy Trilogy:
Perpetual Winter
The Bee Queen
Hive

Standalone novels:
Artifact
Demons on Her Shoulder
Her Quiet Legacy
All Saints

The Curly Fan Club:
Dead Straight
Bad Hair Day
Side Parting